T0333002

BY SEANAN McGUIRE

WHAT IF...

WANDA MAXIMOFF AND PETER PARKER
WERE SIBLINGS?

MARVEL
WHAT IF...

WANDA MAXIMOFF AND PETER PARKER
WERE SIBLINGS?

SEANAN McGUIRE

3 5 7 9 10 8 6 4 2

Del Rey
20 Vauxhall Bridge Road
London SW1V 2SA

Del Rey is part of the Penguin Random House group of companies
whose addresses can be found at global.penguinrandomhouse.com

Penguin
Random House
UK

Marvel: What If . . . Wanda Maximoff and Peter Parker Were Siblings?
is a work of fiction. Names, places, and incidents either are products of the
author's imagination or are used fictitiously. Any resemblance to actual events,
locales, or persons, living or dead, is entirely coincidental

© 2024 MARVEL

Seanan McGuire has asserted her right to be identified as the author of this
Work in accordance with the Copyright, Designs and Patents Act 1988

First published in the US by Random House Worlds, an imprint of Random House,
a division of Penguin Random House LLC, New York in 2024
First published in the UK by Del Rey in 2024

www.penguin.co.uk

A CIP catalogue record for this book is available from the British Library

Hardback ISBN 9781529914351
Trade paperback ISBN 9781529914368

Book design by Edwin A. Vasquez

Printed and bound in Great Britain by Clays Ltd, Elcograf S.p.A.

The authorised representative in the EEA is Penguin Random House Ireland,
Morrison Chambers, 32 Nassau Street, Dublin D02 YH68

www.greenpenguin.co.uk

MIX
Paper | Supporting
responsible forestry
FSC
www.fsc.org   FSC® C018179

Penguin Random House is committed to a
sustainable future for our business, our readers
and our planet. This book is made from Forest
Stewardship Council® certified paper.

For Hillary.
I will see you in the Big Country.

WHAT IF...

WANDA MAXIMOFF AND PETER PARKER
WERE SIBLINGS?

THE CRIME SCENE

WANDA IS SENSITIVE TO SOUNDS, ALWAYS HAS BEEN. IT CAUSED a lot of problems when she and Peter were little—he'd chew with his mouth open on purpose to gross her out, or try to sneak out of the top bunk in the middle of the night, forgetting the creak of the ladder would wake her every time. Predictable noises can fade into the background, can become part of the daily song of life in New York City, but new sounds stand out, no matter how quiet they are.

The sound of blood running down a man's arm to his hand, then farther down to his fingertips, gathering in heavy drops before it falls, *plink, plink, plink,* to join the pool forming around him, that's a new sound.

Wanda Parker has seen dead people before—saw dead people before she can remember, saw her biological parents die when she was too young to know her own name, saw her uncle Ben die when she was too old to ever get the final image of his open eyes out of her mind, saw Gwen Stacy die when the world fell apart and everything changed forever—but she's never heard this sound. This is the sound of everything going wrong. This is the sound of the future, *her* future, collapsing.

This is the sound of Captain America's story crashing to an end.

She hasn't touched him since she arrived at the manor, and

certainly not since she came into the room to find his body sprawled in the leather armchair, where he'd clearly been waiting for her arrival. He doesn't look like he had time to fight back; there are no defensive wounds on his hands, and his shield is still leaning against the side of the chair, unmarred by bloody fingerprints. Those would be unavoidable if he'd been able to reach for it at all. But it's clean, unlike his hands. Unlike the floor. Unlike the front of his uniform, which is coated in blood, all of it drying at different rates, so that his chest becomes a jigsaw of brown and burgundy and bright, bright red. She's never really thought about how much those colors mirror her own costume. Maybe she should have considered that before she dressed to match her brother. Maybe she should have taken more time to *think*.

He didn't have time. Whoever attacked him was fast, and knew enough to know exactly where to slash America's First Avenger and get past his preternaturally resilient skin. Cap's throat is a ruin, a shredded mass of flesh that looks more like chopped meat than anything that should be part of a person. It's horrific. It's the worst thing she's ever seen, somehow even worse than Uncle Ben, even worse than Gwen lying bent and broken at the base of the Brooklyn Bridge. At least when those horrors had occurred, she hadn't been alone.

She's alone now. She's never felt this alone in her entire life.

The only sounds are the wind outside the open window, her own strained breathing, and the steady drip of blood to the floor. She should call someone. She should call someone *right now*, before this frozen moment passes and she's found, alone with the cooling body of the man who may well be—have been—the world's greatest hero.

She needs to move. But before she can, there's a new sound.

A key is turning in a lock.

She found Captain America's body in the living room of the Avengers Manor. That's where he was when she arrived for their one-on-one meeting, the door unlocked and ajar, mockingly inviting her in. She had been so excited, so hopeful, and it already feels like another lifetime, another version of herself. That hopeful girl is the second casualty of this horrific scene, as dead as Captain America himself.

Her invitation had indicated that Jarvis would see her to Captain America when she arrived, but no one had come to meet her when she rang the bell, and a gentle push against the unlatched door had set it swinging open easily. She hadn't wanted to keep Captain America waiting, and so she'd let herself in, automatically closing and locking the door behind her as she did, a habit born of a thousand lectures from Aunt May about responsibility and home security. Right now, she wants to thank Aunt May more than anything. Without those lectures, she wouldn't even have the split-second warning she's just received. This is when she should run.

She still can't bring herself to move, and as what feels like all the rest of the Avengers crowd into the doorway behind her, she knows how bad this looks. She knows exactly what this looks like, and the press has nailed both her brother and her to the wall so many times for things that didn't look even half as bad that she can barely breathe. Her hands are clean, but that won't matter; her gloves wouldn't show the blood.

Jewel—she remembers when her name was Jessica, when she was the shy girl in the back of Spanish class, not making eye contact with anyone, and right now, what Wanda wouldn't give to see that girl again—is the first to recover from her shock, the first to meet Wanda's eyes and whisper the word she currently fears most in all the world:

"Murderer," says Jewel, and it's the loudest thing Wanda has ever heard.

The other Avengers pour past their teammate, filling the room, surrounding a terrified Wanda, and she doesn't think, she just reacts: She doesn't hesitate as she reaches into the cascading light that fills and illuminates the world, the chaos that sings in her veins like a lullaby from the old country, her biological mother's long-forgotten voice calling to her across the void. She fills her hands with red, red, red, like blood, like chaos, like freedom, and she wraps it around herself, a terrified girl in a ruby cocoon, and like Dorothy flashing out of Oz in the blazing light of two stolen shoes, she's gone, leaving the Avengers blinking away afterimages, incarnadine ghosts that don't change anything about a brutal situation.

Captain America wanted to give the Scarlet Witch a chance to prove that she wasn't a villain after all, and now he's dead, and she's fled from the scene of the crime.

"We have to find her," says Hawkeye, voice grim. "She has to pay for this."

No one disagrees.

SOMEWHERE OUTSIDE WANDA'S REALITY, YET PROFOUNDLY INSIDE IT AT THE SAME time, in a universe that exists between word and definition, where all understanding is born, a woman stands watching a mirror that is also a window as it cuts from the hectic activity in the Avengers Manor to Wanda, who is now falling through the red-light void of infinity. Watching Wanda when she moves through chaos requires tricking the mirror into stacking universe inside of universe, a fractal chain of possible realities that is its own kind of chaos. She can't do it for long, but it feels important to keep an eye on this Wanda, especially since her mirror sought out the young heroine of its own accord. This is a Wanda at the beginning of her heroic career, in her early twenties and still unbruised in some foundational ways. This is the age where Wanda almost always joins the Avengers, universe after universe, world after world.

Probably not this time.

Our strange Watcher saw the whole scene as it played out, saw the one who held the knife, saw Captain America die, gasping for breath as his own blood blocked his throat. She's the only one in the entire cosmos who understands the whole situation.

And she's the one who can't do a thing about it. A single tear runs down her cheek as America Chavez forces herself to keep her eyes on the window. She has a duty to fulfill, after all.

She has to watch what happens.

THE FALL IS SHORT; THE FALL IS ETERNAL. WANDA TUMBLES through space for a matter of seconds and a matter of years at the same time, and it doesn't matter which is true, because the result is the same: A red-rimmed portal opens some five feet above the marble floor of the Sanctum Sanctorum foyer, and she falls out of it, landing on her stomach hard enough to knock the air out of her. She bangs her elbow at the same time, and it seems ridiculous that something so small should cause her such intense pain, especially right now, but it does; she curls into a tight ball, hugging her elbow to her chest, and she's grateful for the pain, because it unlocks the hard knot of panic behind her lungs long enough for her to take a great, gasping breath and begin to sob.

It's a terrible, primal sound, the wailing of an animal just smart enough to understand that it's been trapped in a way it can't escape from, and as much as it hurts to hear, it hurts Wanda even more to make. Doctor Stephen Strange, who has been waiting for that sound—or something like it—for the last hour, drops the book he's been pretending to read and bolts out of his office, cloak billowing behind him as he runs the short distance to the foyer.

He could teleport. He could open a transit portal much more skillfully and easily than Wanda did—unlike her, he knows what he's doing, is not a student in the foundational stages of his education, and when he made the journey, the time inside the portal and outside it would both be precisely as long as he wanted it to be. Right now, though, he wants to give her a chance to catch her breath almost as much as he wants to reach her. He knows her too well to believe that she's experienced the entire hour between the call that told him she was a fugitive and now. For her, the terrible events of the afternoon, whatever those events actually were, may have been only moments ago.

But still, he runs. Still, he will not make her wait. He slams into the door between them, flinging it open, and is rewarded with the sight of Wanda Parker, twenty-two years old and clearly scared out of her mind, dressed in that ridiculous costume she calls her "super hero uniform," curled tight and sobbing like her heart is fatally broken. He steps into the room, and that sound catches her attention as the slamming door did not; she uncurls and sits upright, raising both hands in stiff-fingered threat. Even in her terror, her form is flawless, and he's obscurely proud of her for that; it took months of training for her to learn how to hold her wrists with the precise amount of tension needed to be sure she could launch into whatever motion was necessary to complete the desired spell.

Not that most spells behave as desired when Wanda casts them. She has a real gift for unintended consequences.

She's not making that terrible sound anymore, but she's breathing hard, short, sharp inhales and exhales that sound almost like panting, and her eyes are bright with fear. Red sparks cascade around her fingertips, the chaos she's heir to threatening to spill out before she can call for it. That, as much as anything else, makes his decision for him: Doctor Strange raises his own hands, palms toward her in a ritual gesture that needs no magic to use and no training to understand.

"It's all right, Wanda," he says, and his voice is gentle, his voice is kind, his voice is exactly what she needs to hear in that moment. "I know what happened. I know it wasn't your fault."

He moves toward her, and is gratified when she drops her hands, although the fear doesn't leave her eyes. "How long was I gone this time?"

"If they contacted me immediately after you vanished, a little more than an hour," says Doctor Strange. "I believe they did, if that helps at all. The Black Knight knew you were going to be there today—he was looking forward to welcoming you to the team. He reached out as soon as he could. As I said, I know what happened."

Of all the Avengers, Wanda is the closest to the Black Knight. Strange has trusted him to patrol with her on occasion, and he's never been anything other than fair and reasonable. She relaxes very slightly, and a spark of defiance lights in her eyes.

"I didn't kill him."

"I know you didn't. You're capable of many things, Wanda, some more dangerous than others, but I don't believe you to be capable of murder."

Wanda scrambles to her feet and races to throw herself into his arms, shaking. She seems much younger in that moment, as if fear alone has been enough to reduce her to the teenage girl he met what seems like a lifetime ago. Doctor Strange isn't much of a hugger, but he wraps his arms around her in return, granting her the comfort she so clearly and desperately needs.

After several minutes, she pulls away, wiping at her eyes with one hand. "The Avengers saw me," she says, voice small, like she's making a confession.

"I'm aware. As I said, they called me."

"I don't . . . I didn't know . . . They must think I did this."

"Yes."

The admission is small, a single word, a single syllable, and yet it hangs between them like a damning incantation, the foulest magic that has ever been uttered. Wanda recoils, shock and betrayal in her expression, and Doctor Strange reaches out to catch her shoulders.

"Breathe, Wanda," he says. "You have to breathe. Most of the Avengers think you did this. Dane doesn't think you did it. I *know* you didn't do it. But fleeing from the scene when they found you—it doesn't look good. We're going to have to work hard to convince them that this wasn't your doing."

"I was scared," she admits. "The way they were looking at me . . . I didn't know what they were going to do. And I didn't . . ." She waves her hands in frustration. "I didn't mean to do the zappy thing. I still can't control it completely. It happens when I'm really scared and really stuck. Can you tell them? Can you tell them I didn't run away on purpose?"

"For all the good it will do, I'll try," he promises.

Someone pounds on the Sanctum door, the sound echoing through the chamber. Wanda recoils, breath starting to speed up again, and raises her hands in a defensive gesture. Doctor Strange sighs. He doesn't want to chastise her, not when she has such good reason to be upset, but he wants her to start thinking. She needs to analyze, not merely react.

"Wanda," he says, voice low and tight. "Wanda, look at me."

She looks at him, and her pupils are bathed in red. Never a good sign.

"Whoever this is, they don't mean you any harm."

"How do you—"

"If someone who meant you harm were to come anywhere near the door, the wards would notify me at once, just as they would if someone who meant *me* harm were to approach. You're my apprentice. You belong here. The wards know and will protect you. You *know* this, Wanda. This is your home. You have to breathe."

Wanda takes a deep breath, the red light flickering and leaving her eyes. "I do. I do know that. I'm . . . I'm sorry. It's just been a really difficult day."

"That's why you're still an apprentice, Wanda. Apprentices have the luxury of panicking. I don't. Now stay here, and keep breathing until I return."

It pains him to step away from her, to leave her alone, but he does it anyway, moving toward the door. She retreats toward the back of the foyer, and he's proud of her for having that much sense; whoever's here may not mean her harm, but that doesn't mean they wish her well. Only when she steps into the narrow cloakroom between the foyer and the sitting room does he finish his journey to the door and pull it open, revealing a deceptively scrawny young man of approximately Wanda's age.

Like her, he's wearing a ridiculous Halloween concoction instead of sensible clothing, and also appears to have regressed in the last hour, reduced to a teenager once more by fear and terrified loyalty. It's all in the way he holds himself with this one—his face is obscured by a red mask, blazoned with the black spiderweb pattern he's established as his own.

"Is she here?" he demands, and he's probably trying to sound authoritative and official, like someone whose questions get answered. The way his voice shakes betrays him. He sounds scared, and small, and Doctor Strange frowns at him.

"She didn't do what she's accused of," he says. "If you've come to bring her to justice, she already lives there."

"I know," says Spider-Man.

"Then why are you here?"

"She's my *sister*, dammit, I have a right to—please. Is she here? Is Wanda here?"

Doctor Strange says nothing, only looks at him and holds his silence.

ON THE OTHER SIDE OF THE COSMIC WINDOW, AMERICA CHAVEZ WINCES AT THE scene unfolding in front of her, the panic in the web-slinger's voice, and cold disdain in the sorcerer's. They're both trying to protect their world's version of Wanda, but they're taking such different approaches to the process that she's not sure they'll ever be able to meet in the middle.

And the middle is where Wanda needs them to be, because every version of the woman America has seen across the Multiverse has been surrounded by death, yes, but they're also surrounded by life. Whether Maximoff or Frank or Parker—or, in a few particularly unpleasant realities, Wyndham—every Wanda walks in an aura of life as much as chaos. Where her feet fall, the world blooms.

And America can't help her.

She balls her hands into fists, glaring at this crystal chamber, once her paradise, now her prison. She can't do anything to change what's going to come, because if she does, if she intervenes again . . .

The risk is something she can't take, and so all she can do is watch.

"Hence the name," she says bleakly, and glances away, looking at another window. This one is open on the same reality, the same timeline, but an earlier point. She wasn't here when this story started, didn't join it until her mirror arrowed in on it like it was the only essential narrative in existence. She needs to understand why that happened. Why *this* version of Wanda, why *this* reality? What makes her the one America has to watch?

"Our story begins . . ." she says, to no one but herself, and the echo of her words is the whistle of the Latverian wind, rushing across the trees . . .

CHAPTER ONE

—

MEET THE PARKERS

"HOW IS WINTER IN LATVERIA THIS MUCH COLDER THAN WINTER IN New York?" Mary looked out the window, its thick panes of glass distorting the snowy landscape. "I want to get home to Peter."

"Peter's fine," said Richard, in the tone of a man repeating something he'd already said a dozen times or more. He didn't take his eyes off the papers on the hotel desk. "Ben and May are spoiling him rotten. You know that."

If he had to leave his son with someone, Ben and May would always have been his first choice, even if they hadn't been family. He turned a page, making a quick mark in the margin, and kept reading.

"I do. And I also know he's nine months old," said Mary, turning away from the window. "Fury promised he'd reduce our field assignments after Peter was born, but here we are in Latveria. This feels like the field to me."

"I know, sweetheart," said Richard. "But these events have been escalating. The reality distortions have gotten strong enough that we can pick them up from North America. That means we need to find their source before there's a disaster we can't recover from."

"There are other agents."

"As good as us?"

Mary didn't answer.

"I'm the one who isolated and triangulated in on the pattern to these events. It would have been a personal insult for Fury to send anyone else."

"You couldn't have done that without the anonymous tips. I still think it's strange for some whistleblower to contact you directly rather than going to the bureau."

It was even stranger that the whistleblower in question had dropped the documentation showing the mathematical cascades at the Parkers' home, rather than delivering it to the S.H.I.E.L.D. offices. It was like someone had *wanted* them to perform the investigation. But that was where things started making sense. There were no field agents better than the Parkers when it came to this sort of event. That was why they were here, following a tenuous lead into the frozen countryside, trying to collect enough data to convince Fury to secure diplomatic clearance for a full team.

Reconnaissance was no one's favorite part of the job. But at least it wasn't boring.

"Whoever it is came to us, Mares, because they knew we'd follow this to the ends of the Earth," said Richard, with the calm, unruffled tone of someone who had had this discussion many times—they weren't fighting, they were reciting two sides of a well-known script. "Science gone awry is a risky beast to wrestle with."

"Yeah, well, most men don't drag their wives into situations where they might get mutated into something less appealing than Xavier's show ponies," said Mary, flopping backward onto the bed. "Will you still love me when I'm sweating acid and trying to hug you with my eighteen tentacles?"

"I'll be getting mutated right there with you, and we will have many loving, acidic years ahead of us," said Richard. He paused, eyes flicking between columns, comparing the numbers. "Mary, come over here."

"What?" She sat up. "Why?"

"Because I think I found the key to predicting where the next event is going to occur. Come look at this."

Dutifully, Mary rose and crossed to the desk, looking at the numbers Richard indicated. Her eyes widened marginally as she studied them. "I think I see it."

"If these figures are correct, these events have been corresponding to specific fluctuations in the Earth's energy field, and the next set of ideal conditions will occur tomorrow night, about seven miles from here. We'll be home by the weekend."

Mary grinned at him, a feral light in her eyes. "That's the sweetest thing you've said since we got here. Now, does that mean you're done for the night?"

"It does. We can get some sleep."

Mary grabbed his tie and hauled him out of his chair. "That's not exactly what I was thinking," she said, in a low tone.

Richard Parker was a brilliant man, and as he caught his wife's meaning, he returned her grin, then swept her into his arms and carried her back to the bed.

Outside their hotel, the wind wailed, and the aurora danced across the sky, an elegant ripple of light created by solar winds entering Earth's atmosphere. It wasn't something that needed to be stopped, but a beautiful reminder that science was a glorious thing when not turned to the wrong ends.

———

RICHARD'S NUMBERS TOLD THEM WHEN AND WHERE AN INCIDENT was likely to occur, but not what form it was going to take. Without more proof, Fury couldn't get clearance to send them backup or support: They were on their own until they verified the math.

They left the hotel at seven the next morning, having only waited until the sun was high enough that they wouldn't be traveling in the dark; they were both armed to the teeth, and Richard let Mary take the lead as they walked to their snowmobile. Of the two of them, she was the better driver *and* the better shot; he handled theory, and she often found herself managing the practical aspects of their fieldwork. While they could both handle themselves in a fight, this division of labor was part of why they were among S.H.I.E.L.D.'s most effective analysts. Anyone could learn to work with a partner. They didn't need to learn it. They worked together instinctively, and trusted each other absolutely.

As they raced into the white-dipped Latverian forest, their snow-mobile's engine revving to a steady buzz, Richard had to wonder—not for the first time since Peter's birth—whether their insistence on working together was going to orphan their son one day. They loved him more than anything, but they knew what they were good at, and more, they knew how important what they did was to national security. Without them, America would be in a more precarious position, and neither of them could live with that. Director Fury had already floated the idea of splitting them up if they didn't want to leave field-work completely, and the idea turned his stomach. It was bad enough being in the line of fire with his wife. If she were out there without him to keep her safe, he wasn't sure he'd ever sleep again—or vice versa. Mary had saved his life as many times as he had saved hers.

The trees whipped by like black slashes against the snow. The evergreens were lush and green, living up to their names, but the oaks and elms were bare-branched and skeletal, adding a haunting aura to the scene. Then, without any warning, the trees were gone, as the snowmobile zipped into a wide clearing that had no business being there. Richard had been poring over maps of the area since his research had started to point in this direction; every clearing and trail wider than a deer path had been meticulously mapped by the locals, who wanted their children to know how to get out of the all-consuming woods when they heard wolves in the distance, or when they wandered too far from their familiar routes.

This clearing was easily an acre of open space where forest should have been. More, there was no sign the forest had *ever* been there; the snowy ground was smooth and unbroken. A matte black cube occupied the center of the clearing, slightly larger than the storage shed Ben built in the backyard of their house in Queens. An adult could stand upright in there, if they didn't mind close quarters; they'd have to do it alone, however. Any company would make the space unbearably crowded.

Assuming there *was* space inside, and it wasn't just a solid piece of . . . something. Mary reversed the snowmobile into the shelter of the trees and cautiously dismounted, service pistol already in her hands and pointed at the ground. She didn't look to see whether Richard was following. They'd been working together for too long for her to insult him like that; he was already sliding down and drawing his own weapon, falling into a defensive position.

"So much for the element of surprise," she muttered.

"This isn't supposed to be here," said Richard.

"*Here* isn't supposed to be here; that isn't supposed to be anywhere." She jerked her chin toward the black cube. Looking at it felt like the visual equivalent of dragging an iron nail across a chalkboard, metal scraping across stone, setting every nerve she had on edge. That thing was dangerous. It was unearthly. She didn't want to get any closer to it, and her job told her she needed to do exactly that, and at moments like this, she wished she'd chosen a less dangerous career. Shark wrestler, maybe, or municipal fireworks quality control engineer.

They continued inching closer, exposed against the snowy background, no backup, no escape plan. If something happened, they could be in genuine trouble.

Naturally, something happened.

The cube began to hum, a single low note that was somehow disharmonious with its overall appearance, making the sensation of nails on a chalkboard even worse. Mary held up a hand, motioning for Richard to stop. He stopped. There was no arguing in the field; they had to trust each other, and know when to surrender the lead. Right now, this was Mary's show.

The hum continued, but when nothing else changed, Mary began inching forward again, Richard close behind. Finally, they were close enough to the cube that they could have reached out and touched it. Instead, they circled the structure, slow and cautious, looking for a seam or opening.

It wasn't until they rejoined the tracks of their own footprints that the thing they sought presented itself. As they returned to the point where they first approached the cube, a doorway appeared in its side. There was no sound; just the opening, a large portion of the wall fading into nothing.

This had *otherworldly* written all over it.

The sensible thing would have been to retreat. "We found an impossible structure made of unidentifiable material" would be good enough for Fury—but it wouldn't be good enough for the Latverian government. S.H.I.E.L.D. would be unlikely to get a larger mission approved without more than "the big cube made us feel weird."

Mary and Richard exchanged a look, nodded, and stepped inside.

The doorway led into a cavernous warehouse larger than the entire clearing. The size was pure arrogance: Fully half of it was unused, wide stretches of concrete floor showed between banks of mysterious machinery and stacks of wooden crates. A figure stood in front of a large monitor display, studying data that flashed by too quickly for even Richard's eyes to follow.

The figure was dressed in gleaming red-and-chrome armor, the front draping into something that looked like an apron, or like an attempt to mirror the fall of a scientist's coat. Their face was covered by a robotic-looking red helmet, and it was impossible to say whether they were man or machine. Their appearance had probably been designed to invoke that confusion.

They didn't appear to have noticed their uninvited guests.

Richard and Mary ducked silently behind a pile of crates, getting out of sight while they planned their next move. Mary holstered her firearm, signing, "What now?"

Richard frowned before replying, hands moving quickly, "We stick to the mission. Gather whatever data we can. Don't engage. Take it back to Fury. He'll decide what happens next."

Anyone watching would have been hard-pressed to decode their gestures, which were a mixture of ASL, BSL, and Auslan, a sign language spoken only in Australia by fewer than ten thousand individuals. As a synthetic communications method with a limited vo-cabulary, it worked for moments like this one.

Mary's answering frown was sharper. "I don't like leaving an unknown superhuman loose in Latveria."

"It's the mission."

Mary nodded, peeking over the crates and watching the figure move from the monitor to a complicated machine that looked like a combination iron lung and livestock incubator. The figure flipped several switches on the side of the machine, causing its lid to slowly lift away from its body and rise into the air.

The figure reached into the machine, picking something up. The wail of an infant split the air, and when the figure turned back to the monitor, it was holding a squalling baby, wrapped loosely in a length of tan cloth. Mary reacted first.

"Forget the mission," she signed, and pulled her gun before Richard could respond. She stepped into the open, gun raised. "You're breaking a dozen European laws right now," she snapped. "We were willing to let that go for the moment, as long as you didn't seem to be doing anything malicious, but you're not even supporting that baby's *head*."

"You say that as if I didn't practically invite you here when I opened my doors to you," said the figure, voice male, aristocratic, and unconcerned. "As for the infant, it doesn't matter. I have a spare."

The baby continued wailing.

Looking almost bored, if a metal helmet could convey boredom, the figure dropped the baby onto the nearest stack of crates, stun-ning it into silence, then thrust both hands toward Mary. Jets of energy shot from his palms, but she was no longer there. She had recognized the signs of an impending attack, and she and Richard were roughly ten yards away, behind a different stack of crates.

Richard caught Mary's eye and winced. He wasn't sure he would have been able to leave the baby behind, but from the look on her face, she wasn't even willing to consider it. They couldn't back up and call for help without letting the baby out of their sight, and if he tried to make her do that, she was going to lose her tenuous hold on her temper. Even if she agreed, help was a day away, maybe more.

"Why did you let us in if you were just going to kill us?" demanded Mary.

"My sensors picked you up when you entered the clearing. You're less disruptive when you're not trying to break in, and my work was at a delicate stage. I've finished now. I can deal with you and not lose any data."

"This doesn't have to be a fight!" Richard yelled. "You can surrender."

"Funny," said the figure. "It's always such a surprise when you primitive things are actually funny. This isn't a fight. Is it a fight when a snake gets into the henhouse, or a fox gets among the rabbits? This is an extermination, and you're the vermin that's intruded on my plans."

Richard nodded to Mary. She nodded back, then turned and began to slink away, moving through the shadows behind the crates, keeping out of sight.

"Vermin? That's not very nice."

"Neither is trespassing."

The baby, catching its breath, started to wail again.

"Still, I'm done here, and I can dispose of you while dealing with the byproducts."

"The byproducts?"

"The, ah, infants you were so worried about."

Richard heard a roar of rage, and the sound of Mary's gun going off, followed by another of those energy bolts, and then a deep, electrical crackling that bore no relation to the previous sounds. He looked around crates he'd been sheltering behind. The viewscreen was cracked down the middle, spitting sparks and spewing arcs of electricity. The red-and-chrome figure was still standing there, but as the electrical arcs spread to the incubator, he shook his head, then crossed his arms over his chest like a corpse being prepared for burial, and vanished.

The viewscreen exploded a moment later.

CHAPTER TWO

—

ACCIDENTS, ABDUCTIONS, ADOPTIONS

THE BLAST THREW DEBRIS ACROSS THE ROOM, KNOCKING THE PILE OF crates Richard was hiding behind over on top of him. He hit his head as he fell, and when he tried to sit up, his vision was blurry, making it difficult to see what was really going on.

Gray-clad legs ran by, heading deeper into the warehouse, and Richard frowned. Why would Mary leave him trapped if she was close enough to get him out? The figure—the robot scientist or whatever he was—was gone, and she could certainly have stopped to move the crates. He slumped, pressing his cheek to the cool floor.

What felt like seconds later, he felt the boxes being hauled off of him, and Mary's voice was asking, "Richard? Richard, are you all right? Report, Parker, *right now*!"

"Relax, Mares, I'm not hurt," he croaked, opening his eyes again.

His vision was still blurry, but not so bad he couldn't see her bending over him, her knee on the ground next to his head, her expression concerned. The light hurt. He winced and closed his eyes. "What happened?"

"That . . . robot was reaching for the baby, so I shot him, but he deflected the bullet into his viewscreen before he shot another energy bolt at me. He teleported out right before the screen exploded. He left the baby." She paused, eyes widening. "The baby!"

That was what was missing, Richard realized. The baby wasn't crying anymore. Had it been crying after the blast? He thought it had. He thought he could remember its screams. But now there was only silence.

Mary scrambled to her feet and ran. She had done enough to shift the crates that he was able to get up, one hand pressed to his aching temple as he turned to look after her.

She was near the smoking remains of the screen, scrabbling through the debris. There was no sign of the baby. That was possibly a good thing—no sign meant there was no blood or other indication it had been hurt in the blast. He paused, registering the color of her snow pants. They were brown, intended to help her blend into the forest. But they'd been gray when she ran past him before. How?

"Richard! Come help me look!"

He shook the question away, dismissing it as a sign of the concussion he was half-sure he'd received when his head hit the ground, and walked across the warehouse to his wife, looking at the rubble surrounding her. Then he moved toward the strange incubator, which had been cracked in half, but was still largely intact, and peered inside.

Two tiny mechanical troughs were set into the body of the machine, surrounded by dangling tubes and wires. One was empty. The second contained a baby, quietly chewing on its fist and looking at the ceiling of the machine with wide, unfocused eyes.

Richard reached inside. He picked up the baby, careful to support its head as the scientist had not, and turned to Mary.

"I found it," he said.

Relief washed across her face as she moved to take the baby, not quite snatching it from his arms, but definitely moving with a speed born of lingering panic. He didn't resist. She no doubt recognized how dizzy he was from the blow to his head, and didn't trust him not to drop the infant. That was fine. He didn't trust himself, either.

"The blanket," she said. He gave her a puzzled look. "It was beige. This blanket is green. He said he needed to dispose of the infants. I think the first one is still missing."

Richard looked at her grimly. "Then we search."

They hunted through the wreckage for the better part of an hour, until the baby they had managed to locate began to cry in tiny, hiccuping hitches. The incubator made a beeping sound. Richard, whose head was still pounding, shot it a wary look.

The beeping continued.

"Mary."

Mary gently bounced the baby, trying to calm it.

"*Mary.*"

She looked up, blinking at him.

"We have to go."

The beeping was getting louder. Richard reached out and grabbed Mary's wrist, dragging her with him as he sprinted for the door.

They were barely outside when the incubator exploded. The cube shook, then began to collapse inward. Mary howled something furious and tried to pull away, moving like she was going to run back inside, but Richard didn't let go. He pulled her toward him, getting an arm around her waist and holding her until the cube finished collapsing into a single point and disappeared. Only then did he release her.

Mary staggered a few feet forward, eyes on the indent the cube had left in the snow. "There was another baby!" She whirled, staring at Richard. "There was another *baby* and we didn't *find* it!"

"And if you'd stayed inside, we would have lost this one," said Richard, gesturing toward the child in her arms. "Mary, we had to."

She didn't answer.

"While I was pinned under those crates, I saw someone run past me. I thought it was you, but it's like you said with the blankets— their pants were the wrong color. I think there was someone else there. That's why we couldn't find the baby. Someone took it. While we were knocked flat, someone took it."

Mary looked at him plaintively. "That doesn't make this any better," she said.

"I know."

She switched her attention to the crying baby in her arms. "We need to get this little one out of the cold," she said. "Let's go back to our hotel."

"I'm ready if you are."

The three of them piled onto the snowmobile, Mary passing the baby to Richard with instructions to hold on tight and let her know if his head became too much of a problem, the baby whimpering but not quite screaming yet, and they drove off into the forest, away from the impossible clearing, away from the beginning, and nowhere yet close to the end.

———

"THE THING I LOVE ABOUT THESE RURAL HOTELS IS THAT NO ONE ASKS any questions," said Richard, dry-swallowing three Ibuprofen while Mary took the baby to the bathroom to clean up what was sure to be a ripe diaper situation. "Leave alone first thing in the morning, come back hours later with a baby, no one bats an eye. Tourists come back with babies all the time."

"They probably do," called Mary. "Black market adoptions are a real thing. That's what's going to happen to her if we can't find her parents. She'll go to an orphanage and probably wind up adopted by some wealthy American couple that wants a pretty little girl to put on their Christmas cards."

"Girl?"

"Yeah." Mary stepped back out of the bathroom, the baby wrapped in a towel and one of her T-shirts. "Wanda."

"How do you know her name is . . . ?"

"You know how sometimes babies have hospital bracelets on them?"

"Yes."

"This one had a tag. Like you'd put on a corpse. 'Subject B— Wanda.' I'm not calling her 'Subject,' and that means her name is Wanda. At least she'll have *something* familiar."

"Mary . . ." Richard stood, only wobbling slightly. "We have to take her to the authorities. You know we can't keep her."

"Right now, we need to take *you* for medical care," said Mary. "Your eyes aren't focusing right."

"I hate concussion protocols, and you're trying to change the subject."

"I know we can't keep her. Her parents are probably worried sick. But we're keeping her with us until we find them. What's the point of any of this if we can't even save a child?"

Richard looked at her determined expression and closed his eyes, trying to reduce the pounding in his head. It didn't work. He sighed.

"The American embassy it is, then," he said.

LATVERIA'S AMERICAN EMBASSY WAS MORE THAN AN HOUR'S DRIVE from their hotel, much of it down narrow, twisting roads barely wide enough to acknowledge the existence of cars. Richard had the distinct feeling the land resented the intrusion, and expected to be freed to reclaim its own in short order. The trees loomed on all sides. For the first time, the dense, old-growth forest was comforting rather than oppressive. Where there were trees, there weren't terrible constructs being fed on the bodies of babies.

Mary had insisted on stopping at the village's small general store for baby supplies and painkillers before they set out, and now that both Wanda and Richard were prepared for the journey, she focused on the road, driving with practiced efficiency. In the passenger seat, Richard cuddled Wanda's swaddled form, feeding her a hastily prepared bottle. The girl had been quiet since they reached the hotel and she'd been relieved of her sopping diaper; she seemed to appreciate the food, however, and had latched on without hesitation.

"We're almost there," said Richard, glancing from Wanda to

Mary. "I'm sure there's a system in place for this sort of thing. They'll know what to do with her."

"Because we can't keep her. Her parents must be worried sick."

"That's right."

"But what happens if they can't *find* her parents? What if she's really alone? Peter would love to have a little sister."

"Peter isn't old enough to have opinions about siblings."

"So it would be like she'd always been there, and he'd never question it. Wouldn't it be wonderful for them to grow up together? She was supposed to be one of two, and we couldn't save them both. What if she can still be one of two?"

"Babies aren't souvenirs."

"I know that."

"It doesn't sound like you do."

"I just want her to be taken care of."

It was barely trending into evening, and yet the embassy was lit up from the outside, powerful floodlights illuminating the driveway and yard. It was a subtle form of protection, and Mary admired its elegance even as she parked the car and moved to help Richard and Wanda out. No one was going to be sneaking up on the place, not with that much light. Nothing here was happening in darkness.

The buildings around it were more modest, their own lights dim in comparison. Mary had to wonder what their staffs thought of their gaudy neighbors. Did the other embassies understand? Or did they view this as one more case of the Americans being too loud, too gaudy, too self-absorbed? It didn't matter either way. She felt safer walking in the light.

The door opened as they approached, a staff member already prepared to assist them up the steps to the door. Richard handed the baby to Mary, not trusting himself to climb the shallow stone stairs with both a concussion and a baby in his arms. They walked up together, showing their credentials to the staffer, and were quickly whisked away, vanishing into the maze of hallways behind the scenes, the ones casual visitors would never see. The embassy doctor came to give Wanda a full examination; aside from some puncture wounds that appeared to have been made by IV needles, he found nothing wrong with her, and gave her a full bill of health after taking her fingerprints to run through the system.

Richard and Mary retreated with Wanda to a sitting room to wait for results, and after an hour, the American ambassador to Latveria appeared in the door.

"The girl does not exist," he said, without preamble.

"What?" asked Richard.

"What?" demanded Mary. "She's right here. She's real."

"Be that as it may, there's no record of her birth anywhere in Latveria or the surrounding countries. Her fingerprints are not on file. Barring the appearance of a relative who can claim her, she'll be placed into the national orphanage to await adoption."

"Can we help you look for them?" asked Mary.

The ambassador looked at her calmly.

"We have our own methods, and they will be searched for, thoroughly. But it seems likely they will all have died trying to keep her from being taken to begin with. I doubt that child has a soul left in the world."

"Well, if you can't find her family, can we apply?" asked Richard.

"Infants are not like lost dogs," he said. "She'll be held for a week's time, to give any family a chance to appear. After that, applications will be considered. I'm sure a stable couple with verified employment would be able to begin at the top of the list. I take it you would like to begin the paperwork?"

"She doesn't have anyone," said Mary. She looked down at the sleeping Wanda. "She deserves better than this."

"Under the circumstances, if you're willing to fill out the forms, and to agree that if a family member can be found who desires custody, you'll return her, I think we can safely let you take her home."

Mary almost laughed. "All it takes is a little mortal peril and adoption is so easy."

"Consider it a gesture of gratitude from both your country and Latveria, which is fond of not being destroyed by super-powers run amok."

"You're welcome," said Richard dryly.

———

EVEN WITH THE BACKING OF THE AMBASSADOR, IT WAS ALMOST three weeks before Richard and Mary pulled onto the street that led to their house. Their luggage was considerably more extensive than it had been upon their departure; babies required more infrastructure than most people realized.

Mary was the first out of the car, Richard close behind, and as they climbed the porch, they found the door open and the light on, May standing in the doorway with her arms outstretched.

"Peter's gone to bed," she said. "Let me see her."

Richard dutifully passed Wanda to his sister-in-law.

May looked down at the sleeping baby, a smile spreading across her face. "Hello, Wanda," she said. "Welcome home."

CHAPTER THREE

———

HOME IS WHERE THE HOPE IS

AMERICA SIGHS, TEARS RUNNING DOWN HER CHEEKS. SO THAT WAS THE POINT OF DIVERGENCE: That was when everything changed. She touches the window, freezing the image where it is, Aunt May holding Wanda, and the Parkers, weary but alive, watching from a few steps away. This has all happened. Even if she wanted to intervene—and she doesn't; this version of Wanda has as much right to exist as any other, born in fire and fear in the snowy landscape of Latveria, separated from the twin she should have had by the machinations of the shadowy entity who gave Richard Parker the figures that would lead him to the High Evolutionary, raised in love and light by her aunt and uncle, her brother by her side—she couldn't. What's done is done, even for a Watcher.

This isn't the Wanda she knew before she took up her post. This isn't a Wanda she ever could have known. But she still doesn't understand how the road from there to here was traveled, how she went from an orphan girl to a supposed killer. Motion flickers at the corner of her eye. She turns to her original window and watches as it jitters in time, flickering through events she's seen a hundred times, past the Parkers and their plane crash, past the spider sinking its fangs into Peter's hand, until her eye catches on something new, and she stops the stream of images on a small home in Queens, familiar and transformed at the same time, remade by the presence of a new member of the family.

Wanda's adoption didn't move walls or change the layout of the house, but everything else is different, sometimes in subtle ways. There are two sets of pencil marks on the wall, telling their own story of growth spurts and catching up. The pictures on the walls are different, Wanda glowering sullenly from her pre-kindergarten dance recital, clearly resentful of being forced into leotard and tutu; Peter at his sixth birthday party, sitting on the floor of a bouncy castle with Wanda tugging his hands above his head, both laughing and laughing and laughing. That's the first thing America really notices as she studies the house in Queens. There's been so much laughter here.

This isn't just a Wanda who grew up with a stable, loving family that had the resources to meet her every childhood need; this is a Peter who grew up with a best friend and companion, who knew that no matter what, he would never be entirely alone. There are photos of them heading to summer camp, swimming in the community pool, playing chess at the kitchen table, expressions drawn and intent. They have grown up so entangled that it seems impossible they should ever have been anything else, impossible that any reality could exist where they're not living out of each other's pockets. This version of Peter deserves to exist just as much as this version of Wanda does: A small change placed her in the arms of Richard and Mary Parker, but every hour since then has been another small change, until both of them have come to a place they could never have seen from where they started.

America takes a deep breath. She's still getting used to the tools of the Watcher's trade, and it's strange how she can always tell what time she's viewing through her windows on the worlds. This window tells her she's skipped forward a little more than fifteen years. Peter and Wanda are sixteen. The Parkers are long gone. Uncle Ben is still alive.

The image in the window shifts, sliding toward America's target. Wanda is waking up.

Her room is fairly standard for a sixteen-year-old American girl: clothes on the floor, bookshelves jumbled not only with books, but knickknacks and toys, little things she's found and squirreled away. Like Peter, she was too young when Richard and Mary died to really remember them, but next to the bed she has a picture from the day she was formally adopted, Richard holding her, Mary holding Peter, all of them facing the camera. The older Parkers are beaming like they've just won the world. Wanda likes to remind herself that while she may not have her adoptive parents anymore, she made them smile like that, once. She made them happy.

Someone with a keen eye could pick out the pieces of Latverian traditional art tucked among the clutter, some brought back by Richard and Mary, some acquired from online vendors once Wanda was old enough to decorate her own space. Richard and Mary had made repeated trips back to Latveria while waiting for her adoption to be fully finalized, trying to learn everything they could to keep her connected to her heritage. Mary had approached each trip with her heart in her throat, half convinced a cousin was going to appear and whisk their newfound daughter away, half hoping it would happen, for Wanda's sake.

But the cousins had never appeared. Three weeks after the recovery of the baby, the Latverian government had discovered the remains of a Roma encampment a little more than five miles away from the mysterious clearing. Everyone there had clearly been dead for some time, their bodies preserved by the cold. Richard and Mary hadn't inquired deeply about the state of the encampment, and the relief on the bureaucrat's face had told them, clearly, that this was the correct choice: What he *had* told them was that among the bodies were a young couple, the woman recovering from a recent childbirth, the man nearby. "It looks like they died trying to barricade themselves in their wagon," the man at the embassy had said grimly. "And we found these in the wreckage."

He had produced two bracelets of chunky wooden beads, hand-carved and polished until there was no chance of splinters. Two beads on each bracelet had been engraved, one with a wagon wheel shape, and the other with an initial. *W* and *P.* The man had offered the W bracelet to Richard, who took it gingerly.

"I don't think we need to worry about family members appearing," said the man at the embassy, and later, Richard would say that was the moment when it had started to feel like Wanda was going to be theirs forever, even as he and Mary had come to understand what a responsibility they had to her, to make sure she knew where she had come from. He had given the bracelet to the baby as soon as they got home, and it rests on one of Wanda's shelves, deeply etched with toothmarks from her toddler years.

The window is holding here. America takes a breath and lets it come alive again, allowing time to move forward in the reflection, allowing Wanda to have her story back again.

THESE ARE THE THINGS WANDA PARKER KNOWS TO BE TRUE, EVEN AS she swims from sleep back into consciousness, another day beginning: that she has been orphaned twice, and somehow still has a family that loves her; that she is American Romani, and doesn't know nearly as much as she wishes she did about her heritage; and that if her brother snuck into her room and moved her things around while she was sleeping, she's going to start her morning with a murder.

Her dreams were strange again last night, colors and shapes and impossible transitions without anything resembling a coherent story. She knows dreams are the mind processing what happened the day before, but she can't see how New York melting like it's made of ice cream is related to something she needs to process. Dreams like that always leave her with jangling, unsteady nerves, and today is no different.

It wouldn't be such an issue if they had an obvious cause, something that triggered them, but no. It's not "eat right before bed, have a weird dream." That would be too easy.

Wanda stretches, yawns, and sits up in bed, delaying the moment of opening her eyes as long as she can. She doesn't understand what Peter gets out of sneaking into her room while she's trying to sleep, or why he won't stop when it's so clearly bothering her. She takes a breath, and opens her eyes.

———

"PETER BENJAMIN PARKER!!!"

Peter looks up from his pancakes, eyeing the ceiling. "Wanda's awake," he says.

"So she is," agrees Uncle Ben, turning away from the stove with spatula in hand to reach for the plate where he's been putting the finished pancakes as they come off the heat. Sunday mornings are his domain: He makes breakfast, and accepts help from no one until it's time to do the dishes. "She sure does have some lungs on her."

"She gets those from Mary," says Aunt May, leaning in to kiss his cheek before crossing to the fridge and pulling out the orange juice.

Peter snorts at the well-worn joke as he turns his attention back to his pancakes.

Ben shakes his head. "Eat up, Peter. I'd say we have about thirty seconds before Hurricane Wanda comes surging down the stairs and things get a lot less peaceful around here. You need to stop messing with your sister."

"I'm not!" he protests, the same way he's protested every time this has come up. "She says I'm sneaking in and moving her things around while she's asleep, but I'm *not*! Even if I wanted to, you know I'd wake her up as soon as I opened the door!"

Aunt May and Uncle Ben exchange a look. "Peter has a point, May," says Uncle Ben. "He's not exactly what the kids are calling 'graceful' these days. Remember when he wanted to go to Wanda's dance class?"

"You mean remember when he got Wanda kicked out of her dance class?"

They both laugh, and are still laughing when Wanda speaks from the doorway: "You both forget I was the one who put the idea of going with me into his head. I wanted to get kicked out. I hated that class."

"Good morning, sweetheart," says Aunt May, crossing the kitchen to give Wanda a kiss on the cheek. "Orange juice?"

"With maple syrup? No, thank you. I'd rather have sticky pancakes than juice."

"You woke up loudly," says Uncle Ben, sliding several pancakes onto a plate for her and holding it out.

"That's because *someone*"—she shoots a venomous glance at Peter, who quails and shoves more pancakes into his mouth, eating like he's afraid food is about to be canceled forever—"rearranged my room again last night. At this point, I'm almost impressed. How did you move the desk without waking me?"

"I didn't," squeaks Peter.

"I'm not sure which upsets me more. The invasion of my privacy, or the fact that you keep lying about it." Wanda pours syrup over her pancakes and sits down. "If you think I'm stupid, you should just insult me to my face, not put together elaborate plans to make me question my sanity and feel unsafe in my own home."

"Wandy, you know I'm not that kind of mean," Peter protests.

Wanda wrinkles her nose at him. "Could've fooled me. You need to cut it out."

"I'm not *doing* anything, this isn't—"

"Oh, so my room is rearranging *itself*, is that what you're saying?"

They're both talking louder and faster, overlapping each other, making it impossible for anyone else to get a word in edgewise—making it impossible for them to even hear each other. They're not playing out a scene, they're reciting monologues, Wanda too upset and Peter too defensive to see the difference.

"Privacy—"

"Hysterics—"

"Maybe if you didn't mess with me for fun, I wouldn't jump to conclusions all the time!"

"Maybe if you weren't such a reactive *brat,* you'd have friends, and you wouldn't have to blame me for everything!"

"*ENOUGH!*" bellows Uncle Ben.

The sound of him shouting is sufficient to stun both teens into silence. They turn to stare at him, forks forgotten in their hands. He shakes his head.

"Do you think it makes us proud to see you go at each other like this?" he asks.

"No, sir," says Peter.

"Do you think it makes us want to point you out and say 'there they are, those two are ours'?"

"No, sir," says Wanda.

"Do you think it makes us love you any less?"

They know the answer—any question that follows two "*no*"s is going to be the same. Uncle Ben loves a chain. But they're sixteen, and orphans, and since they've started fighting with each other, the world has felt like it was falling off of its axis, knocked askew by a conflict they can't stop themselves from having.

To say puberty hit them like a hammer is to be facile but entirely accurate. Their tempers are short, their hormones are high, and there's nothing they can't fight about. Things they've always taken for granted seem suddenly malleable, like it all might slip away. Uncle Ben counts to ten in the silence, then steps over to lean down and brace his hands on the table.

"Now you listen to me, and you listen good," he says. "There is nothing either of you could do, ever, that would make me or your aunt love you one iota less than we do. We've loved you both since the moment we met you, and if we've loved Peter longer, it's only because we've known him longer. And don't go getting squirrelly about blood, Wanda. Your aunt May isn't biologically related to Peter any more than I'm related to you, but we're still family. It hurts us to see you fighting. You're all you've got, the two of you against the world, and no matter how much we love you, we'll always be those old fuddy-duddies you inevitably leave behind."

"You're not old, Uncle Ben," says Wanda.

He laughs, and if there's a note of relief there, they all politely ignore it. "Oh, I'm old as they come, but there's life in the old man yet. Now do you think you can stop tearing strips off your brother long enough for us to have a civilized breakfast?"

"I can try," she says, looking back down at her pancakes.

"Peter?"

"Sure," says Peter.

"All right, then." Uncle Ben finally gets his own plate, and he and May join the teens at the table, the four of them making an almost storybook tableau as they eat. There's no more yelling. There are a few sharp looks, but that's a small price to pay for peace.

———

THE RHYTHM OF LIFE IS WELL ESTABLISHED, FIGHTS AT THE BREAKFAST table notwithstanding, and it quickly reasserts itself. Peter bikes over to the library come mid-morning, while Wanda stays home and tries to put her bedroom back in order. It's difficult, with so much of the furniture moved in the night, and eventually she has to call Uncle Ben to help with the desk.

"I thought you said you were considering moving this over here anyway," he says, gripping one end in preparation for the lift and shove that will put it back where it belongs.

"I was," says Wanda.

"So why . . . ?"

"It's the principle of the thing." She shrugs. "This is *my* room. He shouldn't be sneaking in here to mess with my stuff, especially not when I'm sleeping. This is my private space, and he knows better."

She sounds so indignant that Ben can't help but smile. She's always been a stubborn one, their Wanda, ready to fight the world if it gets in her way. He's not used to seeing that stubbornness aimed at her brother, but he supposes it was inevitable—children challenge things as they get older. Parents, generally, but siblings as well. They'll always be close. By the time they finish high school, they may be less joined at the hip, and that might not be the worst thing ever. Peter needs to learn to stand up for himself: Wanda needs to learn to be alone with her thoughts without panicking. This is just another part of growing up.

It's sort of nice to see her so possessive of her room. He remembers when they moved her out of the room she used to share with Peter, how she cried herself to sleep for the first week, how he and May both had to pretend they didn't know Peter was sneaking over to sleep with her. The trick with Wanda and Peter has always been pulling them just far enough apart that they remember they can be happy on their own.

"If he says he's not, I'm sure he's not, Pumpkin."

"So you think I moved my desk by *myself*? In my *sleep*? Am I also renting a forklift in my sleep?"

"The desk's a puzzle, but we'll figure it out. We always do."

—

ONCE HER ROOM IS RESTORED TO NORMAL, WANDA SITS ON THE BED and stares at the wall, at its welter of colorful posters, pictures, and postcards. Peter got her a book of Latverian postcards for her birthday last year—adoption day, really, but it's the same thing as far as she's concerned—and he wrote "Wish you were here" and "Love you" on the back of every single one, down in the corner in his meticulous handwriting, so she could still use them if she wanted to.

She does use them, just not the way the printers probably intended. They're a window onto a world she could have belonged to but never did, a place she feels homesick for without wanting to ever visit. That isn't where she belongs. That's a beautiful story from her past, and she can tell it without wanting to live it.

The pictures remind her of her parents, both the ones she barely remembers and the ones she doesn't remember at all, and of her brother, who she remembers better than anyone else in the world. She sighs, rubbing her forehead with one hand. She knows Peter didn't move her things. If she stops to think about it, the way Uncle Ben always tells her to do when she's losing her temper, it's obvious he can't have done it, even if it was his sort of prank—which it's not. He doesn't have the upper-body strength to move her desk without dragging it across the floor. There aren't any drag marks, and the sound would *definitely* have been enough to wake her up.

But by the same token, she can't have moved it while in some sort of weird sleepwalker's haze: She doesn't have the strength, either. She just wishes she could stop jumping straight to blaming him for it. It's not nice, and it's not rational, but she keeps *doing* it.

She picks up the wagon wheel bead from the shelf where it rests, turning it between her fingers and trying to find comfort in the tactile reminder that it was all real, Latveria really happened, and even if she doesn't remember anything, that country is still her own. She still existed before she was here, and she chooses this life every day. This life is worth choosing.

The day is slipping by, sunlight fading into shadow, and it's sunset when she puts the bead back where it belongs and heads downstairs for dinner, Peter's empty chair like an accusation that Uncle Ben and Aunt May can't stop glancing at. Aunt May turns to Wanda, a concerned frown on her face.

"Did Petey say anything to you about staying out late?"

"No," says Wanda, and stabs her mashed potatoes with her fork. "He doesn't tell me anything anymore. Not since he went on that field trip."

That was where it started—the anger, the blaming. He went on the field trip while she was home sick with a stomach bug, and something happened. She's sure of it. He came home quiet and crumpled in on himself, the way he did when Flash had been bullying him, but for the first time, he hadn't been willing to talk to her about it. He'd gone to his room and closed the door, and closed her *out*.

He's been weird since then. It's been weeks, and he's been sneaking around, jumping when she comes into a room, and generally acting like he has a secret. They've never had secrets, not from each other. She knows every crush he's ever had, every girl he's ever dreamed of asking to the movies, and he knows every time she's turned red when a classmate asked to borrow her pencil. He was there for the summer when she discovered boys and fell off the high dive into the deep end of the community pool. They don't *hide* things.

But he's hiding something from her, and he's not at the dinner table, and it makes her so mad she can't see straight, so mad that the anger keeps leaking out around the edges of who she is, too big for her body to contain. As Uncle Ben and Aunt May exchange unhappy looks, she focuses on her food, and on her stubborn determination to find out once and for all what he's been hiding from her.

After dinner, she goes upstairs and turns right, going into Peter's room, rather than turning left and going into her own. His bed is made. He's always been tidy like that, and used to tease her for the controlled chaos of her own bedroom when they were littler, when they were in and out of each other's space every five minutes. She never thought she'd miss those days. She sits on the edge of the bed, resting her weight on her hands, and she waits.

She waits and she waits, and somewhere in the midst of waiting, she drifts off to sleep and slumps slowly sideways, her head landing on Peter's pillow, her feet still planted firmly on the floor. The dreams are there almost immediately, reaching up to grab her and pull her deeper down.

It's the window sliding open that wakes her, followed by the sound of Peter falling catastrophically to the floor. Wanda is sitting bolt upright in an instant, hands raised defensively, staring at the open window.

Peter fell because his desk has been moved to underneath the window, making the opening a few inches shorter than he expected it to be. The sight of him crumpled on the floor in front of the desk is a lot less surprising than the outfit he's wearing, skintight red-and-blue spandex with a spider on the chest. She blurts the first thing that comes to mind:

"Is *that* why you swiped my sewing machine last month? Peter, what the hell. You know I would have helped you with your seams."

"Wanda, what are you doing in my *room*?!"

They stare at each other for a long moment, caught up in the inanity of their respective questions. Wanda is the first to recover.

"This is why you look guilty when Uncle Ben reads articles about Spider-Man, instead of getting curious about the physics of a man being able to flip around on a string of web like an arachnid, isn't it? *You're* the Spider-Man."

"I am," Peter admits. He stands in front of his relocated desk, expression going perplexed. "Why did you move the desk?"

"I didn't, but if I had, you'd deserve it for starting this. Why did *you* move *my* desk?"

"I told you, I didn't move your desk! And I didn't move this one, either. I wouldn't have tripped on it if I'd— Is this really the conversation we're having right now? You just learned that I'm Spider-Man—I'm a freaking *super hero*—and you want to talk about desks?"

"Yes," says Wanda.

"Why?"

"Because if we're talking about desks, I don't have to be mad at you for hiding this from me. And I really, really want to be mad at you right now. It happened during the field trip, didn't it?"

Peter blinks. "I—how do you . . . ?"

"That was the only time you went out without me for long enough to go getting super-powers, jerk face. You were all weird when you came home from that, and you wouldn't tell me what was wrong. You *hid* this from me."

"I got bitten," says Peter. He holds up one hand, back toward her, like she could still see the mark. "A spider they'd been experimenting on got loose, and it bit me."

"That's bad lab safety," says Wanda, almost automatically. Inside, she's numb with horror. A spider bite isn't something worth bringing up weeks later, unless it was a bad one. Some sort of venomous spider, something that *hurt* him.

Peter laughs nervously. "I guess you could say that," he says. "It bit me right on the back of the hand, and it hurt . . . so bad, Wandy. I'd never felt anything like it. I flailed, and it went flying, and Flash and his goons started laughing at me, called me all sorts of awful things for being afraid of a little spider. I didn't see it clearly enough to know what species it was, so I just drew a circle around the bite to mark the progression of the inflammation and went to bed early, to sleep it off."

"You should never try to just 'sleep off' a potentially dangerous bite, Peter!" says Wanda. Her horror is transforming into anger, grain by grain. Oh, she wants to be so mad at him, her brother, the boy she loves more than anything in this world, and she wants to hug him so tight he can't breathe. The thought that she could have lost him is all-consuming, almost pushing rationality away. "That was—"

"A pretty boneheaded move, huh?" Peter rubs the back of his neck. "I wasn't thinking too clearly. I felt terrible. So I just went to bed."

"We all thought you'd caught my cold." She felt bad about that for days. "You mean it was the spider bite?"

"Yeah. Only when it stopped hurting and I stopped feeling bad, I felt *amazing*. Like, better than I ever had before. I didn't need my glasses anymore—my eyesight's perfect. And look." He picks up the desk with one hand, effortlessly moving it back to where it belongs.

Wanda stares. "You *could* have been rearranging my room."

"But I wasn't, I swear. I've been too busy learning how my new super-powers work. I can jump, and stick to walls, and I'm strong—it's like I have the proportionate strength of a spider! It's incredible!"

"I'm just glad you still eat solid food . . ."

"What?"

"Never mind. Just if you start getting the urge to wrap people up in cocoons and drink them, please tell me before I agree to have lunch with you again?"

"Sure . . ." says Peter, bewildered. "Wandy? We okay?"

"I don't like that you hid this from me. We don't have secrets, Peter. We've never had secrets. This makes me feel . . . bad."

"I'm sorry. I just needed some time to figure it out for myself. I was going to tell you, I promise I was."

"And you promise to tell me if anything else happens, or if these new powers of yours change? If you got them because a venomous spider bit you, they could turn bad on you."

"I promise."

He sounds so sincere, and so afraid she's going to judge him for this, that Wanda sighs, stands, and crosses to wrap her arms around him, holding him tight. "You're my brother and I love you, nerd," she says. "Never do anything like this again."

"Cross my heart and hope to live a long, peaceful life, ending in death from extreme old age, stick a needle in my eye," he says.

"That doesn't rhyme."

"I didn't think you'd want me to hope to die."

She smiles. "No. Guess not."

She doesn't think she's going to get any more sleep tonight, but when she returns to her own room and her own bed, she's out almost as soon as her head hits the pillow, falling into the tangled tapestry of her dreams as if she'd never woken up in the first place. Monday mornings mean alarms instead of waking peacefully at her own pace, but she's not surprised when she sits up to find her entire room has been rearranged again.

She should be even more convinced that Peter did it, now that she knows he's Spider-Man—and oh, she's going to be processing that one for a while, but at least he's not keeping secrets anymore—but he was so surprised last night when his desk had been moved that she no longer suspects him. Something else must be doing this, but whatever it is, she doesn't feel like it means her any harm.

Maybe Richard and Mary have finally come home. Or maybe her birth parents have followed her across the ocean, pieces of her past come to protect her by criticizing her taste in interior décor. "Good morning, ghost," she says to the room, and gathers her clothes for the day, taking them with her to the bathroom. If the house is haunted, she's not going to change where a poltergeist might be watching.

Downstairs, Peter looks up at the ceiling, following the sound of her footsteps. They learned years ago that staggering their alarms by twenty minutes led to fewer fights over the shower, and he gets up first because if she gets to the bathroom first, he winds up standing in the hall for half an hour waiting for her to finish. As long as she's ready to go on time, Aunt May and Uncle Ben don't care who gets up when, or who beats who to the door.

Wanda comes downstairs clean and damp and smelling of cherries—one of those fancy shower gels she saves her allowance to buy, and defends tooth and nail from any attempts to borrow. She smiles at Peter as she moves to serve herself from the skillet on the stove, mixing scrambled eggs, bacon, and breakfast potatoes together to pile on a piece of toast.

Anything can be a sandwich if you try hard enough, that's Wanda's motto, and if you can't try hard enough, you're a quitter. She sits down to the sight of Aunt May's beaming face. "What?" she asks.

"You didn't come downstairs yelling at your brother for the first time in a week," says Aunt May. "I'm just glad to see peace in our time again."

"Whatever," says Wanda.

Peter crosses his eyes at her, and she nearly snorts eggs out of her nose trying not to laugh with her mouth full. Aunt May and Uncle Ben exchange a look.

"Teenagers are weird," says Uncle Ben.

"And we have two of them," says Aunt May.

"We have two of them," he agrees, and beams at her. "Aren't we lucky?"

Wanda and Peter roll their eyes in unison as they rise and clear away their breakfast dishes, then move to kiss their guardians on the cheek before heading for the door. The routine is practiced to the point of becoming virtually instinctual; as long as there's nothing unusual happening, they can just go, and never stop to think about it.

"Bye, Aunt May!" calls Wanda.

"Bye, Uncle Ben!" calls Peter. And then they're gone, and the last normal day goes with them.

CHAPTER FOUR

WITH GREAT POWER . . .

"SO YOU'VE BEEN IN THE PAPERS A BUNCH," SAYS WANDA, ONCE they're about a block from the house and don't need to worry about being overheard by their guardians.

"Yeah," says Peter. "I can make a decent amount of money doing tricks for the shows downtown. There's always a circus around that needs a strongman, or someone who'll pay you to balance on the top of a pole or whatever. I may never be, like, ultra-famous, but I figure I can bring in enough that Aunt May and Uncle Ben won't have to worry about money as much. I heard them after the last trip to the grocery store. Eggs went up again."

"So we don't eat as many eggs."

"You say that like it's easy."

Wanda sighs and keeps walking, trying not to let her displeasure show. Finally, she says, "I don't think you're listening to me."

"I'm listening to exactly what you're saying."

"I think you're listening to the words, but not to what I mean."

"Subtext is just a way to build plausible deniability. What *do* you mean?"

"I mean Uncle Ben always says—"

"Oh, no," he groans. "Don't trot out that old chestnut."

"—with great power there must also come great responsibility," she finishes. "Maybe you should be using these powers for something better than making a few bucks on a school night."

"It's not a few bucks, Wandy. It's real money. I'm going to wrestle tonight for one of those private rings, and if the betting goes my way, I could make *hundreds*. Enough to cover our school costs for the rest of the year! I may not be making a difference for the world, but I can make a real difference for our family, and that's what matters."

She frowns at him, unable to articulate exactly why this feels so wrong. Finally, she says, "Just until we're done with school, though, right? Then you'll do something better?"

"There's nothing better than taking care of my family," says Peter. "Oh, hey—can you cover for me tonight? Tell Aunt May and Uncle Ben I'm at the library or doing something with the robotics club? I'm going to be late, and it's so much easier if I don't have to sneak around."

"Yeah," says Wanda. "You know, you wouldn't have been sneaking around these last few weeks if you'd just trusted me."

"Yeah, yeah," says Peter. "Sorry none of those awful talks about puberty included 'how to tell your sister you've developed super-powers.'"

"Well, they should have," she says primly, and he laughs, and everything's going to be just fine. Everything's normal.

Everything's the way it's meant to be.

THE SCHOOL DAY IS, IN FACT, NORMAL: CLASSROOMS, CAFETERIA, CHATTER IN THE HALLS. America watches for a time, entranced by the normalcy of it all, by the way lives unfold across the Multiverse, different and the same all at once. She watches Wanda sit in front of a brown-haired girl in her Spanish class, unaware that she and Jessica Jones are both destined for heroism. The accident that will give Jessica her powers is still some time away, while Wanda's own apotheosis is fast approaching. Reluctantly, America taps her mirror and tells it to skip ahead again, seeking the next big change. What will happen when Wanda's powers fully manifest? When Peter's secret is revealed? What then?

America's first jump forward brought her to the previous day because that was the moment Wanda found out what Peter had become; that could be a wedge driven between them, or a binding secret that draws them even closer. She's surprised when her scan snags on the next major point in their story less than a day later: The image resolves on Aunt May, Uncle Ben, and Wanda at the dinner table, Peter nowhere to be seen.

"I DON'T LIKE HIM MISSING MEALS," AUNT MAY IS SAYING, ANXIETY IN her tone. "He's a growing boy."

"Having been a growing boy in my own day, he can miss a meal every now and again," says Uncle Ben. "Besides, didn't you say he's at Harry's house tonight?"

"Mm-hmm, with the rest of the robotics team," says Wanda. She doesn't like lying to them, but she's surprisingly good at it. When she and Peter were younger, she was always the one tasked with getting them out of trouble. Uncle Ben had realized early that when something was broken, they should ask Peter about it if they wanted the truth. "He'll be home by curfew."

"It's odd for them to call a meeting with this little notice," says Aunt May.

"I don't know exactly what happened," says Wanda. "I feel like he said somebody broke something, so they're having to reassess their competition plan for the season? You should ask him when he gets home."

"We will," says Uncle Ben, and Wanda resolves to catch Peter before they can interrogate him, giving him the scant details she's been forced to fabricate.

The rest of dinner passes peacefully, transitioning into an ordinary night of homework and light chores. Wanda fills out her math worksheet at her relocated desk, not bothering to go to the trouble of moving it back; she'd been saying she wanted it under the window, after all. Her only objection had been to the intrusion, not the placement.

She's still in her room, getting ready to brush her teeth and put on her pajamas, when she hears the window across the hall pushed roughly open. Peter's been coming and going silently for weeks— something must be wrong if he's coming in with that little concern about being heard. He could be hurt.

Fear is at the forefront of her mind as she rushes out of her room to Peter's door, opening it without pausing to knock or ask whether he's okay. If he wanted Aunt May and Uncle Ben involved, he would have come in through the front door. Something must be really, really wrong.

What's wrong is that the man who just climbed in Peter's window isn't Peter. He's older, taller, thicker in the middle, dressed in dark gray, like he wanted to blend into the night while he was approaching the house.

And he's carrying a gun.

That's the first thing Wanda really registers, burning through her shock and leaving her with nothing but her fear. She takes a deep breath, still standing with a hand on the doorknob, and screams as she turns to run away, trying to slam the door at the same time.

It doesn't work. The man recognized what she was about to do as soon as he saw her go pale, and is already lunging for her; his foot in the door stops it from closing, and then he's barely a step behind her, grabbing hold of her upper arm with his free hand and jerking her to a stop.

"This place looked empty," he snarls, pulling Wanda against him so he can lock his arm around her neck. She claws at his arm, trying to pry it off, but it's like an iron bar trapping her where she is. "Shouldn't have screamed. You saw my face. I'm sorry, kid."

Wanda thrashes, but she's caught; she's never been particularly athletic, and this man clearly knows what he's doing. She's never been this frightened, not that she can remember, but this man, this strange man, he came in the window, he thought the house would be empty, this is a robbery. He has a gun and she's seen his face. She's watched television. She knows how this ends.

Adrenaline floods her body, and her nerves begin to fill with the unsteady, jangling static that she associates with her dreams. If she could see herself, she would see her pupils lighting up red, like someone has lit a candle inside her skull. The gun grinds into her temple, and the jangling gets worse, until her entire body is tingling the way her arm does when she lies on top of it too long in the night and it goes to sleep. Pins and needles fill her top to bottom, stabbing and scraping, and her skin is too tight, her bones are made of ice and her muscles are made of light, she's burning up, she's—

"Is there anyone else here?" The question is rough, almost a growl.

She manages to shake her head. If he thinks she's alone in the house, maybe he won't go looking for her family.

"Bad luck," says the man, and she feels the muscles in his arm tense as he prepares to pull the trigger. It's like the world has slowed down, casting everything around her in bright, burning relief.

She doesn't hear the door at the end of the hall open. She doesn't hear Uncle Ben step out of his room, the baseball bat he keeps under the bed for emergencies in his hands, ready to defend what matters.

The red gathers around her hands, fingers lighting up like Fourth of July sparklers, as she continues to claw futilely at her captor. Then, with a sensation that's almost but not quite like sneezing, the red light jumps from her hands to his flesh, knocking him back several feet, his shoulder slamming into the wall and his finger tightening on the trigger, just before he loses his grip on the weapon. The sound of the shot is almost unbearably loud in the narrow hallway. Wanda claps her hands over her ears, recoiling.

The man doesn't grab her again. Instead, he turns and runs for the stairs, not looking back.

Wanda feels hollowed-out, empty, and it takes her far too long to lift her head and be sure he's running away. Relief washes over her. She turns, intending to run to the door at the end of the hall and wake Aunt May and Uncle Ben, but freezes as she sees what's behind her.

Their bedroom door is open. Uncle Ben is on the floor, not moving, a red splotch spreading across his chest. Aunt May is standing over his body, hands clapped over her mouth, holding the screams inside while her eyes bulge more and more. She's pale as a sheet. Aunt May's going to faint soon, Wanda knows, and the thought seems like the best idea she's ever had in her life, and she collapses, limp, to the hallway floor.

———

PETER DROPS BACK TO STREET LEVEL WHEN HE SEES THE POLICE CARS parked on his block, their lights flashing a steady tattoo of red-blue-red, and his spider-sense starts to scream. He changes back into street clothes behind a bodega, then starts along the sidewalk, trying to seem nonchalant. He's worried his cover story was too thin, that Wanda slipped and told on him, that Aunt May insisted on calling the Osborns to be sure he was all right and learned there was no club meeting. She would have called the cops if she thought he was missing. Or Uncle Ben would have done it, to teach him a lesson about responsible behavior.

That lousy organizer shorted him the money he was expecting to make tonight, and he's already in a foul mood. He works himself deeper and deeper into his resentment as he walks, until he's furiously angry with every member of his family.

A thread of fear begins working its way through the fury as he gets close enough to see that his suspicions were correct—the front door of his house is standing open, and there are uniformed officers on the porch. There's no sign of Aunt May or Uncle Ben, or Wanda. A few dozen neighbors are scattered around the street, watching the house with the rapt horror of people witnessing a train wreck, and he wants to grab them, to shake them and demand to know what's going on.

He doesn't. If he's about to learn something horrible, he wants to hear it from his uncle Ben, from the one man who's always been able to convince the world to make sense. He wants to hear it inside his own house, which has always been safe and solid, a sanctum of sorts, a place he could retreat to when the need arose.

He approaches the porch. One of the officers steps forward, hands on her belt.

"Can we help you, son?" she asks.

"My name is Peter Parker," he says. "I live here. This is my house. What's going on?"

The officer is well trained; she barely grimaces, the muscles around her eyes and mouth tightening like she wants to say something, but knows better than to cross that line, and Peter knows. He knows that once he steps through that open door, everything is going to change. This is a moment as pivotal as the spider's escape from its cage.

(Watching from the other side of the mirror, America aches for him; why is it that every version of Peter Parker must stand in this horrible, frozen fragment of time, facing the end of the world? None of the other heroes she knows are tortured like this across the realities. None of them are denied even the possibility of a happy ending. The worlds are never kind to Peter Parker. America can only hope this moment won't destroy him.)

"Your aunt is inside," says the officer, and steps aside. This kid and his impending trauma are above her pay grade. So she lets him walk away from her, with his earnest eyes and the tight note of pre-emptive anxiety in his voice.

—

PETER STEPS INTO THE WELL-LIT BUBBLE OF THE LIVING ROOM. THERE are three more officers standing around and talking in hushed voices, like they're in a church or something. Aunt May sits on the couch with a fourth officer, slumped with her hands between her knees and her head bowed. She looks like she's been emptied out, drained of the vitality that makes her who she is. There's blood under her fingernails.

He's not sure why he notices that detail over any other. His spider-sense is going off so loudly at this point that he thinks it's a miracle he can hear anything else—danger, Peter Parker, danger, *danger*—but it doesn't feel like the kind of danger he can do anything about, and so he answers with polite platitudes as one of the officers approaches him, asking why he's getting home so late on a school night, asking where he's been, asking whether he saw anything—

Wait. Saw anything? Peter blinks, snapping out of the veil of numb confusion and jangling anxiety that was settling over him, and asks, "What's going on? Where's my uncle? Where's my *sister*?"

The officer's look of discomfort is pronounced and sincere, and that's probably why Peter doesn't punch him when he says, "Mr. Parker, there's been an incident. An intruder broke into your home through a bedroom window on the second floor shortly after ten P.M., and an altercation ensued—"

"Those are really fancy words for whatever you don't want to tell me," says Peter. "Where is my *family*?"

"Your aunt's been given a sedative," says the officer. "She's fine, as you can see. Now, if you don't mind, can we get back to my questions?"

"Not before we get back to mine."

"Son, I'm not the one who should tell you these things."

"Well, you've sedated my aunt, so who is?"

"We had to sedate her to keep her from hurting herself," says the officer, but Peter isn't listening. His attention has been caught by motion from the stairs, and the brief spike of hope that it's Wanda or Uncle Ben is extinguished as quickly as it came. A paramedic steps into view, holding one end of a stretcher, and he knows, he *knows*. The only question is who's going to be on the stretcher when they finish bringing it down.

And may the spirits of his parents forgive him, he doesn't know who he's hoping it will be. How do you decide between two of the people you love best in all the world? So he doesn't let himself hope. He stands perfectly still and watches them come down, until the familiar shape of Uncle Ben appears, covered by a white sheet and not moving, but still distinct from anyone else it could have been. Peter looks, helplessly, back to the officer he's been talking to.

"Where is my sister?"

"Upstairs," says the man. "But you can't—"

It's too late. Peter is fast—faster than anyone without preternatural reflexes—and he's primed to move; he's already halfway to the stairs, running past the paramedics to the second floor.

There are more police in the hall, surrounding the door to Aunt May and Uncle Ben's bedroom, but not quite obscuring the bloodstain on the floor. Wanda is nowhere to be seen.

Her bedroom door is open, and Peter rushes toward it, grabbing the frame and looking in.

Wanda is curled into a ball on her bed, knees against her chest and eyes closed. Her breathing is regular, and doesn't change as he steps into the room.

"Wanda? Wanda, can you tell me what happened? Where's Uncle Ben?" The question isn't fair: He knows the answer better than she does, he just saw them carrying Uncle Ben's body out the door to the waiting ambulance. He asks it anyway.

Wanda doesn't react.

"Wanda?" Peter moves toward her, puts a hand on her shoulder, and shakes. He's not expecting her to move like some sort of rag doll, totally devoid of resistance. She rolls onto her back, limbs flopping in all directions, and as he recoils, her eyes open. Her breathing doesn't change; he doesn't think this means she's woken up.

Her pupils are pinpricks, but that doesn't matter in the face of the fact that they're glowing red as rubies, so bright he can't look at them for long. He doesn't know what's going on. He doesn't know how this could have happened.

He just knows that, somehow, this is his fault.

He sits down next to her bed, elbows on his knees and forehead in his hands, and waits for the world to start making sense again.

CHAPTER FIVE

——

WHERE WANDA WENT

WANDA DOESN'T LOSE CONSCIOUSNESS IMMEDIATELY AFTER SHE hits the floor; she's awake long enough to pull her knees to her chest and wrap her arms around them, trying to comfort herself through the reminder that she exists, she's here, she's not a figment of anyone's imagination. It doesn't work the way she wants it to, and she whispers Uncle Ben's name just as she feels the floor drop away beneath her, and she's falling, she's falling, like Alice down the rabbit hole she's falling, into a tunnel of endless red light.

As this happens, America's mirror frosts over with the spider-webbed electric pattern of a lightning strike, becoming momentarily white as a caul. Then the whiteness shatters and she's watching Wanda plummet through the red, the younger woman's chaos magic somehow reaching across universes to entangle her viewport. It's almost like an invitation, and so she steps closer, and she does her duty: She Watches.

This isn't like the fall America saw (is going to see?—oh, chronology is always difficult, and when you're standing outside the time of a hundred different timelines, all moving at their own pace, it becomes borderline impossible) her take in the future, where she'll pull her entire body into the swirling chaos tides of her magic; Wanda's body remains on the hallway floor, empty and abandoned. It's only Wanda's mind that falls, plunging into an infinity that she knows, on some level, can go on forever; she could keep falling until the sun burns out, if she can't bear to go back.

The realization that it's a choice and she can stop falling if she wants to changes things. Wanda doesn't have eyes in this interior space, but she opens them all the same, and sees what surrounds her, sees the red light that should be terrifying and somehow feels like home, like safety, like a promise of nothing ever hurting her again; sees the sheets of deeper red "glass" floating all around her, above, below, and to the sides, shooting by as she falls. They look as if they're made of the light, just pressed close and turned solid, until they become objects rather than ambience.

She tries to focus on one of the larger sheets as it comes into view, and sees a carmine image of Richard and Mary, her own infant self in Richard's arms, the living room behind them. There's a banner on the wall, partially blocked by their heads, that says "Happy Adoption Day, Wanda Parker!" She doesn't remember that day, but it's obvious when it is; she remembers the banner, which she and Peter found in the attic when they were five and ran through the house, pretending to be airplanes flying important messages relating to some nebulous war. The banner snapped and fluttered perfectly, right up until it tore in two. She still has a piece of it in her memory box.

She's so focused on the moment she doesn't remember that she doesn't see the sheet directly beneath her until she crashes into it, and through it, with a sound like breaking glass and a sensation like plunging into freezing water. Then the sensation passes, and takes her with it, and the red tunnel is gone, and something else is left in its place.

——

PETER AND WANDA ARE SIX YEARS OLD. PETER IS OLDER BY EASILY SIX months, and he never lets her forget it—at this age, it means he's taller, stronger, faster in ways that will fade for the next several years, and while he may not know it consciously, he's enjoying his brief superiority while he has it. They've been with Aunt May and

Uncle Ben all summer, and it's been *wonderful*. Their aunt and uncle don't spoil them, really, but they're freer with the ice cream and TV nights than their parents tend to be. They've been to the zoo *three times,* which is something Mommy and Daddy never have time for, with their work and their travel and their everything.

The Parkers love their children and the children love their parents, but sometimes it's nice to be around people who aren't responsible for bedtimes and daycare drop-offs, who can focus on the love instead of the discipline.

Mommy and Daddy are at work again. What they do doesn't make much sense, but it has something to do with doing science, and they travel a lot to do it. Peter and Wanda don't mind. One of Peter's favorite bedtime stories is about how work took his parents to a faraway place called Latveria, and when they came back, they didn't bring a silly souvenir, they brought him a whole *sister*. That's better than a postcard or a snow globe, and now he's a little disappointed every time they go away and don't bring him back another sibling.

Wanda isn't disappointed. Having a brother feels right, like it's the way the world is supposed to be, and she doesn't want to share him with anyone else. She doesn't want to be one of three, or one of many; she wants to be one half of two, always and forever.

But Mommy and Daddy are at work, and Peter and Wanda are tearing around the yard like only young things can, all boundless energy until the moment the exhaustion takes them and they collapse, giggling, into the grass. Aunt May has been supervising them since lunch; Uncle Ben will come out with lemonade soon, and they'll all be together, and it'll all be perfect.

Inside the house, the phone rings; the sound drifts through the open kitchen window. Wanda freezes where she is, listening. She's a more anxious child than Peter: What he sees is that his parents went away and brought him home a sister, but what she sees is that things can change. She sees the underlying chaos of the world, even if she doesn't have the words to describe it yet, and she's eternally on edge for the moment where things change again.

Wanda is the one who hears Uncle Ben's voice shift, tone going shocked and distant, who hears him start crying. Out of them all, Wanda is the first to understand that something is truly wrong. The dreaded change she's been waiting for since she was old enough to know that she had parents before the Parkers has finally arrived.

Uncle Ben appears at the back door, tears running down his cheeks. He steps outside, and he goes first not to May, but to Peter, sweeping the boy into a crushing bear hug. Wanda still hasn't moved. She doesn't know the shape of this change, but she feels it in the air, feels it like electricity, like static, and she hates it, how she hates it.

Uncle Ben puts Peter down and turns to Aunt May. There's no discussion, no question of telling her in private; this isn't news either one of them knows how to break, and so it's best to just get it out in the open. No secrets in this house.

"May," he says. "That was . . . an associate of Richard and Mary's. We're going to get a more formal notification sometime tomorrow, but he wanted us to hear it from someone who knew and loved them. Their plane . . ." He pauses to take a choked, uneven breath. "Their plane went down while they were on their way home. There were no survivors."

May bursts into tears, loud and undignified, and Peter looks afraid. He still doesn't understand what's happening. Planes are supposed to go down. That's what landing is, when you think about it. He looks at Uncle Ben, seeking comfort, and finds only more tears. He turns to Wanda, and finds her crying, too. She's not smarter than he is—she just knows the phrase *no survivors*. She's heard it used about an encampment in Latveria, when people asked where she came from. *No survivors* means no one's coming home.

No survivors means she's lost another set of parents, and everything is going to change.

Peter rushes to her, as he always does when she's unhappy, and wraps his arms around her in mirror of Ben wrapping his arms around May, and pulls her close. She keeps crying, letting him hold her; she doesn't pull away. He looks at Ben, waiting for his beloved uncle to make this all make sense, to explain why everyone is crying.

Ben finally releases May and turns to Peter and Wanda. He looks old. He's always been old—all adults are old, that's what being an adult means—but he's never looked it like this, never looked like the weight of the whole sky was pushing down on his shoulders, threatening to push him to the ground.

He looks at them, at Wanda's tears and Peter's confusion, and he takes a deep breath, choosing his words with painful care.

"Peter, Wanda," he says, very seriously, "the plane your parents were taking to get home to us has had a bad accident. It crashed. I'm sorry. They're not coming back. They died."

Peter needed to hear it put that bluntly. Wanda's tears make sudden, terrible sense, and that realization shocks Peter into tears of his own. For a time, the four of them stay in the backyard, holding one another and crying, until the children start to droop with exhaustion and Ben and May carry them inside, tucking them into their respective bedrooms but leaving the doors open enough that they'll still be able to hear the house.

Peter is tired, first from playing and then from grieving, but he's not ready to sleep yet. He slides out of bed and creeps across the hall to Wanda's room, slipping through the partially open door. Downstairs, Ben looks up at the soft creak of the boards in the hallway and manages to smile despite his own ongoing tears.

"They have each other," he says. "They'll be all right."

"But, Benjamin . . . will we?" asks May.

Wanda is awake, but not in the bed. She's kneeling in front of the dresser with the little bag she packs whenever it's time to go between their house and the house they sometimes share with Uncle Ben and Aunt May. She's crying, steadily, and pushing her clothes into the bag with a robotic steadiness. She doesn't look around.

"Wandy?"

She sniffles, but gives no other reply.

"Wandy, why are you packing? We're not going home if Mommy and Daddy aren't coming to get us."

"No survivors," says Wanda.

"I don't—"

"There were no survivors when Mommy and Daddy brought me to live here with you," she says. "If there's no survivors now, the people who let them keep me are going to come and take me away again."

Peter's shout is loud enough to bring Uncle Ben and Aunt May thundering up the stairs; they were halfway expecting it. Neither of them has any experience with the grief of children, but they know children's emotions tend to be huge, confusing things, less bounded by the experience and moderation of adulthood.

They reach Wanda's room to find Peter kneeling next to her, arms around her shoulders, rocking them both back and forth. "No," he's saying. "No, no, no, no."

"Oh, Peter." Aunt May is quick to move to scoop him up. He screams and clings to Wanda tighter, until she lets go and steps back, bewildered. "Peter, I won't ask you what's wrong, but why are you yelling?"

"No!" he repeats, focusing on her. "I don't *care* if our parents are dead, that doesn't mean you can take Wanda away! She's my sister, even if we don't have parents anymore! She's *mine*."

Aunt May understands at once. She puts a hand over her mouth, glancing at Uncle Ben before looking back to Peter. "Oh, my darlings," she says. "You don't need to be afraid of that, ever. Richard and Mary talked to us years ago about what would happen to you if anything ever happened to them. They did all the paperwork. We're your guardians. Both of us, and both of you. We're a family. Nothing is going to take us away from each other."

"Really?" asks Peter, sniffling.

"Really."

"Wandy, you don't have to leave!" yells Peter, twisting to face her.

Wanda smiles for just a moment, then bursts into tears again. Uncle Ben comes to join the group embrace, and they hold one another and cry as the afternoon wears on.

. . . and Wanda falls out of the memory, plunging through the other side and back into her sixteen-year-old self, scrabbling to return to a moment when her beloved uncle was alive, even if the parents she sometimes isn't sure she really remembers weren't. Six is old enough for memories to have formed; sixteen is far enough away for those memories to have twisted out of true. Does she really remember Mary's voice, or does she remember an amalgam of pleasant maternal voices from television? Does she remember Richard's cologne, or the cologne of her third-grade teacher? She doesn't know. Maybe she never will. They died a long time ago. She mourned them then, and she's not mourning them now. They gave her her family. That was enough.

That has to be enough.

She plunges into another sheet of frozen red time, and is sitting in the kitchen, Aunt May on the phone talking to someone unseen. Wanda has a book of word games she's been working on all week—school's out for summer, and she doesn't like the library as much as Peter does, can't spend hours on hours there without getting bored. She's happier at the kitchen table doing jumbles and crosswords and being able to go and get a glass of juice whenever she wants to, instead of having to use the water fountain, which always tastes like metal and makes her teeth feel funny in the back of her mouth.

She is twelve years old. Old enough to have decided she and Peter don't always have to be in the same place, doing the same thing: Sometimes it's safe to let him out of her sight for a little while. She cried herself to sleep for three years after Richard and Mary died, but she's a big girl now, and she hardly ever cries at night anymore.

Aunt May thanks the person she's been talking to and hangs up, turning to Wanda. "Wandy," she says, somewhat abruptly. "How do you feel about going on an adventure?"

Wanda lifts her head and blinks at Aunt May, then puts her pencil down and appears to think very seriously about the question. "Is it the sort of adventure where I get into trouble for going without Peter?"

"No, Pumpkin, this is the sort of adventure you're expected to have without Peter."

Wanda's seriousness turns wary. "I don't want to go shopping for underwear again."

Aunt May laughs. "No, no, it's nothing like that! It's— You know how Richard and Mary adopted you from a place called Latveria?"

Wanda nods. "I remember."

"All right. Well, the people we think were your parents before them were from a group called the Romani. I've bought you books about them, but that's not the same as getting to know them. They're your heritage, the way all the people in the old photo albums are Peter's."

"Okay," says Wanda.

"I've been trying to find Roma people who would be willing to talk to you about your family. It's been hard, because there are a lot of different kinds of Roma, and most of them are fairly insular— they don't want strangers gawking at them like they're some sort of carnival act."

Wanda, who doesn't think she'd like that either, nods to show her understanding.

"Because of where Latveria is, your family was probably related to one of the groups we call Hungarian or Wallachian Roma, and I haven't been able to find anyone from those groups who's willing to meet with you. But there's a restaurant near Hell's Kitchen that belongs to a group of Romanichal—a different sort of Romani— and they agree with me that while it's not as good as finding your own people for you to talk to, it would be good for you to talk to *someone*. So they're willing to let me take you to meet them."

As always when someone brings up her time before the Parkers, Wanda feels fear clench in her stomach, a sharp feeling of abandonment yet to come. She manages to push it down, reminding herself that Aunt May loves her and would never try to give her to anyone else. Aunt May is her family. "Okay, Aunt May," she says. "Will you leave a note for Uncle Ben and Peter, in case we're not back before they are?"

"I will," promises Aunt May, who was concerned that Wanda would fight harder about the idea of going to talk to a bunch of strangers about the family she doesn't remember. "Go get your shoes."

As Wanda scampers off, she sees May moving to clear her papers off the table, leaving the kitchen as clean as they found it. There's always something else to be done . . .

This memory is shorter than the one that came before it. Wanda has barely had time to relax into it before she's crashing out the other side, falling, falling like she's never going to hit the bottom.

She slams into the next pane of "glass," buffeted by memory and carried along by chaos, and it feels like the red light that fills the world is trying to help her and eat her alive at the same time. Wanda falls into the memory and she's still twelve, still small and attentive in the way of young girls with sharply honed survival instincts: She and Aunt May are wearing the same clothes they had on in the kitchen. This is the same day. They're standing on a sidewalk in Manhattan, looking up a flight of stairs to an unassuming door under an awning.

There's a window, with the name *Dosta* written on it in gilt paint, and a small menu on a stand promises the finest in Italian cuisine. Based on the foot traffic, that can't be true; they haven't seen anyone go inside while they've been standing here, and they've been outside for a while, Wanda clutching Aunt May's hand like a lifeline.

"It doesn't change anything if we go in there," says Aunt May. "They're not going to take you back to Latveria. I'm not going to love you any less if you want to get to know more about where your parents came from. It's *okay* to want to know those things. Knowing your roots helps you know who you are. Richard and Mary would have wanted this for you."

"Really?"

"Really-really. They loved you so much. But they still looked for your birth family. They wanted you to understand where you came from."

Wanda takes a deep breath and finally starts up the stairs. She doesn't let go of Aunt May. Together they approach the door, and Wanda raises her hand to knock before Aunt May shakes her head.

Smiling, she says, "It's a restaurant. We can just go in."

"Oh." Cheeks burning, Wanda opens the door.

Dosta is small and cozy, and despite the menu, it doesn't smell like Italian food. The air is sharp with chilis and garlic, heavy with oil. Wanda inhales appreciatively, looking around. The décor is dark, the tables small and wooden, and a variety of staff members are scattered throughout the room, apparently in the midst of their standard tasks, whatever those are. A tall man with hair like Wanda's and skin a few shades darker than her own medium tan approaches, two menus in his hand.

"Welcome to Dosta, ladies," he says. "You've missed our lunch specials, but we're delighted to have you join us for dinner."

"We're not here for dinner," says Aunt May. "Hello. I'm May Parker. I believe we spoke on the phone? This is my niece, Wanda."

The man shifts his attention to Wanda, and she swallows the urge to step behind Aunt May. She's not a child anymore. She can do this. "Hello, sir," she says politely.

He smiles. "Ah, hello, tikna. So you're the child who needs to learn where her people come from, no? Where was your familia?"

The word is similar enough to *family* that Wanda takes a guess. "Latveria," she says. "About two hours from the capital."

"Ah." The man returns his attention to Aunt May. "We're of a different family, here. But we'll teach her as we can, if you can trust us with her. Say, two hours a week, to begin with? We'll teach her the proper Romani jib, and what she needs to know, and how to cook the things her stomach needs to know to long for."

"I think we can trust you," says Aunt May, and smiles before looking down at Wanda. "What do you think, Pumpkin? Spend the summer taking some extra classes?"

Wanda doesn't want to be left alone with strangers, but she does want to know the things the man is promising to teach her, and she wants to know more about the world her original parents came from. So she nods, and everyone is smiling, everyone is happy, this was the right choice for her—

Out of the memory and into the next, only a flicker this time, passing through so quickly she could blink and miss it.

Peter, angry that Wanda is doing something without him, angry that she wants to learn to talk to people in a way he can't, and Wanda, reassuring him that she'll always be his sister, no matter what happens, they can never change enough to lose each other.

Never.

CHAPTER SIX

—

FALLING FARTHER IN

WANDA IS GETTING MORE CONTROL OF HER DESCENT. SHE'S STILL plummeting through the chaos, but she's aiming herself now, seeming to pick and choose from the memories below her in a way that speaks to learning how this place and power work. This is her magic, finally awake and filling Wanda's hands, giving her a tutorial of sorts on the way she'll be expected to interact with it from now on. She's plugged into the chaotic heart of the universe, and she's not unwinding it, and it's not consuming her, because this is her birthright. She belongs here.

The next memory she falls into is two years later. Puberty has seized control of the Parker household: Doors are slammed more often than they're opened in invitation, questions are answered with huffs and rolled eyes rather than explanations. Peter still goes to the library. Wanda still goes to language lessons at Dosta; she's learning how to cook, quite well, even if the things she says are mildly spiced leave Peter choking and lunging for a glass of milk. They will survive these days.

Wanda is at the restaurant when the memory begins, going over her lesson for the week with Django, the man who greeted her on her first day, and stirring a pot of spaghetti sauce at the same time. They do make some basic Italian recipes, as part of an effort to stay open—Roma cuisine is specialized and not quite popular enough to keep them afloat without the extra money brought in by pastas and risottos. Questions of child labor have been sidestepped by pointing out that this is a family business, and Wanda is family. They just don't specify *whose* family.

Wanda doesn't mind. It's nice to have people who want her enough to claim her as family, and it's nice to have a place she can go when home seems too small and too crowded, when she and Peter inevitably butt heads over something that would have been small two years ago, before they started growing into the adults they would eventually become, and the growing complexity of their lives made everything so much harder than it has to be. Peter has the library, and she has the restaurant. He's learning to cook, too, from Aunt May, who insists it's a life skill they both need to have mastered before she's going to let them go to college—but college is in the future, a problem for versions of themselves who have yet to be born, and right now Wanda is making spaghetti.

The bell over the door rings. Django rises and goes to see who's come in, leaving Wanda to her sauce. She focuses on what she's doing, adding more garlic, more chilis. The spices are still her favorite part. She loves being able to eat things that catch fire in her mouth, light up her senses, and clear her sinuses at the same time, bringing new colors into the world. Sometimes when she bites into something particularly wonderful, it feels like she can see those secret colors only shrimp can perceive, the ones the human eye isn't built to understand.

She's so focused on her sauce that she doesn't hear Django coming back until he's pushing her aside and reaching for her bowl of chopped chilis. "Hey!" Wanda protests. "That's my batch!"

"Yes, but we have a pair of special guests, and they came specifically for our spaghetti."

Wanda blinks. No one comes specifically for their spaghetti, or their lasagna, or any of their other supposedly "Italian" dishes. They may be the sales that keep the restaurant open, but their spice profiles are entirely wrong for what they're meant to be. No one who actually *likes* Italian food comes here looking for it.

"What?"

"They heard it was the hottest in the city. One of them wanted to find out for himself, and he dragged his friend along." Django dumps the chilis in. "Go, be useful, see if he wants a drink while he waits for his takeout order, hurry!"

And so it is that Wanda, who never works front of house, finds herself shoved out of the kitchen and staring in openmouthed disbelief at the handsome, familiar face of one Johnny Storm, also known as the "Human Torch," a member of the Fantastic Four. He's standing next to another blond, broad-shouldered man, but as his friend is studying the pictures on the wall, he takes second place to the handsome teenager she recognizes from the magazines, the one half her classmates are entirely in love with, and the other half pretend they'd be too good for. The *super hero*.

"Guh," she says.

The Human Torch smiles—he smiles *at her,* specifically—and says, "I have that effect on people. I sort of wish I didn't, but I guess it comes with the territory. Are you all right, miss?"

Wanda swallows. There's a cocky note in his voice that she recognizes from Flash when he's talking about sports, or Peter when he's talking about science. It seems to be the tone boys use when they think they're just about the coolest things in the whole universe, and she tries not to encourage it from Peter. She doesn't need to encourage it from Johnny Storm. She's not sure he has that many people in his life who tell him when he crosses the line.

"I'm fine," she says. "Django sent me out to ask if you wanted some water?"

"That would be great."

Wanda busies herself with getting a pitcher and a pair of glasses, not dawdling, but not pushing herself to move particularly fast, either. Waiting is another thing Johnny Storm could probably stand to do a little more of.

He smiles again when she hands him the glass, and she's heard people say Captain America is handsome, but she guesses they've never seen the Human Torch up close to make a proper comparison. This man is . . . well, he's *perfect*.

But then his friend turns to accept the second glass, a polite smile on his own lips, and it's *Captain America*. Johnny Storm is not only here, in *her* restaurant, but he brought *Captain America* with him. Captain America, who saves the world the way Peter does extra credit for science class—casually, nonchalantly, and like it's nothing special.

She can't decide whether she wants to hug Django or kill him for leaving her here alone. Somehow, she manages not to swoon or sigh. Just leans against the counter with fourteen-year-old nonchalance and asks, as casually as she can muster, "You really came all this way for the spaghetti?"

"It's not 'all this way'—you have to have seen the Baxter Building. It's right over there. On 42nd and Madison." Johnny points with the hand not holding his water glass. "And yes, I did. My brother-in-law ordered some a few weeks ago, delivery, and he said it was so hot it was basically inedible. I wanted to see if he was exaggerating. Steve here agreed to come with me, because he's never met a family-owned business he didn't want an excuse to give money to."

Captain America looks abashed. "He's not mentioning that I owed him lunch for helping us with a little problem last week, and this is how he wanted me to repay him."

With these two, "little problem" could mean anything from a leaky faucet to an invasion by a parallel dimension. Wanda looks at them and decides they don't want her to ask. They're not here being super heroes, they're here as Johnny and Steve, men who want spaghetti, and she'll treat them like it, even if she's going to write about this in her diary later, even if she wants to squeal and clap her hands. The Fantastic Four save the world almost as often as Cap and the Avengers do, but they do it with science, and that makes them amazing, while Captain America basically *is* science, and that's amazing, too. She could talk to them all day. She'll still be talking to science, even if she's talking to science as Johnny and Steve, and not a pair of super heroes.

She opens her mouth to say something witty, and what comes out is, "You gentlemen like spicy food?"

"I don't have the stomach for it," admits Steve. "I love it, but it doesn't agree with me. I'm going to pick up about a gallon of milk before we sit down to eat our lunch."

"Yogurt will help even more," says Wanda. "And maybe add an order of jaxnija to your lunch—it's a pretty straightforward meat and bean soup, and ours isn't too spicy. It'll help to fill you up."

"Thanks for the tip," says Steve, with audible sincerity.

Wanda smiles at him. He's easy to smile at, and not just because he's so good-looking; something about him radiates sincerity, and an earnest desire to make the world a better place.

Johnny smirks at him and holds up the hand he was just pointing with. It bursts into flame. "I always pick spicy when it's my turn to choose," he says. "All of me is as heat-resistant as my skin. Things without a decent spice level might as well be made of library paste. I remember liking egg salad before we got our powers. Not so much these days."

"You'd like mine," says Wanda automatically. Her cheeks burn as she realizes what she just said. "I mean, if you add enough paprika and some hot curry powder, you can make egg salad with bite."

"Maybe I should consider you when I'm looking for a private chef," Johnny says, and Wanda's cheeks flare again, even though she knows he's joking, she knows he doesn't mean it—he's too old for her, and he's a *super hero*! Super heroes don't tease ordinary girls they meet in restaurants.

Something about the way he's standing tells her he's also teasing to keep her attention on him, rather than on Steve. She's seen Peter do the same thing, when he didn't want his bullies to be focusing on her. She's torn between being insulted that Johnny Storm is acting like she might be a bully, and charmed that he's protecting his friend. Captain America is a hero. He saves America. He saves the world. Steve, though . . .

Steve seems a little shy and out of place, like he just wants to exist without being observed.

Heroism must be hard sometimes. It's natural to want a break.

And so she keeps her eyes on Johnny, she smiles and returns his teasing with as much sincerity—none—and when Django appears from the back with a bag of takeout containers, she looks over and says, "We need an order of jaxnija, mild, and some plain yogurt."

Django blinks, then grins. "As madame wishes," he says, and hands her the bag, disappearing again.

"Thanks for remembering," says Steve.

"Anything for a friend of Johnny Storm," she says, and is rewarded when Johnny laughs. She likes that sound. She wants to hear it again.

Django returns with a second bag, which he offers to Johnny with a flourish. "On the house," he says.

"I'd argue, but we did save your block last week," says Johnny, extinguishing his hand as he takes the bag. "Tell you what: If this is as hot as Reed says, I'll be back for more, and I can pay next time."

"Call ahead," says Wanda abruptly. "If I know you're coming, I can make a special pot with the spice levels I use at home, maybe give him a better second impression."

"As long as I get the real stuff, works for me," says Johnny, and winks at her before he turns to go.

"Thank you, miss," says Steve. He digs a few bills out of his pocket and shoves them into the tip jar while Django is focused on Johnny, then turns to follow his friend out the door.

Wanda doesn't swoon as soon as they exit. But it's a near thing. She's seen the Fantastic Four save the day plenty of times since she started hanging out in Midtown, but having one of them up close— talking to one of them—is different. She can't even *think* about being that close to Captain America, or she's going to catch fire just like Johnny, and she's not as fireproof as he is.

Django gives her a knowing look. "First crush? Don't worry about finishing the sauce, I've got it good to go. Why don't you head on home for the day?"

Wanda doesn't argue, just gets her things and heads for the subway.

She's still walking on air when she reaches the house, unlocking the front door and letting herself inside to find Peter with his home-work spread out across the dining room table. She would normally grouse at him for that, calling him inconsiderate for not leaving space for anyone else, but right now, she doesn't feel like grousing. She feels like beaming. So she does, radiating happiness at him until he has to notice.

"What?" asks Peter.

"Guess who *I* met today?"

"I don't know. The Queen of England?"

"No. Captain America and the Human Torch." She flops into an open chair, letting her head loll back. "They're even cuter in person, you know. The Human Torch wanted our spaghetti."

"Nuh-uh! No one wants your spaghetti! You put too much hot sauce in it."

Wanda looks affronted. "I don't put *any* hot sauce in it. I use chilis, and a lot of other things. And he did so. He likes spicy food."

"Yeah, well—I'm going to be a super hero, too, someday, just like the Fantastic Four. And when I am, Johnny Storm is gonna see that he should be *my* best friend, and I won't need a stupid sister anymore."

Wanda laughs, and is still laughing as he shoves his chair back and stalks out of the room, all wounded teenage pride and an envy he doesn't even have the words for. She's laughing as she falls out of the memory, and the falling Wanda is still smiling, her joy having been enough to break the panic that had been consuming her.

There's another memory coming up fast, and Wanda twists in the air, adjusting her position so she crashes straight into the ruby "glass," landing in a classroom during her lunch period only a year ago. She's fifteen, taller, gawkier, no longer quite as scrambled by the chemical changes in her own mind. The chaos in her is stronger, too, even if she couldn't see it at the time.

Other students are scattered around the room, divided into pairs, one each on either side of a chessboard. An adult stands be-hind Wanda, one hand on her shoulder, caught in the middle of an introduction.

"—already know Wanda Parker, but she's going to be joining us, starting today," says the man. "Give her a warm welcome while we put her through her paces and find out where she falls on our skill ladder. Go find an open opponent, Wanda."

He doesn't need to tell her twice. She steps away as soon as she's given permission, moving to join a girl who looks a few years older than she is, on the top end of the high school age range, and reaching for the box of pieces.

The rest of the hour is a fairly standard series of chess games, but as time passes, a pattern emerges. Wanda seems to have an incredible grasp of innate probability. She reads the board like a map, and every road points straight and true to victory. She's a gracious winner, probably because she's been playing board games with her family for her entire life, and she's an equally gracious loser—not that she loses often.

The light flickers outside the classroom. This memory is less linear than the ones that came before it: They were single moments, caught and kept for their importance in Wanda's life. This is an aggregate, a display of something that truly mattered, but mattered because it lasted so long, stretched over so much time, and changed her life in some way.

The games come and go, and Wanda wins more and more often, comfortably reaching the top of the club's skills bracket, until she's having trouble finding opponents, until even the teacher doesn't always want to sit down across from her. Still, she keeps showing up; she's happy to help new members get their feet under them, and she likes having the extracurricular on her transcript.

About midway through the year, the light flickers and the chessboards are left on their shelves, replaced by hands of cards. Only about half the faces are familiar, and the clock says school hours have ended for the day; this is some sort of unsanctioned club, a game that isn't meant to be happening here. Peter, who never came to the chess games, sits at a desk in the back of the room, waiting for Wanda to finish so he can walk her home. He's focused on his math homework, not paying attention to the room at all.

In the poker circle, Wanda has just won her fifth hand in a row. She's pulling in her winnings, smiling slightly, when one of the other students throws his cards at her and jumps to his feet, face red.

"You're cheating!" he yells. "You're a cheater, but no one says it, because we all know you're Mr. Connolly's favorite! He doesn't care if you cheat, as long as it means his precious chess club keeps winning!"

"I don't cheat," says Wanda, shocked by the accusation. She wasn't expecting it, that much is clear; she was playing clean, and this came out of nowhere.

"Yes, you do," snaps the boy. "You're a dirty gypsy, and all dirty gypsies cheat!"

Wanda gasps, the blood draining from her cheeks as the boy storms for the door. But Peter is already there.

"What did you call my sister?" he demands.

"She did a whole report on it," says the boy. "She's not ashamed of it. I just called her what she *is*."

"That word is a slur," says Peter. "She told you in the report you're talking about, and even if she hadn't, you threw it like a rock. You apologize right now."

"I don't apologize to cheaters," says the boy.

Peter punches him.

It's not a very good punch, more enthusiastic than effective, and the boy punches right back, sending Peter's head snapping backward. Wanda is on her feet by then, and as the boy closes on Peter, she closes on him, until it's two on one, all of them hitting and pulling hair and scratching.

The sound attracts the janitor, who opens a supposedly empty classroom to find a brawl and an illicit card game. He physically breaks up the first; his presence ends the second.

Peter and Wanda are sent home with a note summoning them to the office first thing in the morning, and while Wanda's crying as they leave campus, her tears have dried by the time they get home. Peter has a black eye and a swollen lip, and Aunt May greets them with dismayed pride, which grows to an offer to take them for ice cream once she understands what happened.

The next morning, all three students meet at the principal's office, along with a surprise guest: Uncle Ben follows them, and makes sure the principal knows, in detail, that the other student started it. He doesn't condone violence, but he won't punish his nephew for protecting his sister. The two get a three-day in-school suspension; the aggressor is sent home for the rest of the week. And they know, without question, that their bond of partnership and protection has survived all the turmoil of the last few years. They are still a unit.

Wanda falls out of the memory understanding why she had to fall into it. It's not unusual for siblings to drift apart during their teen years, when different interests and friend groups tend to develop; Wanda's growing association with her heritage and Peter's studies could easily have come between them. Wanda needed to remind herself how tight their bonds are drawn.

She's still falling, but slower now, and there are no red sheets beneath her. She opens her eyes, and they're red from side to side. No sclera, no irises, no pupils. She sighs, and stops, then rotates slowly in the redness, until her feet are pointed downward. Floating, serene, she spreads her arms.

"Enough," she says, and the word is a scream in the void, and the tunnel of red shatters into nothingness.

———

IT'S BEEN THREE DAYS. UNCLE BEN'S BODY WAS TAKEN AWAY BY THE police and surrendered to the coroner; it has since been released to the funeral home, and they're planning to bury him at the end of the week. Peter still can't believe it. How can Uncle Ben, one of the most *alive* people he's ever known, be contained inside a little wooden box forever? He should be back by now. He should have gotten tired of this game and come home.

He's never coming home. Peter knows that, knows it from the hollows in Aunt May's cheeks and the silence in the living room, the way the house doesn't seem to breathe anymore. But he can't believe it. Not really.

Maybe it would be easier if Wanda were home. But it's been three days, and she still hasn't woken up. He's been sitting with her at the hospital whenever they'd let him, listening to the beep of the machines that tell him she's still alive, holding her hand and waiting.

Just waiting.

"Wanda," he says. "Aunt May can't stop crying. She's afraid . . . she's afraid she lost you both that night. But I know she didn't, because you wouldn't do that to us. You wouldn't go. Not if you had any choice. You're the most stubborn person I've ever met, and you'd find a way to come back just so you could yell at death for not wanting to eat your spaghetti." He sniffles, and squeezes her hand. "Wanda . . . I can't stop crying, either.

"I know you like to say the rules for you aren't the same as the rules for other girls, because you're my sister, and the rules for me aren't the same as the rules for other boys, because I'm your brother. But this is bigger than opening my backpack without asking, and the rules aren't *that* different for you. You have to wake up now. It's a rule. Because the rule is no one is allowed to take my sister away from me, and that means you, too. You have to wake *up*."

Wanda opens her eyes.

Peter doesn't notice at first; he's still looking at his hands. "I can't do this without you. Aunt May can't do this without you. The guy from the restaurant keeps calling the house—Django? And he's really worried about you, too. Please, Wanda. Please."

Her hand tightens slightly in his. He looks up, excitement and fear in his eyes, and jumps to his feet as he sees that her eyes are open. "Wanda!"

He moves to hug her. She pushes him away. He blinks, shaking his head, and clearly decides she didn't recognize him in the moment: He goes to hug her again, and this time when she raises her hands, what greets him is not a shove but a shimmering wall of red energy, like a ruby shell wrapped around her, keeping him at bay. He stares, fear and confusion in his eyes.

"Wanda . . ." he says.

She turns her face away, ducking her head so she can't see him anymore. "You don't understand, Peter, you weren't *there*," she says. "It's my fault. I killed Uncle Ben."

CHAPTER SEVEN

—

... THERE MUST ALSO COME GREAT RESPONSIBILITY

THERE'S NOTHING PHYSICALLY WRONG WITH WANDA; CHECKING HER out of the hospital only takes about an hour, the doctor—who knows Peter and Aunt May better than her own patient at this point—earnestly telling her she needs to sit down at once if she feels faint or like she's in danger of passing out again. They send her home with a bag of antianxiety meds intended to "take the edge off" if she feels like it's all getting to be too much, but on the whole, the episode is chalked up to shock and trauma and not expected to recur.

She and Peter ride home in uncharacteristic silence, like neither of them knows quite how to begin. But once they're back where they belong, the silence shatters. "This wasn't your fault, Wandy," says Peter, getting her settled on the couch—she started to hyperventilate when she saw the stairs, and even though the upstairs hall has been cleaned, not a trace of blood remaining, he doesn't want to push it yet. Aunt May is in the kitchen, reheating some of the chicken casserole one of their neighbors dropped off. "They caught the man who broke in here, and I'd . . ."

He pauses for a moment, expression twisting, turning sick with guilt. "I'd seen him before. He broke into the wrestling ring where I was all evening. Stole the night's proceeds after the organizer refused to pay me. And I let him go. Said if they didn't want to pay me, I wasn't going to do them any favors. I said it wasn't my *job*." He looks down at his hands. "I have these abilities now, I could have been doing so much good with them, and I said it wasn't my *job,* and now Uncle Ben is dead. Because of me."

Wanda shakes her head, and it's hard not to interpret her refutation as agreement, like she believes him when he says this is his fault.

Her words don't agree.

"He grabbed me," says Wanda. "Upstairs, when I came out of my room, he grabbed me, and I'd seen his face, and he was going to . . . he was going to hurt me, Peter, and I was so scared that I just grabbed his arm, and all I could think was how much I wanted him to get away from me. I pulled this—this light out of myself, and it was red, and it filled my hands and I pushed it at the man, and it went into him, and he let go. But when he did, he stumbled. The gun went off, and . . . Uncle Ben . . ." She starts to cry, great racking sobs that shake her entire body.

Peter wraps himself around her, trying to comfort her. "It wasn't your fault. It was mine."

"You're *wrong,*" she manages, through her tears.

"Do you *want* to be responsible for this?"

"More than I want *you* to be!"

They're almost yelling now, Peter still holding on to her, both of them aware that they're careening toward words that can never be unsaid, lines that can never be uncrossed.

There's a crash behind them. Peter lets Wanda go as he straightens, and they turn to see Aunt May in the kitchen doorway, one hand clasped over her mouth, the other clutching her chest, just above her heart. The tray she was bringing for Wanda is on the ground at her feet, its contents scattered in all directions. She's crying, but there's no sound, only tears rolling down her face.

As they watch, she sinks slowly to the floor, still not saying a word. Wanda scrambles to her feet, while Peter vaults over the back of the couch, both rushing to May's side, moving to comfort her.

"Aunt May, it's okay!" says Wanda. "We're sorry, we won't fight!"

"Just breathe," says Peter. "That's all you have to do right now, is breathe."

She lets go of her mouth and her shirt to put her arms around them, pulling them into a hug. "It was *not* your fault," she says, urgently. "Neither one of you. No one made that man break in here with his bad intentions and his gun, and neither of you pulled that trigger. I can't stand to see you fight, not after everything we've lost. Please. I need you to believe me. This isn't on you."

They exchange a look over her head, and they don't believe her, neither of them; it's written in their eyes. They both have good reason to take the blame, and even better reason to agree with her. So they nod, very slightly, and agree without words to do the unthinkable: They agree to lie to Aunt May.

"All right," says Wanda.

"We believe you," says Peter.

They clean up the mess and heat another portion of casserole, and they spend the rest of the night pretending everything is normal. As if anything will ever be normal again.

—

WHEN THEY GO BACK TO SCHOOL AFTER THE FUNERAL, EVERYONE knows something happened. Most people know there was a death in the family, but someone's mother works at the hospital, and the word has gotten out that Wanda was admitted around the same time. It takes no time at all for the school rumor mill to escalate this to her having been committed, and to assign her the title of Uncle Ben's murderer.

Peter gets into more fights trying to quash the rumors about Wanda than he ever has before, although ironically, he's worse at fighting now than he was before he became Spider-Man—he has to hold back too much for fear of hurting his opponents, and it makes it easier for them to get hits in. He cuts class more, and his teachers look the other way, as long as his grades don't slip.

People have started seeing Spider-Man more during the day, and that's good for Peter's secret identity—no one's going to think he can be Spider-Man and getting an A in AP Math at the same time—but Wanda worries that he's getting careless, especially as the headlines have started to feature costumed villains, not just run-of-the-mill muggers and thieves. A few team-ups with the Fantastic Four have also made the news. He's not staying in the little leagues anymore, and he's going to get hurt.

Wanda worries, but she doesn't tell him to stop, just bandages the injuries he comes home with and helps him get the blood out of his costume without Aunt May catching on. It doesn't feel like her place to interfere, not when she knows he blames her for Uncle Ben's death, not when she knows he's right to blame her. So she doesn't say anything about the risks he's taking, and he doesn't say anything about the red light he saw in the hospital, the red light she still doesn't understand, and they're both walking on eggshells whenever they're around each other.

Eggshells break.

Wanda doesn't get angry about the things people say between classes, although she droops a little more each day, visibly wilting as she makes her way through the halls. She's never had many friends, but the ones she does have begin deserting her, rats fleeing the sinking ship, and her grades start to suffer. Peter does what he can to help, but there are limits, especially when he's getting sent to the office on a daily basis for fighting with his sister's tormenters. There's no end to the creative cruelty of high school students who smell blood in the water, and by the second week, he's heard more ways to question someone's mental health than he ever could have guessed existed, all of them aimed at Wanda.

He feels like grief and guilt are eating him alive, but he hasn't failed her yet, and he isn't going to fail her now. He can't let her down again, not when he knows she blames him for Uncle Ben's death—not when he knows she's right to blame him. So he'll fight for her, and hope it can be enough.

But he can't be with her all the time. It's their second week back at school when the boy who called her a cheater during their illicit card game steps in front of her on the stairs, stopping her from getting to her next class.

"Murderer," he says, voice dark. "My dad's a cop. He says when they got to your house, there was blood everywhere, and your aunt was telling some faked-up story about an intruder, but there wasn't any sign of one, just you and the blood. He's not sure that guy they caught is actually to blame. You know what I think? You killed your uncle, you crazy bi—"

She doesn't get expelled because everyone who sees this go down sees that she never touches him. He just seems to lose his balance while standing perfectly still, and then he goes tumbling down the stairs, slamming into walls on the way down. It's a stroke of incredible bad luck: By the time he reaches the bottom, his left arm is broken in three places, and his right hip has been shattered. He may never walk right again. Wanda doesn't move while this is happening, doesn't try to stop him, doesn't even twitch.

She just watches him fall.

A few people will say later that they saw a strange red light in her eyes, but that's not really possible—she's not a mutant, and surely only mutants have light-up eyes.

It's not until the screaming starts that she seems to snap out of her fugue and realize what's going on. She recoils, staring down the stairs after her tormenter, and then she turns and runs away.

She doesn't stop when she reaches the landing. She keeps going, down the hall to the main stairs, down those to the door, and off campus entirely. She runs all the way to the subway, and no one bats an eye or tries to stop her; running teens aren't an unusual sight in this neighborhood, and it's late enough in the afternoon that she could have good reasons for being off-campus.

She takes the train to Midtown, hugging her knees to her chest and enduring the glares of commuters who don't like her putting her feet on the seat. When she gets to her destination, chosen out of instinct and panic as much as anything else, she uncoils cautiously, deboards, and heads for the subway exit.

Dosta is open, but not busy this early in the day. The restaurant mostly serves as a social center between the lunch and dinner "rushes"—never very rush-y from what Wanda can see—allowing the local Roma community a place to gather. She staggers through the door with tears on her cheeks and shaking hands, seeing half a dozen familiar faces scattered around the space. The air smells of oil and spices, and it's so comforting, so familiar, so *right,* that she immediately bursts into fresh tears, stopping where she is, unable to go any farther.

"Hey, hey, hey, what's this? Come, little sparrow, come, stop crying." Django is suddenly there, stepping out of the kitchen to enfold her in a hug as comforting as the air around them. He pulls her toward an open table. "Come, come. I was wondering when you would fly back to us. Your aunt told me what happened. We're all so sorry, Wanda. So very, very sorry."

She clings and cries until it feels like there are no more tears in her, like she's spent them all on her admission to this safe, welcoming space, and when he finally lets go, it's only to fetch a glass of water and a basket of bread, which he drops in front of her like it's the most valuable thing in the world.

"You haven't been eating; you will eat now," he says, tone leaving no room for argument. "You will eat, and you will tell us what's brought you here in such a state. Grief is a powerful predator, but this doesn't look like the tracks of its hunting. This looks like fear. What happened?"

Wanda sniffles, picking up the water and taking a cautious sip. It's crisp and cold, soothing to her dry, dehydrated mouth. "They're . . . the kids at my school, they're calling me terrible things. They say I killed my uncle. And I'm not sure they're wrong."

"Did you hold the gun? Did you pull the trigger?"

"No. But the man grabbed me before Uncle Ben came out of his room, and he was going to hurt me, so I fought back, and—and the gun went off." She trusts these people implicitly, trusts them with her life, but she doesn't want to tell them about the light in her hands, or the way her dreams glow red now, bright from within with a power she doesn't fully understand. Once she knows what's happening, maybe then she can be a hero like Johnny Storm and protect the Uncle Bens of the world, maybe then she can tell people and wear her heroism on the outside. But for right now, she thinks Peter has the right idea. Some things need to stay hidden if they're going to stay safe.

"It went off when he fell back. He didn't even *aim* for Uncle Ben, and it only happened because I tried to get away. If I'd just let him shoot me, none of this would have happened." She starts crying again, hard and unrelenting, shoulders shaking with the force of it.

Django's arms enfold her again, pulling her close and holding her until her tears taper off. "That doesn't make it your fault," he says, fiercely. "Blame doesn't work that way. You fought to get away because you wanted to live, and surviving is in your blood, little sparrow, it's what you were made to do. You are the daughter of the ones who survived, the descendant of the ones who didn't die before you could begin, and you honor everyone who came before you by staying alive. You honor your uncle by surviving. He didn't choose to die, but I bet if you could have asked him, he would have. He was your parent in everything but blood, and parents die for their children all the time. It's what they do."

She pulls away, wiping at her eyes. "I don't . . . I don't want him to be . . ."

"I know."

"I can't go back there. Not with the things they're saying about me."

Django shrugs. "So you stay here."

"You can't tell my aunt."

He pauses at that. "She's just buried the love of her life. You want to vanish on her when she's already grieving? Child, I thought you were a better soul than that."

"I'll text her," says Wanda. "I'll tell her I'm safe. Just not where I am."

Django, who knows May Parker is a clever woman, doesn't say anything. She'll figure out where Wanda is from the briefest of messages, and then she'll come or stay away, depending on what she needs, depending on what she thinks *Wanda* needs. They're all trying to take care of one fragile, grieving teenage girl right now, and he's willing to let her take the lead.

"Text her," he says, and steps away. "You can stay here. Kezia has a spare room, and I'm sure she'll be happy to let you sleep there until you're ready to go home."

"Thank you," says Wanda, fervently.

"Don't thank me. We have a large party tonight, and there are going to be a lot of dishes." He goes back into the kitchen, and Wanda picks at her bread, sniffling.

Still better than being at school.

———

PETER ISN'T HAPPY WHEN HE HEARS WANDA WON'T BE COMING HOME that night, but he understands; he tells Aunt May about the boy who fell, and how he'd been tormenting Wanda, causing some of the other students to say she pushed him. But there's camera footage of the stairwell, and the administration knows Wanda never laid a hand on him; she's innocent. The other student will be out of class for at least a week, maybe more, while he receives care for his injuries, and his parents are furious.

They call that night, and as he listens to them yelling through the phone, he thinks Wanda had the right idea when she made herself scarce. He sneaks out his window to go patrolling, and even the sirens and sounds of Manhattan at night are more peaceful than home.

The next day is a little better. Most of the student body has accepted that the bully fell; they're not blaming Wanda anymore, and no one seems surprised that she would run, given the things that were being said about her. Some of them even show regret for their own part in the bullying. Peter begins to hope that when she comes back, things might improve.

The second day wears on his nerves. He doesn't like having

what remains of his family split up like this: His attempts to text her himself have been met with silence, and she's turned off location sharing on her phone. He's not used to being unable to find her. He doesn't like it. Even when she was in the hospital, he knew where she was. Aunt May seems content to wait for Wanda to come back on her own, but Peter isn't, and he knows where she's likely to have gone to ground.

The dinner rush is just getting under way, and Wanda is in the kitchen making risotto when a ruckus rises from the front. She looks over her shoulder. The Human Torch still comes in for take-out, but he's a frequent enough customer that no one makes this sort of fuss about him anymore. Even super heroes can become old hat when they're around enough. They don't see Captain America as much, but he actively discourages people making a fuss about him, and it doesn't have the right tenor for Steve. The ruckus continues, until she turns down the heat, puts her spoon aside, and goes to see what the noise is about.

In the front, Peter is standing next to the hostess stand in full costume, his mask pulled over his face and one hand on the back of his neck. To someone who doesn't know him, that pose probably looks nonchalant, even relaxed, but Wanda sees the tension in his shoulders and the way he holds his head; she steps into the open, and asks, "What's going on?"

Peter's head snaps around. "Wanda Parker?" he asks. She's almost amused to realize that his voice is pitched lower than his norm; he's trying to maintain his secret identity, and it's adorable. "Your aunt sent me to look for you."

"Did she?" asks Wanda.

Peter nods. "Yes, she did. She's worried about you. She asked me to bring you home."

Before Wanda can reply, Django is there, beaming at Peter. It's his "talking to people who really need to leave now" smile, the one that normally comes after someone says something insulting to a member of the staff. "Our Wanda can make it home on her own when she's ready."

"Please," says Peter, and a bit of his real voice seeps through, coloring the word. Wanda looks at him and realizes Aunt May didn't say a word about coming to get her; the only one who's worried here is Peter, and he's ready to risk his secret identity to get her to come home. "It's been two days, and her aunt is very worried."

"I'm missing school, Django," says Wanda. "If they're sending super heroes to play truant officer, I should probably get back to it."

He looks at her with bemused disbelief, but steps away from Spider-Man. "If you're sure you're ready, my dear—but that means we have another super hero for our wall!" He gestures grandly to the wall where pictures of the staff with various members of the Fantastic Four and a few bonus Avengers have appeared over the years. "Ari, fetch the camera."

One of the waiters scurries off to do as he's been asked. The smile Django turns on Peter this time is less toothy, more welcoming. "We'll send you off with takeout, as a thanks for coming to get our girl. You'll love our stew. It's the most popular dish on the menu."

Spider-Man nods as Django ducks into the kitchen, trapped by his own choice of masquerade, and Wanda smiles, trying not to let her amusement show. Peter hates the stew. Too much spice for him. Watching him try to eat dinner without crying will almost be worth having to leave—almost.

And then Django is back with a heavy white paper bag, and Ari is snapping Peter's picture as he holds the food. Then they're out the door, and at last, after everything, Wanda's going home.

———

SWINGING IS AMAZING, AND THEY'RE HALFWAY TO QUEENS BEFORE Wanda has reached two conclusions—first, that she never wants to take the subway again, and second, that her brother is a jerk. She punches him in the arm when he sets them down in an alleyway, and he yelps, more surprised than hurt, but rubs the spot while he looks at her plaintively. It's amazing how easy it is to read his expressions through the mask. Maybe that's another spider-power.

"You hid this from me!" she accuses. "We could have been swinging for *weeks,* and you hid it!"

"Ow, Wandy," he says, without heat. "I wanted something for me for a little while before I shared it. I was always going to tell you. You know I was."

"I guess I do," she admits. "But swinging is amazing. Can we do that all the time?"

"Not yet," says Peter, letting her go and stepping away. "That jerk who fell down the stairs—I know you didn't push him."

She grimaces and looks down at her feet. Even with the mask between them, she's not ready to see his face when she talks about her impossible, unpredictable powers. "I sort of did," she admits.

"How?"

"The same way I pushed that robber. The . . . energy is still inside me, and he upset me so much that it just came out without my telling it to. I couldn't help it."

"That's what I thought might have happened," he says. "Wandy, we have to get this power of yours under control, whatever it is. You can't just keep hurting people without meaning to."

Wanda winces, certain without asking that he's referring to Uncle Ben. "I don't *want* to hurt people!"

"So we find someone who can teach you not to." Peter looks at her earnestly. He's not going to let her make the same mistakes he did. He can't.

"Oh, and who's going to do that? At least we know you got your powers from a science accident, like the Fantastic Four. I just *have* mine." She pauses, swallowing to force back her anxiety. "Maybe I'm a mutant."

The way she says it makes it clear that this is something she's thought about a lot, and Peter doesn't want to dismiss it out of hand. Wanda has always been looking for a community, even when she didn't realize she was doing it. If thinking of herself as a mutant helps, she should do that. At the same time, he needs to reassure her that it won't change anything.

"I'll love you whether you're a mutant or not, but either way, I think we need to talk to the Fantastic Four before something else happens," he says. "If they can't help you, maybe they'll know someone who can."

"Okay, Peter," says Wanda, voice small. She shifts the takeout bags she's been holding since they left the restaurant from one hand to the other. "Is Aunt May really mad?"

"No. She knows where you've been, and why, and she's not upset. Now come on. Let's go home."

CHAPTER EIGHT

—

FIELD TRIP

AUNT MAY IS DELIGHTED TO SEE WANDA HOME, AND EQUALLY delighted by the fact that she brought dinner, although she scolds them both lightly for bringing so much food on the subway. Dinner is normal, bedtime is normal, and Wanda's dreams are filled with cascading red light. She seems to have reached an accord of sorts with her powers, and no one's rooms rearrange themselves in the night. Everything is, remarkably, calm.

The next day is Saturday. Peter waited for the end of the week to bring her home, guessing she wouldn't want to face their class-mates immediately if she had a choice in the matter. He's at her door bright and early, knocking before he lets himself in.

"We need to decide what you're going to do about a secret iden-tity," he says.

Wanda, who has just woken up and has yet to brush her hair, blinks blearily at him. "Huh?"

"If we're going to take you looking for a super hero mentor, we need to decide which you is going," he says. "Is it going to be Wanda Parker, high school student who sometimes makes weird sparks come out of her hands, or is it going to be the Red Light, newest hero of Manhattan?"

"I am *not* calling myself 'the Red Light,'" says Wanda.

"Why not? You make light, the light is red."

"Does the phrase 'red-light district' mean anything to you?"

This time, Peter blinks at her before his cheeks flare red with embarrassment. "Check. Not a good code name. We'll think of something else."

Wanda sighs, pushing her hair out of her face. "Why do I even *need* a secret identity?"

"So whoever teaches you knows that you have something to protect, and that you don't want to bring hero business home to hurt your family. And in case you ever want to use your powers in public. It can be dangerous to be known as a superhuman. Especially if you find out that you're a mutant, after all. You want that mask so that you can still be normal when you need to be."

"Is that why you have a secret identity?"

"No, I wanted a secret identity so I wouldn't worry Aunt May and . . ." He stumbles, but manages to finish. ". . . Uncle Ben. And so the other kids at school wouldn't find out and make fun of me, or ask me to take them web-swinging, or anything like that. I'd love to be popular. But not like this. I want to be popular for Peter Parker, not Spider-Man."

"I get it," says Wanda. "I think . . . I think I want to go with a secret identity, because they already think I'm a freak after what happened to . . . on the stairs. Suddenly being a freak *and* a super hero and maybe a mutant would just be too much. Secret identity is better."

"Okay. So you'll need a mask."

"I don't want one like yours, that covers your whole face. It would ruin my hair."

Peter smirks a little. "And your hair is really the big concern here."

She wrinkles her nose at him. "I'm already going to have to tie it back if I don't want some criminal or other pulling on it, leave my vanities alone."

Peter sobers. "Criminal? You've already decided you want to fight crime, then?"

"If my powers are useful for that sort of thing, yeah, I guess I do." Wanda shrugs. "Somebody needs to. The Fantastic Four are great for space crimes and science crimes, and the Avengers are great for really big crimes, but we need heroes on the streets here in Queens, to keep the people safe. To stop things like . . . like what happened here."

Peter winces, glancing briefly away. When he looks back, his voice is graver, laden with pain. "Yeah. I guess. So not a whole-head mask. Do you have anything else?"

"Peter, I didn't mean you—"

"Because we can get you another mask if we need to."

"I have the eye mask I wore last Halloween," says Wanda. "It has red sequins on it."

"Are you going to wear the rest of your Halloween costume with it?" asks Peter, only half-seriously.

"Not last year's costume—I don't want to show up asking for help dressed like a little devil—but I have the one I wore the year before, and it still fits," says Wanda, much more seriously. "Who are we going to talk to?"

"I fought those weird water guys with the Human Torch last week, so I was thinking the Fantastic Four for a start. What do you think?"

Wanda sighs. "I think I'm going to look ridiculous in front of Reed Richards, and it's going to be worth it."

——

SHE DOES.

When Spider-Man swings into the plaza in front of the Baxter Building, it's with a red, pink, and silver confection of a Glinda the Good Witch tucked under one arm. She laughs breathlessly as he sets her to her feet and steps away, leaving her to shake her skirt back into position.

"Better than traveling by bubble," she says. "Are they expecting us?"

"You can't exactly call the Fantastic Four for an appointment," he says, in what she's rapidly coming to think of as his "hero voice":

It's a little deeper than his normal voice, a little more bombastic. She would still know it was Peter even if she didn't *know*, but she can see where someone who doesn't know him like she does might be confused. It's like he's reading a monologue for their freshman-year drama elective, the one neither of them had really wanted to take, filled with aspiring thespians and kids who thought yelling was the same thing as acting.

She'll need to develop her own hero voice, something to keep people from guessing her identity. But that can come later, when she knows she's going to *be* a hero, when she understands what she can do. She reaches for Spider-Man's hand, and he lets her take it, seeing her nerves for what they are, understanding how badly she needs the support.

Side by side, they walk into the lobby of the Baxter Building.

The receptionist is surprised to see Spider-Man standing there—who wouldn't be?—and even more surprised by the presence of the unknown, clearly anxious girl at his side. She calls up to the top floor, where Reed Richards is more than happy to meet with them, and so Spider-Man and Wanda find themselves ushered into an elevator with no buttons, whose doors slide smoothly shut before it whisks them all the way to the top of the world.

It's so smooth that it doesn't even feel like the elevator is moving, but Wanda can see the city rushing by through the window, getting smaller by the second as it dwindles below them. She stays close to Spider-Man, trying to hide how dry her mouth is, how sweaty her palms are; this feels like she's preparing for the final exam to end all final exams, a single test that will determine the course of her entire future.

It doesn't help that she's dressed like she's planning to go to a children's birthday party as soon as they're done here. The dress that fit fine when she was fourteen is too tight in several places, and is more than a little over the top for an older teenager: One of her friends had been committed to taking her younger brother trick-or-treating that year, and so the whole gaggle of girls had gone all-out on their costumes, trying to look as ridiculous as possible. She

doesn't have any ostrich feathers or anything, but she has more sequins than is reasonable, and her long, full skirt makes it clear that
whatever kind of costume this is, it's not the sort you wear for fighting crime. Anyone unfamiliar with John R. Neill's original Oz illustrations would probably have trouble pegging her for Glinda.
She looks like a generic medieval noblewoman done up in ruby and
rose.

Spider-Man lets go of her hand when the elevator starts to move,
but keeps his hand on her arm, reassuring her through his presence.
Finally, the elevator doors open, and they step out onto the floor
reserved for the Fantastic Four. There's another reception desk, this
one unmanned, and a comfortable-looking conversation nook. The
couches look a little odd, rough in a way Wanda wouldn't have
expected from a place with the budget of the Baxter Building, but
she's too overwhelmed by the futuristic lines and sleek emptiness of
everything else around them.

This is an office space, not a home, and it looks like exactly what
it is.

"The couches are fireproof, so that when I do interviews out
here and get excited, I don't set them on fire," says a voice from
behind them, and they turn to find Johnny Storm in his civilian
clothes, idly tossing a ball of flame up and down like a baseball.
"Hey, Spidey. Who's your friend?"

"The, uh, Red Wonder," says Spider-Man. "She's new. Powers
just manifested recently. We were hoping Reed might be able to
help her figure out how to get them under control."

"Really?" Johnny looks at Wanda with open interest, and she
bites the inside of her lip to keep from smiling. Based on his expression, he doesn't recognize her at all, which means the mask is working. "What do you do, miss?"

"I make light," she says, trying to do the same trick with her
voice that she can hear Peter doing with his. To her dismay, it comes
out sounding like she's trying to be seductive, which is the last thing
she wants.

Johnny laughs. "I'm sorry—you should see the look on your

face. You're obviously trying to maintain a secret identity, same as Spidey there, and I totally respect that, but if you're going to do a voice, you need to work on it a little more. That one is *not* ready for public use. How about I promise not to try and guess who you are, and you just go ahead and talk normally, huh?"

"This is all so stupid," says Wanda. "I'm sorry. We shouldn't have come here. We should go."

"Hey, no," says Johnny. "If you have powers, you need to know how to use them. Spidey's a pretty smart guy. He wouldn't steer you wrong by bringing you here, and there must be something about whatever it is you do that makes him think Reed can help. So come on. Show me what's going to impress my brother-in-law and that big brain of his."

Wanda tries to reach for the light while Johnny and Spider-Man watch—she has to think of him that way, no matter what, or she'll slip and use his real name. She's going to respect his secret identity if it kills her: She has to show him she *can* respect it, that she can be the one he trusts when the rest of the world seems like too much—and nothing happens. There's a pit where the power ought to be. Panic surges up to fill the empty space, and she grabs the panic instead, focusing everything she has on the fear: fear of failure, fear of embarrassing herself in front of Spider-Man and, *worse,* in front of *Johnny Storm,* who still gets the grace granted by the last lingering scraps of her teenage crush, fear of success. If she does this, if the power comes when she calls, what does that mean? What does that make her?

Nothing is ever going to be the same again if the power comes when she calls.

That's it: That's the tipping point for her fear. It fills her until it overfills her, until it spills out in cascading geometric shapes traced in red light that shimmers and dances as it dissipates. There's no heat—this isn't fire, isn't Johnny's territory. It's just brilliance.

"Whoa," says Johnny, and he sounds so impressed that the fear dials back, just a little, and the light flickers. "What *is* that?"

"I'm not entirely sure," says Wanda. "It can move stuff, although I've never done it on purpose—it was rearranging my bed-room while I slept before I started calling it intentionally. But when I push it into other people, it seems to twist their luck around. Only bad luck so far, but . . . I feel like I could do good luck, too, if I tried hard enough and knew how to twist it. It's hard to describe."

"I know what you mean," says Johnny. "When I first started catching fire, it was like I was going through this whole second pu-berty, only this time there weren't any words to explain what was happening to me, no helpful road maps from people who'd already done it. It was just happening, and I had to figure it out on my own."

"Yes," says Wanda, relieved. "It feels sort of like sneezing and sort of like stretching when I've been holding still too long—like there's a release inside my whole body at the same time. I'm not very good at calling it when I want to yet, but I think I will be, with more practice."

"That's why we need to find someone who can train her," says Spider-Man. "If she's slinging around pure entropic energy, that could be catastrophic in a residential setting."

"That's for the science nerds to figure out, I guess," says Johnny, waving the issue carelessly away. "Come on, both of you. I was just here to make sure you really needed to speak to Reed. We try to be considerate of other local supers, but Spider-Man isn't what I'd call an everyday guest."

"I could be," says Spider-Man.

Johnny laughs, and waves for the two of them to follow as he turns and heads down the hall, leading them to a pair of tall frosted-glass doors. They look remarkably fragile for something this deep in a super hero stronghold, and that thought clearly shows on Wan-da's face, because Johnny smirks as he reaches for the handle.

"The glass is some super-advanced chain polymer thing that Reed cooked up in the shower one day. It's basically unbreakable. And when I say 'basically,' I mean 'Ben took the last cruller so I tried to hit him with a fireball and then Susie slung him across the room, and neither fireball nor flying Thing was able to so much as chip the glass.'"

"You take your donuts very seriously around here, got it," says Spider-Man.

"You have no idea," says Johnny, and opens the door.

The conference room on the other side is spacious and pleasant, with a single large apparently oak table in the middle, chairs surrounding it, and comfortable couches and armchairs ringing the room, providing less formal seating. Susan Storm is seated in one of the chairs, and she stands as they enter, directing a warm smile at Wanda, who feels her cheeks redden under the comforting, maternal gaze of Johnny's older sister.

"Hello," says Susan. "Who would you be?"

"Susie, you know Spider-Man," says Johnny. "This is his friend, the Red Wonder. She's trying to figure out her powers, and they thought we might be able to help."

"There needs to be a school for this sort of thing," says Susan.

"There is," says Reed, coming through a door at the back of the conference room. He has a pile of papers in his hands, which currently seem to hold the majority of his interest, and his neck is too long by a factor of two or three, making him look unnervingly like something created by The Jim Henson Company for a new Muppet adventure. "It's just limited in who it accepts into the student body."

"I understand the mutants needing their own space, but we need training for all the other types of hero," says Susan. "Miss Wonder, how did you get your powers?"

"I don't . . . I don't know," says Wanda. Susan tilts her head, hearing the empty ache at the core of Wanda's words. The girl doesn't know where she got her powers, but the way she says it makes it sound like it's only the tip of a great iceberg of secret stories, things she'll spend her whole life trying to uncover.

Susan doesn't have a problem with secrets as long as they don't threaten her family, and her heart aches for this girl, who has so many questions, and may never get any of them answered. "If you don't know—"

"I don't, they just *happened* one day, I don't."

"So you might be a mutant," says Susan.

Spider-Man stands up a little straighter. "She's not."

"We don't know—"

"There's nothing wrong with being a mutant, and it's awful how people keep trying to make it out like there is, but she's not a mutant," says Spider-Man. "I know her. If she were a mutant, I would know."

"I don't think it works that way," says Wanda. "But I didn't have a science accident or get exposed to strange chemicals or anything like that. My powers had been coming on for weeks, and then a man broke into our house, and they just happened. I hit him with this weird light from my hands, and the gun went off and then I . . . I fell into the light, and it swallowed me whole."

She feels Spider-Man go tense beside her. They haven't talked about her catatonia since she woke up; he doesn't know what it was like for her, or what happened while she was trapped inside her own power.

"I fell for a long time inside the light, and it showed me things I'd almost forgotten, memories like they were movies, like they were happening in real time all over again." She looks solemnly at Susan. "It felt like it was trying to tell me everything was going to be okay, like it's a part of me but it doesn't *belong* to me, and it needed me to know it wasn't going to hurt me. When I woke up, my brother was waiting for me. He'd been waiting the whole time. Talking to me, telling me he needed me to come back to him. And the light was there with me, too. I put it between us like a wall, and he couldn't get through."

Johnny frowns. "All that makes sense, if you're tossing—what did you call it, Spidey?"

"Pure entropic energy," says Spider-Man. "But that's just a guess."

Reed looks at Wanda for the first time. He blinks at her costume, then asks, "Glinda the Good Witch? From the Neill illustrations?"

"It was a Halloween costume," says Wanda. "If Spider-Man gets a secret identity, I figured I could use one, too."

"I already told her she needed to work on the voice thing," says Johnny, helpfully.

"It's a good idea at your age, especially if you don't know where your powers came from," says Susan. "As Spider-Man says, there's nothing wrong with being a mutant, but not everyone is so enlightened, and some people are bigots. They might react badly if they thought you were one of them. Someone could get hurt."

She leaves the question of whether it's Wanda or the bigots who would get hurt unanswered.

"Powers?" asks Reed.

"The Red Wonder here came with Spider-Man to ask for help getting her powers under control," says Susan. "I sent Johnny to meet them and find out if there was any point to our speaking with her, and she impressed him enough that he brought her back."

"Huh," says Reed. "And you do what, Miss Wonder . . . ?"

"I twist luck into knots," she says. "I think there's more to it than that, but I don't know exactly what yet. This is all really new to me, and I'm still figuring it out."

"It's mostly been bad luck so far, which is why I think it's some sort of probability or entropic energy manipulation," says Spider-Man.

"Fascinating," says Reed. "Sue, could you bubble our new friend? It goes with the costume, I think, and we're high enough up that if she's throwing entropy around, we don't want it to hit the structure."

"Of course," says Susan. "Miss Wonder, do you mind?"

"No, ma'am," says Wanda before, like Glinda, she is encased in a bubble, visible only in the way it bends the light. Her voice sounds distant and a little muffled when she says, "Oh, this would have been great for my Halloween party! Now what?"

"Now show us what you can do," says Reed. "Hit the force field as hard as you can."

He puts the papers on the table and reaches behind himself, arm extending farther and farther until it retracts to a more normal length, now holding a small gray object that looks like a scanner from one of Peter's science fiction shows. He points it at the bubble containing Wanda.

"Proceed," he says.

Wanda reaches for the place she found the power before. She's not as afraid this time, but she's more familiar with the sensation of calling it on purpose, and after only a few seconds, her palms fill with light. They don't glow, exactly, although her eyes do: The light appears out of the air, summoned into being by her thoughts, rather than pouring out of her body. There seems to be no end to it. She calls more and more, filling the space inside the bubble with scintillating ruby prisms made of geometric shapes that merge and bend and break apart, ever-shifting and unreadable.

Sue Storm gasps. It's a small sound, but her eyes are wide; she looks like she's been poked with a pin. She rises from her seat, making a twisting gesture with one hand, and the bubble around Wanda gets thicker. In response, the red light begins to crawl over the inside, moving like something alive, twisting and writhing against the invisible barrier.

"Sue?" asks Reed.

"I'm fine," she says, voice strained by the effort of keeping Wanda contained. "You're pretty strong, Miss Wonder. But is that all you've got?"

Wanda makes a sharp motion with her hands, moving them through the air in front of her like she's tying a knot, then turns both palms, joined, toward the barrier wall. A jet of red light shoots out of them, hitting the barrier, and it shatters.

Sue drops back into her chair, lowering her hands, expression stunned. Wanda turns to Spider-Man, hair matted to her forehead with sweat, breathing hard.

"How did I do?" she asks.

"Very well, Miss Wonder," says Reed, before Spider-Man can speak. "Spider-Man's guess was partially correct—this is probability manipulation, but it's more than just that. Right now, the probability is the bulk of what you're doing, Miss Wonder. You're telling the universe how you want things to happen, and events are falling into line. Susan's shields are virtually flawless, but there are still little weaknesses that can be exploited. Your power found the weakness in her bubble and hit it just right to shatter the whole thing. That's the kind of coincidence you can't count on—except that it seems *you* can. For you, good and bad luck are the same thing, and they're always going to fall the way you want them to."

For a moment, he looks almost anxious. But that can't be right. He's a super hero, not just a superhuman, and he can't possibly be afraid of *her*, or what she can do. She's imagining things in her arrogance and her need for answers.

"Oh," says Wanda. Too many things make sense when he explains her powers like that. Poker games and coin flips and everything else that could have been impacted by luck bending one way or another.

Other things don't make any sense at all. She's lost two sets of parents. She's lost Uncle Ben. No one can look at her life and say that she's never known bad luck. But maybe that was just because she didn't have control. Maybe if she gets enough control, nothing bad will ever happen again.

"Have you always been good at pattern recognition?"

She nods, and another piece falls into place, another little element of her life makes sudden, shining sense.

"There you are," says Reed, with the faintly smug tone of a clever man who has just solved a very difficult problem.

"Dear," says Susan.

"What?"

"She came here looking for help, not just labels. Can we help her?"

"Ah. Us? No. But my recorder registered an unusually high quantity of chaos energy in the power she was slinging around, and there might be someone I can call." He returns his attention to Wanda. "Are you truly serious about getting someone to help you understand what you can do?"

Wanda nods vigorously. "I am. I don't want to hurt anyone else." And if she got the control to protect Peter and Aunt May in the process, well, that would just be a bonus.

"The man I'm thinking of may be able to teach you, but he'll demand your absolute loyalty. There won't be any secret identities. There won't be any setting your own schedule. He respects the need for a good education, so if I'm guessing your age correctly, I'm sure he'll work around your schooling—but that's it. Don't think he's going to understand dating and homecomings and all the other attributes of teenage America. You still want this?"

Wanda laughs, very quietly. "Mr. Richards, I'm a nerd. I've always been a nerd. And now I'm a nerd with super-powers, which is a bit jarring, and not necessarily something I would have asked for if it had been up to me. I was never going to go to homecoming, and if someone is willing to teach me to control this, I'm perfectly happy to let them know my name."

"And is everyone in your life willing to make the same choice?"

Wanda doesn't look at Spider-Man. It feels like every fiber of her being is wrapped up in not looking at Spider-Man, like not looking at Spider-Man has become her primary motivation in life. It's surprisingly easy and surprisingly difficult at the same time, like hanging from the rope in gym class. After a certain point, all you have to do is just not let go.

"All right," says Reed. "I'll make the call."

———

TWO HOURS LATER, SPIDER-MAN AND WANDA ARE STANDING OUTSIDE the creepiest-looking townhouse in Greenwich Village. It looks like the sort of place that hosts a haunted house every Halloween and is only visited by people from outside the neighborhood, because all the locals are too smart to come inside, even with an invitation. Wanda blinks, and the outline of the townhouse flickers, now almost ordinary, now straight out of a horror movie.

Clutching Spider-Man's hand tightly in her own, she asks, "What are you seeing right now?"

"Are you feeling all right?"

"Just . . . humor me, okay? What do you see?"

Spider-Man swallows. "Townhouse. Brown, probably needs a coat of paint. Definitely needs the windows washed. Dead leaves around the stairs. Dirty. Not sure I want to get any closer without a tetanus shot loaded and ready to go."

"And see, when I look at it, it's black, with gray trim. The ironwork keeps shifting into new shapes, and I recognize some of them from the energy I generate. The windows are clean, but they're all these different carnival colors, and there's an eye in the middle of the door."

"An . . . eye?"

"Not, like, a human eye. I think it's made of bronze and stained glass. But it definitely makes it seem like the house is looking at us."

"How are we both seeing something different?"

"Mr. Richards said the man who lives here could train me, right? Maybe he works with the same sort of energy, but his makes . . . illusions, I guess."

"At times, it does, but my 'energy' is more rightly bent toward the manipulation of reality itself—as, I believe, is yours."

Wanda jumps. Spider-Man, whose spider-sense impossibly didn't register the man walking up behind them, is able to look calmer and more collected as he slowly turns around. Both look at the man, who looks back with much more open, if dignified, curiosity.

He's old enough to be one of their teachers, with black hair graying at the temples and a carefully groomed mustache. But the way he's dressed . . . he wouldn't look out of place at their school gaming club. He's combined a blue tunic of some sort with black pants and a billowing red cloak that moves of its own accord, paying no attention to the wind.

His eyes quickly dismiss Spider-Man, and he focuses on Wanda, taking in her costume with a small smirk before he says, "I presume you're the potential apprentice Richards was sending to see me?"

"Yes, sir," says Wanda.

"I am Doctor Stephen Strange, this world's Sorcerer Supreme, and I can feel the magical energies coming off you from here. I'm willing to try to teach you, if you're willing to learn."

"Yes, sir," repeats Wanda, and the die is cast. Time, once again, to see if the roll lands in her favor.

———

AS REED PREDICTED, THEY'RE BARELY INSIDE THE HOUSE—WHICH Strange calls his "Sanctum Sanctorum"—before he turns and says, "Your name, please. I like to know who I'm working with, and whatever inane super hero moniker you've settled on for the afternoon won't tell me enough about you yet."

"Wanda," she says, and reaches up to remove her mask, revealing smeared red eyeshadow and inexpertly applied mascara. "Wanda Parker."

"It describes you well, but it's not, I think, the name you were born with," says Doctor Strange, beginning to walk a slow circle around her. Spider-Man might as well not be here for all the attention he's getting from the man; Strange's focus is on Wanda. "Do you have that name to offer me?"

"I was adopted," says Wanda, defensively. "If you're going to say being adopted means my name isn't my own, this isn't going to work out."

"I would never say anything of the kind. We wear many names during our lifetimes, and they change with us, like a butterfly moving through the stages of its metamorphosis. Your name is Wanda Parker, and that name rings true to me, the way Captain America's name rings true for him, for he's more myth than man in this modern era. Someday the moniker I mocked may be a truer name to you than the one you offer now, as Sorcerer Supreme often is for me. For your sake, I hope that day is very long in coming, for it will mean a metamorphosis that leaves this Wanda in the grave."

"I see," says Wanda, who doesn't, fully, but is willing to try.

"And why are you here, Wanda Parker, whose original name is a secret even from herself?"

"I want to control my powers, and Mr. Fantastic said you might be able to help me." Wanda pauses, and frowns. "But you're a sorcerer . . . isn't that, you know, magic? I thought super-powers were more about science?"

"Energy is energy, and it can pass through many stages. Some energy has qualities to it that make it what we would consider 'magical.' If Reed sent you to me, he thinks your powers are more about magic than science." Doctor Strange makes a flourish with one hand, and a rotating symbol appears above it, golden lines against a background of air, fuzzy around the edges, like it's etched from literal light. "Can you do this?"

Wanda tries to imitate his flourish, conjuring a scarlet symbol of her own. It isn't identical to his, but he studies it like it's a masterpiece, finally reaching out and plucking it from above her hand, turning it over in his long fingers. Both Wanda and Spider-Man blink at this, and again when he puts it back, dismissing his symbol at the same time.

"Chaos magic of the purest kind," he says. "Reed was right to send you to me. It would be irresponsible to leave you untaught and in the world. You could destroy so much more than you understand. I have no choice, now that you're here."

"Don't say that like it's my fault," says Wanda, air around her jittering for a moment with sparks of red static. "I didn't *ask* to come to you. I didn't ask for chaos magic, either!"

"Peace, please," says Doctor Strange. "Chaos goes where it will, and while you may be an obligation, you're one I'm willing to accept. An apprentice is a glorious thing, taught and nurtured correctly." His gaze snaps to Spider-Man. "And you, boy. There's nothing magical about you."

Spider-Man jumps, then moves defensively closer to Wanda. "No, sir, there's not, but I take her safety very seriously."

"I'm not going to hurt her."

"I think I'm a better judge of that than you are." Spider-Man's eyes narrow.

"You may be, but you're not going to be my charge. I have nothing to teach you."

"Where she goes, I go."

"Many men have said as much of many women. Many men have broken their words."

"You don't get to push me away just because you want her magic!"

"And you don't get to keep things from me. Do you want to tell me your secret identity now, Spider-Man, or do you want to wait until I make it one of the many conditions of you being here during any part of her training? You won't be able to be here for all of it. Some of the work we'll be doing together could be very dangerous for the non-magically inclined."

This is a moment of transition. Wanda can feel it in the air. If Spider-Man turns and walks out, this is where they begin to drift apart. America can feel it, too. She tenses as she watches the image in her window, not sure which outcome she's hoping for, but certain that these two are better together than they are apart.

Seconds tick by before Spider-Man reaches up and pulls his mask off, blinking at Doctor Strange in sudden vulnerability. "Peter Parker, sir," he says. "Wanda is my sister."

Doctor Strange smiles.

CHAPTER NINE

—

A STRANGE LIFE

PASSING WANDA'S LESSONS OFF AS A STUDY GROUP IS EASIER WITH both of them attending; Aunt May doesn't question it; if anything, she's glad to have her two teenage appetites out of the house three nights a week, especially if they're out preparing for their futures. It's just that the futures they're preparing for aren't the ones she's thinking about. They take the subway to Greenwich Village, where Peter hands Wanda off to Doctor Strange before he goes on his nightly patrol. He's starting to develop his own cadre of recurring villains, and while they worry her, she's more proud of him than she can express. She thinks Peter's proud of himself, too. He's too well-mannered to brag the way Johnny Storm sometimes does, but he walks taller after he helps stop something truly dangerous from happening.

He's also started walking taller because he's seeing someone, a girl named Gwen Stacy that he met during an academic decathlon. Wanda likes her. She's funny and acerbic and mean when she needs to be, and has a heart big enough for the whole complicated, broken, wonderful person Peter has become. Wanda's not ready to call him a man yet, hero name notwithstanding, but he's on the border, and so is she. Gwen makes him happy. She likes things that make her brother happy.

While Peter keeps the city safe from its evolving assortment of threats, Wanda learns to control her evolving and nebulously defined powers. According to Doctor Strange, she has an inherent connection to the chaos at the heart of creation, somehow channeling it into the red light that pours from her fingers, warping it into whatever she desires it to be. It comes more willingly all the time, and seems to enjoy their time together, filling her with the bubbling warmth of true affection.

Her power primarily manifests as energy bolts and what she calls "probability blasts," little shocks of light that can twist luck to the good or the bad, depending on what she wants it to be. She can use it to shield herself, and it isn't long before she's showing signs of changing the fabric of reality to suit her whims. Or to suit the chaos—it likes being with her, but that doesn't mean it's always going to listen, especially not when she asks for something she doesn't utterly desire.

"Concentrate, Wanda," says Doctor Strange, every time he catches her focus slipping, every time she turns a brick into mice or ice cream or wind instead of moving it a few inches to the left. "You have the potential to be formidable, if you can only learn to concentrate."

"I'm trying, sir," she replies, and she is, truly: She's doing her best. But she has school and lessons and her time at the restaurant, and Reed's warnings aside, she's not used to being quite this overbooked. Her concentration is slipping out of nothing more than exhaustion.

It's been more than a month since she had a night to just sit and do whatever came to mind, to restore herself. Doctor Strange pauses, looking at her expression. Then he sighs.

"Sometimes I forget what it was to be young and forever at the beck and call of forces outside my control," he says. "Adulthood is its own flavor of wearying. Work and commutes and the like will leave you exhausted as often as not. But they generally ask less of your mental energy than eight hours of schooling and however many more of homework. Let's take the evening."

"To do what?"

"Nothing of any importance whatsoever."

Wanda sags, guilt warring with relief. She shouldn't be this happy to be released from her obligations—she's here because she needs to learn these things. The more they learn about her power, the more dangerous it becomes, and the more dangerous it will continue to become, until she achieves the kind of control that Doctor Strange seems to find so effortless. At the same time, he's correct. If she continues to push herself when she's already this exhausted . . . she can see the possible outcomes spread out before her like chess pieces, and far too many of them are bad.

"All right," she says. "Is there a kitchen in this place? There has to be a kitchen. You eat, and sometimes there are snacks, so there must be a kitchen."

Doctor Strange blinks, taken aback by her question, but nods and beckons her to follow him deeper into the Sanctum.

So it is that when Spider-Man finishes his night's patrol—no villains tonight, but two muggings, a carjacking, a lost child, and a vehicular misdemeanor—he returns to collect Wanda from a house that smells like freshly baked chocolate chip cookies. He follows the smell to the Sanctum kitchen, which is less medieval and imposing than the rest of the house, having been visibly remodeled sometime since the invention of indoor plumbing. Wanda and Doctor Strange are seated at the kitchen island, a plate of cookies between them, glasses of milk close to hand.

Spider-Man stops, blinking, before he removes his mask.

"Peter!" says Wanda cheerfully. "I made cookies. Come get one."

For everything else he is, Peter Parker is a teenage boy who's been swinging around New York City for hours doing heavy physical activity. He joins them enthusiastically, and only spares half a thought for the oddity of sitting down to milk and cookies with the Sorcerer Supreme.

Stephen Strange can look dignified and untouchable with a milk mustache. Somehow, that's not the most imposing thing about the man. Peter and Wanda manage not to laugh, although it's a close thing.

(America, alone in her chamber outside of the reality she observes, has no such need for restraint, and guffaws with abandon in the silence. These are the moments that make the Watcher's burden lighter, and she treasures them, rare as they are.

She treasures them all.)

SIX MONTHS TO THE DAY AFTER WANDA'S ARRIVAL AT THE SANCTUM, she stands on a rooftop, looking out over the streets. Spider-Man is beside her, and he looks so professional and heroic in his costume, compared to her red tights and apprentice's tunic. At least she has a better mask now, covering her eyes and arching upward as it reaches the crest of her cheekbones, forming high points that frame her face and make it harder to tell the actual shape of it. It looked ridiculous when her mentor put it in front of her, insisting any student of his would be properly obscured, lest she bring shame upon his teachings when she inevitably fumbled in her first public missions.

His words were cold, even cruel, but after six months of his tutelage, she hears the affection behind them, the genuine concern he masks with sarcasm and perfectionism. He's a lonely man, her Stephen Strange, and her presence in his life—and Peter's, come to that—has been a welcome warmth, a softening and a brightening he doesn't always seem to understand. He welcomes her, that much is more than clear, and while he may have accepted her as his apprentice out of obligation, he teaches her now out of the joy of seeing her grow in power and in confidence, seeing her become the sorcerer he knows she has the capacity to be, even as Peter grows into his heroism. In his own way, she thinks Strange loves them both, but he's not well practiced at that form of affection, and so he does what he can to hide it, as she now hides her face.

The mask is a shield, of a sort. When she wears it, she could be anyone. She's not Wanda Parker, adoptee, imported immigrant, girl turning woman who still carries the close-guarded guilt over Uncle Ben's death cradled next to her heart; all Peter's protests have done nothing to shake her conviction that without her, the uncle they both adored would have lived. His story of standing by and letting the burglar run unhampered into the night is so out of character that it feels invented, like he's making up reasons to steal her guilt. She loves him, will always love him, but that little lie grates every time they speak. He couldn't even let her have her own regrets?

But when she wears this mask, she's free of all that. She's a mistress of the mystic arts, trained by Earth's Sorcerer Supreme. She has years yet to go before she can leave her post as his apprentice, but still, he believes her ready for public patrol, chaperoned by a more experienced hero—and when she's masked, she can tell herself it doesn't chafe to hear him call her brother more experienced. It's just the truth. Peter got his powers before she did, started using them in public right away, and has an almost instinctive understanding of what he can do, what he's capable of. She's got more potential and less comprehension, and that's the balance she would have chosen, if she'd been given the opportunity to choose.

Spider-Man turns to face her, oddly expressive mask showing her his concern, and she nods firmly. They're ready. *She's* ready.

He wraps an arm around her waist and she leans into him, letting him support her weight as he steps up onto the narrow rim around the roof. Then he steps off, web-line grasped firmly in the hand not holding her up, and they're swinging, they're in glorious free fall, and it feels like flying. It feels like freedom. Wanda wants to laugh, but bites it back. Laughter would be childish, would be amateur, would be a sign of how inexperienced she is.

So they swing in silence, and the red cloak clasped around her shoulders flutters in the wind their swinging creates, and oh, they must be a terrifying sight from below. Any evildoers out doing evil will be terrified if their shadow falls across the scene of a crime.

She's been allowed to join Peter tonight because none of the city's costumed criminals have been active in the past few days; it seems unlikely they'll run into anything truly dangerous, and Peter has promised to swing them away if they do. Her master wants her to get a feel for the streets before she starts facing true threats, and while the restriction bristles, she's secretly grateful. She doesn't want to fight someone with a code name and a catchphrase yet. In that regard, she *can* admit that Peter is the more experienced hero, and more, that she's content for him to stay that way, at least right now.

They land on a fire escape, and Spider-Man's feet make no sound as he touches down, while the hard soles of Wanda's shoes clang faintly, making her wince. He turns to frown at her through his mask. She shrugs, making an exaggerated "sorry" gesture, and he sighs.

The silence of this exchange must mean he brought them down to stop a crime, and she turns her focus away from him to the street below, scanning for any sign of what caught his attention and brought them here. He doesn't move to help her, but she can feel him tense, and knows he *wants* to help, knows what an effort he's making to be still; this, too, is her master's doing, a condition of letting her go out into the world like the hero she yearns to be. Spider-Man is her guide, her guard, and her partner on this night, but she must find her dangers on her own.

Everything is dark below them, and seemingly still. No convenient screams or demands that someone surrender a purse or other valuable. Wanda raises her hands to chest-level, palms out and fingers overlapping but not interlaced, and when she pulls them apart, a web of red light follows, illuminating the fire escape. Spider-Man tenses again, this time with surprise rather than anticipation.

Wanda doesn't let herself look at him, focusing instead on her web, which she pulls wider, until it forms a dome of softly glowing red around them. This done, she exhales and looks to her brother. "The light won't give us away," she says. "It's a basic obfuscation spell. No one can see or hear us right now. My master, I suppose, if he's scrying our location, but no one else."

The caveat is as much warning as anything else: This isn't true privacy, and they may be watched, just not by their presumptive targets.

"Huh," says Spider-Man. "And this is just a thing you can do now? How long have you been pulling this little trick?"

"A few months. Didn't you wonder how I kept disappearing when it was time to do the dishes?"

"You little—"

"Please. You use your powers to make the dusting faster, I can use mine to make the dishes someone else's problem."

He laughs. She smirks, pleased with herself, and something in the darkness below finally moves.

Wanda's attention snaps to the street. There are two lights out on this stretch of the block, which explains the darkness, and as her eyes adjust, she sees the reason Spider-Man brought them here. There's no way he saw the two men lurking in the deepest part of the shadow from above, which means his spider-sense, nebulous thing that it is, told him where to drop out of the sky; it's not fair that he got a super radar for trouble to go with all his other advantages, but there's no point in saying so. All the arguing there is won't change the way the cards were dealt.

She points to the two men. "That's what you picked up on, isn't it?"

His nod is tense.

"They don't mean well."

It's not a necessary statement, but since when has either of them been interested in counting their words?

"But they haven't done anything yet." She looks at Spider-Man, frowning. "It doesn't matter if they have bad intentions, we can't stop them until they start something, or we're bullies profiling people who happen to be in the wrong place at the wrong time. And if we know they probably have bad intentions and we just stand here waiting for them to hurt someone, how are we *heroes*?"

"Good question," he says.

Wanda sighs. "It's not always as cut and dried as 'good guys good, bad guys bad,' is it?"

"Sadly, no."

"My master put you up to this, didn't he?"

"He may have asked me to find something morally complicated if I could," he admits. "It's good that you want to get out here and do the work, W—"

"*Don't,*" she says, sharply.

"Incarnadine, but the work has consequences. Putting on the mask means accepting the responsibility for what may happen while you're wearing it. For example, while we've been debating the morality of standing by while the two fine gentlemen below us get into trouble, they've found some trouble to get into."

Wanda gasps as she looks down. The men have moved. They're outside the band of shadow now, following a woman down the street. She's walking fast, holding her purse close to her body, like she can watchful attention her way out of the circumstances that brought her here this late at night. It's not going to do what she's hoping for.

Wanda doesn't have Spider-Man's skill at moving quickly, so she tugs on his arm and points, showing him where she wants to go. She snaps her fingers at the same time, and the dome around them pops like a soap bubble, leaving them exposed to the nighttime air. The sounds of the city rush back in to fill the space she's opened, and Spider-Man scowls as he realizes she's just stopped him from arguing. Then he wraps an arm around her waist and jumps down, carrying her with him.

They land silently behind the two men, and the next minute or so is like something out of a comedy routine: the woman, walking fast and anxious, her heels clopping against the street like the foot-falls of an anxious horse, the sound echoing off the nearby walls; the men following as silently as they can, the occasional scuff of their feet covered by the clattering of hers; and Spider-Man and Wanda behind *them,* moving with utter silence, his feet muffled by preternatural lightness, hers by supernatural shielding. If anyone came rolling down the street now, they would take it for a parade.

No one comes. The men finally get close enough to make their move, and the one in the front grabs the woman by the shoulders, jerking her to a halt, while his friend dashes forward to get in front of her, a smug smirk already forming on his lips.

Turning to face her means he sees behind his friend, however, and he freezes as he spots the two costumed heroes, the color draining from his ruddy cheeks, leaving him frozen and waxen-looking, lips moving in silent protest of what he's seeing. The woman, shriek-ing, fights to break free of the hands that hold her, to no avail—the man had time to prepare his grab, to sink his fingers into the soft part of her arm where his grasp would be at its strongest. He holds fast, and she thrashes to no avail.

"Hey," he hisses. "Hey, what gives? We can't just *stand* here!"

The man whose job it doubtless was to rob the poor woman while his partner held her down raises one shaking hand and points behind his accomplice. The woman, sensing a chance at rescue, stops her thrashing, and the man who holds her looks over his shoulder.

"Spider-Man!" he gasps. "And . . . Spider-Man's date?"

"Ew," says Wanda reflexively. Later, she'll look back on this moment, on her introduction as a working super hero, and want to die from the embarrassment of her first word on the streets having been *ew*, but in the moment, there isn't anything else to say.

"Don't make assumptions," snaps the man's partner. "Just be-cause he's got a lady with him doesn't mean there's anything ro-mantic going on."

"Never implied romance," says the first man, sullenly. He turns, dragging his victim with him, and pushes her in front of him like a human shield. She squeals and thrashes, trying to escape. "Platonic dates can happen."

"Are your muggings always like this?" Wanda asks Spider-Man, sourly.

"About half the time. Something about me makes criminals chatty," says Spider-Man.

"We're not criminals!" says the man who spotted them first.

"Oh, no? Then I guess you won't mind letting the lady go?"

"We're not done yet," says the man.

"With your crimes," says Wanda awkwardly, remembering to project her super hero voice. It's less seductive now, although it makes her sound like she's getting over a head cold.

"Man's got to make a living," says the man sharply.

"I am *Incarnadine*," says Wanda, giving her current code name the hard intonation her master suggested. A properly dropped name could give you the upper hand, if it was intimidating enough.

Both men frown. The woman keeps struggling, but stops shrieking, and all three of them look at her.

She's a big, powerful super hero now, in mask and costume and everything. She doesn't squirm. She wants to. She wants to sink into the sidewalk and disappear.

"What does that even *mean*?" asks one of the men. "Spider-Man, sure. He has spider powers. We understand what that's about."

"It's a shade of red," begins Wanda, before Spider-Man shakes his head and makes a "cut it out" gesture. She stops, cheeks flushing. This isn't the time for definitions.

"I have questions about the spider thing, actually," says the other man. "If spiders are so powerful, how come I can put them in a paper cup and throw them outside? Is your greatest weakness a paper cup?"

This is *not* how Wanda wanted her first patrol to go. She's almost relieved when the first man produces a knife.

"Go *away*, whatever your name is," he says. "We're busy."

He moves toward the woman, who stares at him for a frozen moment before she starts screaming again, louder this time, struggling to break free. Spider-Man leaps into the air. On the scale from "assaulting people who've done nothing wrong" to "stopping a crime" the line is apparently drawn when someone produces a weapon.

Wanda shifts her weight onto her trailing foot, bracing herself in case she needs to dodge, and raises her hands to chest height with her fingers spread wide as she pulls energy out of the air. It fills her palms and swirls down to wrap itself around her wrists, tingling against her skin. She can never find the words to describe this moment, but it feels like she's holding hands with the universe, and the universe loves her. She knows the universe loves her best of all.

This has happened in the time it took Spider-Man to leap into the air and come down against the side of a nearby building, sticking there like there's nothing odd about it, like gravity is meant to be treated like a toy. The men are both tracking him with their eyes, dismissing her. That's their mistake.

They may not realize they've already broken the law, but grabbing someone without consent is assault in New York State. That means she's in the right to make them stop. She brings her hands down, and a sheet of red light shoots out from her location toward the people on the sidewalk, cutting cleanly between the woman and the man who holds her. He yelps in surprise as it pushes back against him, and most important, he lets go.

He trips as he stumbles back from this would-be victim, knocking his head into the brick wall. Not hard enough to knock him out, sadly, but hard enough that he yelps again, this time in pain, and puts a hand against his now-aching temple.

Spider-Man makes his own gesture, faster than hers, and the man with the knife becomes the man without a knife as a line of webbing jerks the weapon out of his hand. The two men, now bereft of both weapon and potential victim, exchange a look before running down the street, trying to get away. Wanda slings two bolts of red energy after them, twisting probability in their vicinity until it screams. One trips over his suddenly untied shoelaces. The other trips over the first.

Spider-Man catches up to them easily, webbing them both to the wall while the woman is turning on Wanda, thanking her over and over again for intervening. She sounds so earnest and grateful that Wanda swallows her first response, which is a critique of the woman's idea about where it's safe for her to walk alone this late at night. And that's unfair, she knows it is—she should be able to walk wherever she wants in her own city without fear—but that's not the world they live in, and it's not going to be that world any time soon, and if this stranger had been more careful, Wanda and her brother wouldn't have needed to intervene.

Wanda manages to smile like the woman's gratitude is the sweetest sound she's ever heard, like it's the medicine she's been waiting for her entire life. She wants to leave. Her master warned her she might have mixed emotions after her first heroic act—sometimes the adrenaline crash following an encounter can leave people too unsettled to deal with the aftermath. She wasn't expecting the thanks and praise to sound hollow, like they were the coin you paid for protection. Like this woman took a risk solely because she knew there were probably going to be super heroes around.

She doesn't want people to be *less* safe because she's in the city. She wants to help make a world where there are no more Uncle Bens—or more accurately, where there are *more* Uncle Bens, where good men don't die for no reason, and if that means people start taking her and people like her for granted, she supposes that's the trade-off. Spider-Man comes back while the woman is trying to shake Wanda's hand and smoothly interposes himself between them, wrapping an arm around Wanda's waist, which she knows is a sign he's about to web them out of there. She's grateful, she is, and she doesn't object as he tells the woman to get herself to safety, then shoots a line out, locking it onto some unseen point in the distance, and launches them both into the sky.

"Do people who don't know you're a total nerd just assume your spider powers include geometry?" she asks, once they're high enough up that no one's going to hear.

Spider-Man laughs, sound muffled by his mask in a way she finds oddly endearing, given that it doesn't muffle his words the same way. "I don't know," he says. "It hasn't come up much, except with Johnny, and it only came up with him because my webbing's flammable, and that means he needs to steer clear of it. I told *him* I got top marks on my AP Geometry final, which he assumed happened years ago, and he asked me to help him with some homework Reed gave him." His voice turns wistful. "I wish *I* had a team leader who gave me homework."

"Maybe you can join the Fantastic Four someday?"

"They're a family group. I wouldn't be comfortable even asking until I was ready to tell them my secret identity, and even then, we wouldn't be family. I'm not looking to be adopted, and Gwen would kill me if I told her I was breaking up with her so I could marry the Human Torch."

Wanda laughs so hard she thinks she's going to be sick, and is still laughing when he sets them down on a convenient rooftop, stepping away from her as he scans the streets below them. Bit by bit, she gets herself back under control, and irritation flares again, reminding her that she's been handled from the start. Her master and her brother colluded to make sure her night would be the learning experience they wanted for her, and not the one she needed.

She turns on Spider-Man, glowering.

"No more ethical tests tonight," she says. "Promise me."

"Doctor Strange asked me to—"

"*He* is my master. *You* are my brother. So promise me no more ethical tests."

He sobers. "I know you need to come out so you can get a feel for patrol, and I know this is something you want to do."

"I sense a 'but' coming."

"But I really wish you'd change your mind." He shrugs. "Doctor Strange doesn't patrol."

"Doctor Strange didn't bury two sets of parents before he was ten years old." Neither did she, technically: Her first set was lost when she was too young to understand what she was losing, and the remains of the Parkers were never recovered. But the sentiment remains.

Spider-Man winces. "I guess not."

"Make you a deal," she says. "I'll stop patrolling if you will."

"It's not the same thing. I have more practice than you do."

"Only because you got your powers first, and started sneaking out before I could make you agree to be careful."

"I thought you wanted me to fight crime."

"I do. But I also want you safe, and every time you get hurt, the part of me that wants you safe gets a little stronger. So I'll quit if you do."

"I'm fast and strong. My powers are almost all physical. I was basically *designed* for patrol," he objects. "You're—"

"Careful," she cautions.

"—not as physically enhanced."

Wanda folds her arms and just looks at him. She doesn't say a word. She doesn't need to say a word. She learned this technique from Aunt May; she's never seen Peter stand up to it for more than a minute.

There's more of a distinction between Spider-Man and Peter than she thinks he realizes, because he holds out for nearly ninety seconds before he flinches and looks away. "I just don't want to see you get hurt," he mumbles.

"And I don't want to see *you* get hurt, either," she counters. "You're my brother. You're the only thing I have in this world that I can always, always count on, and if you get captured or badly injured while you're in costume, I might never know what happened to you. So I won't get hurt if you won't."

"Promise?"

It's the sort of promise no one can make, and they both know it. But they're both teenage super heroes with enough stubbornness baked into their bones to believe that they're somehow different from everyone else, and so they link pinkies and say, in unison, "I promise."

BEYOND THE WINDOW, IN HER OWN REALITY, AMERICA FLINCHES AND SIGHS. THAT'S NOT a safe promise to make. She wishes they'd known better, but it's too late; they can't take it back, no matter how much she wishes they could.

Some things are just begging fate to intervene.

CHAPTER TEN

—

HEROIC MEASURES

THEY STOP TWO MORE SMALL CRIMES THAT FIRST NIGHT: A CARJACKING
and an attempted mugging. Wanda never quite shakes the feeling
that Spider-Man is steering her toward ethical questions—the car-
jacker is younger than they are, scared and half-starved, clearly desperate. They stop her crime and give her twenty dollars and a jacket
Wanda's magic summons out of a handkerchief before they direct
her to the Taco Bell a few blocks over, following until she gets there.
"Super heroes are never going to be the solution to all this city's
problems," says Spider-Man, somewhat morosely. "Too many
things need systemic change, and systemic change needs money.
Maybe if Iron Man decides he wants to buy himself a better social
safety net, or Thor decides the gods of Asgard need to get involved
with the foster-care system, but until that happens, we just do what
we can. We're patching holes in the drywall."

"It's better than doing nothing," says Wanda, and Spider-Man
doesn't argue.

The mugging isn't any better than the carjacking—the near-
victim is a corner dealer who's almost more upset at being saved
than he was at being threatened. They wind up leaving him webbed
alongside his assailants, all three of them struggling to break free
before the police arrive.

"Are there any easy answers?" asks Wanda, as they swing back
toward the Sanctum.

"Sometimes," says Spider-Man. "Appreciate them when they

come, because they're rare, and they make the job a lot easier. Simple situations, and super villains."

"Does that mean you'll take me to fight a super villain?"

"Do you *want* Doctor Strange to turn me into a newt? Don't push your luck, *Incarnadine*," he says, dropping them to the Sanctum roof. Doctor Strange has left the rooftop entrance unlocked for them, and after Wanda pauses to tell the bees about their evening—they have three hives currently, all of them thriving, their innately mathematical little lives and chaotic flight physics making them an easy connection for her powers—they descend into the warmth of the house.

She hasn't realized how cold swinging above the city like that was. Spider-Man removes his mask as they walk down the stairs, and she's with Peter again, her beloved brother, not the more experienced super hero who's been her supervisor all evening. She relaxes, some of the stiffness going out of her posture. The secret identities are necessary for a whole bunch of reasons, but she likes it better when she's not walking around with a super hero she doesn't really know.

She knows they're the same person, but the masks change things. Peter glances at her, a certain pleading in his eyes, and she realizes her own mask is still in place. Chagrined but not entirely sure why, she reaches up and removes it, and they finish their descent as themselves, as they have always been when it was just the two of them. As they're meant to be.

"I think we need to work on my code name," she says, before Peter can start rehashing the night's criminal encounters. She knows he'll want to review everything they said and did and saw—she agreed to it before they went out—and she's not ready yet. "It doesn't work if no one knows what it means."

"Incarnadine is a shade of red," says Peter. "You liked it this morning."

"I like how it sounds sort of like 'incantation,' and I was thinking it might give people a clue what they were about to be up against—it seems polite, and it helps with the branding."

Peter wrinkles his nose. "I hate how you think of it that way."

"But it's a real factor," she says. They've reached the ground floor; she unclasps her cloak and hangs it on the rack next to the base of the stairs, starting toward the kitchen. "It's easier to manage the psychological side of super heroics when people know what to expect. It's why you call yourself 'Spider-Man,' instead of, I don't know, 'the Moth.' "

"I don't have moth powers!"

"You have bug powers."

"Spiders are arachnids, not insects."

" 'Bug' has been genericized sufficiently that it basically means any small creepy-crawly thing that might get stuck in your bathtub," she says. "But you're not 'Bug Guy,' either. It's not precise enough. You want to warn your opponents about what sort of enemy you'll be, and also tell the people you're protecting what to expect from you. So I was going for 'red' and 'incantations,' and it didn't quite work the way I wanted. It's not a good code name if no one can pronounce it."

"You've just hit on why I didn't call myself 'Arachnid.' "

"That, and all the super heroes I know except my master—"

"Who's only a super hero on a technicality."

She wrinkles her nose at him. He stops talking. "—think you're an adult, because your name has 'man' in it. Even when you say stupid stuff or slip and admit to needing to be home by curfew, they take you for an adult." She's heard Reed talking to Doctor Strange a few times when he's come to the Sanctum for a supernatural consultation, and he assumes Peter is Johnny's age, old enough to be starting college. He's called him an inspiration more than once. She hasn't relayed this to her brother. No need to inflate his ego more than his various successes already have. "If you'd called yourself 'Arachnid,' you know someone would have dubbed you 'the Arachkid' by the end of your first active week of patrol, and everyone would downgrade their estimate of your age."

(In a room that both does and doesn't exist, outside the boundaries of this slice of reality, America leans away from the window to shake her head. She's seen a lot of Wandas across a lot of worlds, but few of them have talked like this. Every Wanda is smart—she has to be, in order to have even a sliver of the control she needs over her powers—but most of them don't talk like it. This Wanda talks like she thinks the best use of an afternoon would be arguing with Reed Richards about scientific theories. The most fascinating thing about this little deviance from the norm is that she knows it's something every Wanda has had the potential to be. She's smart, she's enthusiastic, and she's eager to belong, a chameleon of sorts for the communities around her. Given a family of smart people who encouraged education as a primary focus, she was always going to turn out this way.)

Peter nods, agreeing with her assessment, and together, the two move into the hall, heading for the kitchen. "So that's a no on 'Incarnadine.' I still say 'the Red Wonder' would work."

"No," says Wanda firmly.

"Why not? I called you 'Wonder' when we were kids."

"And I made you stop because it made me uncomfortable. Now, if you called me that, you'd get so relaxed that you'd slip and call me 'Wanda' or 'Wandy' in front of the wrong person, and they'd figure out our secret identities in no time flat. They'd be able to follow us back to Aunt May, and *she* doesn't have super-powers. She'd be a sitting duck for anyone who wanted to follow us home!"

"Like the burglar who killed Uncle Ben," he says, subdued.

Wanda sighs.

They have this argument more regularly than they should, each of them carrying their guilt over what happened close to their hearts, like oysters jealously hoarding bits of grating gravel. Peter let the burglar go, but that's where his involvement ended; the man had no reason to think Spider-Man was in any way connected to the Parker home. If they stretch the realities of the situation until they cry, they can look at the fact that the man came in through Peter's window, where the light being off meant the entire front of the house was dark; if Peter had been home, the man might have chosen a different target, and someone else would have died.

In her bitterest moments, Wanda wishes she could will that world into being, shift the man's target a house or two down the street, kill one of their neighbors and leave her beloved uncle alone. And that's why it's so important she become a hero: She may not have sent the killer to someone else's window, but she's thought about it often enough, and she knows she'd do it if she could. Given how much potential her master says her powers have to rewrite the universe, she needs to hold herself above that sort of petty wishing. No matter how much she wants it.

Because Peter let the burglar go, but she interrupted him, she got herself caught, she blasted him with her first, subconscious use of her powers. She bends probability, she knows that now: She shot that man so full of bad luck that it's a wonder a piano didn't fall out of the sky and smash him where he stood. She can't imagine some of that bad luck didn't spill over into the gun, so that it went off erratically, putting a bullet through the most important man in her life. Peter let the burglar go. She let the burglar do the rest.

They exchange a look, rife with guilt and self-recrimination, and neither of them says a word, and neither of them needs to. If they speak, they'll start to debate who owns the lion's share of the guilt all over again, and this is a time for joy. Her first patrol was a success. She's proven she can, at least potentially, survive on the streets of New York. This isn't the time to go ripping open old wounds, and so they keep them carefully sealed as they proceed onward, into the kitchen.

Doctor Strange is there, sitting cross-legged in the air several feet above the kitchen island. His eyes are closed, but he cracks one open as they come into the room, making a show of looking them up and down before he opens the other eye and asks, in his ever-sonorous voice, "Well?"

"Sir, you know I can't take you seriously when you're floating," says Wanda. "There are other rooms you could do that in."

"I knew the two resident walking appetites would head immediately for the food when they returned, so this seemed to be the best place to wait for you," he says, drifting backward until he's no longer directly above the island. This makes his floating more impressive, as he's now easily six feet above the floor, rather than a mere three feet above the island.

Peter isn't sure why a greater height is that impressive, but it is. He can't float an inch, so it probably shouldn't matter as much as it does.

"Why were you waiting, sir?" asks Wanda.

"I only have one apprentice. If I lose you, that looks like sloppiness, and the other sorcerers will judge me."

Wanda smiles, almost teasing. "Since when do you care what the other sorcerers think?"

"An excellent point, Apprentice. Concern revoked: Go out and get yourself killed for all I care, I'll be here regardless." He drifts downward, uncrossing his legs, until he's standing on the kitchen floor. Peter glances down. Nope: standing a few inches *above* the kitchen floor. Still impressive. "How was your first outing?"

"I don't appreciate you and Peter conspiring against me," says Wanda. Doctor Strange lifts his eyebrows, attempting to look innocent. He doesn't have the face for it: The man could make donating feather toys to a kitten rescue seem sinister. But he's trying, and Peter silently gives him points for that.

Wanda, on the other hand, definitely doesn't. She rolls her eyes, then heads for the fridge, pulling it open to extract the fruit salad she made earlier. The Sanctum Sanctorum, like all good creepy Victorian manors, has an orangerie attached at the back. It doesn't exist to anyone outside the house, but inside, it's a thriving grove of fruit trees and shrubs. There's no such thing as seasonal fruit, not here. Even when fresh fruit is expensive beyond words in the rest of the city, the house of Stephen Strange has mangos and strawberries.

Peter thought it was unfair the first time Wanda said she'd make them blueberry waffles if blueberries weren't currently eight dollars for eighteen ounces at the bodega, and Doctor Strange responded by walking them back to his private garden to pick whatever she needed. Now he accepts it as part of how the house operates, and every meal he eats here is a meal Aunt May doesn't have to pay for. Doctor Strange can afford it.

"Conspiring?" asks Doctor Strange. "Whatever do you mean?"

"I mean setting up ethical puzzles in the form of crimes, so I have to make decisions about when and whether to intervene," snaps Wanda. "I mean treating my patrol as some sort of test."

"But it was a test, Apprentice. A test of whether you could handle yourself in the real world, even with your brother by your side. Peter won't always be there to help you. Someday you'll have to make those judgment calls on your own, and when that day arrives, you'll be prepared to weigh the situation and reach a conclusion rather than jumping wildly into action. You'll be better prepared than your peers to survive. That, much more than your temporary good graces, is my goal. I want you to learn to control your gifts, to hone them to their full potential, and to stay alive long enough to use them for whatever purpose they are intended. If a few ethical questions help you achieve those goals, then those questions will be well worth asking."

Wanda sighs heavily, put-upon as no teenage girl has ever been. "All that, *and* they didn't understand my code name."

" 'Incarnadine' is a lovely vocabulary word, but not so excellent for shouting in the heat of battle."

"See?" says Peter, while Wanda looks stung.

"I understand the theme you're trying for, but it might be better to get less multisyllabic, for the sake of your target audience. Most muggers didn't win their school spelling bees, sadly."

"I still like 'Red Wonder,' " says Peter.

"I told you no," snaps Wanda. "You'll slip and use my real name."

"Consider, then, 'the Scarlet Witch,' " says Doctor Strange. "It plays to your color scheme and your inclinations, while invoking the Scarlet Pimpernel, who was the model for many modern caped heroes. You could do far worse as a lineage."

"The Scarlet Witch," says Wanda to herself, feeling out the words. They feel right enough. They feel like they might work. "I think I like it. But how do we get people to *use* it?"

"I have an idea," says Peter thoughtfully.

"This truly is a remarkable night," says Doctor Strange.

The kitchen is warm, and the fruit is fresh, and laughter takes the night until it's time for them to head for home.

———

THE NEXT NIGHT, SPIDER-MAN AND THE SCARLET WITCH STAND ON another rooftop, this one in Queens, close enough to Midtown for her to see the outline of the skyline in the distance. They're both in costume, and Spider-Man has been setting up cameras for the last five minutes, leaving the Scarlet Witch to shiver and draw her cloak closer around herself.

"I refuse to believe you take this long to set up every time you're getting pictures of yourself for the paper," she says.

"I don't have to these days," he replies. "Everyone knows who Spider-Man is. I just need a few clean motion shots, and I can do that with a camera webbed to a fire escape and set on a timer. You're new, and we don't know how your powers will photograph. I've got a few digital cameras, a few using traditional film, and even a Polaroid. We'll find out what works best for you."

"We don't know that I won't make all your cameras explode into pigeons."

"If you do, I'll use my phone and get a *great* picture."

Wanda sighs, heavily. Peter always makes light of the way her spells can go awry, even as her master uses it as a justification to keep her from going on any patrol more dangerous than sweeping for petty criminals. But it's true. Sometimes she misfires, and when she misfires, things can get deeply weird. Reality bends to her whim, and sometimes even she doesn't know what she wants.

Petulantly, she says, "I don't see why we need to do this."

"Again, you're new. Some good pictures of you 'leaked' to the press will establish you as someone to watch out for. We'll do another shoot in a few weeks, with both of us, and let that lock our partnership into people's heads."

The Scarlet Witch frowns, wrapping a lock of hair around her finger as she watches him fuss with the cameras. "And this doesn't seem, I don't know, dishonest?"

"You have powers, you want to use them to fight crime, you're planning to protect the city—what could be truer than getting a little positive PR out ahead of the curve?" Spider-Man hesitates. He doesn't like to remind her how uncomfortable her powers can make people who aren't as relaxed about chaos magic as Doctor Strange. Finally, he says, "Remember, even Mr. Fantastic was a little uneasy when you first showed him what you could do. It's better if we rub off a little of the newness, start building familiarity."

"Familiarity breeds contempt," she says, somewhat sourly.

"And novelty brings in big money," he says. "I can get top dollar for these shots, and we need the cash."

Wanda grimaces but moves where he tells her to move, and begins to summon cascades of light as his cameras click all around her, capturing the moment for tomorrow's news.

———

WITH AS MUCH THOUGHT AS THEY BOTH HAVE TO SPARE THESE DAYS for questions of money and its absence, eating their meals at friends' houses when they can—and their definition of "friends" includes both Doctor Strange and the Fantastic Four, as well as leftovers from Dosta on the nights when Wanda goes for her language and culture lessons—it's a small mercy that Peter's powers mean they can mostly skip the subways. If Aunt May thinks it's strange how rarely she has to top off their MetroCards, she's putting it down to them begging for swipes or sharing the same card to make the money she *does* have to give them last twice as long.

She would be horrified to learn how much time they both spend worrying about the house finances. She thinks she's doing an excellent job of hiding how tight things have become since Ben's death, and neither of them is going to disabuse her of that. Let her have the small mercies she can conjure for herself, and they'll find the rest on their own.

They land in the safety and dimness of an alley, Peter returning to his civilian clothes while Wanda shimmies out of her tunic and stuffs it into her backpack. They emerge as two ordinary teens—and like any two ordinary teens, their extraordinary evening is almost immediately consumed by more mundane concerns.

"I forgot to finish my physics homework," moans Wanda. "I have to turn it in tomorrow morning."

"You'll be better off going to bed and knocking it out in the morning," says Peter. "If you try to stay up all night finishing it, you're just going to get fuzzy-headed and make mistakes. I know whereof I speak."

"Stop trying to sound smarter than me," she says, shoving him. "You're just showing off."

"Yeah, but next year we're both off to college, and how am I going to show off for you then? We'll be in different dorms. I'll have to call you if I want to impress you with my brilliance."

"Don't remind me," she says, morosely. "You're going to be so busy with studies and your girlfriend and being Spider-Man that you're going to forget all about me."

"Hey. Don't get glum. You'll still be my only sister, and that counts for something, no matter what. We'll team up all the time. I don't trust any of the other local capes with you, and you'd miss my scintillating wit."

Wanda smiles at him, but her mood doesn't bounce back as they walk. Empire State University is giving Peter a full ride on a science scholarship, and he's been trying not to rub her nose in it since the results came back. She'll be attending Metro College in New Jersey; they have a better math department, and even without a full scholarship, tuition is reasonable enough that she should be able to handle it. If nothing else, probability loves her. She'll just buy a bunch of scratchers from a few bodegas and she'll be able to cover the whole shebang.

Of course, with the way her luck tends to twist, if she does that she'll win the big jackpot, millions upon millions of dollars, and she won't be able to collect without attracting the world's attention. Not a great idea if she wants to keep making steps into the world of super heroism, where it's better that the eyes of the world *not* be on you before you put the mask on. She'll just have to take more paid shifts at the restaurant, something Django has been increasingly willing to let her do, and eat as many meals as she can at the Sanctum.

She can do this. *They* can do this. They're almost adults now, and Aunt May can't take care of them forever, even though Wanda knows she'd be willing to kill herself trying.

Peter knows he killed the mood, and so he walks quietly with her for a while, neither of them aware of just how closely their thoughts align. He kept his new powers a secret at first, because they were strange and frightening and he had no way of knowing how his sister would react, but since telling her, he's come to depend on the release of having at least one person in his life who knows the truth about him, what he is, where he spends his time. Being at two different schools, in two different *states* . . . he can't see how that can fail to start putting distance between them.

There's already distance there, always has been. It began when they were tiny, when they first understood that "adopted" meant they weren't related the way he and Uncle Ben were related, that there would always be people in this world who didn't think they were truly family. It got wider when puberty hit, turning them into strangers from themselves, turning the world upside down and complicated even before the introduction of super-powers to the situation. And it grew wider still when Uncle Ben died, and neither of them was willing to yield responsibility to the other.

He's afraid one more chasm between them might be the last one, and he's not sure he'll survive that. He's smart enough to recognize how much he depends on her to be his rock, and to know some people would call that unhealthy, would say one person can't carry the full weight of another. And to them he would say, sure, when you're not dealing with super-secrets on top of everything else. His relationship with Wanda carries too much weight because there's no one else to lift it, and he's lifting almost as much for her. Only "almost" because her master shoulders some of the weight of Wanda's secrets.

He hates that he envies Doctor Strange, but he does.

And then they're rounding the corner between them and home, and Peter reaches over to give Wanda's hand a reassuring squeeze, as he always does when he gets near the house without his spider-senses telling him he's walking into trouble. No burglars this time. No bullets. No bodies.

Wanda exhales, shoulders untensing, and flashes him a quick, grateful smile. This is a small ritual, like so many others, and like so many others, it developed entirely on its own, with no intent from either of them. It comforts her more than she can say.

The porch light is on, and that is also a comfort. Aunt May is probably still up, waiting for them to come home from whichever study group they're supposedly at tonight, and she'll make hot cocoa and they'll talk until it's time for bed.

This is what home is: a lit porch light and a cup of cocoa with the people you love. Smiling, Peter and Wanda walk toward it.

AMERICA TURNS AWAY FROM THE MUNDANE LITTLE MOMENT, EYES BURNING WITH TEARS she doesn't quite shed. This isn't fair. The distance between here and the events she witnessed in the Avengers Manor seems insurmountable, but she knows it's only a few years. How did they get there? How did they get to a point where people would see this Wanda and jump immediately to murder, to villainy, to all the accusations you hurl against someone whose track record is less than savory? These are happy children—and she knows they'd bristle at that label, but she's seen versions of them from the cradle to the grave a dozen times over, seen them early, seen them ancient, and these are children in her eyes—who love each other so much that anyone who encounters them for an instant will see it. They're not villain material, either one of them.

People still surprise her. This entire reality surprises her, not just in its existence, but in how *right* it is, how much sense it makes. Peter Parker has always been an essentially lonely person, and Wanda has always been a compass searching for true north, for a direction she can point to and feel safe pursuing. He wants to be needed, she wants someone who will let her need. This timeline seems ridiculous at the surface, but fits together better and better the deeper down she goes.

And somewhere between here and there, it's all going to fall apart. She doesn't want to see that happen, wants to turn away and let these versions of the people she knows be happy and together and untouched by what's to come. But she can't do that. She's their Watcher, and their world came to her attention for a reason: She has to watch. She has to understand why this world, out of all the possibilities there are, needed her to witness its events. Something that's seen won't be forgotten.

For whatever reason, the cosmos wants these people to be remembered.

America waves her hand, calling for the next pivotal moment in their lives. The window skips forward again, and she leans, somewhat regretfully, closer to watch what follows.

CHAPTER ELEVEN

—

MUTATION

A YEAR AND A HALF OF APPRENTICESHIP HAS TAUGHT WANDA MORE than she could ever have imagined about magic, the way it's done, its limitations, and its dangers. She can read incantations in Greek, Akkadian, and Latin, and has partially translated some old spells written in a form of Romany she doesn't quite speak but can puzzle her way toward via the words she *does* know and the spaces between them. Doctor Strange says those spells are not safe to use, since there's no predicting what they might do without an accurate translation, but she knows he's proud of her for getting as far as she has. He doesn't say it, but then, he rarely says it. His expressions of satisfaction with her performance usually take the form of homework and access to new parts of the Sanctum.

When she presented him with the first of her half-translated spells, he unlocked a solarium with walls made of crystalline glass perpetually bathed in light from the full moon that always hung precisely overhead, even if it was noon when she went inside. Technically it's probably a "lunarium," but that isn't a real world, and her master has a tendency to sniff and tell her she's not Shakespeare yet when she makes up words: She can't just mutilate the English language for her own amusement. Too many people have done that for too many years, and it's delicate now, a thing to be handled with precision and care.

She thinks he's making a joke when he says things like that. It's hard to be sure, because his sense of humor is bone-dry and easy to choke on, but she's starting to get a grasp on it.

Magic is dangerous. Dangerous and wonderful, structured and mercurial, a contradiction that never resolves. She sits cross-legged on the floor in the middle of the room reserved for her studies, hands resting on her knees, and concentrates on the candles around her. They outline the chalk circle containing her; they decorate the shelves and surfaces of the rest of the room. Even her master holds one, a sardonic expression on his face as he leans against the wall.

He's a sometimes necessary variable to these exercises. "You won't always have the perfect conditions under which to perform a working," he's said, so many times that she can summon his exact intonation to mind if she tries. "That's part of why I allow you to go on patrol with that ridiculous brother of yours. Your magic thrives on chaos. You must learn to feed it the variables you can survive, to keep it from creating variables you *can't*."

She's supposed to be calling fire, to be lighting those candles. She understands the science behind the request as well as if not better than she understands the magic: All she needs to do is excite the molecules until they combust. But somehow knowing makes it harder than it should have been. It's like her magic, her chaotic, capricious magic, hates to be understood. It wants to be surprising and free, to do things no one expects. That's why, the last time she was asked to light the candles, she summoned a wave of fire that reduced everything in the room to ash, burning hot enough to even char the Sanctum walls. The Sanctum is meant to be untouchable, and those streaks of ash frightened her more than she really had the words for.

But her master had only looked at them, like they were a spider he'd found in his bathtub or an inconvenient solicitor, sighed, and closed that room for the remainder of the week. "You'll learn control, Apprentice," he'd said. "I would hardly be a qualified teacher if you didn't."

Lessons are easier now that she's in college, and harder at the same time. There's no one making sure she gets out of bed in the mornings, no one bringing her cocoa and cookies while she labors over her homework; she sometimes thinks half her professors wouldn't notice if she stopped coming to class. But the classes themselves are more engaging, filled with students who *want* to be there, rather than being forced into their seats by academic requirements. The discussions are vigorous and lively and interesting, and she thinks she might be happy to spend her whole life at college, learning more and more, the world ripping wider and wider around her as she understands the ways it works.

But her homework, when it comes, is more difficult. It takes more time to complete. She goes on patrol with Peter four times a week, and that happens on his schedule, not hers, since he's the one who has to swing all the way over to her dorms to collect her. Thus far they've managed to keep him from being spotted on campus, but the papers have been talking about how Spider-Man is spending more time in New Jersey, and it's a matter of when, not if, someone sees him where a super hero shouldn't be. She's always on the cusp of falling behind, and that's before adding in her lessons with Doctor Strange or her shifts at the restaurant.

It's a real job now, became one the day she turned eighteen, although she spends half her shifts in language lessons and feels guilty about the fact that Django insists on paying her anyway. "You're family, and you give us your labor; you make us better through your time. We thank you as we can."

It's hard to argue with that, and she wouldn't succeed if she tried—if she tried too hard, he'd just call his mother, who's ancient and terrifying. She understands English perfectly, but she refuses to speak it, and so Wanda always feels like she's been shoved back to her first days in the dining room when Django's mother comes to call, trying to understand and make herself understood across an insurmountable gulf. She doesn't want to argue hard enough to invoke the nuclear option, and so she takes her paychecks and her complimentary meals, and she eats better than half the people in her dorm, and she ignores the way her roommate grumbles about the smell of spices.

Her roommate is another math major, from Indiana, and from the way she reacts to even the mildest trace of heat in her food, she's never been anywhere more challenging to her Middle American palate than a Taco Bell. Not liking spicy food isn't a crime, even if Wanda sometimes feels like it ought to be, but she's been working at the restaurant long enough that the smell has seeped into her skin, and her roommate acts like this proves Wanda doesn't shower. It's offensive and upsetting, and it turns out "my roommate is racist in a way I can't quite articulate" isn't a reason to request a new room.

It should be. Wanda's sure of that.

But her lessons with her master are worth all the rest of it. Those are the moments where she can plunge her hands into the magic that runs through her, the magic she still can't explain but comes closer and closer to understanding, and bend the world to her will. The magic doesn't have to worry about dropped term papers or missed assignments. Her master understands the other draws on her time, and while he expects her to prioritize her magical studies as much as possible, he speeds and slows the curriculum as needed.

He still acts like teaching her is some sort of a burden, but she knows it isn't. He shows her in a thousand little ways, in the solarium and the fruit trees in the orangerie, in the way her most-used spices always seem to show up in the kitchen, never running out, even the ones she had to bring with her back in the beginning. He appreciates her company, she's sure of it. And sometimes he's proud of her.

She wants him to be proud of her tonight.

So she reaches deeper into the wellspring of chaos, and whispers silently for the molecules to get with the program already, to do what she knows they want to do and start vibrating fast enough to light those candles. She doesn't think about the fact that this time, if she fills the room with a private inferno, her master will be right in the path of the flames. She just focuses on the air.

"Where too many people go wrong is in focusing on the fire," he'd told her, when he explained this exercise. "The fire is what we're hoping for. The fire is what's coming. Right now, in this moment, what you have to work with is the air."

She focuses on the air until there's a soft whooshing sound from everywhere around her, and she opens her eyes to find herself sitting in a dazzling star field of lit candles. Every one of them is burning, even the one in her master's hand, and nothing else is on fire. Wanda beams at Doctor Strange, too overjoyed in her success to restrain herself to polite apprentice manners.

"Sir! I did it!"

"Yes, I can see that," he says, and with a lazy wave of his free hand, all the candles are extinguished. "Now do it again. One at a time this time. We need to work on your precision. Not every problem is a nail in want of a hammer. Sometimes you must be a scalpel."

Wanda's smile melts into a sulk as he turns and leaves her alone. She slumps back into her circle, then resumes the position and closes her eyes again. Time to get back to work.

Always the work.

———

A WEEK AFTER THAT, SHE COMES DOWN FROM THE ROOF WITH PETER behind her and what looks like the lion's share of a burrito splattered across her costume and her hair. She's removed her mask: There's an outline of filth around the skin that it protected. Peter has also removed his. His skin is clean, his expression sour.

Her master is in the sitting room when they descend the stairs. He lifts his head and then his eyebrows, questioning without a single word. Peter steps forward to start explaining, and Doctor Strange stills him with a quick gesture of his hand.

"No," he says. "I want to hear this part from her. Wanda? What happened?"

She stops, and swallows, throat working hard to finish the gesture. "I—we—there was a woman outside the cinema on West 42nd, and some jerks decided they could knock her down and take her purse. She had her son with her. He looked like he was about our age, maybe a year or two younger, and when they pushed his mother over, he didn't move to stop them, he didn't say anything, so we stepped in, and we—and we—"

She runs out of words, looking desperately to Peter, who winces. He doesn't want to disobey Doctor Strange, who he finds rationally terrifying, but he wants to let his sister squirm even less. When Doctor Strange gives a nod of permission for him to go ahead, the relief is indescribable.

"We stopped the muggers," he says. "It was pretty easy—no super-powers, and no firearms. Just some people who got desperate and thought they'd find easy pickings at a movie theater. It only took us a minute to take their knives and knock *them* down. And that's when the lady's kid . . ."

He stops, struck silent by the same force that stopped Wanda's tongue, and looks at his feet. For a long moment, there's nothing.

Nothing but the memory of Wanda reaching down to help the woman off the pavement, and the boy rushing forward like a linebacker, shoving her away from his mother with all the fury he hadn't bothered to direct at the muggers, knocking her back by several feet.

"Don't you touch my mother, *mutant*," he'd snarled, and that word had been every terrible thing she'd ever been called while they were at school, every slur both applicable and not. There had been a wide assortment of them, delivered by people who couldn't tell Wanda's race at a glance, only that something about her said "I am not like you" to their schoolyard-honed sense for sniffing out the other. The boy's voice had struck Wanda silent before she could protest, and it's the ghost of that silence that clings to her now, stopping her from telling her side of the story, even as it had stopped her defending herself.

The boy's declaration had been solitary, but when Wanda had just stared at him in horrified hurt rather than refuting his accusation, the rest of the crowd waiting for their movie had gotten involved.

Spider-Man's public association with the Fantastic Four has

largely shielded him from people who want to accuse him of being a mutant. Wanda has no such associations in the eyes of the public. The legitimacy Peter gets from the team doesn't extend as far as her. She's his strange sometimes-partner with the indefinable powers and the word *witch* in her name. Some people assume she's a villain for that alone. Others want her to hex their exes, or pose with them outside the theater that's showing *Wicked*.

But no one knows where she came from, and the rumors of mutation have been gaining speed.

". . . they threw things," says Peter finally. "They threw things. At both of us, but mostly at her, and hitting me with a bag of popcorn or a burrito isn't easy. Wanda, though, she just . . . she just stood there and took it."

Wanda doesn't say a word, simply stands miserable and filthy, bits of rice and sour cream dripping from her hair. Doctor Strange stands, and Peter knows that every time he's been afraid of the man, he's been absolutely right to be: The Sorcerer Supreme is suddenly terrifying, his shadow too long and his gaze too sharp as he moves toward Wanda.

"Why is she still covered in their detritus?" he asks, voice low and cold.

"I . . ." manages Wanda. She pauses, swallowing again, then says, "I couldn't. I wanted to clean myself, but I *couldn't*. Every time I tried, my magic ran through my fingers like it was water, and I knew if I . . . if I grabbed it hard enough that it couldn't get away, it was going to hurt those people. *I* was going to hurt those people. They didn't deserve what I could do to them."

"Didn't they?" asks Doctor Strange.

"No," says Wanda, with more strength. "They were being . . . being ignorant and small, but that doesn't mean I should hurt them. Only villains hurt people for disagreeing with them. For being . . . for being different from what they are."

"As you say, although I would argue that bigotry is no disagreement, but a fundamental failure of personal character," says Doctor Strange. He moves his hands in an arcane gesture, and Wanda is clean, like she had never been dirtied to begin with. "I am proud of you, Apprentice, for not lashing out. Perhaps you and your brother should go to the kitchen, and fix yourselves something to eat. Tomorrow is Saturday: You have no classes. I would thank you both to spend the night here, so we may take an outing in the morning."

"Aren't you going to come and eat with us, sir?" asks Wanda.

"I have business to take care of," says Doctor Strange. "I'll be back shortly." He turns and walks toward the front door, leaving them alone.

A moment later, they hear the door open and close, gently. Peter and Wanda exchange a look.

"Field trip, I guess?" says Peter.

"Come on," says Wanda. "There's leftover chicken from dinner, and I can fry up some potatoes."

"Just try not to burn the skin off the inside of my mouth," says Peter, and he follows her.

———

THE OIL IN THE PAN IS HOT AND POPPING WHEN PETER—SITTING ON the ceiling like gravity is something that happens to other people, and not a thing he should ever need to worry about—leans back on his hands and says, "Doc just said we should spend the night, not that we had to stay inside the whole time."

"Don't call him 'Doc,'" says Wanda, chopping a potato into even cubes. "He hates it, and I don't want him to turn you into a newt."

"He wouldn't do that," says Peter. "I mean . . . Wait. Is that a thing he can do?"

Wanda makes a noncommittal sound and keeps chopping.

"Okay, just hear me out, all right? You've had a hard day, I've had a hard day, your day was worse, we could both improve our days by going out for pancakes and milkshakes at the Starlight Diner."

Wanda stops chopping and turns slowly to face him, the knife still in her hand. "Pancakes. I told you I had leftovers for dinner, and you want to go for *pancakes.*"

"Yeah." He smiles his most winning smile, the one that's been charming her since they were babies, and she frowns.

"And this has nothing to do with a certain Miss Stacy liking to hang out there after her classes?"

"No, never!" He manages to sound almost shocked by the suggestion. "I mean, if she is there, I wouldn't object to joining her . . ."

"You're buying."

That's when he knows he's won. His smile broadens. "Of course I'm buying. I'm your big brother."

Wanda turns off the burner and puts down the knife before picking up a bowl and starting to fill it with water so she can put the potatoes in the fridge. Midway through the gesture, she stops, sighs at herself, and waves her free hand. The chopped potatoes reassemble and unpeel themselves, becoming whole again. Peter looks impressed.

"I didn't know you could do that," he says.

"I've been practicing," she replies. "I'll get my coat. We're swinging?"

"We're swinging," he confirms.

Half an hour later, when Doctor Strange comes home, it's to an empty house and a note on the counter saying that they'll be back before midnight. He shakes his head with frustrated fondness before taking Wanda's leftover chicken out of the fridge and reheating it with a snap of his fingers. Sometimes they can make him feel so *old.*

———

THE STARLIGHT DINER HASN'T CHANGED IN THIRTY YEARS, AND WILL probably stay the same for thirty more. The linoleum is permanently just a little grimy, the Formica tables are scratched and dull, and the vinyl booths have been patched a hundred times over. Still, the air smells fresh and cool, rich with frying burgers and fresh fries, and the light is steady and reassuring. A jukebox plays in one corner. It could be any time, and that time is going to last forever. In the Starlight Diner's artificial lighting, they're immortal.

In the corner booth, a familiar blond head is bent over an open book. Peter smiles a small, besotted smile and swaggers—yes, swaggers—in that direction, leaving Wanda to snicker into her hand as she follows him.

"Gwendy!" he declares, dropping into the seat next to his girl-friend, who looks up as his arm goes around her shoulders.

Wanda can't imagine ever being that casually unaware of her surroundings. Maybe she could have been once, but that was a long time ago, and things were different then.

"Do you think sticking a *y* on the end of someone's name makes you clever?" asks Gwen. "Because it doesn't make you clever, it makes you sound like you're casting a children's show. Hey, Wanda."

"Gwen," says Wanda with a smile. She moves to the other side of the booth, sliding in and eyeing Gwen's half-eaten club sandwich thoughtfully. "Munchies?"

"Munchies and math homework," says Gwen. "I sent your brother here a text to see if you'd both like to join me. My treat."

"You don't have to do that."

"No, but I want to."

Wanda smiles again, and when the waitress comes to check on them, orders a club sandwich and a vanilla milkshake, while Peter gets a burger and a cup of coffee. It won't keep him awake. He has a metabolism that treats caffeine like the setup to a joke that never gets delivered.

Wanda thinks she's doing a pretty good job of hiding the way the night's earlier events are playing and replaying in the back of her mind, an endless litany of prejudice and blame. And maybe she is . . . to anyone who doesn't know her as well as Gwen does, who isn't as perceptive. Gwen smiles at Peter, lowering her eyelashes, and asks, "Can you go get us some extra napkins? And maybe put something on the jukebox?"

"There's old-fashioned and then there's wasting my quarters," teases Peter, before he kisses Gwen's hand and goes to do as he's been asked. Gwen immediately shifts her focus to Wanda.

"Do you want to talk about it?" she asks. "Sometimes it's easier to talk with someone who hasn't known you since diapers."

Wanda can tell it's a genuine offer. But it's not like she can tell Gwen she was assaulted because people are prejudiced against mutants and terrified of her powers. Even if she could share her secret, Peter has one, too. But the words come bubbling up anyway, alongside tears she's managed to avoid all night.

"Sometimes, people can just be so *awful*," she says, and it's a weight off her chest to say it out loud. "And vile. And entitled. And crude. And just . . . just awful."

Gwen reaches out and grabs her hand, holding it silently until Wanda calms down.

"Yeah. You're absolutely right."

Gwen lets go of Wanda's hand as Peter makes his way back, turning to smile at him. "What took you so long, Parker?"

"It looked like you and Wanda wanted a moment," he says.

Gwen laughs, and the lighter mood returns. It's not long before Wanda's helping Gwen with her math while idly dipping fries into her milkshake, ignoring Peter's theatrical gagging sounds. Gwen just smiles, and the evening is long and lovely, and by the time they go their separate ways, Wanda's almost forgotten the movie theater, the boy with the irrational fury in his eyes, the burrito hitting her chest.

"Thank you," she says, as Spider-Man swings them back toward the Sanctum. "I needed that."

"We all did," he says, setting them down on the roof. "Now get some sleep, Wandy. I dunno what your weirdo master is going to do with us tomorrow."

Wanda nods, and opens the rooftop door, and goes back inside.

MORNING BREAKS BRIGHT AND EARLY, WITH PANCAKES AND FRIED eggs and the daily news, the headlines labeling Spider-Man as a menace once again—how Peter can be so blasé about that is something Wanda may never know—and a smaller article about a batch of tainted butter at a downtown theater sickening an entire auditorium of moviegoers and leaving them regretting their choice of evening entertainment. Wanda looks sharply from the paper to her master when she reads that, but he's enjoying his coffee, and pays her no mind.

They finish quickly, and Wanda washes the dishes with a wave of her hand, halfway grateful for the opportunity to show off for Peter, who doesn't get to see the proof of her growing control nearly as often as she wishes he could.

He looks suitably impressed, and they follow Doctor Strange to the solarium, where he's chalked a complicated ritual circle on the floor. They've had nearly two years to get used to him: They step into it without question, and he joins them a heartbeat later.

This is a rare one. He doesn't just move his hands. He speaks, the way Wanda often has to, when she's attempting a complicated working. She feels for Peter's hand, gripping it and squeezing it tight. Neither of them is in costume, but he's not as comfortable with the mystic arts as she is, even if he follows where she leads in these matters; he needs the reassurance.

The circle lights up, white-gold and gleaming, and in a flash of brilliance, they're gone.

THEY REAPPEAR ON A DRIVEWAY WINDING ITS WAY THROUGH A BROAD expanse of carefully maintained green, a stone fence and iron gate behind them, a manor house at the driveway's end. Wanda drops Peter's hand, and gasps as she realizes they're wearing their costumes, Spider-Man and the Scarlet Witch instead of the Parker siblings.

"We're visiting an associate of mine," says Doctor Strange. "It seemed better not to put you in the position of feeling like I expected you to reveal your identities. Just because the two of us are forced to face the public, that doesn't mean I expect the same from you. Do you understand?"

"Yes, sir," they say, in almost unison.

"That said, this man already knows your identities. His particular gift is mind reading, and he's powerful enough that he often does it without intending to. He's known about you both for years. We're keeping your secret from the others you may encounter here."

"Others, sir?" asks Peter. Wanda asks nothing, only stares at him in silent understanding.

She knows where they are. She's never been here, but she's heard descriptions, and she . . . she knows where they are.

"If they're going to label you a mutant, you may as well know what that word means in flesh as well as on paper," says Doctor Strange. "And some of these mutants may have things to teach you. Magic chooses its own vessels. Sometimes people never know why they were chosen. If genetics are enough to call it home, then some people's mutations may put them into contact with the mystical. It's a simple enough thing to check."

"Yes, sir," says Peter, and squeezes Wanda's hand again, before the three of them start walking down the long driveway toward the mansion.

Later, Wanda will look back on this moment and compare it to approaching the Baxter Building, the way she'd put on her Glinda the Good Witch costume like it was some sort of armor against discovery and judgment, like this was a game and their powers would go away when the book was closed and the real world came flooding back. Then, she had walked with Peter and no one else, but now she walks with her brother and her master, three penitents on the way to the Emerald City.

Maybe this is where she can finally find out where her powers come from. Maybe this is where she comes to understand herself a little better. It's hard not to resent Doctor Strange for deciding this on her behalf, but if he'd asked her, would she really have been able to get past her own fears and prejudices and say yes? She's not sure, and so she's just glad to be here.

She should have been here years ago.

It's staggering. It feels almost inevitable, a feeling that doesn't fade as they approach the door and Doctor Strange rings the bell, and the door is opened by a tall, broad-chested man with blue fur covering his entire body, most of which is on display thanks to a costume Aunt May would call little better than swim trunks.

The man is silent for a moment, blinking at them. Then his face splits in a wide grin that displays several impressively large, sharp teeth, and he steps to the side, saying jovially, "I wasn't aware we were expecting a house call today, Doctor! Who are your aides?"

"You recognize them, Dr. McCoy," says Doctor Strange, stepping inside with Peter and Wanda close behind. "We're here to see Xavier. He's expecting me. Please let him know that we've arrived."

"No introductions?" asks the blue man. He looks to Wanda and sighs. "Such a shame, when manners are set aside. Very well. The professor has no doubt known of your arrival for some time, but he still respects the forms of things. If you would follow me, I'll take you to him."

The foyer is huge and grand, all pale wood and airy light. It makes the house in Queens where Peter and Wanda grew up feel cramped and small in a way the Sanctum Sanctorum never has. The blue man leads them toward a hallway, lowering his voice as he continues:

"We're a working school, and class is in session, so I'll thank you to keep your voices down and not disrupt our teachers. Logan especially gets annoyed when people interrupt his lesson plans." He chuckles, like this is somehow hilarious.

Doctor Strange is less amused. "Logan's lesson plans generally take the form of punching people," he says. "I doubt he's conducting class inside on a day like this."

"Allow me *some* enjoyment, as you come here all clandestine, dragging two of our fair city's newest and most exciting heroes in your wake! A man cannot live on seriousness alone."

"Perhaps not, but there will be time for pleasantries after our meeting."

"I'll hold you to that," says the blue man, and walks to a pair of closed doors, pulling them open and waving the trio through.

The room beyond is large, dominated by bookshelves and a floor-to-ceiling window behind a massive oak desk. A man sits there, bald head gleaming in the sunlight, and it's not until he pushes back from the desk that Wanda realizes he's using some sort of high-tech wheelchair. It floats a foot or so above the floor, much the way her master sometimes floats, and a blanket covers his legs.

He glides toward them, the motor of his chair virtually soundless. She can't see how he's controlling the movement of the chair; that must be part of the technology that powers it. She glances to Peter, and despite his mask, she can tell that he wants to start asking questions and maybe taking pieces apart as badly as she does. It's rude to analyze someone else's mobility devices, but an urge isn't rude, only acting on it. Wanda keeps her hands behind her back, holding her patience as best she can.

"Hello, Stephen," says the man, once he's close enough. His accent is one Wanda knows well, that particular blend of money and manners that comes from the cultivated gardens and walled houses of the upper crust, local and foreign at the same time, like wealth elevated them to an entirely different nationality. He directs his greeting at Doctor Strange, naturally enough.

Wanda's master smiles with a rare degree of genuine fellow-friendship, teeth flashing white below the black border of his mustache. "Charles," he says, his own iteration of that same accent coming through more strongly than it normally does, a mimic fitting into his surroundings. "You're looking well as ever."

"As are you, Stephen. As are you. Now." The man—Charles—turns his attention to Wanda and Peter. His gaze is kind but intense; he seems to see everything there is to see about them. Wanda feels grubby and small under that regard, like she should have taken more than one shower that morning. She doesn't feel judged, just . . . unworthy, in a distinctly uncomfortable way. "These are . . . ?"

"Professor Charles Xavier, please allow me to present my apprentice, the Scarlet Witch, and her . . . associate, Spider-Man."

"Splendid," says Charles. "I've heard much of both of you. Why, some of my students have crossed paths with you in the city, when they've gone on their own patrols. I've been hoping to meet you myself."

"It's nice to meet you," says Peter.

"A pleasure," says Wanda, inching a little closer to her brother, like she thinks he can protect her from this whole strange situation, like there is any protection from this situation. She glances to Doctor Strange, who remains perfectly calm. Oddly enough, that helps. He brought them here, and he wouldn't look so relaxed if there was any danger.

"You're both aware that I'm a reader of minds, if the quadratic formulae our arachnid friend is filling his thoughts with are anything to go by, and while it's true that I glance at your surface thoughts at times without meaning to—young man, if you're going to use math to keep me from seeing things you'd prefer go unseen, please be sure your equations resolve, or you're going to give us *both* a headache, and I don't think either of us is going to appreciate it."

Spider-Man grimaces and turns his face away, chagrined. Professor Xavier continues: "While I may 'hear' things you think loudly, or in my specific direction, I won't go prying, and anything I happen to 'overhear' that you didn't intend to tell me will be kept in strictest confidence, unless you're planning some grand act of super villainy that needs to concern me, or might impact the safety of my students. We're mutants here. We understand that sometimes secrets are a form of self-protection, and I won't go looking for yours."

"Manners are the first rule of the telepath," says Doctor Strange. "You can trust Charles, or I wouldn't have brought you here."

"Now that we've settled that, young lady." Professor Xavier shifts his attention to Wanda. "Your teacher tells me there was some unpleasantness last night. People throwing the word *mutant* at you like some sort of curse. He says you're concerned they might be right."

"Not . . . not concerned, so much," says Wanda haltingly. "We don't know where my powers come from, just that I have them, and I've always wondered, a bit. Being a mutant might . . . might make some things harder for me, but at least it would answer the question of why I'm like this. Most of the people I know with powers know how they got them, and I just want to know the same thing."

"It will be easier for you if you're not a mutant, it's true," Professor Xavier admits. "But we have a quick way of finding out."

"I don't like needles," says Wanda. Spider-Man takes her hand, squeezing it reassuringly.

Professor Xavier smiles. "No needles, I promise. This is entirely noninvasive. And Spider-Man? I promised not to dig, or to share your secrets, but a bit of advice: If you're not going to tell the world she's your sister, people will make assumptions when they see you holding her hand like that. They're not fair, and they're not reasonable, and you should be allowed to give comfort to your friends, but they're inevitable, and rumors are difficult to quash. If people start calling her your lover before you inevitably admit your true relationship, you may face backlash beyond what you are prepared to deal with."

Spider-Man drops her hand like it's suddenly become too hot to hold, and Wanda recoils, expression disgusted.

"I don't want to throw up on your rug," she says. "Please don't make me."

"Very well, then, let's go," says Professor Xavier, and steers his miraculous floating wheelchair out of the room, the trio following.

Spider-Man recovers before Wanda does. He leans toward her, murmuring, "Never thought I'd meet someone who makes your boss seem relaxed. You think the stiff upper lip and too many syllables come with being a senior superhuman? Are we going to get their vocabulary when we get old?"

"Hush," she says. "You're already obnoxious enough without swallowing a dictionary." But she's smiling, and Spider-Man grins to see it.

The blue man is gone when they emerge from Xavier's office. They follow Xavier through the halls of the house to an elevator—and that, more than anything else, proves this place is too large to be reasonable—who needs an elevator in a private home? A few of the doors they pass are open, and glancing through them, Wanda sees classes in progress, students younger than herself or Peter learning about super-powers like it's a normal part of a curriculum. Some of the students are older, college age and more. The range causes her to look to Professor Xavier, a question burning at the front of her mind.

"We're fully accredited," he says, seemingly out of nowhere. "Our students can use their degrees to transfer to any other program in the country, if not the world—Oxford has acknowledged our system, although not every major university has. Latveria, for example, has yet to extend academic reciprocity to any of our students, and I doubt they're going to. All mutants are welcome here, regardless of age or education level. Those with physical mutations frequently find it difficult to manage any sort of formal schooling before they come to us. Our adult literacy program is always quite full."

So if she's a mutant, she'll have peers. People her own age who understand what it is to navigate the world as a super hero and an outsider. The thought is more tempting than she expects. She's a Parker and she always will be, but that doesn't change the fact that she's always been just a little bit to the left of everyone around her, not American enough, not *right* in some indefinable way people have always been able to see and seize on. She's had teachers say to her face that the Roma were wiped out in the Holocaust, that they're fantasy creatures like unicorns or elves—or witches, she supposes. She can pass for white without much trouble, even when she isn't trying, and sometimes that makes her want to scream, like she's denying herself just by letting people look at her and draw their own assumptions.

It's a complicated thing to be an adoptee, especially a transracial one in a country that barely acknowledges people like her exist. She has all the privileges that come with being a middle-class American white girl, and she enjoys them, even while she feels like she doesn't really deserve them and never will.

Professor Xavier flashes her a reassuring smile, clearly picking up on more of this than she meant to project, and together, the four of them get into the elevator, which takes them far below the foundations of the house, dropping deeper until Wanda begins to worry about the structural stability of anything driven this far into the earth. Just as she's really beginning to fear what's going to happen next, the elevator stops and the doors slide open, revealing a long white hall that's even more out of a science fiction story than the Baxter Building.

She and Spider-Man are enthralled, stepping out to stare at their surroundings in silent awe. Professor Xavier and Doctor Strange exit behind them, exchanging an indulgent look. Clearly, this is a common response among people seeing this place for the first time.

Professor Xavier steers himself past them to take the lead. "This way," he says needlessly, and they follow him through the gleaming world toward an unknown destination, passing closed doors and large glass viewing windows on rooms as high-tech as the hall. It's hard to keep moving with so much fascinating science only feet away, but they do. Wanda doesn't want to disappoint Doctor Strange, and Spider-Man doesn't want to inspire him to give him one of those looks that says "your sister is my apprentice, and you are extraneous to our needs," and so they keep going, until they reach a metal door. Professor Xavier presses his hand against the plate set into the wall, and the door slides open, revealing a room on the other side, almost entirely black.

A catwalk extends from the door to a lit platform in what Wanda assumes is the center of the room. Only that betrays the potential size of the space; the blackness is all-consuming, making it impossible to distinguish individual walls. A rail keeps them from falling an unknowable distance to the floor below.

Professor Xavier leads them along the catwalk, and when they arrive, it lights up, a screen appearing in the air in front of him, and a strange helmet descends from the ceiling. Xavier grasps it in both hands, turning to address Wanda gravely.

"This is Cerebro," he says. "With this machine amplifying my natural abilities, I can detect every mutant mind in the world. We have a subtle frequency to our thoughts that non-mutants don't have, and it's consistent enough that I can find it. If you're a mutant, you'll show up here."

Wanda swallows and nods, afraid to even speak. Xavier lowers the helmet to his head, and lights begin to appear on the screen.

She waits to see if a light will appear for her.

———

DOCTOR STRANGE HAS STAYED INSIDE TO CATCH UP WITH PROFESSOR Xavier before taking them home. After extracting a solemn promise from Spider-Man not to grab Wanda and swing away, he allowed him to take her out onto the manor grounds for a walk in the fresh air.

Wanda is quiet as they walk, has been quiet since Cerebro confirmed she wasn't a mutant. Spider-Man keeps stealing little glances at her, trying to understand, until he finally grabs her arm and pulls her to a halt.

"Hey," he says. "What's going on in that head of yours? I'm not that professor guy. I can't read your mind. And let's both be grateful for that." He makes an exaggerated face, the expression carrying through his mask, and Wanda laughs, just a little.

"I would have moved out when we were both fourteen," she says.

"Ah, yes. The year you were in love with Jeff Goldblum."

"At least I wasn't crushing hard on Beverly Crusher."

"Hey, don't insult the best doctor in Starfleet!"

She laughs again, more heartily this time, then shakes her head. "And I'm—I don't know. Being a mutant seems really hard. It definitely causes them a lot of problems, and way too many people hate them for no good reason. We have powers. They don't hate *us* the way they hate the mutants."

"Let's just be grateful for that, okay?" says Peter. "I don't *want* things to be harder than they already are."

"Neither do I. It just . . . it doesn't seem fair, you know? They say it's because anyone can be a mutant, your kid could be a mutant, and that's scary, but anyone can have an accident, like you did. Our science teacher could have been the one who got bitten by the spider. Or Gwen. Or me, if I hadn't been sick that day."

"You'd be terrifying with spider-powers *and* chaos magic," says Spider-Man.

(In her chamber, America blinks and makes a note to herself to look for *that* timeline, which surely must have branched off this one at least once; the Multiverse seems to have a fondness for Spiders, and makes them out of whatever raw materials it can find lying around.)

Wanda laughs a third time at that, most heartily of all. "Can you just imagine? I'd be webbing people and then hexing them, and it would get all sorts of messy and complicated, and no. It's better this way. I think this may be the best way things could have gone for us."

"I think it is," says Spider-Man. "It could be better. Fewer people could be dead. But if you were going to have magic either way, at least this way we get to be super heroes together, and no one gets left behind. It was killing me, keeping secrets from you."

"Same," says Wanda. "It's just not fair the way people treat mutants. They're people, too, even if they're not the same kind of human people, and anyone can get bitten by a radioactive spider or hit by radioactive waste or, I don't know, dunked in a pool of radioactive chaos magic. It all comes down to radiation in the end."

Spider-Man glances around, making sure that they're alone, before he asks gently, "Wanda, are you *disappointed* not to be a mutant?"

"No. Yes. I mean . . . they're a community. You look at them, you look at this place, and it's obvious that they're a community. I guess part of me wanted to know that I belonged to something bigger than myself. That I had real roots. It's selfish, but there you go."

"Your family is your roots," he says.

She smiles at him. "I know. I just got transplanted a little, that's all."

"You're not sorry about that, are you?"

Wanda hesitates. "No," she says finally. "I'm not sorry I'm a Parker, and there's nothing in the world that I would give you up for. But sometimes I wish I *knew*. Where I came from, how I got here, whether it's part of where my powers come from. Being a mutant would have been an answer."

Peter nods. He doesn't have anything to say to that; he's always been more privileged here than she is.

"So I'm disappointed, but I'm not sad. Does that make sense?"

"It does, yeah."

"Let's go back." They turn then, side by side if not hand in hand, and start back toward the manor.

They're almost there when a tall blond woman in a green leotard comes walking briskly through one of the gardens, waving in their direction. They pause to wave back.

"Kushti divvus!" calls the woman, once she's close enough not to need to shout. She keeps heading toward them, moving to seize Wanda's hands. "Pey Romani!" From there, she talks too fast for Wanda to follow, the words just slightly out of tune with the ones Wanda has been studying in her language lessons, and she is suddenly, forcibly reminded of how careful everyone at the restaurant is in their discussions with her, the way they simplify their vocabulary and steer away from difficult concepts. She's been studying for years, but she has the working conversational grasp of your average eight-year-old. There just isn't enough immersion outside of controlled environments, and important as her language lessons are to her, she's never been able to give them the attention that they desire.

"I—I'm sorry," Wanda stammers, "I . . . kek mandi jinnavvas?"

"Oh." The woman's face falls at once, and she releases Wanda's hands. "I'm so sorry, when the professor told me—I assumed. I should have realized—I'm sorry." Her accent is British, more apparent when she's speaking English than when she's speaking whatever dialect of Romani she was just using. Her ears are pointed. There's no other visible sign of her mutation. "I'm Meggan."

"No code name?"

"It doesn't matter as much for me, since I'm obviously a mutant," says Meggan, tapping the point of one ear. "Normal people don't wander around looking like they're going to offer you a strand of hair in exchange for carrying the ring to Mordor. Anyway, I *am* sorry. Professor Xavier told me there was a young Roma woman visiting, and I thought I'd come say hello. I should have realized that even if you spoke Romani, you wouldn't necessarily speak the same dialect I did. Communication can be hard when there's a continent in the way, and you don't have the dominant media forms reminding everyone how a sentence is supposed to go."

"Ah," says Wanda. She glances at her hands, then extends one toward Meggan. "I'm Doctor Strange's current apprentice. They call me the Scarlet Witch. But I'd love to meet up and speak Romani with you the next time you're going to be in the city. Does your professor have a way of contacting my master?"

"The telephone, usually," says Meggan, with a hint of amusement. "If we meet off the grounds, any chance you'll let me know what else people call you?"

"Yeah," says Wanda. "When we meet away from here."

"It's a date." Meggan takes her hand and shakes, smiling. "I went from people calling me dirty because I was Romanichal to people calling me dirty because I was a mutant. I'd play my name close to the chest, too, if I thought I could get away with it, even temporarily. Must be nice to walk in the world and not have people already think they know you."

"It is," says Wanda.

"I'll wear a hat," says Meggan, almost flippantly. "Not out of shame, mind—neither of us has a thing to be ashamed of—but because I want to have a nice day with you. I'll call your master as soon as I know when I'll be free, all right?"

"All right," says Wanda, and watches as Meggan heads back into the garden, a natural disaster that touched briefly down and is now moving on.

"What just happened?" asks Spider-Man.

"My apprentice has made a playdate," says Doctor Strange from behind them, sounding amused. Him appearing out of nowhere is so common that neither of them flinches, they only turn to look at him. "Now shall we go home?"

"Yes, please," says Wanda, and so they do.

CHAPTER TWELVE

———

BURNING BRIDGES

GWEN STACY IS EASY TO LIKE. SHE'S SMART, AND SHE'S FUNNY, ONCE you get to know her—her humor is drier than Peter's, less quippy and more sharpened to a killing edge. When Gwen drops a comment about something, there had best be someone nearby to stanch the bleeding. The first time he brought her to the house, she had charmed Aunt May in a matter of minutes, while she and Wanda had eyed each other warily, two tigers occupying the same hill for the first time. Peter had been gleefully oblivious to the tension between them, only caring that the two most important women in his life were meeting the girl who was vying to become the third.

Then Gwen had smiled at Wanda, sudden as a sunrise, and asked, "You got your hands on the new Gaiman novel yet?" and everything had been fine.

If Wanda has her lessons with Doctor Strange and at the restaurant complicating her college experience, Peter has Gwen. Smart, sweet, suspicious Gwen, who isn't going to stay in the dark forever; she's going to figure things out sooner or later. Wanda has been prodding him more and more, trying to make him understand that lies are acid to love, and it's going to be worse the longer he waits. She barely forgave him for hiding his powers from her, and they had a lot more history together than he has with Gwen, and he had been a super hero for a lot less time when she found out. He needs to tell her.

But his second secret life has already sunk its sharp little teeth into Gwen's world. Her father is dead—they're all members of a terrible, deeply specialized club now, the Association of Orphans, and her enrollment is entirely down to the acts of Peter's enemies. He came back from Captain Stacy's funeral completely wrecked, staggering into the Sanctum Sanctorum and interrupting Wanda mid-lesson as he collapsed in front of her, burying his head in her lap. She'd been afraid, when he did that, that something had happened to Gwen as well; that his heart had been broken beyond repair.

But no, it had just been guilt eating him alive, digging its own sharp teeth into his heart over and over again. He couldn't tell her after that, he'd argued: If he did, he'd lose her, and then she'd be alone.

Wanda could almost see the logic in that, could understand when he let Gwen leave for Europe without stopping her from shifting her life onto a new track, and she'd kept in touch with Gwen the whole time she was away, the two women exchanging letters across an ocean, both censoring themselves carefully for the sake of the other's sensibilities—although while Gwen was protecting Wanda from the depth of her feelings for Peter, Wanda was protecting Gwen from a mountain of secrets that weren't hers to share.

It was almost a relief when Gwen said she was coming back to New York. It was oddly easier to lie to her in person, and Wanda missed having another girl her own age around to talk to. Gwen's spice tolerance was much higher than Peter's. When they wanted privacy, they just went to the restaurant and shared an appetizer platter, spices burning their tongues and laughter filling their mouths.

It was perfect. It *is* perfect. Wanda knows it's going to be that good again, it has to be, because this isn't how it ends. Not in the dark, not with the cackling voice of the Green Goblin hanging in the air, waiting to be whipped away by the wind. He's been one of Peter's most persistent villains since the beginning. Wanda has faced him several times now, both by Spider-Man's side and on her own, never intentionally—she's gotten in trouble with her master each time, even though she's never sought out the Goblin. She likes to think she's held her own against the villain. Hex bolts are good for taking out glider engines, and his pumpkin bombs rarely explode when they're close enough to her to do any real damage, but she hasn't been able to catch him. Neither has Spider-Man, not yet, not for long enough to make him stop.

And now here, tonight. Wanda was at the Sanctum preparing dinner for herself and her master, this being one of her rare nights off from both the restaurant and patrol; she's not in the habit of cooking elaborate meals for Doctor Strange, but she's supposed to go on a picnic with Meggan and Gwen tomorrow and she wants the leftovers. Lasagna is not a good picnic food unless it's eaten cold out of a Tupperware and has that gluey consistency that comes for pasta after twelve hours in the fridge keeping it all together.

She was there, and then Peter was there, coming through the window in the exact way her master tells him not to, begging her to come with him, because there wasn't any time, and the Goblin had Gwen. The Goblin had snatched her and carried her away, and Peter needed to get her back before something terrible happened, because something terrible was *going* to happen, oh, yes. Something terrible was already happening.

Wanda had stopped and stared at him, ground beef and oregano dripping from her fingers, not sure how to react. And then her master had come, and with a wave of his hand, she'd been dressed for the city night—red tunic, mask across her eyes—concealed from the world.

"Go," was all he'd said, and somehow that had been the most alarming thing of all. Doctor Strange was a man of many words where she was concerned—too many, sometimes, more enchanted with the sound of his own voice than he was with the enchantments she called from her open palms. For him to command her so bluntly was frightening and strange, and she had dropped her suddenly clean hands and run after her brother, following him out the window and into the night. Then his arm had been around her waist and they had been swinging through the air as they had so many times before.

But this time had been different, hadn't it? The air had crackled with a taste like an impending storm, even though the sky was clear, and for the first time, Wanda had felt like she was tapping into Peter's spider-sense, actually *tasting* danger on the wind. It wasn't a pleasant spice. It didn't make the air any sweeter, or make her feel any more alive. If anything, it made her want to go back to the Sanctum and pull the window shades closed behind her, sealing out the world while she wrapped herself in the softest blanket she could find and huddled in the room set aside for her use on the nights when she slept over. She had been afraid.

She's still afraid now, standing on the bridge where Spider-Man set her down, with the wind doing its best to shove her from her perch and send her plummeting to the river far below. It's so distant and dark that it looks black as an asphalt highway, and if she hits it from this height, she knows it'll be just as hard as that highway. This isn't a fall a person without physical enhancements can survive.

The Goblin knows that. The Goblin is *counting* on that, as he dangles Gwen like bait—and how did he know to go for her? How did he know she was the way to hurt Spider-Man? Peter has always been so *careful*. After the Green Goblin learned of Peter's secret identity—and by extension, Wanda's—they had managed to force him into a web of electrical wires doused in volatile chemicals. Logically, the shock should have killed the man. Instead, thanks to a little well-twisted probability, it had given him severe amnesia, and neutralized the threat he represented.

So how did he get his memory back? How did he *know* to aim for Gwen? He rises higher on his glider, one hand around Gwen's throat and the other covering the lower half of her face, the woman too terrified by the distance between her and the ground to even struggle. Her eyes find the Scarlet Witch where she stands on the bridge tower, silently begging for help.

And there's nothing she can do. With the wind and her own emotions as heightened as they are, if she hits the Goblin's glider with a hex bolt, she's likely to send Gwen plummeting to her death.

She's been working on her levitation, but it's still a clumsy thing, unreliable and likely to fail her before she can do anything. The Scarlet Witch isn't going to be the one to save Gwen tonight. That will come down to Spider-Man, as it so very often does, and they both know it. They both *believe* it. Maybe all three of them believe it. This is a game to the Green Goblin, a game that will eventually end in Spider-Man's humiliation and unmasking, but nothing more.

Surely nothing more.

Spider-Man has been swinging around the bridge for the last five minutes, trying to grapple the Green Goblin without knocking Gwen from her place on the glider, trying to stop the man without jostling him enough to make things worse. The Scarlet Witch has managed a few twists of probability to help him hit harder and dodge more easily, but like Spider-Man, she's limited by the need to avoid Gwen, to pull her punches.

The Goblin isn't pulling his. His taunts have become wilder and wilder as the fight stretches on, and as Spider-Man once more swings and misses, the Goblin urges his glider higher, until he's eye level with the Scarlet Witch. His mask covers his face, but she's been a masked hero in her own right long enough to know that he's smiling at her, cold and cruel; the expression shows in the way his throat tenses and his ears lift, ever so slightly. Wanda thinks she'll be seeing that smile in her dreams for the rest of her life.

It's better than what comes next, as the Goblin flies even higher, to the very top of the tower, where he shoves Gwen away from him and onto the structure. She shrieks, the first sound she's made in minutes, and clutches for the bridge, struggling to anchor herself while the Goblin glides a few feet away and turns to taunt Spider-Man.

No. He's not taunting Spider-Man. He's taunting *Peter*. This is personal, personal enough to bring bile flooding the back of Wanda's throat, where it burns like the fires of perdition, searing and strangling her.

"I have your *woman,* Parker!" shouts the Goblin. "And just like I knew you would, you brought your pathetic sister in your rush to save her! I can kill either one of them and leave the other to blame you! Or you can kill yourself, and they can both live! Choose!"

He's not holding Gwen anymore. Hex bolts are back on the table. The Scarlet Witch eyes the angle between them, summoning the chaos from deep within herself and preparing to sling it.

Gwen stiffens, face going even whiter than it was before, and Wanda realizes that somehow, despite everything, she didn't really believe the Goblin's claims that Spider-Man, the monster who failed to save her father, was also the man she loved. But identifying the Scarlet Witch as his sister was a step too far—she's evidence that what the Goblin is saying is the truth. Because the mask has never really been enough, has it? Gwen has seen her hair, her mouth, heard the way she laughs. Wanda's tried to keep Gwen and the Scarlet Witch apart, but it hasn't always been possible, not with the tangled way their lives have gone. Gwen knows it's her, and if Gwen knows the Scarlet Witch's true identity, she knows Spider-Man's as well.

Gwen's eyes go to the fast-moving red-and-blue streak that is Spider-Man, and she whispers a single word, one that the wind whips away and helpfully carries down to the Scarlet Witch on her lower platform, as if anything could be helpful right now. "Peter . . . ?" she whispers.

The Goblin tilts his glider downward then, covering the distance between himself and the Scarlet Witch in an instant. He's fast—she's always known he was fast, has seen him fight Spider-Man more times than she cares to count, dodging blows and web-lines that would have flattened a normal human—but he's never aimed that speed at her before, and her hex bolt goes wild, shooting off into the sky to give some asteroid or cable satellite a blast of unusually bad luck. He has her by the back of the cloak before she can ready another bolt, jerking her roughly upward to deposit her next to Gwen.

Gwen turns to look at her with wide, wounded eyes, not grabbing for the safety she must surely represent. The Scarlet Witch is someone familiar, someone well-known and—she thought—

well-beloved, but Gwen looks at her like she's an extension of the Goblin, like she created this untenable situation.

"Gwen . . ." she begins, and stops, words dying as the hurt in Gwen's face morphs into disgust.

Spider-Man and the Goblin are finally fighting with the fierce abandon she's more accustomed to seeing, trading blows and bombs and—no doubt—piercing quips she can't quite make out over the whistle of the wind and the occasional explosion. Balling his fists together, Spider-Man brings them down on the Goblin's head, and the Goblin loses control of his glider, sending them into a spin that knocks Spider-Man loose. Somehow still conscious, the Goblin turns his glider toward the two women clinging to the bridge.

Gwen's face shifts again, fear returning, and she scrambles to get behind the Scarlet Witch. It doesn't do her any good: The Goblin is already there, and as the Scarlet Witch shoots a bolt of pure bad luck into his glider engine, he grabs them both.

"Spider-Man!" he howls, ignoring the way his whining engine starts to sputter. "I offered you both their lives for yours! Now you get to choose—which one lives?"

And just like that, they're falling.

———

THE WIND IS LOUDER THAN ANYTHING ELSE HAS EVER BEEN. WANDA grabs for the air as she falls, forcing back the fear, reaching for the currents of chaos that always surround her. Her master moves through space as easily as he does time, appearing and disappearing as if distance were just a notation someone made in a workbook, not something that applies to him. He's been trying to teach her the same skill, but she understands the physics too well, knows how far the Earth can travel in an instant, how impossible it is to do the math of motion.

She's never been able to throw herself into the void the way he does, because she's all too aware of how unlikely it is that she'll survive to come out the other end. Only now she knows the physics of her fall just as well, and she knows what happens when she hits the bottom. Bridge or water, it doesn't matter; from this height, she's dead either way. And by throwing them both, the Goblin has created an impossible choice. Sister or lover? Family or future? She can't force Peter into this decision, she *can't,* not when her magic is willing to save her if she just stops fighting and trusts it to know what it's doing.

The Scarlet Witch falls, and there's a flash of red, and from the perspective of those on the bridge, she's not there anymore. Not that any of them are looking. The Goblin is fighting to maintain control of his glider, which is making a horrible whining sound, like it's getting ready to explode; Spider-Man is focused on Gwen, not because she's his girlfriend, but because she's a civilian. He knows the Scarlet Witch can take care of herself, and if he's putting more faith in that than he should, he has to put his faith in *something* right now.

And Gwen? Gwen is falling. Gwen is falling forever, dropping out of the sky like an angel cast down from the heaven. She claws at the air as she drops, desperate for a lifeline.

The night is deep and cold, and Gwen Stacy is falling.

———

WANDA IS ALSO FALLING, BUT UNLIKE GWEN, WHO FALLS IN desolation and the dark, she falls through crimson, the world around her reduced to a glowing tunnel of endless red. It reflects forever in all directions, like she's dropping through a funnel made of mirrors. The cascade of light and color is geometric and fractal, perfectly orderly when she looks close enough, infinitely chaotic at first glance.

This is her magic. This is her version of the void.

This is home.

"Great," she says to the cluttered nothing. "So I got here. Now how do I get out?"

That's where her mind always freezes up. Her master says transit is easy: Just picture your destination exactly as it is, and put
yourself there, like you're a doll and a great hand has moved you
around the dollhouse you normally occupy. There's no space between, no transit. There's here and then there's there, and skipping
between them is as easy as a thought.

But Wanda has never been able to picture her destination without getting stuck in the complicated math of figuring out how far
the world will have traveled in even the split second it takes her to
move herself. So she freezes, and she falls, and she can keep falling
forever if she doesn't find a way to break the stalemate; not even the
Sorcerer Supreme will be able to find her here, in this cascading
column of chaos. This place belongs to her.

This place *belongs* to her. She forces her breathing to slow, moving deliberately in the air until she's seated cross-legged, the way she
always is when she's beginning a new working; she rests her wrists
upon her knees and closes her eyes, shutting out the geometric cascade.

But not the red. The red remains, bright as a sunrise, vivid as a
rose. The red never leaves her, no matter what, and now she pulls it
close, like a cloak, like a shield, and she tells it exactly what she
wants it to do, and her power, to her surprise and delight, listens.

Took you long enough. It's not words so much as it's a feeling,
but it wraps around her all the same, and then it's gone, and she's
standing on the bridge, far below the place where she was, where
she fell.

She doesn't know how long that took—time can be strange inside the chaos—and so she looks desperately around, searching for
Gwen's broken body on the pavement. She doesn't find it, and so
she finally lifts her eyes, and there's Spider-Man, frantically spinning a web as he rushes to stop Gwen's fall.

He understands the physics as well as she does, the limits of the
human body, the speed and the inertia and the laws of motion and
everything else he has to account for. He understands them, but he
doesn't live them, not anymore: His own body has tolerances so far

above those the rest of them have to navigate around that maybe it shouldn't be a surprise when his web-line catches Gwen's foot and jerks her to a sudden, inescapable stop.

The wind is loud, even this low, and the ocean is loud, and everything is loud, the world is a sea of sounds, and still Wanda hears the brutal finality of the snap as Gwen's head is thrown back by the abrupt end to her fall. She allows herself to keep hoping that she heard wrong as Spider-Man swings down to the bridge, lowering Gwen to the pavement, and hurries to gather her in his arms.

He begs her to open her eyes, to wake up, to do anything but lie there limp and not breathing. They've started to gather a crowd, or maybe the crowd has been there all along: Stopped cars are backing up on the bridge, and a police cruiser comes toward them, lights flashing blue and red.

It's the red light that catches Spider-Man's attention. For the first time, he takes his eyes off Gwen and looks wildly around, only calming when he finds Wanda standing frozen, watching him grieve. Her own grief is lurking, still buried under shock and trauma.

"Fix it," says Spider-Man, and he sounds more like Peter than he ever has when in costume, he sounds like he's eight years old and demanding she put a broken toy back together. There's anger, yes, but underscored by pleading desperation. "Don't just *stand* there staring at me, *fix* it!"

"I—" Wanda manages, and is relieved to find that she still has a voice to answer with. "I can't. I'm sorry, but I can't."

"You mean you *won't*," Spider-Man protests. "Use your magic, rewind time, and fix it. Make it so the air is softer, so she doesn't break when she stops falling. I've seen you unbreak dishes and unpeel potatoes and I know you can do it, so do it."

"P—Spider-Man, my magic doesn't work that way," she says. "Fixing a dish isn't like raising the dead. I can't bring her back. I'm so sorry. I would if I could. I loved her, too."

"*Bring her back!*" he howls, and it's every protest against the unfairness of the world that has ever been, all wrapped up in a single pained demand.

Tears run down Wanda's cheeks—when did she start crying?—as she shakes her head and says, "It was all I could do to get myself down here safely. I can't, and I won't, and I'm sorry."

"You can do anything *you* want," he spits, pure venom in his tone. "If *you* want it, it happens. Your magic always works when you need it to, but when *I* need you, it doesn't work at all—or maybe it puts you first. I saw you disappear, and then my catch went wrong. Did you take everyone else's luck to give yourself a safe landing?"

Wanda can't speak. Peter can't seem to stop.

"Why is it always the people I love who have to die? You've been the common denominator every single time."

Wanda rocks back on her heels, as stunned as if he'd slapped her. "Ex*cuse* me? It's not my fault you forgot how human anatomy works! And it's not my fault you couldn't catch her safely! Don't you try to pin this on me."

Spider-Man sneers at her. "You never belonged here. I never wanted you anyway." Wanda's voice deserts her. In one swift accusation, he has thrown everything she's ever been afraid of in her face, and she can't even answer him, not with people getting out of their cars for a better look at this superhuman showdown, not with the police getting closer. She needs her brother right now.

What she has is Spider-Man, outraged beyond all reason, lashing out as he looks for someone to blame. "You've been nothing but bad luck since I met you! You're a jinx, and everything you touch falls apart! You've been cursed since they brought you home—they should have left you in Latveria, instead of inflicting you on me!" If she weren't crumpling under the weight of his words, Wanda would be proud of him: Even lost in his grief and anger, he managed to stop himself from revealing their familial connection where civilians would hear him. "Fix her, right now, make this right, or I swear, I will never speak to you again!"

He raises a hand, and for a moment, she thinks he's reaching for her, thinks maybe Peter is fighting his way back to reason from beneath the mask of pain that's clouding his thoughts. Then she sees the way he's holding his fingers and realizes he's about to web her, his sister.

So she does the only thing she can do. She uses her powers against him before he can hit her, calling up a rolling wave of chaos, red and blazing in the darkness, that catches his web before it can make contact, walling him off from her.

"I guess you're never speaking to me again," she says, and turns, and walks away.

CHAPTER THIRTEEN

—

DIRGE

SHE DOESN'T GO BACK TO HER DORM, AND SHE DOESN'T GO BACK TO Queens: Neither of those places feels like home right now. She goes back to the Sanctum Sanctorum, walking until she can't walk any farther, then flagging down a taxi. It takes four tries to find a cab-driver who's willing to take her on promise of payment when she gets to her destination: She's never needed to rely on public transit or vehicles while in costume, and she doesn't have a wallet with her.

The driver seems to think she was at a costume party and abandoned by an unfeeling friend or partner; he asks a few questions to make sure she's not too drunk to function, and then settles into a quiet that's rare for a New York cabbie, driving her to the Sanctum without further comment. Doctor Strange is outside when they pull up. Wanda's heart gives a lurch of relief and gratitude at the sight of him, and stumbles into his embrace while he's still trying to pay the driver.

They don't have a hugging relationship. They both like it that way. He's never been physically demonstrative with her, seeing it as a violation of the master-student relationship, and she takes her cues from him, and keeps her distance. They don't hug. But here Wanda is, clinging to him like she's going to die if he lets her go. He finishes paying the driver, makes a gesture that will ensure said driver forgets the whole thing, if not the generous tip that he's been given, and then turns to the substantially more difficult task of getting Wanda into the house.

She's sobbing by that point, and Doctor Strange is abstractly amused to see that she's not what anyone would call a "pretty crier": She's all snot and sniffling noises, red eyes and pallid complexion, and he finds himself looking her over for signs of obvious injury as he steers her up the stairs and through the doors into the safety of the Sanctum.

She keeps crying, but he's able to free one arm and guide her through the foyer without needing to worry about her tripping over unseen obstacles. She's always calmer in the solarium, and so he walks her there, finally peeling her away to settle her into a plush chair. A platter of cocoa and scones is already sitting nearby, supplied by the Sanctum. He tries not to remind Wanda that the house takes care of its own: She takes so much satisfaction from the kitchen, from knowing she does something he can't. Moments like this one are an exception.

He sits across from her, watching for signs of her tears beginning to slow. Eventually, she notices the scones and picks one up, nibbling like she's afraid he's going to slap it out of her hands. His heart breaks a little to see her like this. Something truly terrible must have happened.

"Wanda," he says. "Can you tell me what's wrong?"

She doesn't answer, just keeps nibbling her scone as she looks at him with heartbreak in her eyes.

A different approach, then: "Apprentice, tell me what happened." He makes his voice sharper, more commanding, but not as sharp as it would normally be if he was giving her an order: He wants her answer, but he wants to tread gently at the same time, to show her he understands her pain, even if he doesn't know exactly why she's feeling it. For a man like Stephen Strange, this is more difficult than any number of open battles or arcane challenges, and he would trade the look on his apprentice's face for a proper fight in an instant if the choice were up to him.

It isn't up to him. Wanda stares in silence for a few seconds more, then closes her eyes and slumps like she's exhausted, like she just realized how long her day has been. "Gwen . . . fell," she says.

"Gwen. Miss Stacy? Your brother's paramour?" He knows exactly who Gwen Stacy is. He's trying to draw her out, to keep her talking long enough for him to learn what happened.

She gives the smallest of nods, nibbling at her scone again, still without opening her eyes.

"Is Miss Stacy all right?"

A shake of the head, and silence.

"She hurt herself when she . . . fell?"

"No," says Wanda, voice very small. "Peter caught her before she could hit the ground. Snatched her right out of the air." Her voice gets even smaller as she says, "I didn't know a neck snapping would sound so much like a rib of celery."

Doctor Strange sits back in his own chair, sudden dread filling his chest. "Wanda, is Miss Stacy still alive?"

They can do a lot with surgical repair these days. She may not be paralyzed, or if she is, she may not be so injured that she'll require breathing assistance. Charles can help her with the adjustment to using a wheelchair; it will be a change, but she's young and resilient. She'll adjust to her circumstances, she'll recover—

Wanda shakes her head again.

"Apprentice—Wanda—is Miss Stacy dead?"

"Yes," says Wanda, voice barely audible. "Physics killed her, I guess, or the Green Goblin, because he's the one who threw us both off the bridge."

"Both—" Alarm washes away dread, as Doctor Strange sits abruptly upright. "You fell off a *bridge*?!"

"The Green Goblin pushed us. Both of us. He wanted to make Peter choose who he'd save. But I couldn't make him choose, because if he chose me, Gwen would die and he'd hate me, and if he chose Gwen, I might hate *him*. So I reached for the chaos, the way you always tell me I can, and I pulled myself inside of it, and it put me down on the bridge."

"You made a magical transit? On your own, unsupervised? You could have been hurt! Or lost forever in the void!"

"Or I could have hit the Brooklyn Bridge face-first. This was better. My magic helped me, and it happened fast enough that I saw Gwen fall. I saw Peter trying to catch her. I saw . . ." Her eyes open as her face crumples, unable to stand the images playing out behind her closed eyelids. "I saw her neck snap when he pulled her to a stop. He didn't save her. He couldn't save her. And I couldn't . . . I couldn't . . ." She starts to sob again, even harder this time, lost in her shock and grief.

"Raising the dead is a complicated art, and not one in which I've given you any training," says Doctor Strange, mistaking her despair for what follows an actual failure. "There was no way you could have brought her back."

"That's what—that's what I told P-Peter, when he told me to fix her. I said I couldn't. I said my magic wouldn't do that. I said I didn't know how. You never taught me how." The tears overflow her eyes and roll down her cheeks, heavy and unstopping. The front of her tunic is wet, a spreading dampness darkening the fabric.

"I don't know if I *could* teach you how, Wanda. Your magic is . . . not conducive to that kind of application. You could study all your life and never become a competent healer. And even the strongest healers have difficulty raising the dead. If you'd been able to catch her spirit before it could escape, you might have been able to force her into an unwilling unlife, a sort of imprisoned continuance. She was your friend. She didn't deserve that."

Wanda nods, dully. "I told him. I told him I couldn't. And he said . . . he said . . ."

Doctor Strange watches her, his own eyes darkening. He can guess some of what Peter said. He's a proud man, and worse, a clever one: Proud, clever men have always said things in the heat of the moment that they've come to later regret. If anything, the surprise is not that Peter said something unforgivable, but that it took him so long to do so.

And even so, Wanda is his apprentice, not her brother. If Peter said something unforgivable enough, it's not Wanda who will no longer be welcome in these walls.

Wanda's voice drops again as she continues, "He said I was a jinx. He said every time someone he loves dies, I'm there, I'm the common denominator. He said I was a curse, and our parents should have left me to die in the snow in Latveria . . ." Her words dissolve there, washed away by another wave of sobs.

Doctor Strange is silent for several seconds before he stands, moving his hands in a quick, complicated gesture. All through the Sanctum, windows slam, locking themselves against the outside world. He lowers his hands and looks to Wanda.

"Your brother is not welcome here until you can look me in the eye and tell me, with honesty, that he's made amends for what he said to you tonight," he says. "Not just apologized, but healed the wounds he's carved into your heart. That day may never come. That's his choice. But I will not have him in my home, in our home, if he's going to show such disrespect for my sworn apprentice. Do you understand?"

Still speechless, Wanda meets his eyes and forces herself to nod.

"Good," says Doctor Strange. "Do you intend to return to your dorm this week?"

Wanda nods again, clearly miserable. "I have exams coming up. I need to study."

"I won't try to forbid you—you're a grown woman, and you have the right to control your education. But I *do* need you to promise not to reach out to him. You're not seeking his approval after he's shown this level of disrespect. Do you understand?"

Wanda sighs and looks away. She knows he's right—overbearing—but right.

"I promise," she agrees. "I can't imagine being around him right now. But he'll probably swing around in a couple of days, offer to pay his weight in disco fries, and promise to be my personal chauffer for the next six months. Minimum."

"He doesn't have to grovel, but he has to be sincere. You can't allow him to treat you this way. I *won't* allow him to treat you this way."

"I'll still be going to the restaurant, you know."

"That's part of your education. I expect you may also wish to continue your lunches with Meggan—she helps your language skills, and you need a social life. Outside your brother, which is perhaps something I haven't encouraged enough."

Shattered and shaken by the death of a friend and the rejection of her brother, Wanda tries for the only valid objection she has left: "I don't have a car, and it'll take hours to get from here to campus on the train."

"I'll get you there."

It's not an offer. Wanda knows when she's been beaten; she nods, almost meekly, and puts her nibbled scone aside before standing. She sways, but does not fall.

"I'd like to go to my room now, Master, if it's all right with you."

"Of course it is," says Doctor Strange. "Just . . . remember to drink water. You need to hydrate."

Wanda (who will wake up tomorrow with a pounding headache brought on by both dehydration and overuse of chaos) nods, and says, "I will," before she turns and drifts, unsteadily, out of the room.

Doctor Strange rises in turn, heading for the foyer. He'll spend the rest of the night sitting with one eye on the door, waiting for Peter Parker to come begging to apologize. He intends to give the boy a piece of his mind, to remind him that what separates humans from animals is that when a human is in pain, they can choose not to strike out at the hands that help them. He wants to look Peter in the eye while he tells the boy how much his sister is suffering. He wants to see how badly Peter is suffering, too. He can't be there for the boy the way he is for Wanda, but there are others who might be, if only he can tell them that they're needed.

He won't get the chance.

Peter never comes.

———

WANDA PASSES THE NEXT WEEK WITHOUT CALL OR VISIT FROM HER suddenly estranged brother. She goes to her classes in all three locations—the school, the Sanctum, the restaurant—and she performs adequately enough at her studies that her grades won't suffer, but she's hollowed-out, empty, and stunned into an unusual silence by what happened on the bridge.

Meggan shows up at the Sanctum after Wanda and Gwen fail to arrive for their scheduled picnic in the park, and has to leave when her empathic metamorphic abilities turn her into a perfect replica of Gwen, causing the heartbroken Wanda to begin sobbing again. Doctor Strange sees her out, and promises that Wanda will call as soon as she's feeling up to it.

Wanda doesn't call.

The death of Gwen Stacy makes headlines across the city and into New Jersey. Jonah Jameson at the *Bugle* is especially enthusiastic about running with the story—a death he can explicitly blame on Spider-Man? A public falling-out between two of the city's costumed nuisances, conducted over the cooling body of a college girl? He's always hated Spider-Man, and has spread some of his vitriol onto the Scarlet Witch due to proximity alone, and now, finally, he has a weapon to wield against them both.

Wield it he does. By the end of the week, he's managed not only to blame Spider-Man for Gwen Stacy's death, but for her return to the city, claiming that the webbed menace lured an innocent young girl to the city solely for the purpose of ending her life. He uses every insult he can get away with printing, and a few Wanda is pretty sure he's going to get fined for, and almost all the pictures he prints with these explosions of slander and disgust have Peter Parker as their byline, snapshots of the self turned against the hand that shot them.

Wanda's classmates, accustomed to her stalwart support of Spider-Man, expect her to be enraged by the offending articles, and are confused when she pushes them aside and refuses to comment. She doesn't want to talk about Spider-Man, she doesn't want to talk about the girl who died, and she *definitely* doesn't want to talk to the classmates who remember Gwen visiting her on campus. Bit by bit, the other students piece together their version of the story: Gwen was a close friend of Wanda's, and her sudden refusal to defend Spider-Man is because she also blames him for Gwen's death.

It's closer to the truth than it could have been. Wanda doesn't fight it, only goes through the motions of her days, then goes back to the Sanctum, or into the city to fulfill her obligations at the restaurant. When Aunt May calls, three days into Wanda's week of solitude, she makes polite excuses for why she hasn't been home, tells her she's been grieving for Gwen, and promises to come by after the funeral.

The funeral. It looms up ahead of her like a tunnel preparing to swallow a train, and like the tunnel, it's full of shadows and unseen dangers, a landscape she neither knows nor understands. Gwen's parents are dead, but her grandparents handle the arrangements, and Wanda receives an announcement. Like all the rest of her mail, it's rerouted to the Sanctum by some spell she doesn't fully understand, and when she sees the envelope, it feels like her own heart stops for a long moment.

Gwen is dead. Gwen is never going to graduate college, never going to get married or have children. More immediately, Gwen is never going to make another grilled cheese sandwich, never laugh so hard chocolate milk comes out of her nose, never slather a corn dog in mustard and try to argue for it as a form of haute cuisine. Gwen is done. She's dead and gone and the funeral is a coda on what should have been a long and wonderful life.

A coda written by the Green Goblin as a gift to Spider-Man. The responsibility for Uncle Ben's death may be tangled and unclear— was it Peter's fault for letting the burglar go, Wanda's for fighting back, or the burglar's for breaking into the house?—but the responsibility for Gwen's death is easier to place. The Green Goblin snatched her, yes. He did it to hurt Spider-Man, and if not for Spider-Man, Gwen wouldn't be dead.

No matter how much she rotates the facts, how closely she examines them, Wanda can't find a way to blame herself. This wasn't her fault.

She holds that fact firmly in mind as she stands before her master with the funeral announcement in her hands, telling him she's intending to attend.

Doctor Strange looks at her with a steady, assessing eye, allowing himself the time to properly consider her words. When Wanda starts to squirm, he shifts position, ever so slightly, and asks, "Will *he* be there?"

"She was his girlfriend, and they were pretty serious. I can't imagine he won't be."

"And do you remember my requirement for you to spend time with him again?"

Wanda looks up sharply, a frown on her face. "You said that was the requirement for him to be allowed here again, not for me to see my brother," she says. "He's my *brother*. I can't tell my aunt May I'm not coming home for Thanksgiving because Peter and I have been secret super heroes since high school, and he said some horrible things to me after his girlfriend got tossed off a bridge by his nemesis! That won't work!"

"I can't control you, Apprentice, but I can ask certain things of you. One is that you respect me enough to respect yourself. If you must speak to him, feel free to pass along my requirements. That might inspire him to begin seeking amends. I would prefer you let him come to you. You can return to your home, of course, and I understand that you'll see him, but don't rush to a rapprochement that can only do you harm. Let him realize how wrong he is in his own time, and let you realize how strong you can be without him."

She looks away, eyes on the floor as she says, "I won't approach him if he doesn't approach me."

"That will be enough to satisfy me. Thank you, Apprentice."

He turns away then, returning to the book he was translating.

Wanda holds her place for several seconds more, until he glances up and asks, with a frown, "Are you still here?"

She flees.

———

THE SKY IS CLEAR AS CRYSTAL ON THE DAY OF GWEN'S FUNERAL. Wanda glares at it as she walks from the subway station to the funeral home. It's small, tucked into the middle of an ordinary business district block, with a long, canopied awning like a high-end hotel, providing cover for mourners and family members trying to get inside. Wanda's not the first one there. Gwen's grandfather is at the door when she arrives, and he doesn't recognize her, but he shakes her hand anyway, before waving her inside.

Her new black dress is a little too loose, chosen that way because looseness makes it more likely to be pristine when she removes it; if she's careful, she'll be able to return it to the store where she got it, rather than turning it into a macabre souvenir of a day she never wanted to experience. She can't imagine wearing it again. For any reason.

The room is half-full, Gwen's friends and distant relatives milling around, looking lost. There's a certain hollowness that fills a person's eyes when they've lost someone, and that void is everywhere Wanda looks. Everyone here is grieving. Everyone here is alone.

She finds a seat near the back, and has barely settled before Aunt May and Peter arrive, Aunt May's arm wrapped around his shoulders, Peter staggering like he's aged twenty years in the last two weeks. Wanda stares but doesn't move, and they take a spot near the front, seemingly without seeing her.

The service is short and heartfelt, nondenominational in a way she thinks Gwen would have appreciated—not that Gwen would have appreciated anything about this. Gwen would have appreciated not being *dead*. Everyone stands when they should, sits when

they should, and listens with the solemn focus of people who have
no idea what else to do. Only Aunt May and Gwen's grandparents
seem comfortable with the ritual of it all. All three of them are crying, but there's an ease to their motions and their words that speaks
to other funerals, other days like this one, other heartbreaks.

To live a long life is to grieve again and again. Those three people have a head start on grieving. Now is when the rest of them
start catching up, whether they want to or not.

When the official ceremony is finished, it's time for speeches,
and Wanda sinks lower into her seat, dimly afraid someone will try
to call on her and force her to the podium. No one does; there are
willing speakers enough. Friends of Gwen's from Europe and from
school, cousins, people Wanda doesn't know. Until Peter gets up,
and Wanda straightens again, suddenly attentive.

He moves to the podium, the glasses he doesn't need anymore
spattered with salt from the tears he's clearly been shedding all day,
and he grips it with both hands, looking at the lectern like he thinks
notes will suddenly appear to help him through this speech to the
other end.

"I had crushes in elementary school," he says. "Everyone does,
I think, except for maybe people who don't fall in love at all, but
they were all just that: crushes. I fell in love with girls at recess and
fell out of love by lunch, when they didn't think it was funny how I
liked to blow bubbles in my chocolate milk, or when their brothers
pushed me down on the playground." His voice is rain to the
parched soil of Wanda's heart: She's never gone this long without
hearing him, not since she got old enough to remember, and she
misses him like she'd miss a limb, like she'd miss her powers.

"I thought I knew what it was to fall in love, because of all
those crushes, and then I met Gwen Stacy. For the first time in my
life, it was like I was talking to someone who understood me, all of
me, and didn't hold a single inch of it against me. She kept up. No
matter what I said, she kept up. She was smart and she was funny
and she was perfect, and I . . ." His voice breaks, and he removes
his glasses to put a hand over his eyes. "I was going to marry that

girl. I swear I was. I loved her more than I knew I could love anyone."

Wanda isn't going to be jealous of Gwen at her funeral, she's *not*, she's not that kind of person, but oh, she wants to in that moment; as she listens to her brother talk about Gwen Stacy like she was the only person who ever really loved him, it's hard not to feel a bolt of discomfort. They were both in danger that night, but he doesn't care that she could have died, only that Gwen *did* die, and it was his fault, not hers, so why is she the one who's all alone? She never thought romantic love mattered more than any other kind. If he really loved Gwen more than anyone else in the world, maybe it makes sense that he's taking her death this badly. She was the only person worth fighting for, after all.

He sniffles and wipes his eyes, then looks up, and for a moment, it feels like he's looking right at her. "I *hate* Spider-Man," he says, with surprising fierceness. Gwen's casket is behind him, and her blandly smiling picture is beside him, and he's preaching Spider-Man's villainy with a confidence Jonah Jameson would envy. "I hate him for what he did, and what he's taken away from me. He's a monster. He always has been, and I hate that he's probably out there swinging around like nothing's changed, like he has a right to call himself a hero. Well, we know the truth, don't we? We know what he's done. He breaks everything he touches.

"I guess he'll have to live with that for the rest of his life, if he ever stops swinging long enough for it to catch up to him.

"Gwen, I love you. I'm always going to love you. I'm so sorry. I'm sorry we didn't have all the time we were supposed to have, all the time we were promised. If I could do it over again, I'd be better, I swear. I'd love you the way you deserved to be loved from the beginning, and I'd protect you. If we could just do it again from the beginning, I'd do it right this time, I promise."

He wipes his eyes and puts his glasses back on and slouches back to his place next to Aunt May. He doesn't look at Wanda again. Not once for the rest of the service.

When the mourners leave the funeral home for the cemetery, a long drive in chartered black cars with flags on the hoods to signal them as part of the funeral procession, no one speaks. Wanda winds up in a car with three of Gwen's cousins, and she's awed all over again by how much family Gwen had, this girl who was an orphan just like she was, yet somehow still has a web of connections tying her memory to the world. Wanda and Peter have Aunt May. And each other, but right now it feels like Peter wouldn't agree that she's part of what connects him to the rest of humanity.

Gwen was so lucky, right up until the moment when she wasn't.

The beautiful day isn't anymore by the time they reach the cemetery; the sky has turned black with clouds. It's a stroke of bad luck in the changeable New York summer, and Wanda knows it's not her fault. It *can't* be her fault. Storm is one of the strongest mutants there is, because she controls the weather. If Wanda's magic were that powerful, she'd know. She just bends individual strands of fortune, just ties moments into knots. She doesn't blacken entire summer skies.

(America knows better. But for all her observations and occasional distant interjections, America is only an observer here. She can't tell Wanda how powerful she is. Maybe that's a bad thing. Maybe it's a good one. There's no way of knowing, not even for her.)

The mourners gather around the gravesite. Wanda stands in the back, head bowed and hands folded, and listens as they consign Gwen's body to the earth. The coffin is lowered down, and Gwen is gone. Gwen is gone, and the world is different now.

Wanda turns to go, and there's Peter, malice in his eyes and tears on his cheeks. She stares for a moment, unable to help herself. She doesn't speak. She's keeping her word. But if he does, she can answer, and oh, she wants him to talk to her. She wants it so badly that when he finally opens his mouth, she barely registers the words at first.

"What are *you* doing here?"

"Peter—" she manages.

He shakes his head. "You're a jinx, and you're no sister of mine. I don't want you anywhere near me."

She makes a low moaning sound and starts to reach for him. And he, her beloved brother, her protector, pushes her away.

She falls to her knees in the cemetery grass, tearing her nylons and breaking a nail. She stares at him. He looms over her, and for a moment, she fears he might do something worse than push her.

Then he turns away. She scrambles to her feet, eyes burning with unshed tears. But these tears, for once, aren't for Gwen. Back stiff with what little pride she can scrounge, she turns and walks back to the car, dirt falling from her knees.

She makes it there before the rain begins.

She'll be able to return the dress.

CHAPTER FOURTEEN

—

PASSAGE

WANDA GOES BACK TO THE SANCTUM AFTER THE FUNERAL. WHERE else is she supposed to go? She can't go home, not when she knows Peter will be there, and while the restaurant is always an option, she's feeling the sort of heartbreak she can't mend with a shift spent serving plates to tourists or hiding in a kitchen. She wants to get out of this dress before she stains it somehow, wash the mud off her hands and knees, and sit alone in the orangerie until she feels like she can breathe.

Naturally, when she opens the door, she finds a blond woman sitting in one of the uncomfortable chairs in the foyer, an unfamiliar black-haired man dangling by his knees from the banister nearby.

Meggan beams and waves at her. "Wanda, hello! Your professor let us in. Thought you might need a bit of company after the day you'll have had."

"I was planning to—"

"Sit and marinate in your sadness, and then cancel another lunch? I was going to suggest a picnic in the park, but it seems the weather has other ideas. I could phone Storm, but she'll get cross if I ask her to mess about the normal passage of things so I can eat sandwiches in the grass." Meggan pulls an exaggeratedly sour face, clearly trying to coax a smile out of Wanda.

It doesn't quite work. Wanda resolutely switches her attention to the stranger. "Who's your friend?"

"Ah, this is Kurt. Kurt, this is Wanda. I've told you about her."

At Wanda's alarmed expression, she puts her hands up. "Nothing I'm not allowed to say to any of the X-Men! Just that you're a good friend, and we've been spending time in the city together. Kurt couldn't join us when Gwen was there, so I thought this might be a good opportunity to introduce the two of you. Keep you from wallowing."

"Why couldn't Kurt join us?" Wanda frowns as she looks at him more carefully. Nothing about him screams mutant; he could be a student from her college.

"Pretense is a luxury among strangers, but an offense among friends," says Kurt. He has a German accent, even heavier than Meggan's British accent, and as he speaks, he does some sort of complicated somersault, flipping off the rail to land lightly on the floor. It's so much like the kind of thing Peter does casually that it makes Wanda's chest ache, finding yearned-for familiarity in a stranger.

"What does that mean?" she asks.

He touches his wrist, and he's someone else. Gone is the skin a half shade lighter than her own, replaced by short blue fur, like velvet. His ears are as pointed as Meggan's, and his hands are three-fingered, matching his feet. Strangest of all, he has a tail, long and sinuous, and his eyes are yellow from side to side, no irises or pupils.

There's a decision to be made here, but Doctor Strange let them into the house, and Meggan is still smiling, although there's an edge of tension as she waits to see how Wanda will react.

Wanda manages to find a smile. "I fell down in the graveyard and tore my stockings," she says. "Can you amuse yourselves long enough for me to run to my room and get cleaned up?"

"I thought we might call for a pizza," says Meggan, edge of tension fading.

"Not a great idea. They can't always find the Sanctum. But I made jaxnija last night, and there's plenty left, if you don't mind reheated soup."

"It always tastes better the next day," says Meggan.

Kurt, meanwhile, is staring at Wanda. "You made jaxnija?"

"It's not bad. I've been working for years at a restaurant that specializes in Roma cuisine. I can make you a sandwich if you'd rather . . ."

Meggan bursts out laughing. "Go get changed before he starts proposing marriage," she says.

Wanda heads quickly up to her room, where she changes into jeans and a warm sweater after placing bandages on her knees. When she returns downstairs, Meggan and Kurt are waiting, two smiling pointy-eared kinfolk she didn't know she needed this badly.

They take their soup to the orangerie and eat wrapped in the blankets Wanda was dreaming of, and everything is warm, and they're alive. Gwen's gone, and Peter's lost in his own labyrinth of self-recrimination and grief, but they're alive. The world goes on.

———

THE WORLD GOES ON, BUT THE WORLD IS DIFFERENT NOW.

Wanda keeps going to her classes, mundane, magical, and culturally fulfilling. She goes home to Queens on the weekend, and Peter is never there; she finds herself comforting Aunt May when the woman weeps over the obvious and inexplicable fracture in her family. Peter still visits, but never when he knows Wanda will be coming. They don't discuss it, but they carve up the holidays and school breaks between themselves like a Thanksgiving turkey. He has a job—first his photography, and then a series of scientific internships—while she has her shifts at the restaurant. It's easy for her to make excuses, for both of them, and for the better part of four months they manage to coordinate without speaking, avoiding each other effortlessly.

Then comes Christmas morning.

The Sanctum is decorated to the extent of Doctor Strange's patience. Wanda thinks the place put up half the decorations on its own, just to tweak the man, who is sometimes too invested in the appearance of profound mystique for his own good: Streamers and boughs of holly deck the halls, and the trees in the orangerie drip with brightly colored glass balls. Candles float in bowls of water in the kitchen, burning without consuming themselves in quiet acknowledgment of Santa Lucia and the light she brings to the depths of winter. Wanda hasn't been able to find much on the holiday traditions of Latveria—apart from Doom's Day, which is well-known enough to have been lightly parodied on an episode of *Saturday Night Live* that has since been removed from circulation, but can still be found on bootleg videocassettes. What she has been able to find tells her that Saint Lucia plays a strong role at the darkest time of year, and is venerated through much of the countryside. Wanda lights candles for the home she never knew and never truly will, and hopes the light can reach the ones she's lost.

She isn't quite living at the Sanctum; she still maintains her dorm room, and sleeps there several times a week, meeting the requirements for residency and telling anyone who asks that she spends the rest of her time with a relative in the city. Her roommate doesn't mind her absence, seeing it as a cheap route to a single room, and as long as her grades stay good, the school doesn't get involved. Still, she spends Christmas Eve in her room at the Sanctum with the tall patchwork glass window, sleeping in starlight and trying not to think about how much colder this year is than last year.

The temperature hasn't changed. But last year, she was wrapped in the warmth of her family, and while Doctor Strange can try, he isn't the same. He doesn't honestly want to be, but he makes an effort for her sake, and she appreciates it, even as she makes apple cinnamon pancakes in the kitchen and waits for him to appear.

"You should go home," he says, as soon as he does.

"I am home, Master," she says, sliding pancakes onto a plate.

"And these doors are always open to you, but I meant your real home, with the people who love and worry about you," he says. "Your aunt will come looking for you soon if you don't at least go home long enough for her to fuss about how you need to eat more."

Wanda shrugs. "Peter will be there."

"Probably."

"He hasn't apologized yet. You told me not to spend time with him until he apologized."

Doctor Strange sighs. He did say that, and he meant it; he means it still. That doesn't mean she can cut all ties this easily. He moves closer to her. "I said you shouldn't seek out his company or his approval. I didn't ask you to avoid him completely. The superhuman community in New York is small. There's no way you can stay away from him forever, even if you have good reason to try."

"After the things he said at the funeral, I'm *very* invested in trying."

"Be that as it may, I don't want to incur your aunt's wrath."

"So you want me to go home, on Christmas, when Aunt May has no idea why we're fighting, and not talk to him if he's not ready to apologize yet?" Wanda slams her skillet down with more force than she would normally use. "Forgive me, Master, but that's the most ridiculous thing you've ever asked me to do. People on the streets are already starting to treat me differently, now that I'm not patrolling with Peter anymore."

"Differently how?"

She takes a deep breath and turns off the stove. "Magic is something people have trouble trusting, you know that."

"I do."

"Well, it just gets worse when that magic has to do with twisting people's luck around. People don't trust me. Not all the way. There's always been a question of whether I was safe to be around, but it mostly got overlooked because I was with Spider-Man. Everyone likes Spider-Man. He's funny, he's a good guy, and if he liked me, I had to be on the up-and-up. And now we're not patrolling together. I'm spending time with mutants, and I'm not going to stop doing that—Meggan has been an amazing friend, and Kurt is a sweetheart: I think I'd be a lot worse off than I am right now if I didn't have them to lean on. I won't even say it's not their fault that they're mutants, because there's nothing *wrong* with their mutations. They have pointy ears and super-powers, I have chaos in my blood, you have magic powers strong enough to scare *me* sometimes, and we're all just people! But people don't trust them because of the way they got their powers, and they don't trust *me* because they don't understand the way my powers work! Too many wicked witches in the stories they grew up on. If I can't even stay friends with Spider-Man, I must be a bad guy."

Doctor Strange lifts an eyebrow. "You've been wanting to say all of that for some time now, haven't you."

"I have," she admits.

"I still don't want you going back to him unless he apologizes."

"Then you don't want me going back to him at all, because he's not going to apologize. I've never met anyone as determined to hang on to their guilt as Peter Parker."

"I suppose it's difficult to meet yourself."

"What?"

"Nothing. I understand that you're in a difficult place right now, Apprentice, but your aunt doesn't deserve your absence over this. Please, go home, eat her roast turkey and mashed potatoes, and come back when you're feeling a bit more anchored in the world outside these walls. The winter fades, the wheel turns, and this, too, shall pass."

Wanda sighs heavily and tries one more argument: "It's been snowing all day, and the trains are running on a holiday schedule. It'll take me hours to get there."

"I'll take you to Queens. I can drop you at the end of the block, so you'll be properly frozen by the time you reach the door, and won't raise any suspicions, and you can call me when you're ready to come back."

Wanda pauses, eyeing him carefully. If he's volunteering to play taxi, he really feels strongly about this. He thinks she's isolating herself, and if she's being honest, she is, to a degree. She never thought she was invulnerable. If anything, she's had a lifetime of being reminded, roughly, that no one lives forever. Her parents, the

Parkers—who she barely remembers; Aunt May has always been much more of a mother to her than Mary Parker ever had the chance to be—and then Uncle Ben . . . people die. Wanda knows that. But Gwen was her and Peter's age. Gwen was bright and beautiful and full of life, and she didn't have powers, she didn't have a way to fight back. She just died, and it wasn't fair, and Wanda isn't sure how to wrap her head around the unfairness of it all. She's trying, but it's so much harder than she ever thought it could be.

But more, every time she's had her foundations shaken—when Uncle Ben died, when her powers developed, when she was bullied or harassed at school, when puberty hit and Johnny Nelson thought her bra straps were designed for snapping—Peter's been there to hold her up and keep her from collapsing. She's braced him just as much. Together, they were strong enough to withstand virtually anything. Alone . . .

Alone, she's not sure she's going to survive this. And that's why she doesn't want to go home, doesn't want to sit in the kitchen in Queens while Aunt May stirs her famous cranberry sauce and the air smells like roasting turkey and mulling spices, doesn't want to be in the place where she's always been safe, because Peter will be there. Peter, who *is* safety, who *is* home and harbor and knowing that things will be okay. He's the other half of who she is, and without him, she feels like she's missing an organ. She wants Peter to realize that what he said to her wasn't just wrong, it was cruel, cruel in a way she never expected from her brother. She deserves better than to go crawling back to him the first time she sees the opportunity.

But if she sees him there, she'll try. She knows she'll try. She'll apologize for things that aren't her fault if it means he lets her back in, and it's not right—it's not fair to her, or to what she's gone through, or to what they are to each other—but it's true. She knows herself. She knows where she's strong and where she's weak.

And when it's her brother, she's weak.

"I really don't think this is a good idea," she says.

"I know," says Doctor Strange.

—

THIRTY MINUTES LATER, SHE'S STANDING ON THE PORCH OF THE HOUSE where she grew up, with snowflakes in her hair and her gloved hands wrapped around each other, shivering. She has a key, but she doesn't really live here anymore, and it feels wrong to just let herself inside.

Breath a plume of white in the air, she unclasps her hands, reaches out, and rings the bell. The low, mellow tone sounds through the air, and she knows it fills the house; it's not loud, but there's nowhere you can go to escape it. Stepping back, she rubs her arms to keep them warm. Even walking the block from where Doctor Strange dropped her off has left her half-frozen.

Do Peter's spider-powers come with immunity to frostbite? They've never discussed it, and she takes a mean little satisfaction from thinking about him swinging across the city with ice on his elbows and turning his web-lines brittle. She doesn't want him to get hurt. She does want him to suffer, just a little, while she is.

The door swings open, and Aunt May is there, lighting up when she sees Wanda. "Oh, sweetheart! I was afraid you weren't going to make it, with as busy as you've been lately—poor dear, you must be *freezing*, come in, come in."

Wanda smiles, teeth chattering, and lets Aunt May usher her into the gloriously, gaudily decorated living room, where the couch is empty—no Peter. Wanda blinks at that, but stops when Aunt May tugs on the shoulder seam of her coat, saying, "You won't warm until you get out of these cold things. Now, come on, dearest, let me get that for you."

Wanda unzips her jacket and lets Aunt May peel it away before removing her gloves and following her aunt to the linen closet. She doesn't want to ask, doesn't want to break the brittle cheer as Aunt May chatters about the weather, about the neighbors, about all the things they haven't had a chance to talk about recently. So she's caught off guard when Aunt May turns and pulls her into a hard hug, so hard that for a moment, Wanda can't breathe.

She inhales, and Aunt May's grip loosens, just a little. "I missed you," she says, still holding on tightly.

Aunt May begins to cry. Wanda doesn't let go. She can't think of what else she's supposed to do. So she holds on until Aunt May pushes away, and then she releases her, staying where she is as Aunt May steps back, out of grasping range.

"Aunt May, what's—"

"I know you two get up to things you don't tell me about. You always have. That's the purview of the young: You have to be allowed to sneak around at some point, and you were such good kids that Ben and I, well, we never worried all that much. Peter wasn't going to get some girl in trouble, and you weren't going to come home with a baby in your arms, neither of you was going to start drinking or sneaking around selling the silverware to buy drugs. So we kept our eyes on and our hands off, and that worked for a long time, until you were grown up and you both drifted off to where I couldn't even keep eyes on. But I didn't worry about you, because I knew you had each other."

"Aunt May . . ."

"Peter isn't coming today." The words are sharp, dropped between them like sheets of glass that shatter when they hit the floor. "He called this morning to make his apologies. He has a lot of classwork to get through, and says it's easier to study when the dorms are empty."

Wanda puts a hand over her mouth, glancing away. "I'm sorry. I didn't—oh, I'm so sorry."

"I know you two aren't getting along, haven't been since poor Gwen died. I don't know what went down between you, and I'm not going to try to force my way into the middle of it—that wouldn't be fair to you, to Peter, or to me. I won't choose sides. But, Wandy, darling . . . I can't lose either one of you. You're all I have left."

"I didn't tell him not to come."

"And he didn't tell me he wasn't coming because of you, just like he's never told me he's Spider-Man. There are things a . . . I never had children of my own, and I would never think to erase

Mary's memory, but I don't think she'd begrudge me saying there are things a mother knows. Not after we've been together for this long."

Wanda doesn't say anything, only stares at her.

"I didn't put it together until Ben died. I knew *something* was going on with Peter, but that was during your 'Hurricane Wanda' phase, and we had our hands full just trying to keep you from bringing the house down around our ears. Borrowing extra trouble by asking Peter why he was sneaking out almost every night seemed like a waste of energy."

"You knew? This whole time?"

"As I said, not before Ben died, but then Peter started sneaking out even more, and taking you with him—there's a difference in the air when you're alone in a house, like all the ghosts you don't want to know are there are getting a chance to catch their breath. I can pretend I left you alone because I didn't want to interfere, but I was so deep in my own grief at that point that I'm not sure I knew *how* to interfere. You were having so much trouble at school, and Peter was fighting, and I had better things to worry about than a few nighttime walks around the block."

"But . . ."

"And then you started showing up in the papers with Spider-Man, and honestly, Wanda, did you really think I wouldn't recognize my own kids? You didn't even change your hair, and there you are with the fellow I already half suspect of being my nephew, waving your hands around and 'muttering strange incantations' according to the reporters who wrote you up. I'm half surprised Django didn't show up at their offices to demand a published clarification."

"Django doesn't know," says Wanda, numbly.

Aunt May gives her a look that telegraphs precisely what she thinks of *that* argument. "That man has watched you grow up just as much as I have, and he noticed when you started running out of there every other session, not staying all the way to closing time."

"You talked to him?"

"Sweetheart, do you honestly think I took you into the city, dropped you on the doorstep of a stranger, and walked away? Django and I have been talking since the beginning. We keep each other aware of how you're doing. He doesn't know you're the Scarlet Witch yet, but he's going to figure it out eventually. I'm not sure whether he's going to be thrilled with you or angry that you've been playing into cultural stereotypes. You know how he gets about that sort of thing."

Wanda's cheeks redden, and she looks at her feet, snow boots still on and leaving a little puddle on Aunt May's hallway rug. "I didn't know—I never thought about you two talking."

"Well, we do. Now tell me what happened, Wanda. What *really* happened."

"Peter and I were both there when Gwen died," begins Wanda, and even that much of an explanation is like ripping open a scab. Sadness and curdled guilt come pouring out, mixing together in a sticky, toxic stew that coats her words, making them taste sour in her mouth as she continues. Aunt May listens with wide, horrified eyes, not interrupting, just letting Wanda speak, and that helps, a little. Aunt May isn't judging her.

A fragment of her guilt cracks off and falls away, and her voice is steadier as she continues. "I used my magic to transport myself to the ground without slamming into it, and Peter used a web to stop Gwen's fall. He—"

She pauses, the sickening sound of Gwen's neck snapping a distant echo in her ears. Softer, she finishes, "He stopped her too fast. The force broke her neck. She died instantly. He demanded I use my powers to bring her back, but that's not how my magic works. I can't heal people."

There's something almost comic about standing here using words like *powers* and *magic* in front of Aunt May, who has always represented the other side of her life, the side where she goes to class and contends with a vaguely racist roommate, not the side where she's apprenticed to the Sorcerer Supreme and may one day inherit his mantle. She doesn't know how to reconcile the halves of her life. They don't fit together.

"Oh, darling. He should have known you couldn't do that. It was obvious you adored Gwen, right from the first time Peter brought her home, but if you could raise the dead, Ben would be standing here with us now. I know that. I'm sure Peter knows it, too."

"I don't care what he does or doesn't know," says Wanda, and the anger in her voice surprises them both. "He said some genuinely *terrible* things to me while he was lashing out, and I can't—I couldn't live with myself if I went crawling back to him without an apology. I'm waiting for him to say he's sorry. To understand why what he said was wrong."

Aunt May is quiet for a long moment. Finally, she says, "He's a stubborn boy, our Peter. He gets that from his father—both of them. Those Parker brothers, they never met a brick wall they didn't think they could force their way through. It makes them capable of doing great things, but it also means it can be hard to make them admit it when they're in the wrong."

"I know. I may be waiting for a while."

"But you're not waiting alone, are you?"

Wanda shakes her head. "No, Aunt May, I'm not alone. I have friends, and I have the restaurant, and I have my master."

Aunt May's expression sharpens in the way of older female relatives whose charges have just admitted to something that might be dangerous. "Your . . . what?"

"When we were trying to help me get control over my magic, Peter took me to the Fantastic Four, and Doctor Richards introduced me to a friend of his. Doctor Stephen Strange. He's the Earth's Sorcerer Supreme."

"I didn't even know we had one of those. It sounds like something you'd order at Taco Bell during Halloween."

Wanda pictures Aunt May saying that to Doctor Strange's face, and can't quite smother a giggle. "Well, we do, and he agreed to take me on as his apprentice. I've been studying under him for several years. He teaches me not to hurt myself or others, and I do some light dusting every now and then. He's the one who insisted you'd want to see me today."

"Well, then, I suppose I owe this man a debt of gratitude, both for taking care of you and for making sure an old woman didn't spend the holiday alone."

"I'm sorry Peter's not coming."

"I am, too, darling, for him. Wherever he is right now, he could be here, with us, drinking my famous hot cocoa." Aunt May fixes her with a stern eye. "So could this 'Doctor Strange' of yours, you know."

Wanda blinks. "I just found out you know about us being super heroes. I don't think I'm ready to see you drinking cocoa with my master."

"You will be," says Aunt May sagely. "Now get those boots off, you're soaking the rug."

"Yes, ma'am."

——

IT TAKES MOST OF THE AFTERNOON AND PART OF THE EVENING, BUT as Aunt May is preparing to pull the turkey out of the oven, Wanda picks up the phone and dials a number with an area code she's reasonably sure no one else shares, waiting for Doctor Strange to answer.

"Are you ready to come back already?" he asks.

"My aunt knows I'm the Scarlet Witch," she says.

There's a long pause. Then, in a sharper tone, he asks, "Did you tell her?"

"No, she figured it out on her own, after she figured out Peter was Spider-Man."

The pause is even longer this time, and Wanda nearly laughs. This shouldn't be funny, and yet . . .

"Do you need me to make her forget? It's a complicated spell, but she lives alone—I could manage it if I had to."

"No." Wanda looks at Aunt May, hoisting the small turkey—barely bigger than a large chicken—onto the counter. "She deserves to know. It's easier if she knows. Better, too. It means she understands why I can't talk to Peter right now."

"So why are you calling?"

"Tell that master of yours the mashed potatoes will get gluey if they sit too long!" yells Aunt May.

"Because we'd like you to come to dinner," says Wanda.

"Dinner."

"Yes."

"Christmas dinner."

"Yes."

"With your aunt, in her home, in *Queens*."

"The house hasn't moved recently, so . . . yes."

The phone goes dead.

Wanda replaces the receiver gently in the cradle, turning to Aunt May. "He'll be right here," she says.

The doorbell rings.

Wanda hurries to answer it, and there's Doctor Strange, still in his customary blue tunic and red cloak, looking entirely out of place with their suburban street spread out behind him like a postcard of a winter wonderland. He's holding a bottle of wine in one hand, and a bunch of white roses in the other. He hands Wanda the flowers as she gestures him inside, and she takes them automatically, blinking down into the petals.

"Where is your aunt?" he asks.

"In the kitchen." Wanda looks up from the roses, shutting the door behind him. He doesn't remove his boots, she notes; he doesn't need to. There's not a speck of snow on them. A lifetime of manners kicks in, overriding the protocol she normally practices in the Sanctum, and she asks, "May I take your cloak?"

"You may," he says, with a lazy wave of one hand. The cloak unfastens itself and floats to drape over Wanda's arm, remaining quiescent as she carries it to the coat closet and hangs it carefully inside.

Doctor Strange waits for her to return, then follows her through the house to the kitchen, looking around as they move. It's not a long trip—just the living room to the hall, and then to the warm confines of the room where Aunt May is already setting the table. She looks up as they enter, smiling brightly.

"Oh, you must be Doctor Strange!" she says. "I'm sorry it's taken us this long to meet—from your side of things anyway. I just found out you existed a few hours ago."

"Ms. Parker," he says, reclaiming the roses from Wanda and offering them to Aunt May. She takes them, smile getting even brighter. It doesn't fade as he sets the wine on the table. "Thank you for the invitation. You have a lovely home."

"It's always better with a full table," she says. "Now sit, sit."

Doctor Strange sits.

"I like him," says Aunt May as she passes Wanda to get the green beans. "You've done well with this one."

"Yes, Aunt May," says Wanda.

They gather around the table, and eat and laugh and toast the year to come, and everything is warm, and everything is bright, and for a little while, everything is good again.

But Peter never comes home.

CHAPTER FIFTEEN

——

REPUTATION

"AGAIN!" SNAPS DOCTOR STRANGE, AS WANDA'S HEX BOLT HITS THE wall and fizzles, not leaving even a scorch behind. "You have to *focus*, Apprentice!"

"I *am* focusing!" Wanda scowls at him, pushing sweat-matted hair out of her face. "*You* try doing better with all these manikins shooting arrows at you!"

The arrows are soft things, constructs of hardened air that dissolve as soon as they hit her; they leave bruises, not wounds on anything but her pride. The manikins she refers to are a ring of woven fabric figures surrounding the circle where she stands, each armed with a bow and a quiver full of arrows sculpted out of wind.

"I have," he says, much more calmly. "I ask you to do nothing I have not already done myself, and right now I'm asking you to focus. If you get caught by another group of criminals like you did last night, knowing how to counter multiple projectiles while still fighting back could be essential."

"Don't remind me," groans Wanda.

Doctor Strange only claps his hands and resets the circle.

Wanda barely has time to take a breath before the manikins are drawing their bows and shooting again. This time, their first volley of arrows is met by a crimson shield that catches and shatters them, while the second hits a more curved shield, bouncing them back. Half the manikins go down, impaled on their own arrows. The other half aim at her again.

Wanda hits her knees, changing the height and angle of their target as she begins firing hex bolts at them. She's getting faster, and another four are down before the remainder can release their arrows. She flings another shield between herself and them, stopping the arrows. Now it's just her against three manikins, and she has time to aim before she shoots them down. Climbing back to her feet, she gives Doctor Strange a challenging look.

"Was that enough focus?" she asks.

His answering bolt of energy slams into the shield she's already thrown up between them. He blinks once in surprise, then nods his approval.

"Much better," he says. "If you can do that every time, I'll agree that you're ready to patrol on your own."

"I'm not a *child*."

"No, but you're my apprentice, and if I have to collect your body from the town morgue, it reflects poorly on me. Not to mention the fact that your aunt knows where I live, and she's a formidable woman. I would rather avoid her wrath."

"Aunt May's not very wrath-y."

"Have you ever died?"

Wanda shakes her head. "Not that I've noticed."

"So you have no idea how 'wrath-y' she might become in the event of your death. As I don't know, either, I would prefer we not find out if it can be avoided."

Wanda folds her arms. "*Peter* patrols alone."

"Peter's powers are more physical in nature. I would prefer he not do so, either, since you'll be utterly impossible to live with if something happens to your brother, but he does better on his own than you likely would. And more to the point, his death, while tragic, would not bring your aunt to *my* door. She doesn't expect me to take care of Peter."

Wanda glowers at him without heat. She knows Aunt May and her master have been talking since the holidays, and for the most part, it's been a good thing—it's easier to explain where she is when she can tell her aunt about the Sanctum, when she can practice her magic at home in Queens. She doesn't know whether Peter is aware yet that Aunt May has figured out his secret. She thinks not, since Aunt May has been getting increasingly annoyed with him.

She'd never noticed how much time she spent playing the peacemaker in their little family. It was something she'd always just done automatically, keeping them all together by keeping them united. And now that she's functionally gone from familial interactions, things are starting to erode.

(That wasn't right, thinks America, watching the scene unfold. There were countless timelines where Aunt May and Peter did just fine without a third person to smooth the ground between them. But she's watched these people for snapshots of years, and she's seen the shape they've made between them: It's not identical to any other Parker family she's seen. With Wanda to lean on, Peter grew up a little less willing to slow down and apologize, a little more determined to stand on his own. And Aunt May had been splitting her nurturing and spoiling between two targets, not piling it all on Peter. This version of Peter Parker is more stubborn in some ways, but also less dependent on a single person for his emotional stability. She can't say whether this is better or worse than the status quo she's used to, but it's definitely different.)

Wanda sighs. "I don't really have anyone else to patrol with."

"What about Meggan?"

"She's going back to England at the end of the month, and also she has a team, a whole team, of people she can work with."

"All right—the Fantastic Four?"

"They're Peter's friends before they're mine. They're polite when we run into each other, but I don't think they like me very much now that they can tell we're fighting. And even if they were down for a team-up, you won't let me move on to real threats. *They* deal with real threats. Same goes for Captain America. We've met enough times to be civil, but we're in different leagues and he knows it."

Her few truly dangerous encounters, junior villains and monsters, had come because Peter thought she was ready, not because her master had approved of them. As far as Doctor Strange is concerned, she'll be dealing with muggings and carjackers for the rest of her life.

He frowns. "I can call Reed—"

"Master, please don't take this as insolence on my part, but don't you dare."

He goes still, save for one lifted eyebrow. "Explain."

"I'm not a child, and I don't need you to arrange playdates for me with the other heroes," she says sourly. "If they don't want to associate with me because they feel like that would be turning their backs on my brother, that's their call, and I'm not going to try to force the issue. I'll just keep going out with the X-Men when they're in the area, and see if maybe I can get the Black Knight to agree to a team-up, when he's in the area. He's okay with magic, and when he's not with the Avengers, he's usually okay spending an evening at street level."

"Okay with magic" is an understatement where the Black Knight is concerned, his own powers deriving from a source of magic as ancient and unpredictable as her master's. They're not close friends, but he's seen her in action enough times to have settled into a sort of grudging respect. They work well together.

"I believe Dane is intending to be in New York over the weekend," says Doctor Strange thoughtfully. "I'll contact him."

"For right now, I cleared out your manikins. You said if I could do that, you'd trust me on patrol by myself tonight. So whether he's available or not, I'm going out."

"I don't like this."

"I know, Master."

"I should have forbidden it when you first wanted to take to the streets with your brother, should have told you that an apprentice's place was by her master's side, not fighting petty crime. But you have the taste for it now, and it's too late to hold you to a higher standard."

"I know that, too, Master," says Wanda, with a sudden smile. She's learned to feel victory coming. She can taste it in the air.

"Very well." He waves a hand. "Stick to the tourist areas, around Times Square. You're likely to encounter more muggings there, and will be less likely to get in over your head."

"Yes, Master," she says, beaming at him, and scurries off to get ready for the night ahead.

—

WANDA'S SOLO PATROL WAS MORE EXHAUSTING THAN SHE'D BEEN expecting. Her ability to use her powers to move is still a tenuous thing, prone to failing at the worst possible times, and that means a lot more walking and climbing of fire escapes than she's used to. Still, she apprehends two muggers and stops a group of teens from breaking a bodega's windows—small acts of heroism to her, who wants to do so much more, but huge to the people whose lives she's just touched for the better.

Still, as she lies in a bath of ice water the next morning, waiting for the dull ache in her hip to subside, she has to ask herself if interceding with such petty crimes is really worth the trouble. She can't imagine someone like Captain America, who launched himself into the throes of World War II after getting his powers, would be impressed by her résumé so far.

That's another thing she's getting better at hiding from her master. How she carefully clips out and saves every article chronicling the Avengers' latest heroics. How she keeps track of who joins the team, who leaves the team, and why. How she might've been working on super hero poses that could work well in a possible group setting. If she can join a proper super group, the concerns people have about her powers will wither on the vine, and she'll finally be free. She'll be a hero. She just needs her chance.

She's finally starting to relax when the quartz sphere on the sink chimes and the voice of her master says sonorously, "The Black Knight is available to take you out tonight. Please be prepared for collection at six."

Wanda sighs and sinks down below the water, letting the cold take her. She asked for this. If she refuses because she's sore, that just proves her master is right to keep her close to home. Still, she resents the need to come back up for air, ice cubes bobbing around her on the surface of the bath.

She wiggles her fingers, reactivating the sphere. "Yes, sir," she says, and that's that: She's going patrolling again. With the Black Knight this time, which means she'll have backup, and can take on greater challenges. Assuming she can find them, and twisting probability means she'll *always* find them.

The day passes in a blur of aches, pains, and lessons, during which she does her best to conceal the first two items on her list. By the time her master tells her the Black Knight is waiting on the roof, she's more than ready to go. She waves and scoots off up the stairs, ready to save the city, or at least a few neighborhoods.

Doctor Strange smiles as he watches her go. She thinks she's managed to conceal her aches and pains from him, but he's not so easily fooled; this is all part of her training. He'll lose her to the hero's life soon enough, to the Avengers or to a team of her own making, and it won't be a proper application of her talents, but she'll shine there, and he knows it's what she wants.

He's here to teach and prepare her for the world, not to hold her back.

And more than anyone else, he can't wait to see her shine.

———

DANE WHITMAN IS NOT A MAN OF MANY WORDS. WANDA SOMETIMES wonders if her expectations for how much people talk have been completely skewed by a childhood and adolescence spent with Peter, but she doesn't wonder all that much if she can help it—right now, she prefers not to think about Peter at all. She's not the one who needs to find her way to an apology, and until he does, all thinking about him is going to do is cause her pain when she's already bruised by his absence. So she tries to focus on the moment.

Besides, patrol with Dane is nicer than patrol with anyone else *because* he doesn't talk that much. She patrolled with Johnny once, and he kept trying to figure out why she wasn't patrolling with Peter. Dane doesn't ask questions. Dane finds bad guys, stops bad guys, delivers bad guys to the authorities, and moves on. He's refreshingly uncomplicated, and she likes that.

They're atop one of the hybrid buildings that surrounds the area, retail on the bottom layer, residential from there up. Getting down won't be an issue. The Black Knight has his flying horse, and Wanda's been working on something recently that she knows is going to blow his mind. Meggan laughed for almost an hour when Wanda demonstrated for *her,* and Meggan's sense of humor is such that if something makes her laugh, Wanda knows it's just going to make less quixotic people stare at her in awe, even if only for a moment.

Sometimes it's nice to inspire awe, not just laughter.

They're up here because an aerial view is almost always better for spotting trouble. Despite years of living in a city that has almost as many super heroes as it does stray cats, New Yorkers have never gotten into the habit of looking up. Tourists do it more, and they're always delighted when they catch a glimpse of someone lurking on a rooftop, even if it's someone the papers have been quick to dismiss as a villain. They come from their small towns and their far-away cities to see super heroes as much as Broadway shows, and normal humans wearing cheap Spider-Man costumes and hanging around to take pictures in front of the big Toys "R" Us just isn't the same.

They've been watching the street for an hour, and while they've spotted three pickpockets and two unlicensed hot dog carts, none of those have been serious enough to warrant intervention by a super hero. If anything, Wanda feels bad for the pickpockets—they wouldn't be working an area with this density of both police and heroes if they weren't desperate, and any tourist who carries that much cash and takes that little care probably needs a few lessons about life in the big city to take home with them. As for the hot dog carts, licenses are prohibitively expensive, and she doesn't work for the city. She's more than happy to look the other way, especially in the current economy.

Then Dane touches her knee, and she looks where he's pointing, following his finger to a figure skulking in the shadowy recess around the door of a closed café. It's dark enough that she hadn't spotted the man at first, and neither have any of the people passing on the street.

Lurking is not a crime, not even in Manhattan. But lurking with a knife the length of your forearm in one hand is a little more questionable, and as Wanda watches, the man reaches out of his shadowy hiding place and grabs a passing woman by the back of the jacket, dragging her into the dark.

Right. That's crime enough, even if the woman has yet to scream. Dane runs for Aragorn, his flying horse, gesturing for Wanda to follow.

She shakes her head, stepping up onto the edge of the building. Before he can call her back, she steps off, and she's falling, the air whipping around her, sweet and fresh and ripe with diesel exhaust and the distant grease of frying foods—the great contradiction of New York. She reaches into the chaos, and red light envelops her feet, slowing and stopping her descent.

Doctor Strange says she'll be able to fly without the momentum of a fall by the end of the year, using magic alone to change her relationship to the air. The idea is exciting. Here is something new, something no one can say is dangerous or strange, even if it's associated with her magic. Almost every other hero she's met can fly. Meggan can fly. It's like it comes as an automatic add-on with most super-powers, like whipped cream on a cup of cocoa.

She's still getting used to the sensation of flight. She's not lighter than air, and the air isn't heavier than normal; it's like she's negotiating a truce with the molecular structure of the world around her, and if Peter were here, he'd probably be asking her to do it in a lab, so he could try to measure it.

She reaches the street before the Black Knight and Aragorn, all of them moving with purpose toward the shadowy alcove. She holds up one hand, calling a ball of red light into it as the crowds begin to draw back, giving them room to work, getting out of the probable line of fire. Some people are pulling out their cameras. She doesn't try to wave them off. As long as they stay back so she and Dane can prevent a crime, a few pictures won't be a bad thing. Show her in a good light.

"Halt, evildoer," shouts the Black Knight, dismounting from Aragorn, the Ebony Blade already in his hand.

Wanda doesn't like that sword. She swears she's heard it whispering a few times, when she got too close to the blade. Surely her master would have said something if it was bad, though? She can't imagine he'd let her go out with a man who carries a cursed sword like it's a pocketknife.

Her ball of light reveals the man in the alcove, illuminating his skintight black jumpsuit with the characteristic yellow bolt down the center, bisecting it neatly in two. The black parts of his costume— because it's a costume, they're all wearing costumes, heroes and villains alike—blend into the shadows around him more than should be possible. He's still holding the knife, but from here, it's obvious that the blade is made of solidified shadow, rather than anything as ordinary as steel.

She knows him. He's not a big-time villain, but he's a super villain all the same. This isn't the sort of street-level petty crime she's supposed to be looking for. Her master would want her to withdraw, to leave this for the Black Knight to handle.

Her master isn't here.

The man with the knife sneers at the sight of the Scarlet Witch and the Black Knight, pulling the woman closer to his chest. He has her arm bent behind her back; her purse is on the ground between them, contents spilled everywhere.

"This doesn't concern you, Avenger," he spits, eyes on the Black Knight.

Wanda fights back a jet of irritation. She's an apprentice, but this is *her* patrol, *her* education; Dane is her support, not the hero in charge of this mission.

"That's right," she snaps. "This concerns *me*. Let her go, Blackout."

"This little lab tech has been thieving from Stark Industries," says Blackout, pulling the woman closer to his chest. "Naughty naughty. She should have known picking up a battery that draws power from the Darkforce would get her the wrong kind of attention. She's not an innocent."

"Please, he's lying," gasps the woman. "Please . . ."

Wanda lifts her hands, the air around them glowing red and crackling with barely contained chaos. She's fought Blackout before, although she's never sought him out; she knows the energies they produce are as likely to cause explosions as they are to cancel each other out if they meet. By forcing this confrontation in a populated area, he's preventing her from using the most effective of her defenses.

The civilians around them are figuring that out, at least. Most of them came to Manhattan hoping for a glimpse of the super hero life, but this is a closer look than they were expecting. Most are starting to scatter, although a few are producing cameras, staying closer than they should in the hopes of getting an impossible shot.

Blackout moves forward a few steps, shoving his hostage ahead of him. The woman, who still hasn't screamed, whimpers. She's holding herself rigid to keep some distance between her throat and the blade, and tears are running down her cheeks.

"This is how this will go down," says Blackout, with perfect calm. "I'm going to walk away, and I'm going to take her with me. Once we're out of sight, I'll release her, and you won't follow me. Got it?"

The Scarlet Witch nods. He's lying, of course; they always are, which makes it okay for her to lie to him in return. He seems to realize that, because he hurls a bolt of solid darkness at her, a shard of the Darkforce dimension pulled into the daylight reality where it doesn't belong. She deflects it with a chaos shield, and it bursts into prismatic shards, filled with rainbows antithetical to Blackout's nature. The crowd gasps, and there's some scattered applause, these people treating the display like a show put on for their entertainment.

Wanda wants to scream. Don't they see how dangerous this is, how much they need to get away? Blackout throws another bolt, and then another after that, and she deflects them both, moving closer without looking to see where they might have landed. No one's screaming, so she didn't hit anybody, and that's what matters right now. The Black Knight advances with her, and they have him pinned, Blackout has nowhere to go, not unless he has the power built up to open a portal, but if he does that, he'll lose the battery he claimed to be looking for, and this will have been for nothing. His pride won't let him retreat.

The Scarlet Witch tangles chaos between her fingers, shaping it into a whip she can use to snap the shadow knife out of his hand. The hostage has to be their first priority right now. She cracks the whip, sending sparks flying.

Later, Wanda will try to replay the moment, and find that she's unable; it all happened too fast to follow. There's a sound in the air, high and thin, like the flutter of a hummingbird's wings—something almost outside the range of human hearing. Then there's a blur that passes in front of her, sending her hair blowing back. It feels like someone turned a hair dryer on her for just a moment, the air heated by the speed at which it's moving.

The blur is only visible for an instant, but in that instant, Blackout and his hostage are shoved apart with superhuman force, Blackout vanishing into the shadowy alcove, the woman falling to the sidewalk, where she doesn't move. There's a snapping sound, and the taste of ozone, and Wanda knows Blackout has opened a portal, abandoning the battery as a bad risk.

Wanda flexes her hands, the red light fading, and looks to the Black Knight.

"What was that?" she asks.

He doesn't have an answer.

One of the bystanders, screaming shrilly, does, and Wanda turns with a grim feeling of inevitability to see that the former hostage is bleeding. Blackout's knife wasn't knocked away with him, it was knocked back, slitting the woman's throat and leaving her dead. The Black Knight hurries to take control of the scene, but even as sirens begin to sound in the distance, Wanda hears the tourists muttering about blame and how carelessly she'd deflected those bolts of darkness before.

This is bad.

———

THE PAPERS KNOW WHAT HAPPENED, OR AT LEAST THINK THEY DO; it's one of the mornings where Wanda wakes up in her dorm room, putting in the required appearances to keep her roommate from trying to take over the whole place as her own. She doesn't have her own newspaper subscription, but several copies are delivered to the common room, and when Wanda wanders downstairs, dressed and damp-haired and yawning behind her cupped hand, she finds half a dozen of her peers clustered around the tables, which can only mean something's happened.

Sometimes it's a natural disaster or a high-profile assassination somewhere in the world, but more often, it's one of the local heroes doing something that attracts public comment. Wanda doesn't approach at first, more focused on getting to the communal coffee machine, but a reasonably cute boy from her economics class waves her down, beckoning her closer.

Wanda's been through a lot, and is in some ways much more serious than most of her peers, but she's not immune to the lure of a cute boy who wants to tell her something. She wanders toward him.

"What's going on, Andy?" she asks.

In answer, he brandishes the front page of the newspaper. "I remember you used to be really into that Spider-Man guy. Well, it looks like his ex-partner's finally gone all the way over to the other side of the line."

And there, in thirty-point type, is the headline that condemns her: WICKED WITCH? SCARLET WITCH MISHANDLES MIS-CREANT IN TOURIST TRAGEDY.

The article is accompanied by a picture of herself and the Black Knight standing menacingly in front of Blackout. The angle of the shot obscures the knife in the man's hand; he looks like he's just holding the woman in front of him, which is somehow not enough to justify the level of force she's being accused of.

The byline on the photo is, unsurprisingly, Peter Parker.

According to the reporter, Blackout had already surrendered when the Scarlet Witch used her terrifying magical powers to knock him away, leading to his escape, and the death of his hostage.

Wanda supposes she can see how someone who just saw the picture might believe this narrative: Her hands *are* glowing in the picture, her chaos whip dangling menacingly, and Dane's sword is large and visibly very sharp. What she can't understand is why no one who was there said anything to the contrary, or how quickly everyone seems to be accepting it. She looks around the group, and sees no defense for her alter ego, no one protesting the clear mistreatment of one of their few female heroes.

She passes the paper back to Andy, murmurs, "I have to go," and exits the dorm, not bothering to get the coffee she came for. She's awake enough without it.

She walks to her first class on autopilot, sits through the lecture without hearing it, and resigns herself to a lost day. She'll attend her classes, to keep herself from attracting too much attention, but she'll spend the night at the Sanctum, in the safe company of Doctor Strange, who knows she didn't do what she's accused of. Even Queens doesn't feel safe right now—Peter could be there, since she's not scheduled to go over tonight, and she's not sure she could survive him believing she's become a villain.

And people who use excessive force against unpowered individuals *are* villains, no question. She's not like that. She's *not*. She just doesn't know how to make the world see it.

She has to find a way.

CHAPTER SIXTEEN

—

FAMILY REUNION

SHE DOESN'T GO ON PATROL FOR TWO WEEKS.

Blackout tries for the battery again. This time, he gets away with it, despite the efforts of half the Avengers. Wanda isn't there. The family of the woman who died is talking about filing a lawsuit against the city for allowing super-powered vigilantes to roam free; their lawyer's promising them a seven-figure settlement. Wanda doesn't care. She knows the law, and she knows she didn't break it. Despite people's ongoing attempts to register mutants, she's not a mutant, and so she's perfectly within her rights to practice her powers in any way that does no harm to the public.

Put her in a room with a telepath for five minutes and she can prove she didn't do anything wrong. Unfortunately, all the available telepaths are mutants, and the public is unlikely to believe them exonerating someone who they've decided has changed sides.

She spends those two weeks moping around the Sanctum, avoiding the house in Queens, and taking a sabbatical from her classes, one aided by Aunt May calling in and claiming a vague family tragedy that will inevitably take Wanda away until it can be resolved. She's still paying her tuition—the administration really doesn't care whether she's there or not, and it'll be up to her to make up the work she's missing. Still, she can't handle going back while she's still in the papers like this, and it doesn't matter what she does— she's still in the papers.

Jonah Jameson doesn't hate her as much as he hates her

brother—she's pretty sure he doesn't hate *hemorrhoids* as much as he hates her brother—but she was associated with Spider-Man long enough that he's happy to mine her sudden villainy for all the sales he can get. Her disappearance from the public eye is taken as proof that she's gone rogue. If she were a *real* hero, he argues, she would come forth and defend herself in the court of public opinion. Her refusal to do so only proves that she's in the wrong.

"Master, have you seen this?" she asks, showing him the latest article, in which she's challenged to explain herself, preferably to the police.

"I have," he replies.

"And?"

"And no apprentice of mine is going to be arrested for something she didn't do. It's ludicrous to even humor the notion for a moment. Stop picking at this, Wanda. I've been painted the villain in my time as well. It will pass."

"Peter's not defending me!" Peter took the picture that condemned her. He not only took it, he *sold* it, which is a bigger betrayal than she entirely has the words for.

"And how would you suggest he do so without betraying your secret identity, or his own? I believe he's still wanted for questioning in connection to the death of young Miss Stacy—claiming responsibility for a murder in front of the police was sloppy of him, even considering the duress he was under. If he tells them you're his sister, they'll just rake the muck more thoroughly, and they'll find something that puts them on your trail. Let it go, Wanda. You can't do anything about it."

"I can't patrol, I can't go to class, I can't change people's minds— what *can* I do?"

"Practice. You're getting better at teleportation. I'd like to see you stabilize your chaos warps and be able to transport yourself from one end of the Sanctum to the other by the end of the week." Doctor Strange looks at her blandly. "I know you're capable of it, Wanda. I need you to be able to do it without the threat of being smeared across the pavement."

Wanda scowls. "I don't want to practice my teleporting."

"Then find something else to do. Just stop dwelling on the news. You can't change the things they're saying; you can only wait for them to see how wrong they are."

Wanda sighs and gathers her armload of newspapers. "I'll be in the kitchen, Master."

"I'll see you at dinner."

She walks away, not willing to throw herself into the void for the sake of saving a few steps. Who needs teleportation? There are other ways of getting around. She's seen rumors about a new speedster in town, someone who can cover distance like it's nothing—

Someone who could move so fast they'd be nothing but a blur to anyone who isn't seeing the world at super-speed.

Feeling like she's just been hit by a bolt of lightning, Wanda hurries to the kitchen and spreads the papers out across the table, looking for mentions of a speedster—and looking for unsolved crimes. It's a hunch, but she's good at pattern recognition, and if she has a hunch, she feels like she should pursue it. It's worth looking into anyway.

There's been a string of home invasions and small store robberies over the last week, mostly in the outer boroughs, but moving steadily deeper into the city. No one's seen the thieves. Even when there's surveillance footage, it never shows a person, just things disappearing from shelves, and occasionally a strange blur. Wanda wonders if there's also a sound like a steel mosquito beating its wings, if there's a rush of wind without a source.

She clips the articles for later and goes to practice her teleportation as she's been told. That keeps her occupied for the better part of the night, and she manages to throw herself into the chaos twice, leaving her exhausted and salty with sweat as she collapses into a chair in the solarium, surrounded by moonlight and silence.

She falls asleep there, and wakes up in her own bed, moved in the night by her master, or by his unseen servants. It doesn't really matter, in the end. She collects the morning's newspapers and repeats her search for this mystery speedster, adding the locations that have been affected to her notes. There's a pattern developing there, one that she can trace if not yet quite predict.

She's drawing her own web, made not of sticky strands but of information, and like her brother's webbing, she thinks she can use it to catch a criminal.

On the third morning, Doctor Strange catches her with the scissors, and fixes her with a stern eye. "Is there a reason you've been defacing my morning news before I can review it, Apprentice?" he asks.

To his surprise, Wanda nods. "Yes."

"Is there a reason beyond trying my patience?"

"You know I didn't touch Blackout. That woman's death isn't my fault."

"Dane has expressed the same sentiment. He says that despite your cracking of the whip you had manifested, Blackout simply flew backward, untouched. I believe that's why you're getting the blame—people are assuming your magic could have interacted with his powers in a way which put the hostage at risk."

"Yes, but it wasn't. There was a high-pitched noise, and a wind ruffled my hair right before the man was thrown into the wall. I think we have a speedster in town."

"I've heard a few rumors to that effect. You have yet to explain why you're stealing the newspaper."

"Whoever it is, they're clearly not interested in being hailed as a hero, or they wouldn't have been so careless with a civilian. So I've been looking at small-time crimes with no clear perpetrator and no video evidence of what happened. I'm building a model of where the attacks have taken place. So far, it looks like that poor woman is the only person who's been hurt, but we can't count on that being the case forever." She looks at him, almost challengingly. "I need the papers so I can find the next pieces of the pattern."

"And what are you going to do if you find this speedster?"

"I don't know yet," she admits. "But I'll have proof that I didn't hurt anyone, and even if we're the only ones who know it, I'll feel better. Please, can I have the papers?"

Doctor Strange hesitates. He doesn't want her getting pulled into a wild-goose chase for some speedster who doesn't actually exist—but he's always told her to trust her instincts, and if her instincts are telling her there's something to find, she's probably correct. He wants her to feel like she can trust him to support her. She's his first apprentice, and he wants to do right by her. Even if Reed has turned his back on Wanda, he'll be there for her until the end.

Finally, cautiously, he nods. "You can have them, but try to leave the financial section intact for me, if you would be so kind."

She snatches up the papers and runs off before he can change his mind.

Today's search yields five more crimes that might fit the pattern. She puts them on the map, then removes two that clearly don't belong. Outliers can exist, but these don't feel right, and at this stage, she's focusing so much on feel that she trusts her instincts.

Looking at what she has now, it forms a clear spiral, starting from a point on Staten Island and looping out from there, getting a little wider every day. Sometimes there are hits on earlier points in the spiral, like whoever's doing this is looping back and revisiting previous crimes, but for the most part, it progresses.

"Master, I'm going out," she says, as she brings the papers back to him.

Doctor Strange looks at her. "Alone?"

"Alone. There's something I need to look into. I've been practicing my teleportation—if I get cornered or anything, I can come back here right away." She's stretching the truth a little. She's been practicing, but she's still not good enough that her return is guaranteed, no matter how surprised she is.

"Mmm," he says, and for a moment, she's afraid he's going to ask her to call Dane or Kurt or someone to accompany her on what still might be a fool's errand. She can understand the importance of backup, especially right now. She just knows she'll be mortified if she has to take a babysitter and her hunch doesn't actually pan out. She's allowed a little pride.

"Fine," he says, finally. "If it means you're willing to leave the house, I suppose you can go out alone. Just remember your uniform."

"Yes, sir," she says, and flees to her room to suit up for the mission. She's going to find this speedster.

She's going to clear her name.

———

ACCORDING TO THE PATTERN SHE'S UNCOVERED, THE NEXT LIKELY target is a small single-family house in Forest Hills. There's no one there when Wanda arrives, dropping out of the sky like a falling leaf. She lands lightly in the yard, noting the lack of cars in the driveway and the lack of light in the windows. The curtains are closed. It's possible the residents are at work; it's barely past noon, after all. But as she makes her way up the walk, she notices the piled-up newspapers by the door, and the small drift of missed delivery notices on the doorframe. The people who live here haven't been home in at least a week.

That may explain why it's an appealing enough target to attract this theoretical criminal. She leaves the porch and circles around the house, well aware of how exposed she is until she's safely in the backyard. They have an apple tree. It's clearly been cared for; these people are on vacation, not gone. The house is not abandoned. That makes her feel a little better, although still self-conscious as she moves to check the back door.

It's locked. But the city already thinks she's a villain, and the probability of a lock failing to hold when someone tries the knob is never zero; a little chaos forced into the tumblers and it clicks open without any sign that it's been interfered with or manipulated.

She goes inside. She finds the living room. She settles on the couch to wait, sitting in deep shadow where anyone who comes through the front door won't see her straightaway. If the owners return home unexpectedly, she can find out just how well that teleportation practice has really been going. Hopefully well enough that her master won't need to come and bail her out of the local precinct when she's already a villain in all the papers.

She reviews her charms and little memorized spells as she waits, taking this as an opportunity to go over the material she's supposed to be studying today. She'll have to go back to real classes soon, or she's never going to catch up, and her financial aid won't look kindly on her failing an entire semester, no matter what excuses Aunt May makes. But it's harder and harder to think of a college degree as something worth pursuing when she's working toward becoming a Mistress of the Mystic Arts, something that will leave her without the need for an ordinary job.

She mostly stays in school for the sake of Aunt May, and because her master encourages it. He was a surgeon before he became Sorcerer Supreme: He'd had what he insists on referring to as an "ordinary life," something that would make sense on a résumé. He believes that experience was a valuable one, and says it helped to prepare him for some of the stranger aspects of the life he leads now. He wants Wanda to have the same chance.

Wanda wants to make them both happy, and so she stays, but she's not sure she'll stay all the way to the end. The diploma just doesn't seem to matter the way it used to, and her priorities are shifting. Peter will stay. She has no question of that. Aunt May will get her college graduation, even if she doesn't get two of them, and Wanda thinks she'll be content with that.

One constant across the crimes she's flagged as potentially associated with this mystery speedster: They happen in broad daylight. That's part of what makes her believe there must be super-powers involved with the incidents—there are never any witnesses. Surely there would be witnesses to *some* of the crimes if they were happening at a normal speed.

She's pondering that when the front doorknob rattles. Just for a moment, but the door doesn't open, and she's still sitting in the corner, waiting for the potential intruder to try again when the jinxed back door slams open and a breeze rushes through the room, a runaway wind blowing out of nowhere. It spins circles around the living room, and with every pass, another small element of the room is gone—a silver candlestick, an antique-looking little clock.

"Stop!" shouts Wanda, rising. The wind doesn't stop, and she hears the buzzing, barely audible but absolutely present. She doesn't have a lot of time. She knew this would happen fast, because that's what speedsters *do,* but she was anticipating slightly more time than this.

In an act of desperation, she resorts to the first trick she learned with her powers: She flicks her fingers out, like she's shaking off a cobweb, and a gleaming red shield springs up all around the outside of the room. The wind continues to circle, and she knows she's trapped her target: Now it's just a matter of time.

"You can't get out, not even if you knock me down," she says. "The shield stays until I intentionally release it."

The wind stops, becoming a man. He's about her age, and his skin is the same shade as hers, pale enough to be believably a tan Caucasian, dark enough for some people to ask questions about how he got so much sun. His hair, in contrast, is whiter than she's ever seen on someone so young. He and Storm could go to the same salon. He's wearing goggles, and he blinks as he moves them out of the way, pushing them back on his forehead in order to stare at her.

"Wanda?" he asks, and she recognizes her name, and she recognizes his accent—Latverian—but she doesn't recognize anything else about him, not even as he moves toward her, dropping his stolen trinkets as he spreads his arms, not like he's preparing to grapple her, but like he's expecting a loving welcome.

"I should have known you'd be the one to find me," he says, and although she doesn't move, he keeps advancing, interpreting her shock for invitation as he wraps his arms around her. "I should have known you'd be looking for me just the way I've been looking for you. I *thought* that was you with the strange man with the sword, but you didn't say anything, and I didn't want to risk your secret identity. That's what you call it here, isn't it? A secret identity? Such a charming euphemism."

Wanda stares at him, struck briefly silent by his ramblings—and by his uninvited embrace, which isn't tight enough to be painful, but is a lot tighter than she expects from a stranger. He lets her go and steps back, puzzlement overtaking his features. "Are you angry that I didn't speak up in the moment? I thought the gift of my intervention would be enough to prove my good intentions."

"I'm sorry," says Wanda, tongue feeling thick and clumsy. "I have no idea who you are."

The stranger rears back like he's been struck, shock and hurt washing across his face, only to be replaced by a sullen anger that looks far too comfortable there: It fits the lines of his features like he was made to scowl at the world, not smile. "Of course you don't know me," he says, voice gone sharp and cold. "Of course they denied you even *that*."

"They?" she asks. "They who?"

"The imperialist bastards who stole you from your rightful place beside me!" he replies. "We were meant to grow up together, two halves of the same whole, cleaving to each other and never to be parted! Those American swine ripped you from our poor weeping mother's arms! They stole you from your family, from your country, from *me*!" His voice breaks on the last word, anguish clearly unfeigned.

Wanda takes a half step toward him, seized by the urge to offer comfort. She has no idea who this stranger is, although she's forming the beginnings of an understanding—one that's sour and bitter in her heart, but still, makes sense of the situation. "I'm sorry, I really don't know who you are," she says. "Can you tell me your name, please?"

"Pietro," he says. "Pietro von Doom."

"Pietro . . ." she echoes. All she can think is that it's a form of Peter: If this man is her brother, she's always had a brother named Peter. She knows the name "von Doom," knows it belongs to a man who fights Reed Richards and the rest of the Fantastic Four whenever the opportunity arises, knows it belongs to a villain. Is this man, this Pietro, a villain as well? She doesn't know yet, but if he's a villain, he still says he's her brother, and dealing with one is going to mean grappling with the other.

Pietro's expression softens at the sound of his name, but the anger remains. It's not directed at her, specifically, but it's strong and hard and present. "Yes," he says. "Pietro. I was adopted by the lord of our glorious nation after our parents passed away, our father under mysterious circumstances, our mother of a broken heart after you were stolen from us. I should have stopped it. We should have grown up together in the palace halls, in beautiful Latveria, under the Latverian sky."

"Pietro, stop," says Wanda. "You're going too fast for me." Everything she knows about her adoption—which isn't much, she's never wanted to go digging, never wanted to learn anything that might mean she'd have to leave—tells her that she was an orphan when the Parkers found her. But how can she have been an orphan and stolen from the arms of her mother at the same time? It doesn't work. One of them has to be wrong.

"I go too fast for everyone," he says. "It's my greatest gift, and my eternal curse. No one can keep up with me. I always knew, dearest sister, that you would come closer than the rest of them, and look, you have—you've caught me, as no one else ever could."

"Okay." Wanda exhales and pushes her hair out of her face, trying to make the space she needs to think. "Okay. Let's say you are who you say you are, and I'm your sister. It's nice to meet you."

His scowl deepens, and for a moment, he looks truly hurt. "You're not meeting me, Wanda, we shared a *womb*. If they hadn't stolen you away from us, you'd know that."

Wanda shakes her head. "No one stole anyone, and even if they had, I was a baby when they brought me to America, which means you would have been a baby, too. There's nothing you could have done to stop them from taking me."

"So you admit they took you!"

"Yes, I admit my adoptive parents took me from Latveria," says Wanda. "I'll have to talk to my aunt to find out the circumstances.

We never really discussed it when I was a kid." She'd been too young when the Parkers died to know what questions she wanted to ask, and the topic had been too painful after they'd been gone. There had just never quite been a good time to bring it up.

Well, it was coming up now, in the form of a white-haired man who looked at her like she was simultaneously the answer to all his questions and the source of all the problems in his life.

"Why are you robbing people?"

"What?"

"I was waiting here for you because you've been stealing things all over the area, and I wanted to make you stop." She pulls herself up a little taller, trying to look more confident than she necessarily feels. "I'm a super hero."

"I knew you would be super," he says. "I am, and you're my twin, so I knew that you, too, must be truly spectacular."

The praise makes Wanda's breath catch in her throat. It's been so long since someone praised her just for existing, not for mastering a tricky bit of magic or complicated incantation. Pietro looks at her like all she has to do is be, and that will make her endlessly magnificent. "I . . ." she manages, before she can't say anything more.

Pietro doesn't seem to notice as he continues speaking. "The things I steal, I take because these people have too much, and I have too little. America is a nation of thieves. They earn nothing, but take everything. I'm simply taking some of what they've stolen back."

"You're hurting people."

"The only person I've hurt is the man who stood too close to you with power in his hands and intent to do harm," he says, voice going cold. "I would hurt him again, if he threatened you."

"Pietro, a woman *died*."

"Not at my hand, and not at yours. Sadly, normal humans are fragile things, and fragile things get broken."

Wanda looks at him, searching for a trace of remorse. She doesn't find one. Finally, she frowns, and tries another approach.

"The Black Knight was holding a sword, and you didn't attack him."

"The man you call the Black Knight is known even in Latveria. He offers no harm to maidens, only to miscreants. His presence told me I was right to hit the man who threatened you so. I've hurt no one undeserving."

Wanda doesn't know what else to say, or how to make him understand that what he's been doing is wrong. It feels like one of the ethical questions Peter and Doctor Strange used to orchestrate for her, when she was first going out on patrol. It feels like a test, and a trap. "Pietro, you have to stop stealing from people. If you don't, you're going to get labeled a villain. People like me, we fight villains."

She doesn't have any villains of her own the way Peter does. But she's still fought plenty of them, and she knows they're a lot more violent and unpredictable than the scuffles she gets into with ordinary criminals. Sometimes she feels like her super heroics are running on training wheels, controlled by the people who feel like they're responsible for her.

They say she's powerful, and then they put limits on her every chance they get, like they're afraid that without limits, she'll overreach and run herself over the edge of the void. Even her master pulls her back whenever she seems to reach too far. It chafes, and yet she can't fully resent it. Not after everyone she's lost.

She doesn't want to fight her brother if there's any way to avoid it. She looks at him pleadingly, then slowly reaches up and removes her mask.

He stares at her exposed face like it's the most beautiful thing he's seen in his life, like he's been waiting to see her for as long as he's been capable of wanting anything at all. He starts to reach for her, then pulls himself back with a visible effort.

"If I become a villain in the eyes of these people around you, you'll fight me?"

She doesn't answer, just looks at him miserably.

Pietro sighs. "Then I suppose I can't be a villain, can I? I came here looking for my sister, and I refuse to lose her a second time over the petty possessions of these people. I'll follow the laws of this uncivilized country, for your sake."

"Thank you, Pietro," she says, and puts her mask back on, releasing the wall of shining chaos at the same time. "Now, this isn't our house; we should get out of here before the owners come back. Will you walk with me?"

Pietro nods, reluctantly, and she offers her arm, leading him back to the door they both used to get inside. She relocks it before she steps out, and he follows, letting her close the door behind him.

Side by side, mismatched but somehow the same, they walk through the backyard to the front, and down to the sidewalk. Pietro is an odd sight in his blue spandex, white hair glittering in the late afternoon sun; Wanda is almost as odd a one beside him, red tunic, cloak, and mask.

Pietro looks antsy walking at the pace of a normal human, jittery and uncomfortable with the pace Wanda's setting, but he doesn't race ahead. "You'll love Latveria, sister," he says, like he's trying to convince them both. "The snow on the mountains still takes my breath away, and the sunrises are lovelier than any other in this world. Father will be so happy to meet you. He couldn't adopt you alongside me, of course—we thought you had died in infancy for the longest time, and when you began appearing in the American papers, we knew you at once, yet didn't know your civilian name. He's already told me he'll give you his name. You'll be a princess of the most beautiful country in the world."

Wanda doesn't know what to say to that. She swallows hard. "I'm not going back to Latveria with you, Pietro. My life is here. My family is here."

"Your family of thieves."

"You're as Roma as I am, Pietro. You know how loaded that word can be. I'm talking about the family who raised me, and loves me, and has always cared for me. I don't need to be a princess. I'm a Parker."

Pietro scoffs.

"What do you mean, you thought I'd died in infancy? You said they ripped me from our mother's arms."

He looks away. "I was, perhaps, speaking hyperbolically. My father knows everything that happens in Latveria. When a terrible man came from outside our borders and abducted two infants, he knew. He sent his people to bring the children home. He *intervened,* Wanda, he took steps to make things right. But there was a great explosion, and his agents told him the second child had died. That I alone survived. By the time he learned otherwise, you were long gone and impossible to retrieve without causing a diplomatic incident—if you had had living blood family beyond myself, it might have been possible, but without that tie, you were already lost to us."

"How?"

"A foolish bureaucrat fast-tracked your adoption by a pair of American tourists."

"Shouldn't that have told you where to find me?"

"The man was a coward. When he realized what he'd done, he burned the embassy to the ground in an effort to conceal his maleficence. He died in the blaze, and we lost your trail. I've mourned you my entire life. I can't wait to take you home."

"I'm not going back to Latveria with you."

Pietro's expression twists, confusion, anger, and agony. "Of course you are. Father sent me here to find you."

"Maybe I'll come for a visit someday, but this is my home. I'm American."

"I can't . . . This isn't how . . . You were supposed to be happy to see me. Aren't you happy to see me?"

"Honestly, not yet. I'm mostly confused. I need to talk to my aunt. I need some time, Pietro, so I can decide what we're going to be to each other. I'm sorry."

"Just come with me. Back to where I've been staying. We can talk in privacy, and I can convince you."

Wanda lets go of his hand.

"No, I'm sorry, but no. I don't know you well enough to go

anywhere private with you yet. I'm happy to talk to you, but until I trust you, I'm not going to be alone with you. Meet me tomorrow morning, at this deli right by the Baxter Building. If you're not there, I'll know you won't stop trying to get your own way, and I'll know I can't be what you want me to be."

He grabs for her hand, moving at an ordinary human speed— when he's not using his powers, he's still fast. He'd be faster than she is, if she weren't using her own powers to lift herself into the air, away from him.

She stops ten feet or so above the ground, ignoring the people who are beginning to stare and point, and says, "Tomorrow."

Then she flies away, confusion and turmoil boiling in her chest.

———

"DID YOU FIND WHAT YOU WERE LOOKING FOR?" ASKS DOCTOR Strange, after she comes crashing back into the Sanctum. She enters through the rooftop door she formerly used with Peter, and that alone is enough to make her ache for the brother she knows and loves, the brother she longs to turn to in this moment of terrible contradiction.

"No, sir," she says. "But I found the speedster."

Doctor Strange frowns. "I thought you were looking for—"

"He's my brother."

"Ah. That does change things somewhat. Have Peter's powers mutated?"

"No, I mean he's my biological brother, from Latveria. He's calling himself 'von Doom,' says he grew up in a palace, and he came here looking for me. He said the Parkers stole me from our parents."

"And what do you think?"

"I think I never really dug too deeply into the way I was adopted." She drops herself, drooping, into the nearest chair. "I loved my family, and Aunt May and Uncle Ben were devastated by losing my parents. Peter was terrified they were going to send me away. So I just never asked. But I remember the Parkers. Not well, but enough. Mary used to sing me to sleep at night, and she was the one who told Aunt May she wanted me to stay in touch with my heritage. Would she have done that if they'd stolen me?"

"People do strange things when guilt grips them," he says. "She might have done that regardless."

"I'll have to talk to Aunt May." She sighs heavily. "I wish I could talk to Peter. I know why I can't, but . . . this doesn't feel like something I should be trying to navigate without him."

"I understand."

"Good, 'cause I don't." She stands, unsteadily. "I'm going to bed, Master. I have an appointment in the morning, but it shouldn't interfere with my lessons."

"Good night, Apprentice. May your dreams show you the answers you need."

She doesn't look back as she walks away.

She's almost to her bed when she realizes she's crying.

CHAPTER SEVENTEEN

—

BETRAYAL

WANDA WAKES TO A WORLD THAT LOOKS THE SAME AS IT DID yesterday, but has transformed beyond all reason. She has questions she never imagined before. She has a brother she's not forbidden to speak to, who eagerly wants to know her. She's stopped a super-powered criminal on her own—and sure, those two people are one and the same, but still, that's something she's never done before.

She feels full of confidence as she dresses and descends the stairs, intending to grab a quick breakfast before she heads out to meet with Pietro. Instead, when she reaches the kitchen, she finds her master barring her way, a copy of *The Daily Bugle* in one hand.

"You were seen," he says coldly.

"I know."

"Do you?" He hands her the paper, and she stares at the front page.

It's an excellent aerial photograph of herself and Pietro. Pietro is holding her wrist, and the timing of the photo makes it look like she's running with him of her own accord. The headline is just as bad.

SINISTER SORCERESS PLANS PARTNERSHIP WITH SUSPI-CIOUS SPEEDSTER?

"They couldn't even keep their alliteration consistent," she mutters.

"A small offense," says Doctor Strange. "They've connected your newfound sibling to the recent wave of criminal activity. You weren't the only one to have noticed the blurring effect of his powers, and apparently he's nearly been apprehended by Spider-Man on several occasions, none of which were previously made public. This picture makes it look like your descent into villainy has been completed, and you're assisting him in his malfeasance."

Wanda's eyes flick automatically to the byline below the picture, printed in such small type that it's easy to overlook if you're not intentionally looking.

Peter Parker.

Her stomach lurches, and she drops the paper to the floor, taking a step back like she's afraid it's going to bite her. "Why would he do something like that?"

"I don't know. I'm sorry."

"I'm sorry, too."

"Why?"

"Because I know you wanted me to wait for him to apologize, and I can't wait any longer." She looks at Doctor Strange, calm and horrified at the same time. "I have to go talk to him. Right now."

"I think you do, yes. It might be better if you called him to come here."

"Yeah, but that gives him a choice, and it would be so much worse if he chose not to come," she says, and pulls a veil of red around herself.

When it fades, only an instant later, she's gone, and Doctor Strange is alone. He picks up the paper, sighing.

Must all young people be so dramatic?

———

WANDA FALLS THROUGH THE RED-RIMMED TUNNEL, ARMS TUCKED tight and legs together, controlling her passage in a way she's barely ever been able to manage; fury is apparently good for something, even if it doesn't leave her in a clearheaded state of mind.

She's going to kill him. He wants to help the world make her out to be a villain—oh, she'll show him why that's not something he wants her to be. She's going to make sure he understands how badly he's just screwed up, and then she's going to kill him, and she's sure Aunt May will understand, once she tells her exactly what he did to deserve this.

She drops out of the red and into the shadows of Peter's dorm room. She knows from Aunt May's careful updates on how he's doing that his roommate failed out of school earlier in the semester, and Peter doesn't have a new one just yet: Like Wanda's technical roommate, he's enjoying the luxury of an unofficial single room until the administration can find someone to move in with him.

He's still asleep, the mound of his body curled beneath his covers. Wanda glares at him. How *dare* he be sleeping so peacefully after the way he betrayed her? He doesn't deserve to sleep peacefully. He doesn't even deserve a *bed*.

Her magic, responding to her anger and the half-formulated desire in that thought, rises, and too late Wanda realizes what it's about to do. She tries to call the chaos back, but an object in motion tends to stay in motion, and a spell once cast tries to complete itself.

Peter's bed disappears. He falls a second later, slamming hard into the floor, and waking up in a tangle of bedding, sputtering as he shoves himself upright and looks frantically around the room. Wanda doesn't know what his spider-sense is likely to be telling him right now—her determination to commit murder faded as soon as she saw him, years of love and trust washing away her anger—but she's still mad enough to be losing control of her powers, and an uncontrolled sorceress is not a safe thing to share a room with.

Peter's frantic scan of the room finds her standing motionless some feet away, and he springs out of the blankets, sticking to the ceiling on finger- and toe-tip. He's wearing Empire State University sweatpants and no shirt, and she's grateful for the former, if marginally discomforted by the latter.

"Do you want to put a shirt on before I start ripping strips off of you for invasion of privacy and behaving like a complete jerk?"

she asks, tone cold enough to leave frost on the windows. Literally: Her magic is still on high alert and ready to respond, and the glass ices over like it's the middle of January, turning opaque with cold.

"Wanda?" Peter drops down from the ceiling, staring at her. "Wanda, what are you doing—"

"Don't you even ask what I'm doing here," she snaps. "You *know* what I'm doing here. How *could* you?"

Peter is a smart man—smart enough not to play the fool when he's clearly been caught out. "You saw the pictures," he says. "I thought I got some pretty good ones, all things considered. Thanks for slowing that guy down enough for me to get his face—everything before that was just a blur."

"Thanks? *Thanks?!*" She balls her hands into fists as they begin glowing again, struggling to contain the chaos that wants to break loose and devour the room around her. "You are a lying, cheating, remorseless *snake,* Peter Parker, and I don't know how I'm supposed to forgive you for that invasion of my privacy."

"Invasion of your privacy? Wanda, you were in public with a suspected super villain! Right *after* you were in the papers for a botched patrol! We don't work that way!"

"'We' don't work *any* way, Peter," she snaps. "*We* don't work together anymore."

"And whose choice was that?"

"Yours, when you decided to call me a jinx. Or did you not realize that was when I stopped letting you use me as your personal punching bag?"

Peter's face falls. "You can't blame me for being upset when Gwen died, Wanda, that's not fair."

"I'm *not* blaming you for being upset when she died! I'm blaming you for forgetting you're not the only person who loved her, and for lashing out at me like I was going to just sit there and take it, like it was my *job* to let you abuse me! I'm not here for you to abuse. That's not what sisters are for. If you even think of me as a sister. After what you said, I haven't been entirely sure."

"I knew . . . after I said it, after you left, I knew what I said wasn't okay, but, Wanda, I didn't mean it. I was in shock, and I didn't mean it."

"That just makes it worse, because if you didn't mean it, you were saying it just to *hurt* me. Can't you see how that's worse?" She looks at him, still glaring, fighting the need to plead. She just wants him to understand why she's angry. She wants him to give her the consideration she's been giving him for their entire lives. "At least if you'd meant it, you would have been telling me the truth."

"I . . . I'm sorry, Wanda." Peter rubs the back of his neck with one hand, looking ashamed. "Is that why you've been avoiding me?"

"Oh, you noticed? Could have fooled me."

He drops his hand, sighing. "I guess I deserved that, but yeah, I noticed. I noticed right away. I was crying, I was *dying,* I was so deep into my grief that it felt like I was drowning, and you've always been the one I could hold on to when things got that bad, and you weren't there. I couldn't find you. But then Aunt May wouldn't tell me how you were, and neither would Doctor Strange, and I realized that I'd screwed up more than I thought I had. I didn't know what to do."

He doesn't seem to notice the way red light licks at the back of Wanda's pupils, rage manifesting in her expression. "You were talking to my master?"

"I wouldn't call it 'talking.' More 'I was asking him where you were, and he was closing doors in my face.' He asked me if I was ready to apologize every time, and when I wasn't, he said I could try again later."

Oh, she's going to have words with him later. But right now, Peter is the target of her anger, and he deserves to be. "You could have tried contacting *me.* Do you still have a phone? Or *you* could have stopped avoiding me. I wasn't the only person keeping my distance."

Peter begins to protest: She recognizes all the signs, the way his shoulders square and his lower back tenses, like arguing for his own innocence is the heaviest thing in the world. Then he stops, sagging where he stands.

"I couldn't, though. As long as I was staying away from you, as long as I was too mad at you to stop and think about why, I wasn't alone in my grief. Gwen's gone. She's really gone, and she's never—" He takes a breath that turns into a broken sob. "She's never coming back. It's all my fault."

This isn't like Uncle Ben: She's not going to argue with him on whose fault it is that Gwen died. She didn't do anything wrong. So instead, she does what Gwen would have wanted: She takes a breath, pauses long enough to be sure, and says, "I'm sorry."

Peter looks at her, tears in his eyes. "I am, too, Wandy. I was just trying to make you hurt as badly as I was hurting. It wasn't fair. I hit you because you were the closest safe target. You're my sister. I love you. I didn't mean to drive you away."

"If you ever say anything like that to me again, I'm going to put a hex bolt through your liver," she warns.

Peter nods. "That's fair enough. If I ever say anything like that again, I'll deserve it."

"I would have broken down and come to confront you a long time ago, but my master told me not to."

"Doctor Strange? Why?"

"He said I deserved better than groveling for your love. I should just get it. I shouldn't have to prove that I'm good enough."

Peter sighs. "He's right. God, Wanda, I'm sorry I ever made you feel like that."

"But that's not why I'm here," she says, remembering her situation. "That picture—what the hell, Peter?"

He winces. "I'm sorry."

"You're saying that a lot today. What were you *doing*?"

"You wouldn't talk to me, you were never at your dorm room or the house, and Doctor Strange and Django wouldn't tell me *anything* when I asked them how you were. I had to do something to know that you were okay."

"So you started following me?"

Peter nods, looking guilty. "I couldn't approach you, not when I was still so sad and so angry and no one would let me in, so it was a way to know that you were still doing well enough to keep up with your patrols, and to see how you were, even if it was always through a telephoto lens. I felt a little bad about it sometimes, but not bad enough to stop. I just wanted to know you were all right. This was how I could know that. It was the only way."

"Okay, first, stalking is still stalking, even when it's your sister. Second, was selling the pictures to *The Daily Bugle* your way of making sure I was all right?"

Peter grimaces, looking chagrined. "I needed the money, and they needed pictures for the articles they were already going to run. I swear, I didn't have anything to do with the first articles about you going villain."

"But you sold them the pictures."

Peter pauses. He looks exhausted; there are deep circles under his eyes that can't be explained by the early wake-up call. It's almost enough to make Wanda wonder what sort of support he's had while she was dealing with things on her own—Aunt May is mad at him, and he's never had a mentor like Doctor Strange has been to her. He makes friends more easily but more shallowly at the same time, and she's not the only one who's been hurting. While she's been healing in the company of the people who love her, he's been alone.

"I guess we should have gotten over ourselves a while ago, huh?" he asks.

"Maybe *you* should have," she snaps. "I've just been waiting for you to realize how badly you screwed everything up."

He looks, for a moment, like he might cry, and she thaws a bit.

"Just don't do it again," she says.

Peter nods. "Yeah, I've been following you. I couldn't come to the Sanctum, so I'd wait for you to come out, and then I'd follow along to see what you were doing. I was stunned when I saw you breaking into that house. I stuck around to see if I could figure out what you were doing, and then the speedster showed up—how did you know? Has he been communicating with you?"

"No. I just mapped out all the crimes that looked like they might be him, and then I went and staked out the next point on my map. He showed up a few hours later. It was all math."

"Math is a super-power," agrees Peter. "But once I saw him, I knew I had to get pictures. People have been wondering about the speedster for weeks, and here was proof he was real, not just some sort of super hero urban legend. I got excited. I guess I didn't think about the fact that you'd be in all the pictures until it was too late and Jonah was asking if I thought you were teaming up with that guy. You're not, are you?"

"Not yet," says Wanda. "I guess I might be in the future. He says . . ." She pauses. This is Peter. She's always trusted him, with everything. And yes, he's hurt her very badly, but she needs to talk to someone her own age about what's happening, or she's going to explode. Her brother seems like as good a confidant as any. "His name is Pietro von Doom. He's from Latveria. And he says he's my brother."

"Like, biologically? From before our parents brought you home? Wanda, that's amazing. I'm so happy for you!" She thinks she sees his face falter just a moment, before he adds, "I hope he was looking for a two-for-one deal, because this means he's my brother, too."

"I don't think adoption is transitive," she says, and she's smiling, even though this is probably what Pietro was afraid of when he talked about her replacing her heritage with American things. She has her American brother, and now . . . her Latverian brother. She can find room in her life for both of them, even if it isn't going to be easy.

"He says he's my twin brother from Latveria, and that when the Parkers adopted me, they didn't adopt him. He's been looking for me. He wasn't completely sure I was the Scarlet Witch, so he didn't introduce himself, but he figured we'd cross paths eventually. And we did!"

"Wanda . . ."

"He's got some weird ideas about American imperialism—which

is a genuine problem, but doesn't mean it's okay to come over here and start doing crimes, no matter how annoyed you are at the state of global politics. But he sounded sincere, and he looks like me. The bridge of his nose, the way his eyes are shaped. He looks like me, and he didn't know for sure that I'd have super-powers—he suspected, because *he* has super-powers, but he didn't *know*—so why would he have bothered coming up with this whole song and dance about being related to a random adoptee from a family that doesn't have a lot of money or diplomatic standing or anything? He could be trying to play me, but I don't feel like it, and I want to find out. I want to talk to him more. And I think that starts with me talking to Aunt May. Some of the things he said about my adoption . . . I don't want to think Mom and Dad could have done anything wrong when they brought me home, but I have to face the idea that it's possible. If we're done fighting, can you come with me to talk to her?"

"Sure, Wandy," says Peter, sounding a bit nonplussed by the cascade of words.

"Thank you."

"But before we do that . . . do you think you could bring back my bed?"

———

SUMMONING A BED ISN'T AS EASY AS VANISHING ONE, AND IT'S another two hours before they leave for Queens, Peter's dorm room once more equipped with all the furniture it's supposed to have, both of them in full costume as he wraps his arm around her waist and steps off the edge of the dormitory roof. There's a glorious moment of free fall before he throws a web-line at the nearest building, pulling them up, and then they're swinging through the city, they're floating, they're flying.

She can fly under her own power now—she'll have to show him soon—but this is still one of the best things she's ever done in her life. She hangs off Peter's neck as they swing, laughing and laughing, glorying in the wind whipping through her hair, the faint chill in her ears, even the way they occasionally swing through a cloud of smoke or steam, chilling and heating up with their environment.

When she flies, her magic wraps her in an envelope of stillness, no bugs in her face or feathers in her hair. When her brother swings, he is one with the city. When she flies, she's apart from it. This is a moment of reunion: She's back where she belongs after more than a year of unwanted solitude. Right now, she just wants to be one with something. So he swings, and she clings, and her laughter is a sweet soundtrack for the moment, carrying them all the way to Queens.

Spider-Man drops into the alley they've always used for changing their clothes, and switches to his own civilian identity in a matter of seconds before looking expectantly at Wanda. She looks back, still in tunic and cloak. She isn't wearing her mask, but that's fixed easily enough; with a gesture of her hand, she plucks it out of nothing and slides it onto her face.

Peter blinks. "Um?"

"Trust me," she says.

"I always do," he replies, looking at her uneasily.

Wanda offers her hands, and when he takes them, she's the one who throws them into the sky, a red light enveloping them as she pulls him close and wills them higher, leaving the alleyway behind. Peter squeaks and clings, and she laughs again, flying them to the house where they grew up, forever familiar, so changed since they both left. It hasn't gotten any smaller; it just feels that way. Maybe they've gotten bigger, somehow.

Maybe they still are.

She lands in the backyard, letting go of Peter. He steps back and looks at her, perplexed. She offers only one hand this time, and when he takes it, they stay on the ground as she tugs him to the back door. "Trust me," she says.

"I do."

"And that means everything to me, believe me."

She opens the door, stepping into the hallway, which smells like tea and cinnamon candles. "Aunt May? We're home."

"'We'?" The reply is immediate, and followed by Aunt May's head poking out of the kitchen, a perplexed expression on her face. It only lasts an instant before it dissolves into a bright, teary-eyed smile. "You've found your way back to each other! Oh, my darlings, I knew it was always only a matter of time!"

"Aunt May?" Peter sounds utterly confused.

Wanda laughs as she lets go of his hand and walks over to embrace her aunt, then removes her mask and cape, putting the one on the little table where they stack the mail, and hanging the other from the coatrack. "I didn't think you'd officially told her yet. Shame, Peter."

"Shame—you *told* her?" His voice peaks and squeaks like it hasn't since puberty.

Now it's Aunt May's turn to laugh. "She didn't tell me anything about *you,* sweetheart, and she didn't confirm anything about herself until I told her it was silly to keep pretending when I knew exactly who she was. Maybe you could have hidden it if there was only one of you, but do you honestly think your old aunt is so decrepit that I wouldn't know when I was living with *two* superpowered teenagers? I would have deserved to lose custody of the pair of you if that were the case."

"You *knew*?"

"Darling, I've known since before you left for college. I've never told a soul. It's been easier since Wanda's known that I know, and now I can talk to that dashing mentor of hers. Doctor Strange is a fine figure of a man."

"Ew," says Wanda. "Gross."

Peter doesn't say anything, just makes a revolted face and steps closer to Wanda while Aunt May laughs again.

Then she smacks him in the arm. He yelps and jumps, startled rather than actually hurt.

"What was that for?"

"Not *telling* me," she says. "I've been leaving hints all year, Peter. Or did you think it was coincidence that my book club did *Charlotte's Web* twice in a row? It was the nicest book about spiders I could find. Most of them make the spiders the villains. I didn't want you to think I thought of you like that."

"I didn't even notice," says Peter, abashed. "I'm sorry, Aunt May. I thought I was protecting you."

"Ignorance is almost never protection, Peter."

It's a perfect opening: Wanda can't let it pass. "That's why we're here," she says. "Because ignorance is never protection, and I need to ask some questions about my adoption."

Aunt May pauses. She's been waiting for this conversation for years, and somehow she had started to fall into the comfortable belief that it was never going to happen. Now that it's here, she honestly doesn't remember how she was planning to deal with it.

"Let's go to the kitchen, dears," she says finally. "This will be easier with a hot beverage in front of us."

———

IT'S THE MOST FAMILIAR OF FAMILIAR SCENES, THE THREE OF THEM around the kitchen table, Aunt May with a mug of tea, Wanda with cocoa, and Peter with his coffee. The only thing they have in common is the cream, which they all take, softening and sweetening the liquids.

Aunt May wraps her hands around her mug, staring into its pale brown depths. "You have to understand," she says finally. "This wasn't one of those cases where an American couple goes to Europe to buy a baby. No money changed hands. They were in Latveria for work—they were following up on some data anomalies your father had identified. What they found instead was an orphaned little girl with no one left in the world."

"Do we know that for sure?"

There's a sharp edge to Wanda's question that brings May's head up, suddenly attentive, like a deer catching the sound of hunters in the trees. "What do you mean, dear?"

"I met a man, my age. His name is Pietro, and he says he knows things about my adoption. Did Mom and Dad ever say anything about a second baby?"

"Richard said . . . he said there were signs that there had been two babies before they arrived on the scene, but that there was only you when they got there. It ripped Mary up inside, knowing there was a child they'd failed to save."

"So I *did* have a brother before Peter." Wanda feels briefly bleached-out inside, like something has been kept from her. But has it? If they thought the boy was dead, would telling her have done her any good? Is it better to grow up not knowing, or grow up grieving someone who isn't ever going to come home?

"We don't know for sure that the second baby was a boy, but it seems like you may have, yes," says Aunt May.

"Why did none of you ever tell me? When you were encouraging me to read up on Latveria, to learn to speak Romany—why didn't you tell me I hadn't been alone in the beginning?"

"Because as far as any of us knew, the poor child was dead before Richard and Mary found you. There was nothing any of us could have done to change the past. It seemed unkind to tell you you'd survived when he hadn't, and then Richard and Mary died, and then your uncle Ben died, and it felt like every time I worked up the courage to tell you more about your adoption, someone else passed away. And you never asked. Which is unfair of me to say, and feels like I'm putting the blame for my silence on you, when it was my cowardice that kept me from saying anything. But it felt like permission at the time. I wasn't telling you something you didn't even want to know. How could I be depriving you of your history when you never asked?"

Wanda knows her aunt is right. How many times did those unspoken questions lead her to disappointment? Like the time her heart broke, even just a little, on a beautiful day in Westchester County. But it is possible an answer has, quite literally, found its way to her.

"Well, my history's here now," says Wanda. She's not angry, not really—her confusion is too big. It fills the entire world. Until she's managed to process what she's just learned, anger is going to be beyond her. "I was born in Latveria, and I had a little time there, but everything I know is here. I'm Wanda Parker, not Wanda von Doom or Wanda whoever I was going to be. And I know Mom and Dad did the best they could. They really told you about him?"

What kind of sister is she, if she never thought to look for him?

"They never saw your twin, only inferred his existence from the place where you were found. Mary couldn't talk about it much. She broke down crying when she tried. Richard . . ." She pauses, gathering her thoughts. "Richard said you were one of his greatest successes, and that was what allowed him to sleep at night despite his greatest failure. They loved you both, so very much. I think, sometimes, Mary forgot she had only carried one of you."

Wanda reaches for Peter's hand, and he takes it, and they hold each other, fingers tangled in the familiar way they spent so long building between them. Aunt May doesn't miss the gesture, and a small line of tension so tight and constant that she's stopped noticing it releases behind her breastbone. Her children are holding on to each other again. They're not alone in the world, which is so much bigger and stranger and more terrifying than she knew when she was their age.

It's going to be all right.

"Why are you asking, dear?" she asks, to cover her relief.

Wanda looks down into the depths of her cocoa. "I . . . Pietro is . . . I think I met my brother."

Aunt May gasps. Peter's hand clenches tightly on Wanda's, squeezing hard.

"I'm sorry, what?" asks Aunt May.

Voice halting, Wanda lays it all out: The strange speedster. His reaction when she caught him. The things he told her, about himself, about herself, about the Parkers. Some of the details are new to Peter; he doesn't let go of her while she's explaining things, only holds on tight, like he's never planning on letting go ever again.

When she's done, she looks to Aunt May, waiting for the woman who has always been able to comfort her to do it again, to make the world make sense.

Instead Aunt May cups her teacup with both hands, face pale, and looks down into the steam. "I am . . . so sorry, Wanda. So very, very sorry."

"Why?"

"Because I wondered, a few times, whether you might have surviving family in Latveria. The way you came to us was so abrupt, so . . . lucky. Like everything had to happen just *so* for it to work out. I thought about contacting the embassy after Richard and Mary died, looking deeper into the circumstances of how it all happened, but I never did."

"Why not?"

"Do you remember when Ben and I told you your parents were gone? How Peter reacted?"

Wanda nods.

"He said we couldn't take his sister away, and he was so angry, and it was so obvious that his anger was masking genuine terror—he'd just lost his mother and father, and he was afraid it meant he was going to lose you, too. Every time I thought about contacting the embassy, I remembered Peter yelling at me, and I couldn't do it. I couldn't take the risk that I'd call them and they'd say I was right to do so, because they needed to take you back. You're my niece, Peter's sister, and this is where you belong. And as time passed without you asking questions, I felt more and more like I was in the right, like there was no point in opening old wounds. I'm so sorry, Wanda. I made the choice for you, and I don't know if it was the right one."

"Pietro doesn't think it was," says Wanda, almost numbly. "He's . . . I don't know what he is. He has powers, just like I do, but he's . . . he's so strange. He's been looking for me for his whole life, and I never even knew he existed. I asked him to step back and stop trying to pressure me. I hope he will. He says he came here looking for me, and if that's true, I guess he'll try to stay on my good side."

"So what are you going to do?" asks Peter.

"I want to get to know him, at least a little," says Wanda. "I can't say whether he seems like a nice person or not, because we've only met the once, but he's my brother and he came here for me. Doesn't that mean I owe him a chance?"

"I don't think you owe anyone anything," says Aunt May. "Blood relation is not the only one that matters."

"I know," says Wanda. "But I also know how it feels to be rejected by family, and Pietro doesn't deserve that. I want to try."

Peter tries to pull his hand away. Wanda doesn't let go.

"No," she says. "I just got you back, you don't get to pull away again. No."

He looks at her, silent and despairing, and that's wrong. Peter babbles. Peter prattles. Peter isn't silently miserable.

"What is it?" she asks.

He shakes his head. She kicks him under the table.

"What *is* it, Peter?" she repeats.

"Am I not enough?" he asks. He sounds guilty about even asking, like he doesn't want to make this about him when it's supposed to be about her.

Wanda thaws, just a little. "You are, for me," she says. "You're all the brother I'll ever need. But Pietro doesn't deserve to be alone because our parents thought he was dead when they adopted me. If they'd known about him, I'm sure we would all have grown up together. We have to give him a chance."

Gradually, the stiffness leaves Peter's shoulders, and he stops trying to pull his hand out of hers. He nods, almost grudgingly. "All right. For you, I'm willing to try."

"That's all I needed from you," says Wanda, and her smile is everything.

CHAPTER EIGHTEEN

—

A NEW BEGINNING

WANDA'S SMILE DIES WHEN THEY LEAVE THE HOUSE, AND NOT EVEN swinging above the city can bring it back. She holds on to Peter's neck as tightly as she ever has, and he shoots anxious little glances at her, trying to figure out what he did wrong, until he finally brings them to a landing on a fire escape, stepping back as he lets her go.

"Well?" he says.

"Well what?" she asks.

He spreads his arms, gesturing helplessly. "I can't apologize if I don't know what I did wrong *this* time."

"I haven't completely forgiven you for saying those awful things and leaving me alone. You wouldn't have said them if you didn't think them, at least on some level. But I'm done with my big mad, and the little mad will fade if you just don't prod at it. No, right now, I'm mad at Django and my master for not telling me you'd come around. How was I supposed to wait for you to apologize when they didn't tell me that you'd *tried*?"

"About that . . ." he says, sounding chagrined.

"What did you do?"

"I only came by the Sanctum twice. The first time, I was still angry, and I wanted to pick our fight back up where we'd left it. Your master told me not to bring that energy into his home, and that I could come back when I was ready to apologize. I didn't see what I needed to apologize for. I left. When I came back, it was because I missed you, and I wanted to see if we could be friends again. But I still wasn't planning to apologize, and he made me leave again."

"Ah." If he hadn't come to apologize, of course her master wouldn't have let him in. It doesn't extinguish her anger, but it banks it; telling her Peter had been there would have just been a temptation she didn't need. "And Django?"

"I swung by the restaurant a few times, once with Johnny, once with Cap, to pick up takeout and ask about you. It's funny. I know he doesn't know about me, but he was perfectly friendly with both of them, and really cold with me. Wouldn't answer when I asked how you were doing."

Peter is the smartest person she knows, but sometimes he can be really stupid. If Aunt May figured them out, and Django figured *her* out, the Scarlet Witch and Spider-Man having a falling-out probably told him exactly who Peter was. "Did you always come in costume?"

"Yeah."

Another sliver of her anger fades away. If Peter had come in costume, asking after Wanda, Django would have had no way to tell her about it without revealing that he knew her secret identity. He'd been keeping an unexpectedly convoluted secret that she had never given him permission to share.

"Oh," she says.

Spider-Man looks at her, anxious and hopeful. "We good?"

"We're getting better," she says, and gestures him closer. "Come on. Swing me home."

It's still early afternoon, and she knows people will see them swinging across the city. Peter's not even trying to hide the fact that he's carrying her, and that's another part of his apology. He drops her on the Sanctum roof, promising to come back that night to take her on patrol, then swings away, leaving her to go inside and face the Sorcerer Supreme.

—

WANDA'S FORGIVENESS OF HER WAYWARD BROTHER DOESN'T
guarantee her master's, and when Peter returns to the Sanctum roof
that evening, he finds the door locked against him. That isn't right—
the door is never locked when he lands on the roof. He rattles the
knob several times, scowling at it like his eyes alone will somehow
be enough to serve as a key.

And maybe they are, because when he tests the door again, the
knob turns and lets him in. The Sanctum seems gloomier than it's
been in the past, the hallways choked with shadows that spring
from nowhere, clinging in defiance of the light. The wallpaper is the
color of an old bruise.

Peter pauses halfway down the hall and, feeling a little foolish,
addresses the walls. "All right, I get it," he says. "You're mad at me
for being unfair to Wanda. I told her I was sorry. We talked through
what happened. She's forgiven me. I can't believe I'm saying this to
a *house,* but do you think you could maybe try to stop holding a
grudge before I trip on a stair and break my neck or something?
That's only going to upset her worse."

The Sanctum, which is a house, however mystical and impressive, does not reply—but as Peter starts walking again, the shadows
thin, finally responding to the light the way physics say they ought
to, and the stairs are as well lit as ever. He descends without issue,
even as he's tempted to stick to the wall and go down that way,
which feels less subject to the whims of angry architecture.

It's nice being back in the Sanctum, even if it does feel like the
house itself is judging his recent behavior. He follows Wanda's voice
to the solarium, where she's in full costume, tucked into one of the
armchairs and explaining some piece of complicated magical theory
to her master. For his part, Doctor Strange looks like a tolerant
teacher allowing a student to explain something he already knows,
for the sake of getting it locked more firmly into said student's

mind. He glances up as Peter steps through the doorway, mouth hardening into a tight line.

Wanda stops talking, accurately guessing what's caught her master's attention. "Master—" she begins.

He motions for her to be quiet, and so she does, as he moves to put himself between the two of them, expression cold. "Mr. Parker," he says. "To what do we owe the pleasure?"

"I'm here to take my sister on patrol?" says Peter, the statement somehow transforming into a question. He clears his throat and tries again. "I mean, hello, Doctor. I'm here to get Wanda, we're going out on patrol."

"Are you, now," says Doctor Strange.

"We are," says Wanda, standing. "I told you this afternoon that we were going out, and you said it was fine as long as I could defend my ideas about entropic decay in folded chaos space. Which I just did, and you were very satisfied by what I had to say, right up until you decided to be mad at Peter again. He apologized. We're good now."

"As easily as that?"

She hesitates. She doesn't want to hurt her brother's feelings, but her master will know if she lies. He always does. "No," she admits. "Not as easily as that. I'm still hurt, and it's going to be a while before I can relax and trust him not to hurt me. But he said he was sorry, and he knows what he did wrong, and he's not going to do it again."

"I can't treat her like she's not worth the world," says Peter. "She's my sister, and I love her more than anything, and that means I can hurt her more than anyone else, and I have to be careful with her."

"Mmm," says Doctor Strange.

"I'm going," says Wanda.

"Apprentice—"

"I'm *going*." She glares at her master. "I know you're trying to protect me, and I genuinely do appreciate it, but he's my brother, and I'm handling it. I promise."

Doctor Strange looks at her for a moment in silence before he nods and, silently, steps away. She's not the gawky, untrained teen she was when Richards brought her to his door. She's not the grown woman she believes herself to be, either; she's caught in the twilight hinterland of early adulthood, when everything is possible, but the experiences she needs to navigate it are still ahead of her. Despite the pressure of his own desires, he can't prevent her from going out and having those experiences. He can't protect her from everything. Sometimes he has to let her go.

As for Wanda, it aches a little to see him so cold to Peter, who used to be the only person in the world Wanda truly believed would never hurt her. It aches more to know that he has reason to be. But he follows them to the roof and waves as they swing away, and he doesn't try to stop them going, and it's better than it could have been, so much better.

"I guess you don't need me to provide the transport anymore," says Peter, when they come to a stop on a billboard. They're both masked: She should be thinking of him as Spider-Man by now, but he was her brother before he was a hero, and she just got her brother back. She's not ready to make the switch when they're alone just yet. Besides, Spider-Man is like a second mask for him, the way the Scarlet Witch is for her: He talks differently, moves differently, even holds himself differently. Right now he's Peter Parker in a spandex costume, and she likes it better this way.

"How do you mean?"

"The flying thing?" He makes an airplane takeoff gesture with one hand, flying it up into the air.

"Ah. Yeah, I can do that now."

"So why am I swinging us?"

"I'm still not the best at it. I can't always take a passenger with me, and even when I can, it's not *easy*. It takes a lot out of me." She shrugs. "If you have to swing anyway, it seems better to conserve my energy until there's something that needs hitting."

"That makes sense. So you've been patrolling alone while I was being a butt?"

"Alone, or with the Black Knight. I preferred alone." Her eyes drop toward the street, scanning for crime and preventing her from the need to look at his masked face. "Most of the people I ran into while I was with him wanted to know how you and I fell out, so they could figure out whether I was the bad guy and they needed to worry about me turning villain. People like you better than they like me."

"Well, that's stupid. You're way more likeable than I am!"

"Yeah, but it's not like we've ever been public about our relationship, so it's not like I could say 'My brother said some nasty things after his girlfriend died, and we're not speaking right now.' "

"Not without blowing my secret identity, and probably yours at the same time," Peter agrees, more quietly. "I'm sorry, Wandy. I didn't know things were that hard for you."

"Would it have changed anything if you had?"

Peter doesn't say anything for a long time. When Wanda looks up at him, he's facing away from her, hands loose by his sides.

"I don't know," he says finally. "I want to say, 'Yes, of course, it would have changed everything if I'd realized how much you were hurting,' but that want comes from the part of me that doesn't want to believe I can hurt you, even a little, and especially not on purpose. So I think I have to say I don't know. I was hurting, and I needed someone I could blame other than myself, because if I was trying to carry that much blame on my own, it was going to break me."

"How about blaming the Green Goblin?"

"That would have been the healthy choice, yes."

Somehow, that's what sets them both howling with laughter, the wind whipping it away and scattering it across the city, where it dissolves into nothing. When they're done, Wanda wipes her eyes through the holes in her mask, and says, "I missed this."

"I did, too. So if you've been patrolling without me, you're probably used to working without the training wheels, huh?"

"Are you asking whether you can stop avoiding the really dangerous fights? Yeah. That would be fine."

She sees him grin behind the mask, and then he's sweeping her under one arm and launching them into the air, webs flinging them into the night.

Wanda just holds on. For tonight, she'll let Peter drive.

—

THEIR FIRST STOP IS A PRETTY STANDARD JEWELRY STORE ROBBERY, notable only because there are six armed men involved. When she'd patrolled with Peter before, he never seemed to find more than three criminals at a time. The men don't have any powers, and they don't put up much of a challenge. They're easily subdued. It's not until Spider-Man is webbing the last of them to the wall that Wanda realizes where they are; he's swung them into Hell's Kitchen. This is Daredevil's territory, and he's normally careful to give the hero without fear a wide berth. They're not enemies or anything, he just respects the other man's boundaries.

"Spider-Man," she hisses. "What are we doing here?"

"Fighting crime," he says, a bit too loudly. "As a team." He picks her up again and they're off. It's not until they've put several miles between them and the crime scene that he says, "Daredevil hears everything that happens in Hell's Kitchen. He must have been busy when that robbery kicked off. He'll make sure people know we're working together again."

"Oh." Wanda has never considered using the power of gossip to bolster her reputation, rather than destroying it. It's a good idea. "Smart."

"I have my moments," he says, before he begins swinging them lower and lower, moving with the sudden focus that means his spider-sense has picked up on something worth pursuing. It's not fair, how he gets to have radar for the bad guys, and she just has to trust in luck and the occasional police scanner.

But then there's the museum, lights on and shouts coming from inside, where a charity gala had been in full swing before it was so rudely interrupted.

"Why does anyone bother having charity galas?" asks Spider-Man, setting her on the sidewalk as he releases his line. "They're like catnip for bad guys. It's as if they want to be assaulted by costumed creeps."

"Any idea who's in there?"

"Nope."

"Let's find out."

The doors are standing open, propped to let the bored and rich come inside to lighten their purses and their consciences at the same time. There's a reception desk, presumably to check tickets for those who have already paid and take money from those who haven't. It's unmanned. One of the chairs has toppled over, and there's a bloodstain on the chair that remains, still bright and wet, reflecting the scattered light from the chandelier.

Spider-Man immediately abandons the floor for the wall, while Wanda calls just enough power to hover a few inches off the floor, emulating Doctor Strange in a way she would once have thought impossible.

Together, they head deeper inside.

(Watching, America has to resist the urge to punch the air and cheer. They aren't fighting anything yet, but they're not fighting *each other*, either. She's invested now. She's been watching them long enough to want to see them find their way to happiness, somehow, however impossible it might seem. She's seen what feels like the ending of this story. She wants them to have a better middle.)

They make their way through the museum, any sound that might betray their presence masked by the screaming from inside the main hall ahead, where lights flash and jitter uncontrollably. Spider-Man gestures for Wanda to take the right-hand door, while he heads for the left.

Inside the hall is a scene of pure chaos. The overheads are swinging in erratic arcs, set off by blasts of sand and water from below. Two figures move through the crowd, grabbing frightened attendees and stripping them of their valuables. One is a man who seems to be entirely made of sand; the other is half man, half solid water.

Together, they have their captives ringed in with walls that seem to be made from the substance of their own bodies, and Wanda assumes it's only scope that keeps them from doing the same to block the exits.

She slips into the room, calling as much chaos as her hands can hold. Spider-Man is almost to the center of the hall, moving along the ceiling on all fours, and she doesn't see what good his powers are going to do here—can you wrap a web around sand? She's not sure hers will be much better.

Then he swings down into the middle of the fray, quipping a sunny, "Mind if I crash the party? *Can* you crash a pre-crashed party? I know! Mind if I *un*crash the party?"

The two superhumans turn on him, scowling, and fire jets of sand and water at Spider-Man. He leaps clear, and both blasts impact the same philanthropist, sending him sprawling.

"Hey!" yells Wanda, not sure what she's going to do with their attention, but sure she stands a better chance of surviving it than the normal humans they've decided to victimize. "Pick on someone your own—no, that won't work, you're twice as big as I am."

The figures grumble a quick consultation between themselves, and the water man starts toward her, leaving Spider-Man to fight the sand man on his own. Wanda squeaks and throws herself flat, hover becoming flight as she races across the hall for the shelter of a display. The blast of water destroys the exhibit, but leaves her only slightly dampened.

Throwing herself back into the open, Wanda hits him with several bolts of charged chaos. His liquid body appears to absorb them without any effect, although a confused expression crosses his face, leaving him looking briefly baffled.

Wanda spins in the air, heading back toward Spider-Man and his own opponent. She has to swerve to dodge a table flung by the villain behind her. It doesn't hit any of the partygoers, but slams harmlessly into a wall as she zips past Spider-Man, extending her hand. He grabs it, and she pulls him with her as she flies onward, until he webs the ceiling and jerks them both abruptly upward.

Wanda takes advantage of no longer needing to watch where she's going, throwing several hex bolts into the sand man.

"You can *move*," says Spider-Man, as below them their opponents circle, moving closer together. "Can you hover?"

"I've got it."

Spider-Man lets her go, and she floats where she is, hurtling more bolts of pure chaos down at the pair. Spider-Man swings lower, flinging webs in their direction, and as more and more of her concentrated bad luck strikes home, his webs start to find purchase on the items the two semisolid villains have pulled into themselves. Maybe he can't web water, but he can web debris, and by tying enough of it together, he's pulling them closer and closer to each other.

They realize the true danger of their situation too late, when the man of water brushes against the man of sand. Wanda sees their brief, horrified expressions, and then they're smashing into each other, two figures becoming one figure with two heads, mud wrapped tight in the strands of her brother's web. She floats gently to the floor, standing back as Spider-Man finishes the process of binding them together.

Outside, the sound of sirens tells them help is on the way.

"Spider-Man!" says a curator, rushing to shake his hand. "Thank you so much. I don't know what we would have done if you hadn't shown up when you did."

"I didn't do it alone," he says, voice again pitched a little louder than it needs to be. "Half the thanks should go to my partner, the Scarlet Witch. Without her hexes, I'd still be trying to figure out how I'm supposed to web a liquid."

Wanda isn't used to this many eyes on her when no one's accusing her of anything. She has to force herself to stand tall, proud, and heroic, a smile on her face and red light cascading around her hands. She feels like a fraud.

"The Scarlet Witch?" asks another partygoer. "I thought she was a villain?"

"She's never been a villain," says Spider-Man firmly. "She just has a power set that sometimes puts her in the wrong place at the wrong time. Sorry about your party, everyone. I hope the night gets better from here."

Then he's scooping Wanda off the floor and the two of them are swinging away from the buzzing room and the bound super villains, out into the cool night air. They make it back to roof level before Wanda starts laughing.

"That was *amazing*," she informs him.

"We make a pretty good team," he agrees. "Let's not fight anymore."

"Peter . . . I'm your sister. We're going to fight. That's what siblings do."

"So let's always make up."

She doesn't want to disagree with that, and so they swing off into the night, looking for more crime to thwart, together again, as they were always meant to be.

—

PETER DROPS HER ON THE SANCTUM ROOF A LITTLE BIT BEFORE midnight, when the stars are specks against the light-washed sky, and even New York is considering the virtues of a quick nap. She waves goodbye as he swings off, waiting until she's sure he's gone before she steps off the roof and takes flight under her own power, heading away from Greenwich Village.

Pietro is waiting behind the deli where she told him she'd be. He looks impatient, like he's been waiting for hours, and maybe he has been, but she suspects it's more a matter of him looking impatient if he has to hold still for more than three seconds at a time. What must it be like, to live life on fast-forward? They're clearly the same age, so he doesn't age faster in the time he's given, doesn't get twenty seconds for each of her one or anything like that. He just stretches the seconds he has further than anyone else can, like Aunt May turning the last cup of flour into an entire batch of waffles when Wanda would struggle to make it into one.

She lands behind him, almost silent, and is unsurprised when he whips around, tense and ready to fight. It bothers her a little, that his first impulse is fighting and not fleeing. He's clearly built to run away, and she's not sure what there is that could stop him if he wanted to try. The fact that he answers surprise with aggression says a lot of things she doesn't want to hear about the way he grew up, the life he lived without her.

"It's just me," she says, hands up and palms outward, showing him that she's unarmed. Not that she's ever truly unarmed, with chaos ready and waiting to fill her hands, but she does what she can.

Pietro continues to look at her warily for a moment before he relaxes, lips spreading in a smile. "Wanda!"

"Not when I'm in costume," she says hurriedly. "Scarlet Witch, please."

"Pah. That's not a name one calls one's sister."

"Maybe not, but it's the name I use when I'm dressed like this."

"Then I would prefer we meet in civilian clothes, but I will call you 'Witch' for now."

"Thank you. I . . . so I talked to my adoptive family."

"And?"

"And they thought you were dead when they adopted me, Pietro. They knew there had been two babies, but they couldn't find you. They thought you were dead, and I had no family left in Latveria. They adopted me to give me a better life, not because they were trying to take me away from you. They didn't know you were there to be taken away from."

Pietro looks at her, a visible ache in his icy eyes. He wants to believe her, but something about his past—maybe the same something that put lead in his heels and anger in his hands when surprised—is stopping him, and it hurts her.

"They didn't hurt me, they didn't cut me off from our heritage, and they didn't *steal* me, Pietro. They want to meet you."

That, at least, seems to shock him. "Meet me? Why?"

"Because you're my brother? And now that I know you exist, I want you to be a part of my life. Well, they're always going to be a part of my life, and that means I need the two parts of my life to come together."

"Do they . . ." He gestures, somewhat awkwardly, at the costumed length of her. ". . . know?"

Wanda nods. "They do. My aunt figured it out, and my brother is like us. He does this, too."

Pietro scowls. "*I'm* your brother."

"So is he. If this is going to work, with you and me and having any sort of a relationship, you have to accept that. We grew up together, he cares about me, and we're a package deal."

"That should have been *me*."

"Maybe, but it wasn't, and we can't change that now. You want to be a part of my life? You acknowledge that he's always going to be a part of things."

Pietro glares at her, hands flexing, open, now balled into fists, open, closed, over and over, until he finally, sullenly, glances away. "Fine," he says, resentment dripping from the word like honey. "I'll meet this 'brother' of yours."

"I'm so glad." Wanda hesitates. This was Aunt May's idea, but even after everything she's been through, Aunt May can be a little idealistic sometimes. Pietro is her brother, yes. He's also a superhuman who didn't think twice before using his powers for crime. She doesn't want to lead him to Aunt May's door.

That's why she says what she says next.

———

"I'M SORRY, YOU DID WHAT?"

It seemed like such a good idea at the time. Now, standing in front of her master and facing the consequences of her actions, Wanda isn't so sure. That's something she has in common with Peter: speaking before she thinks.

"I invited my brother to join us at the Sanctum for dinner," she says, meekly.

" 'Us' meaning . . . ?"

"You, me, Peter, and Aunt May."

"And we're doing this here rather than at your aunt's house, which is, I'm sure, what you had been authorized to extend the invitation for?"

"I didn't think it was a good idea to invite a superhuman I'd only just met to come to my aunt's house," she admits. "Aunt May doesn't have any powers. If he's not as trustworthy as he says he is, he could hurt her."

"Well, at least you have that much sense remaining," says Doctor Strange. He pinches the bridge of his nose. "When is this meal meant to take place?"

"Tomorrow night."

"I see. And he knows . . . ?"

"He knows you're my master, and the Sorcerer Supreme, and that he won't be able to get back in if he upsets you."

"Or if he upsets *you*, Apprentice. As you've already learned, I don't care if you claim someone as a sibling. If they fail to respect your position in this house, they will not be welcome here. Now or ever."

"I understand."

"And who's to handle the menu?"

"I will, Master. I don't spend half my time in a restaurant for nothing."

Doctor Strange looks at her, this young, idealistic, still hopeful woman he's taken as his responsibility, and he wants to thank Richards for the gift she's been and curse him at the same time, because it's been a long, long time since he's opened himself up enough for the potential harm he can see hurtling toward him, unstoppable and oncoming.

("I know how you feel," mutters America, alone in her stronghold, still watching. Always watching.)

"Very well," he says. "Tomorrow night. Don't make me regret this."

"I won't, Master," she says, relieved, and beams at him even as he turns and walks away.

CHAPTER NINETEEN

—

DINNER PARTY

DOCTOR STRANGE HAS TO ALLOW THAT THIS FARCE, POTENTIALLY disastrous as it is, may have been worth it just for the smells filling the house. Wanda spent the morning at Dosta, and came home with several sealed trays of already prepared food, which she added to the piles of groceries that have been the target of her ongoing preparations. Apparently, her second family is as excited by the idea that she might reunite with someone from her past as she is.

The air smells of spices and roasting meat, red wine and rich sauces, and baking bread above all else. It's a feast in every breath, and it will taste even better when it's spread across the table to be devoured. May Parker arrived an hour ago: She's in the kitchen with Wanda, the two of them cooking together, the process rendered easy and smooth by years of sharing space, juggling pans over limited burners, and chopping things on narrow counters. The size of the kitchen here at the Sanctum is a treat, he knows: Wanda's told him as much enough times, usually when she feels like he's being unappreciative of what he has.

He's the master here, but there are times when he feels like this house is as suited to her as it is to him, if not more so. She'll be here long after he's gone, and the thought is more comforting than anything else: He's leaving a legacy, a tradition of stability that his office has needed for some time, that he didn't know he was searching for until he had it.

There's a knock at the door, and he turns to answer it, walking the short distance rather than waving his hand and opening it from the other side of the room. Peter isn't impressed by him anymore, and he wants to loom at this new "brother" Wanda's gone and acquired. He's aware that most men dealing with women her age in a mentoring position are looming at boyfriends, not brothers, and he almost envies those men for the simplicity of the relationships they're navigating. Boyfriends can be chased off. Brothers, not so much, or not so easily, at the very least.

The door opens to reveal an anxious young man whose hair could use a visit from a brush, holding a bottle of sparkling apple juice the way most men would hold a bottle of wine. Doctor Strange sighs and steps back, waving him inside. "Peter."

"Sir." Peter Parker steps into the Sanctum Sanctorum. He wants to go exploring, to see how this strange old manse has changed while he's been persona non grata in its halls. Instead, he nods politely to the master of the house, and offers him the apple juice. "I brought cider."

"So I see. Your aunt and sister are in the kitchen, if you'd care to join them. I'll be there shortly."

Peter stands there awkwardly for a beat before he appears to realize Doctor Strange isn't going to take the cider. As he turns away, he glances back and asks, "Waiting for Pietro?"

Doctor Strange nods. "Indeed."

"You know, 'Pietro' has the same root meaning as 'Peter.' Isn't it sort of funny that we have the same name?"

Doctor Strange looks at him without blinking, that steady, unwavering gaze that always makes Peter feel about two feet tall. He refuses to allow himself to look away.

Finally, after far too long, Doctor Strange gives a grudging nod. "We may never know where Wanda's power originated, but the chaos has been with her as long as she's been alive—it only needed time to mature before she could begin using it to her own ends. I believe she may have been bending probabilities longer than any of us could know for certain."

"So, what, you think she was always supposed to have a brother named Peter, and she just bent the luck until it gave her one?"

"Stranger things have happened, says the sorcerer to the hero with the proportionate strength and speed of a spider."

Peter pauses again. "Did you just make a joke?"

"I'll never admit it if I did. Now go. I'm tired of you."

Chuckling under his breath, Peter walks away.

Doctor Strange resumes his wait.

About fifteen minutes later, there's another knock, and again, Doctor Strange moves to answer the door by hand. He doesn't know why, exactly, but he doesn't want to show this stranger the extent of his power—and that includes the little parlor tricks he barely notices anymore. There are times for bold displays of power, and times to play one's cards close to the chest, hidden from all who don't yet need to see them. This is one of those times.

This time, the man on the doorstep is unfamiliar, although he carries a ghost of Wanda in the shape of his face, the slope of his shoulders, even the angle of his limbs. They could never have been identical, but he wonders if they realize how similar they are, differences in coloration and gender notwithstanding. The man has white hair, blue eyes, and empty hands. He's wearing street clothes, at least—based on Wanda's descriptions, Doctor Strange had been more than half afraid he wouldn't understand discretion, would show up in spandex. Instead, he wears brown slacks, a gray hoodie, and a blue windbreaker. He could blend into any crowd.

"Welcome," says Doctor Strange. "You are . . . ?"

"Pietro von Doom," says the man. "My sister invited me here for dinner."

"I am the master of this house, Doctor Stephen Strange. You may call me 'Doctor' or 'Doctor Strange,' as you prefer." Doctor Strange steps to the side to let him pass. "Enter freely, as you mean no harm."

Pietro looks unimpressed but unsurprised by this archaic greeting, as befits someone who, by name, grew up in the care of Victor von Doom. The man may not have Doctor Strange's mastery of the mystic arts, but few do, and he's more than just a dabbler—anyone raised in Doom's house would understand the importance of ritual and hospitality. Although not, it seems, the value of bringing a guest gift; in that regard, Aunt May's tutelage has already proven superior.

Pietro steps inside. Doctor Strange shuts the door, and Pietro pales, feeling the shift in the air around him, the way it slows and stills, becoming a contained thing: This is the territory of the Sorcerer Supreme, and he has no power here.

"This way," says Doctor Strange, and gestures for the unsure speedster to follow as he walks through the foyer, toward the dining room.

They don't often take their meals in such a formal setting. It's too large by half for just himself and Wanda, much less for him alone; but as this night is an event of some occasion, it seemed petty to make his apprentice host her family at the kitchen table. The dining room table is a long expanse of polished oak, lit from above by hanging chandeliers and from the side by a roaring fireplace, its light orange and red and dancing over the cutlery and waiting plates. Half the food has been moved into place, and as they arrive, Wanda and Aunt May emerge from the kitchen door with additional trays, Peter following with a basket of rolls and what looks like an entire roast leg of lamb, which he holds carelessly with one hand as if it weighs nothing at all.

Doctor Strange has seen Peter throw a car. The lamb is effectively weightless in comparison.

"Pietro!" exclaims Wanda, putting her dishes down on the table and beaming at him. Then she pauses, blinks, and looks at the food, suddenly abashed. "I'm sorry. I cook when I get nervous, sometimes, and I was really nervous today. Me, nerves, and a full kitchen, not the best combination."

"It smells amazing," blurts Pietro, and Doctor Strange warms to him, just a fraction. "Did you do this all by yourself?"

"Oh, no," says Wanda. "My aunt May helped a lot, and I picked up some things from the restaurant where I work before I came over. Aunt May, this is my biological brother, Pietro."

"It's a pleasure to meet you, young man, and I hope you realize any family of Wanda's is family of mine," says Aunt May.

Doctor Strange doesn't think she catches the way the corners of Pietro's eyes tighten when she says that, like he doesn't appreciate her offering him that connection. "Charmed, I'm sure," says Pietro, and bows lightly at the waist, one hand tucked against the opposite hip, the other bent behind his back. It's courtly and old-fashioned and so very Latverian. The hidden hand could hold anything, could be preparing an attack from close range.

Still, Aunt May looks delighted by the show of manners, smiling at Pietro as she sets her dishes on the table. "I'll be right back, dears," she says, and kisses Wanda on the cheek before she vanishes into the kitchen once again.

Peter hasn't said a word. His silence is uncharacteristic enough to be notable. When Doctor Strange looks at him, he's eyeing Pietro like a leashed dog confronted with another canine. He looks a little unsure, a little confused, like he somehow thought this moment wouldn't actually arrive, like Wanda's newfound brother would forever remain hypothetical and out of reach.

Pietro is the one to break the silence. He looks Peter languidly up and down before he asks, "The American brother, I presume?"

"I'm sorry," says Wanda. "Pietro, this is Peter, my adoptive brother. Peter, this is Pietro, my biological brother."

"Nice to meet you," lies Peter.

"Likewise," lies Pietro in return.

Doctor Strange manages to resist the urge to roll his eyes.

———

NOT LONG AFTER, THEY'RE ALL SEATED, FILLING THEIR PLATES. THERE was no possible way to seat everyone without making someone uncomfortable, and so they gave up trying after a few seconds of staring at the chairs like they were some sort of ridiculous logic puzzle. Peter and Aunt May are on one side of the table, Pietro and

Wanda at the other, with Doctor Strange at the head of the table, close enough to knock the two younger men's heads together if he feels the need.

"Where did you learn to cook sarmi?" asks Pietro, moving several stuffed cabbage rolls onto his plate. "It smells amazing."

"Aunt May wanted me to get in touch with my heritage once I was old enough to understand what 'adopted' meant, and that I had ancestors in a part of the world that I didn't share with her and Peter," she says. "She found a restaurant owned by a Romani family, and she convinced them to let me study there, to learn the cuisine and the language, so I'd have a better idea of where I came from."

"She treated you like a scullery in your own home?"

Wanda blinks. "Oh, no, not at all. I didn't cook at home hardly at all, and the cooking lessons were so wrapped up in my language lessons that they felt like the same thing. For a long time, I couldn't remember my verb tenses unless I was making risotto while I did it. I wanted to cook more than they let me."

"I don't have a great stomach for strong spices," says Peter. "Wandy has always impressed me, but I couldn't always eat the results."

"I see," says Pietro, suspiciously.

"We had chores," says Wanda, missing the thrust of his suspicions. "I did the dusting and the dishes most days, and Peter would do the mowing and take out the trash, until we both turned twelve and confronted Uncle Ben about the sexist divisions of household labor. After that, we took turns doing whatever needed to be done."

"Uncle Ben?" Pietro looks around, as if he thinks they might have somehow hidden a sixth body from him.

"He passed several years ago," says Aunt May, reaching for a piece of bread. "It was very tragic, and we still miss him very much."

"I think we always will," says Wanda. "My adoptive parents died when we were very little. Aunt May and Uncle Ben basically raised us."

"If the people who adopted you died, why were you not returned to Latveria?" asks Pietro.

"We didn't know she had any family there to go back *to*," says Aunt May. "And even if we had, we were all the family she'd ever known, and she'd just lost her parents. She and Peter were both distraught. Splitting them up wouldn't have made things any better, and could have made them quite a bit worse."

Pietro scowls and looks at his plate, stabbing a bit of rabbit stew with his fork.

"I really have been happy here, Pietro," says Wanda. "How about you. Tell us what it was like to grow up in Latveria."

"I don't need your charity," growls Pietro. Wanda shies away, looking startled.

"I wasn't . . . I just want to *know*. I didn't get to grow up there, so I want to know what it was like."

Pietro is quiet for a long moment, still looking at his plate. Then, haltingly, he says, "Our parents were dead and my sister was gone, stolen across the sea by people who didn't speak our language or understand our ways. I was found by a footman of the king, traveling on official business, and he took pity on me, carrying me with him to the palace, where our beloved monarch claimed me as his own. I was raised in the palace halls, given access to the finest tutors Latveria had to offer—and when those were insufficient, the finest tutors in the *world*. I wanted for nothing, but there was a void in my life, one that had always been there, as far back as I could remember. When I was seven I went before the king my father and asked him why I ached so, what I was yearning for. He told me then that I had had a sister, once, born of my mother, and lost to us before I had come to him. As soon as he said that, I knew what was missing, and what I had to find. I began my search immediately. All I've done since then has been bent toward the goal of one day bringing you home."

"I must wonder," says Doctor Strange, tone carefully neutral. "How did he know she existed, if you were a foundling without a name or family when you came to him? How, if he hadn't been aware of the circumstances of your sister's adoption before that?"

Pietro says nothing, only stabs his stew again, skewering a bit of meat. Doctor Strange frowns. The silence is allowed to hang for several seconds, but Pietro offers no answers.

"I'm sorry you felt like that," says Wanda.

"I suppose you didn't," says Pietro, and he makes no effort to hide the bitterness in his voice, to soften his tone in the slightest. "I suppose you never knew anything was missing."

"I'm sorry, but no," says Wanda. She sounds genuinely regretful. "I wasn't lonely. I didn't have *time* to be lonely. I had Peter, and my aunt and uncle, and my classes, and my life was always very full. I wish you'd been in it, but I didn't know to miss you, so I never knew you were gone."

"I see," says Pietro, and stands, shoving his chair back with a scrape of the legs against the floor. "Thank you for your hospitality, Doctor Strange. You have honored your household, and I will carry word of your reception to my father. Everything was delicious. May, it was a joy to meet you. Wanda, as you have so precisely replaced me, I will not trouble you again."

Then he's gone, racing out of the room at a speed that none of them can follow. The front door slams less than a second later, and Doctor Strange sighs, making a gesture in the air.

"Our guest has gone; the wards are sealed," he says. "He won't be back unless invited."

Wanda looks like she's about to protest. He quells her with a glance.

"No," he says. "I know he's your brother, but no. He won't come and go as he pleases, not until we know him better. He can ring the bell like any other uninvited guest."

Wanda sags, looking down at her still full plate, and sighs heavily. "I hoped that would go better," she says. "Did I do something wrong?"

"You weren't miserable," says Aunt May, voice gone cold. Wanda and Peter both glance at her. "You were too young to remember, but when you were both little, we went to a few playdates with children from your nursery whose parents thought it was such a shame that poor Peter would never have a 'real' sister, that Wanda would never have a 'real' family. They were sure you must both be uncomfortable, because we were forcing you together when you weren't meant to be. Some of them even implied that when you got older, we'd have to send Wanda away or there would be problems, because Peter would never really be able to see her as a sister."

She stops talking, reaches for her glass, and takes a long drink, ignoring the horrified way the siblings are looking at her, the disgusted expressions on their faces. Wanda and Peter exchange a glance.

"Ew," they say, in unison.

It's a childish, sincere sound, and Doctor Strange laughs, bright and oddly merry in the doleful atmosphere of the room. Aunt May looks at him and smiles, and then she's laughing, too, and it's just Peter and Wanda looking disgusted and unhappy.

Peter looks at Wanda across the table. "I'm sorry that didn't go the way you wanted it to."

She shrugs. "You didn't do anything wrong, and neither did I. I feel like he came tonight already primed to be upset because I didn't immediately ask him to take me back to Latveria to live in a palace and never think about America again."

"I can still be sorry."

"You can." She smiles at him, almost shyly, and says, "I think you're the brother I was supposed to have, and that's why everything worked out the way it did."

"You think so?"

"I do. Besides, you're useless without a sister to show off for and tell you what to do, and how else were you going to get one?"

"Don't look at me," says Aunt May, still laughing. "I was never planning on motherhood. You two were a very sideways surprise."

"There's still so much food," says Wanda, sadly. "I don't think we can ever eat all this."

"Why don't we put away enough for dinner tomorrow, and pack the rest up to take to the soup kitchen where I volunteer?"

asks Aunt May. "They know me, they'll accept home-cooked food from me, and that way you know it won't go to waste."

"I shall accompany you," says Doctor Strange ponderously. "It's a nice evening for an outing."

Wanda and Peter exchange a look, too startled to say anything.

———

THERE ARE ENOUGH TAKEAWAY TRAYS FROM THE RESTAURANT TO pack everything up, and a little judicious manipulation of space from Doctor Strange sees them packed into a single cooler too heavy for any of them but Peter to lift. He hoists it like it's nothing, making Aunt May smile and Wanda mutter about showing off. But she's smiling, too, as she and Doctor Strange step into a circle of salt and semiprecious stones, moving through a ritual they both know by heart. They pause when they're halfway through, gesturing for Peter and Aunt May to join them in the circle, and after a momentary hesitation, they do.

There is a flash of mingled red and orange magic, Wanda and Doctor Strange working in concert, and the four of them are standing in the dark living room of the house in Queens. Aunt May squeaks, clapping her hands over her mouth. Peter shoots Wanda a look. "And you call me a show-off."

"I can only manage myself without help," she says.

"This seemed a faster way to transport the food and prevent Pietro following us back to the house if he's lurking around outside and feeling uncharitable," says Doctor Strange.

Wanda frowns and looks away, not liking the easy assumption of Pietro's villainy any more than she liked it when people were assuming it of her. But she doesn't protest, and more than anything, that says he made the right decision. She doesn't want to think quite that ill of her brother, but she doesn't argue; she can see the value of doing it this way.

Doctor Strange doesn't comment on her discomfort, instead focusing on Aunt May. "Ms. Parker, if you would lead us to the soup kitchen?"

"Of course," says Aunt May, lowering her hands and gesturing for the rest to follow her.

Wanda falls into step with the others, and as a group, they exit the house and walk down the street to the train station. They only have to go two stops, but the sight of Doctor Strange on a subway is something Wanda won't soon forget.

The soup kitchen is delighted by their large offering of fresh, homemade food, and they find themselves pressed into helping with service, standing side by side with the volunteers who were already on duty for the evening. Doctor Strange maintains a stern but non-judgmental expression the entire time, like a college professor collecting papers from his students; the woman currently in charge pauses to tell Aunt May she can bring him anytime, as that sort of unblinking, unvarying calm is very soothing to some of their regulars.

Wanda is pleased when some of the people, upon receiving their first serving of something unusually spicy, brighten and come back to ask for seconds. As those are the dishes some others won't touch at all, there's plenty to go around. By the time the food runs out, everyone is content and full, and they gather their trays in preparation for the trip to Aunt May's house.

Peter and Wanda walk side by side as they trail back to the subway, their shoulders almost brushing. "I'm glad you're my sister," says Peter.

"Me too," Wanda replies.

Doctor Strange teleports himself home as soon as he's said good night to Aunt May. Peter changes into his costume, and Spider-Man loops his arm around Wanda's waist before the two of them step off the roof and swing away into the night, and everything is peaceful and everything is calm and everything is exactly as it should be.

(America can imagine an entire future from this moment, a version of the world where everything goes perfectly and just as it should: one where Spider-Man and the Scarlet Witch become the foremost heroes of their generation, fighting side by side against threats both physical and mystical, never backing down, never giving up on what's right and necessary.

She can imagine it. She just can't see it.

Because in the end, that's not what happens.)

CHAPTER TWENTY

———

INTERFERENCE

THE NEXT FEW WEEKS ARE A BLUR OF CLASSES AND PATROL. WANDA and Peter rediscover the groove of patrolling together, and before long, it's like they never stopped. Her ability to fly makes it easier on both of them, as does her master's willingness to let her grapple with minor super villains. She's not restricted to muggers anymore. The papers still don't quite believe she's on the side of good, but their articles begin to take on a less negative tone—all save *The Daily Bugle*, which treats her affiliation with Spider-Man as proof of her villainy. Wanda doesn't mind so much, until Jonah writes an article accusing her of seducing Spider-Man to the side of evil. She minds that a *lot*.

Sisters aren't that uncommon, and so they solve the Jonah Jameson problem by having Spider-Man web a large sign to the front doors of the paper, that reads:

SHE'S MY SISTER, YOU DOOFUS!

That changes the tenor of the articles the papers run about the two of them together. Wanda hadn't realized how much it bothered her that so many people were trying to spin their association as a "will they or won't they" sort of thing until it stopped, but now that it has, she's not even worried about handing out another clue to her secret identity.

They're returning to a rooftop after busting a bank robbery when a low buzz rattles her eardrums, and Pietro appears in front of them. She doesn't question how he got up there without flight: He's fast enough that she's fairly sure he can run right up walls.

He stands there, sneering at them both, supercilious and cold. She smiles as she turns to face him. "Pietro! I haven't seen you in weeks! How are you?"

"Did you really think it would be that easy to replace me?" Pietro asks. It isn't a demand; it's a calm, mild question, voiced in the same tone he would use to ask if she wanted something to drink, or if she needed to put on a sweater. Wanda still stiffens. Something about the way he's holding himself is alarming, no matter how calm he sounds.

"What do you mean?"

"I mean, we've barely met and here you are announcing your relation to another man in the local papers! Claiming him publicly, when you've never afforded me the same courtesy!" His calm breaks, replaced by a raw and obvious ache that she almost but not quite recognizes as a cousin to her own. How she hurt during the days when she thought her brother had rejected her, how she grieved for the life she'd always assumed they would have.

She and Pietro haven't known each other half as long as she and Peter have, but in his own way, he's grieving the same loss. So she forces her tone to stay as steady, and says, "We only did it because the editor of one paper was trying to imply that we were sleeping together, and it was too gross not to respond to. If you want to start patrolling with us, we can tell them about you, too."

"We'd be happy to have you," says Peter.

"A family team-up," says Wanda.

"I refuse to be second-best in the terrible little drama that is your life," says Pietro, with absolute chill. He looks to Peter. "And I refuse to be replaced."

Wanda has no warning before Pietro moves. Peter, with his spider-sense, does, and leaps into the air as the speedster rushes through the space where he was standing, a blur that resolves into sudden, furious stillness.

Pietro looks up at where Peter sticks to the wall. His hands are balled into fists; his tone is no longer calm. "Come down here and face me like a man!" he snaps. "Show some courage, coward!"

"One, not a coward. Two, actually passed physics. At your speed, a solid blow could put me in the hospital—you'd kill some-one non-enhanced. So no. I'm not coming down there to let you hit me and break half my ribs. You're going to have to learn to live with disappointment."

Pietro turns. That he does so slowly enough for Wanda to see him move means he's doing so deliberately: He *wants* to be seen. The look he gives her is dangerous, cold, and terrified. He's afraid of something. It doesn't feel like he's afraid of *her*. What could he possibly have to be afraid of?

"If I am not to have a sister, so be it," he says. "But I won't carry the blame for failing to bring a daughter of Latveria home. I'm not the only one who wants to see your smiling face in the palace halls, phen." He spits the Romany word for "sister" with such venom that it very nearly becomes an insult. The fear is still there, layered thick, and it's the fear that makes him dangerous. A frightened ani-mal will bite, every time.

Wanda's hands are up before he finishes speaking, but even that isn't fast enough, could never be fast enough; he slams into her with the speed of a freight train, one arm wrapping around her wrist and jerking her off her feet. She's never moved this fast in her life. It's so fast that the *air* hurts, cutting at her lips and eyes like it's become somehow solid and bladed, and still Pietro is running, Pietro isn't slowing down.

He's saying something, but she can't understand it, his words consumed by the blurred sound of the world around them and the impossible speed with which he speaks.

"Put me *down*!" she snarls, kicking against him, and it's only when he lets go that she realizes she's made a mistake, because she's flying, hard and fast, toward the ground.

In the instant between release and impact, she finishes the mo-tion she started before she was grabbed, and then she's falling into the red, down into the chaos, momentum bleeding away in this place where physics is hers to toy with and command. She falls until she no longer feels like she's falling, and then she tumbles out of the red and onto the roof where she left Spider-Man only a few seconds ago.

He rushes to her side as soon as she finishes rolling across the roof, helping her into a sitting position and checking her over for injuries.

"I'm so sorry," he says. "I should have realized he was going to go for you next, I should have seen—I'm just so sorry, Wanda, you didn't deserve that."

"No, but it's over now, and he's not going to do that again. I won't let him." Wanda looks at Spider-Man, pushing herself back to her feet and dusting off her costume with a few quick brushes of her hand. "For right now, take me home. I think I'm through patrolling for the night."

Spider-Man nods, and if anything, he looks relieved. Pietro can't access the Sanctum without Doctor Strange allowing him—and that's not going to happen.

They swing back to the Sanctum in silence, and if they embrace a little longer than usual before Spider-Man reluctantly lets go and swings away, neither of them can really be blamed.

——

IT'S EARLY THE NEXT AFTERNOON WHEN DOCTOR STRANGE COMES TO find Wanda in the orangerie. She's gathering fruit from the grass beneath the pomegranate tree, brushing them off and placing them carefully in the basket she has waiting for the crop. "Apprentice."

"Sir?" She doesn't drop the fruit she's holding, but straightens as she turns to face him, already attentive. She doesn't have class today, either college or private work with her master, and so this is a rare intrusion, a possible opportunity for more learning . . . or a sign that she's done something wrong and is about to receive a reprimand.

"Walk with me."

He turns and strides away, cape billowing behind him. Wanda

drops the pomegranate into the basket and chases after him, eager to catch up.

When she falls into step beside him, he glances at her, the way she carries herself. She has always paid him the deference owed to a master, but she grows more confident by the day and year. She could study under him for another decade or more, and still not learn everything he knows, but he begins to feel that she could learn even more if she did her studies out in the world, on her own. Their time today, precious as it has been, is ending.

"I have been looking toward your future, Apprentice."

"My future, sir?"

"You can't be an apprentice forever."

"Can't I?" Wanda sounds alarmed. He glances at her again, trying to read her concern in her face. "I'm not ready to stop studying. Not until I finish college at the absolute least."

"Are you saying you know better than I do?"

"No, sir! I just . . ." She stumbles, hesitates. If she contradicts her master, she's a bad student; if she doesn't, she may no longer be a student at all. The dilemma is clear. She looks at him, pleading for him to understand. "I don't want to go."

"And I won't force you. No matter what changes between us, you will always have been my student, and I will always have been your master. But life marches on, and things can't continue as they are forever."

"So what do you want me to do?"

"I've been speaking to the Avengers."

Wanda stops walking as she stares at him. He continues for a few more steps, then stops and turns around to look at her.

"Captain America remembers you fondly, and the Black Knight has put in a good word for you," he says, as smoothly as if there had been no pause. "The captain is very interested in meeting with you. He thinks you could be an asset to the team."

"Asset?"

"Yes. They don't currently have anyone with remotely your power set, and as you've been getting more and more control over your abilities, you've been making yourself more and more valuable. The fact that you've reconciled with Spider-Man only gilds the lily."

"Wait, are they willing to talk to me because they think it'll help them recruit Peter? Because he doesn't want to join a team—and he doesn't need to, his powers mean he can solo this city as much as he wants. And if they only want to talk to me because they're hoping to get him, I don't want to have anything to do with them. I'm not a path to Peter."

"No, they know your brother isn't going to join up just because you do, although there's some natural hope that he might be willing to consider an auxiliary position if it would mean working with you more. They want you for what you can bring to the table. They want the Scarlet Witch. Are you willing to speak with Captain America?"

Wanda's mouth is dry and her palms are damp, anxiety bleeding out every pore. Is she willing to meet with the face of America, the man who stands for the country that took her in and raised her to be a hero in her own right? Is she ready to step out of the safe shelter of her master's care and stand on her own two feet?

"I . . . can," she says.

And Doctor Strange smiles.

———

"THE AVENGERS? REALLY?"

"I told them you weren't going to join up just because they recruited me."

Spider-Man sticks to the side of the wall as they talk, sitting cross-legged and leaning back on his hands. He looks perfectly comfortable that way, and Wanda resents, just a little, that she can't treat gravity that much like a suggestion, or a toy.

She's sitting on the edge of the roof with her hands between her knees and her cape snapping gently in the breeze, attention fixed on her brother. They're both masked; they were on patrol when they took a break to talk, and Wanda decided to tell him what was going on.

"They've been trying to get me for ages," he says, and for a moment, Wanda's afraid he's going to make this moment all about himself. Then he grins behind his mask, and says, "I'm glad they've finally seen sense about which one of us they should be focusing on. Oh, Wandy, this is *amazing*! You're gonna be such a good Avenger!"

"I *told* them getting me didn't mean getting you," she says again. "I love you, but I don't want to work with you, we would drive each other crazy."

"Exactly." He sounds annoyingly relieved, and still excited on her behalf. "But if you want to, you absolutely should. I think it would be good for you."

"Good for me? How's that?"

"You've always been good at group projects, and being on a super team is sort of like a group project. You know Jewel? She went by Jessica when we were kids—Jessica Jones. Well, she says they take turns cooking for the whole team. You can make them your world-famous spaghetti and scorch all the skin off their tongues."

"My spaghetti is delicious, you just have the spice tolerance of a toddler!"

"Your spaghetti is an act of biological warfare!"

"Are you seriously proposing I commit an act of biological warfare against *Captain America*?"

Spider-Man is laughing, and she's laughing, and the night is bright and clear and she's going to do it. She's going to go to the Avengers, and talk to Captain America, and see if she can find a place with the team. She's going to step out of the shadows, and try.

CHAPTER TWENTY-ONE

CRIME SCENE

THE NEXT DAY, DOCTOR STEPHEN STRANGE AND WANDA PARKER appear outside the Avengers Manor in a swirl of mixed red and orange power. He stands behind her, his cloak billowing out to form the shape of a half-broken sphere, sheltering them both. Then the magic fades and his cloak drops back to a flat, unmoving piece of fabric.

"This is where I leave you," he says.

Wanda looks up at him, afraid. "What?" she squeaks.

"This is your meeting. Your . . . job interview, if you will. Most people don't bring their masters with them when they interview for a new position. I'll be at the Sanctum when you're through."

He steps back and then he's gone, the swirl of power that carries him away orange with no trace of red. Wanda stares for a long moment before she turns again, looking back at the manor.

It's larger than the Sanctum, at least from the outside. She's sure it has a fixed number of rooms that never change, a floor plan that remains steady from day to day, a staff made mostly of flesh and blood, not summoned spirits. Still, it feels enough like the place she's come to think of as home that she's able to take the first steps toward the door, and once she's taken the first steps, the next ones come more easily.

Soon, she's at the front door. She rings the bell before she notices that it's standing slightly ajar, cracked just enough to let a little wind blow through. She pauses before pushing it open. According to her master, Jarvis, whoever that is, is supposed to meet her and take her to Captain America. She wants to stand on ceremony. She wants to wait.

She can't. Curiosity wins out, and she nudges the door, sending it swinging wide to reveal the foyer beyond. It's a large room, impressive, but not grandiose the way the Sanctum is grandiose. It's not even as ridiculous as the X-Mansion. Those little comparisons carry her over the threshold, and she's inside, she's in the Avengers Manor.

Alone. "Hello?" she calls. "Is anyone here?"

There's no response, and so she begins making her way deeper into the manor, pausing every few feet to call again, hoping that someone will come to break the stillness. No one does, and when she sees an open doorway to her right, she hurries a little, rushing to get there.

"Hello? Is anyone . . ."

The sentence dies half-formed as she stares at the room in front of her in silent, wide-eyed shock, the ghosts of her unspoken words still clinging to her lips. Captain America's body is slumped in a leather armchair, his throat a shredded ruin of torn flesh and broken skin. Blood drips down his arm, running along the length of his fingers before falling to join the puddle forming on the floor.

He can't have been dead for long. His skin is still flushed, not waxen and white, and while she's not getting close enough to touch him, there's a certain visible stiffness to people who've been dead for more than an hour. She's seen it more times than she likes to consider, and he doesn't have it.

A key turns in a lock somewhere behind her, and the door opens, and then the Avengers are crowding into the doorway, all of them, staring and yelling as the enormity of the scene in front of them begins sinking in.

"Murderer," says Jewel, and the frozen moment shatters, the Avengers pouring into the room to take up positions around her, ready to stop her from escaping.

Wanda grabs the chaos more fiercely than she ever has before, filling her hands, and yanks it down around herself, painting the world with red. She falls into the dark of the space that belongs only to her, plummeting through frozen sheets of memory, dropping down, down, down what feels like forever, Alice lost in the rabbit hole, Wanda lost in the chaotic, ever-expanding dark.

And then she slams into the Sanctum floor, too panicked and distraught to have controlled her descent in any meaningful way, and curls into a ball, and cries. She cries like her heart is broken, like she's dying, and she continues crying as her master rushes out of the depths of the house to gather her close. Her uncontrolled teleportation brought her here because this is where she has always been safe: even above the house in Queens where she grew up, where she was happy, but where her uncle died and where she learned she was an orphan twice over. The house in Queens is not safe. The Sanctum is safe.

She tells him what has happened, and he's dismayed, but not as dismayed as he might have been had she been in possession of more control over her descent: He already knows some of the situation, knows Captain America is dead, knows the other Avengers are searching for her in connection with his murder. She fell for a lot longer than she realized. She feels like she's still falling now.

And then there is someone at the door, the front door, and she knows, down to the bottom of her, that the Avengers have come for her. Everyone knows she's Doctor Strange's apprentice: Where else would she run if she did something as terrible as what she's been accused of?

But no, it's Peter, her Peter, and he knows she didn't do this, and he's going to defend her. He's going to help her get away from all this. He can't bring Captain America back, but he can protect her. He can. Peter says something. Her master replies, the two of them trading words, mistrustful and cold, and this is wrong. This is *wrong*. They already got past this; they apologized, she knows they apologized, she knows Peter is on her side again.

Unless that was all a chaos dream, and he's here to hurt her. She doesn't know, and that's the worst part of all.

Doctor Strange steps out of the doorway, making his invitation clear. "Yes, Spider-Man, the Scarlet Witch, my apprentice, is safe where she belongs; you may enter, if you intend her no harm."

Wanda relaxes a little. If their rapprochement was a dream, her master wouldn't be letting Peter into the Sanctum.

She picks herself up from the cloakroom floor as Spider-Man is darting through the door and looking frantically around. Doctor Strange sighs, closing the door and turning to watch the young man search the foyer. Young things have no patience. It would be more annoying if it weren't so universal, but as things stand, it's deeply frustrating.

"Wanda," he calls. "You have a visitor."

Wanda bites her lip, grappling with the need to go to Peter and the screaming sense of danger in her blood, before she takes a breath and emerges from the cloakroom, pale and shaking but present, no red sparks in her eyes or around her hands.

"Hi," she manages, voice barely a whisper.

Gravity means very little to Spider-Man: Somehow the proportionate strength and speed of a spider includes jumping twenty feet across the foyer to pull Wanda into a tight embrace, which she returns with a gasping, grateful sob, clinging to him like he's the only lifeline remaining in the world. He holds her in much the same way, and Doctor Strange looks away, not wanting to intrude. He can't let them have this for long. They have much to worry about, and even more to prepare for. But experience has taught him that getting between the two when they're not ready for it never ends the way any of them would like.

Wanda pulls back, crying again, and gestures at the mask that covers Peter's face with one hand. "I can't see . . . please, let me . . ."

"I'm sorry." Peter pulls back in turn, and pulls his mask off. His hair sticks up in all directions, and the tear tracks on his own cheeks are glaringly obvious. "I know you don't like it when you can't see my face. But secret identities work better with a mask. What happened? Are you hurt? I ran into the Black Knight, and he wouldn't tell me what was going on, just that he was looking for you. *All* the Avengers are looking for you. Wanda—"

"Captain America is dead." It seems strange to say it so bluntly, like it's just another fact. Snow is cold, water is wet, and Captain America is dead.

Peter recoils, shocked and distressed. Wanda doesn't flinch. She knows her brother better than anyone in the world; some days she thinks she might know him better than she knows herself. She doesn't see any blame in his eyes, no recrimination, no fear. He doesn't think she did this. No; he *knows* she didn't do it, because he knows her, and he's the only person in the world who would never question whether or not she was capable of such a thing.

Let everyone else there is think she's a villain, she'll still have her brother by her side.

"Your sister is wanted for questioning in relation to the murder of Steven Rogers, otherwise known as Captain America," says Doctor Strange, words almost serene. "It's a terrible thing, what she's accused of, and yet it's no surprise. If anything, this should be a relief."

"A relief?" demands Peter. "How?"

"Death has always surrounded Wanda, all the way back to the very beginning," he says. "Where she walks, death follows. It was going to catch up to her soon enough, and now that it has, we can face it together." He glances to Wanda, and his expression is complicated, concerned mentor and caring father figure and close friend all at the same time. "She doesn't have to do it alone."

(America flinches at the simple truth of the sorcerer's words. He's right, of course; he knows what he invited into his home when he agreed to teach Wanda to control her powers. He doesn't know how pivotal the changes to this world's version of Wanda have been to his very reality, but the rest . . . he knows. He's had plenty of time to sample and study her chaos, and he probably understands her magic as well as Peter understands her heart. Worse yet, Peter and Wanda both know that; they won't question him.

He's right, and he's also wrong. *Where her feet fall, the world blooms.*)

"It might be best if we get away from the windows," says Doctor Strange, and so they make their way through the Sanctum to the kitchen, scene of so many good memories, the door to the dining room firmly closed to keep its less pleasant memories at bay. They sit at the kitchen table; Peter gets some day-old cookies from the jar, and Doctor Strange makes cocoa, and it would feel normal, even cozy, if not for the storm she knows is raging outside.

Captain America is an icon. He's beloved of what sometimes feels like the entire superhuman community—even some of the villains look up to the man. He was the first of them and he's the best of them, the beginning of an era that's still unfolding, finding its shape and footing. And now he's dead, and it looks like she did it, and no one's going to believe she didn't, not even if Xavier goes into her head and proclaims her innocence. Anti-mutant prejudices run too deep, and she's too well-known as a sympathizer; there will be people who think Xavier is lying on her behalf, and the rumors will keep going. As long as one person thinks this was her doing, she won't be safe.

Just a day ago, she and her master were discussing the fact that she would eventually have to leave the Sanctum: can't be an apprentice forever. Now it feels like she'll never be able to leave, like she's going to live and die here, because no place else will ever be safe for her, not for very long. She'll be a fugitive her whole life. She'll never be a hero again. She'll—

Peter's hand on her wrist pulls her out of the spiral she was tumbling into, and she snaps back to the table, to the people she trusts to protect her even when the rest of the world refuses. She looks at them and sighs deeply. She can't let herself devolve into fear when they still believe in her, when they still need her. It wouldn't be fair to repay the trust they've invested in her with that kind of cowardice.

"What do we do now?" asks Wanda.

"We can't go straight to the Avengers, they'll never believe you," says Peter. "Part of that's on me—if we hadn't been fighting for so long, they might have fewer questions about your allegiances, but it doesn't matter whose fault it is when it's real and true and something we'll have to work around. I think we start with the question of who knew you were going to be there today. Were you actively set up, or were you just in the wrong place at the wrong time?"

"I . . . didn't tell anyone," says Wanda, slowly. "Meggan and I were supposed to have lunch on Friday, and I was going to tell her then how the meeting went, but I didn't tell her it was coming. You knew, and my master knew, and Captain America knew, but that's all I'm sure of."

"If Captain America knew, we can assume some of the other Avengers may have known," says Doctor Strange. "Jarvis would certainly have known, but the rest of the team—I can't be sure he told them without asking. I could call the Black Knight, but . . ."

"If you call while I'm here, you're leading them to me," says Wanda. "Dane might be able to get past the wards. He's been allowed access often enough that we can't be sure they'd bar him."

"What if you went somewhere else?" asks Peter. "You could do your teleporty thing and go someplace safe, so even if he does show up to search the place, you won't be here for him to find."

"I'm not going back to the house," says Wanda. "If there's *any* chance they have a way of finding me, I'm not putting Aunt May at risk."

"I don't believe they can track you when you move through chaos, or they would already be at our door," says Doctor Strange. "Still, I support not putting May in danger. She is a very dear woman, and she deserves better than to have the forces of good led to her door to seize her child."

Wanda frowns. "I can go to the restaurant," she suggests.

"What?"

"Master, you need to contact the Black Knight. Knowing how many people could have used this as an opportunity to hurt me tells us the shape of the crime, and establishing that you're not sheltering me here makes us all safer. I want to be able to sleep at night without fear that Hawkeye will be shooting an exploding arrow through my window. Unless the wards block those, too?"

"Not specifically," says Doctor Strange. His tone implies that the wards *will* before he's finished adjusting them.

Wanda rises, putting her half-eaten cookie aside. "Call Dosta when you're done and it's safe for me to come home. Django will hide me. I don't have to tell him what he's hiding me from—he's Roma in America. He knows that sometimes a back room with an unmarked door is the greatest treasure we have."

"Remember to change into street clothes before you go," says Peter.

She looks at him witheringly. "I've consistently managed that much since I figured out how to use my powers, and you know it," she says. "I'll see you when it's safe."

She leaves the kitchen then, heading for the stairs.

In the end, she changes her clothes, and takes her wallet and her backpack, but nothing else. She still believes, truly, that she's coming back.

——

THE SCARLET WITCH IS A WANTED FUGITIVE, BUT WANDA PARKER IS an ordinary college student, and she reminds herself of that as she emerges from the underground station into the bright afternoon light, blinking in the sun. She teleported from the Sanctum directly into a sheltered alcove in the subway, startling the homeless man who had been sleeping there enough that he woke with a shout, forcing her to stagger back, mumbling swift apologies. Ten dollars of her pocket money was enough to calm him even more than the apologies, and now here she is, free and untroubled, on the streets of New York City.

She has never felt more exposed.

She walks quickly to the restaurant, forcing herself to stand up straight and keep her eyes off the pavement. Hurrying is nothing strange in Manhattan. Hurrying like you're trying to escape from something can be. She needs to look natural.

Then she's at the stairs, and heading for safety, for the familiar space that's been first a second and then a third home to her for so many years. Her heart grows lighter with every step, her breath coming more easily, because she knows she can stay here as long as she needs to. She knows Django won't ask any questions. Her family isn't here, but she'll still be protected.

But when she opens the door, she finds a diner seated near the window, where he has a perfect view of the street below. He's flirting with one of the waitresses, and the cadence of his voice is smooth and easy, although she only understands one word in three: He's speaking what sounds like Wallachian Romany with the confident ease of someone who's been raised to the tongue.

Wanda's lessons have been in Anglo-Romani, the dialect spoken by Django and his family, but not all the staff come from the same region, and it seems Pietro has unerringly found the ones who share his mother tongue. He winks flirtatiously at the woman, who giggles behind her hand, then waves his laden fork at Wanda, offering a cheerful greeting in the same language.

"I'm sorry," she says, as she approaches. "I don't speak that dialect. Hello, Pietro. What are you doing here?"

His expression folds inward, flirtatious charm becoming cold unhappiness. "Our shared tongue is one more thing this nation stole from you. You should speak it as beautifully as I do, should have learned it long before you learned this filthy English, but here you are, robbed of one more thing that was yours by right. How are you not furious?"

"Because I'm happy," she says. "And because I *do* speak Romany, just not that dialect. This country did its best to make sure I didn't lose track of where I came from, or who my ancestors were. It's not perfect, and my family's not perfect, but at least an effort was made. What are you *doing* here?"

"You already asked me that."

"Yeah, and you didn't answer, so I get to keep asking until you do. You really want that?"

Pietro frowns. "During our . . . ill-fated supper, I saw some of the takeaway bags from this place. Do not restaurants in America print their logos on bags as a form of advertising? That's how it works in Latveria. I saw the name, I liked the food, I sought out the place. Do these people know who you really are, sister? Do they know where you come from?"

"They know I was adopted as a baby, and they know my aunt brought me to them so I'd have some sense of my culture," she says.

"Ah, but I mean who you *really* are." His voice drops and he leans closer, trying to be subtle. "Do they know you're a princess of our kind? Do they know where you were last night?"

"You were adopted into royalty, I wasn't, and I don't tell them about every moment of my day," she snaps. "*Why* are you *here*? I thought I made it very clear that I was done humoring your nonsense. What do you want from me?"

"You need to come to Latveria with me, Wanda." The statement is blunt, and seemingly honest. He looks at her unflinchingly as he makes it. "My father insists on meeting you."

Again, Wanda hears the fear there and wonders what it means. She takes a deep breath, pinching the bridge of her nose before she says, "I *don't* want to. You were going to hurt my brother. You nearly hurt me. I don't trust you, Pietro, and you've given me no reason to. What could you possibly say to change my mind?"

"I want you to come home with me, back to Latveria. My father the king would be your father as well, if you allowed it. You belong there, not here. You should be a jewel of our homeland, not grit in the tread of America's booted foot. I want my sister. I want us to be the family we should always have been. The gaje like to accuse us of stealing children, to say we destroy beautiful things, but they stole you from me. They destroyed the childhood we would have shared with each other. They had no right to take you away from me."

"They weren't taking me away from you. No one knew you existed. They were taking me away from a situation where I would have been alone."

"And that justifies leaving *me* alone for all these years?"

"It does when no one knew that you existed! My adoption was *legal*, Pietro. There were *records*. If your father the king was that concerned about getting you in touch with me, he could have facilitated it a long, long time ago. He didn't because he knew there was nothing to facilitate. He knew I was a Parker, and I was never coming back to Latveria, not even for a brother I'd never had the chance to know! I'm sorry you feel like something was stolen from me, and I'm sorry you feel like I was stolen from you, but this is my home. This is where I belong."

Pietro flinches, and the hurt in his expression hurts her in turn. He's still her brother. Even if she doesn't want to go with him, he's still her brother. She hates seeing him so hurt, and so afraid.

"He didn't know until you were in the papers . . ."

Meaning the man she mostly knew as an enemy of the Fantastic Four hadn't started encouraging Pietro to seek reunion until he knew about her super-powers. Pietro's fear starts to make a little more sense.

"Even with the Avengers whispering your name to every open ear in this city, seeking for proof you killed their greatest hero? Come with me, Wanda. Come *home*. If you come home, you won't have any more blood on your hands, ever. You'll be free. You can thrive and blossom and become exactly who the world meant for you to be, before you were taken from us. You can have your life back. Your *real* life."

". . . the Avengers are looking for me?" Her voice comes out as barely more than a whisper, thin and broken and sad. She knew they were looking for her—she wouldn't be here if she didn't know—but she thought they were restricting their search to the super hero community. If they've already reached the rumor mill, this is worse than she thought.

Pietro nods. "They think you killed their captain. They think this is all on your head, and they may not know your real name now, but they'll learn it. They'll unmask you and your false 'brother,' and they'll have you both stand trial for crimes you never committed. Which means you'll have no defenses, because there *is* no defense when you're accused of a thing you didn't do. Come with me or no, your life here is over."

Wanda's head is spinning. She's not thinking about how hard she's worked to keep her extracurricular activities a secret: She's thinking about Aunt May, and how it will destroy her to see her children tried and punished for things they didn't do. She's thinking about how hard she's worked to make a name as a hero, to make up for her sometimes unnerving powers and the way they tend to influence the way people see her. She's thinking about her life, here, in this city, in these places.

She's thinking about what she could do in Latveria. About how she could experience the very places she's only seen through taped-up postcards. About how she—maybe even she *and* Pietro—could find out more about her birth parents. About how, possibly, the Scarlet Witch could help some other people for a little while.

She's thinking about her master, and how much she's going to miss him.

It might be good to lie low for a little while. So she looks Pietro in the eye and asks, hesitantly, "If I come with you, will you help me come back here when I'm ready? I'm not leaving forever. I don't think I can."

"Of course," says Pietro. He stands, offering her his hand and throwing money onto the table at the same time. The coins land on his plate, sinking into the sauce. He doesn't appear to notice. "Whatever you want, sister. You know I only want you to be happy."

She still hears the fear under his words, but it's lifting now, replaced by hope. That helps her to believe him. He may not like the world that raised her, but he sounds sincere when he says he wants her happy. Wanda reaches, cautiously, for his offered hand. As she does, Django emerges from the back; one of the waitstaff must have finally told him she was here. He approaches, a worried look on his face.

"Wanda, dearest, are you all right?" he asks. "Is this man bothering you?"

Pietro says something sharp in Romany. Django looks at him blankly, another victim of divergent dialects, and doesn't soften.

"I know you've had a hard day," he says. "It's all right, you're safe here. I have some of your favorite stew on for the daily special. You'll feel better once you've eaten."

Wanda pauses. The way he's talking, it's like he knows something is wrong. But he can't possibly know something's wrong, unless—she looks at Django's face, carefully searching for what she already knows she's going to find there.

"Django? Why would you think I'm not safe outside here?"

"The world is always so fast to think poorly of us, given half the opportunity to do so," he says solemnly. "To be Roma is to be hated without cause or evidence, always. We protect our own."

"That doesn't answer the question."

He sighs heavily. "Wanda, chavva, you've been my responsibility, in part, since you were still the child I see you as. You always will be. Did you really think I wouldn't know your eyes, whether or not there was a mask in front of them? You've done so much good, and fought so fiercely, and we know you didn't do what you're accused of. We know you never could."

Wanda's breath catches in her throat as she stares at him. It's not new information, that Django discovered her—and Peter's—secret, but that truth remained unspoken between them.

"Since the first time they put your picture in the papers, we've known. And we've kept your secret—yours and that gaje brother of yours."

The realization chills her to the bone: Wanda has only been allowing herself the polite fiction of a secret identity. She's put them both in danger without ever realizing there was a risk. They're not safe. They never were.

She turns back to Pietro, offering him her hand. "We have to hurry . . . please," she says. It's to save the people she loves as much as it is to save herself, and she doesn't listen to Django's protests as Pietro tugs her, ever so gently, out of the restaurant and onto the step, under the awning. Everything is bathed in shadow, even with the sun directly overhead, and she closes her eyes for a moment, enjoying the darkness.

"It's all right, Wanda," he says, still guiding her. "I'll never let you fall. And I know you didn't kill that puling captain. You would never slash a man's throat so messily. You're a proper lady, in your own way."

Wanda stops walking, trying to pull her hand out of his. She fails as he grips her tighter, trapping her where she is. His expression is politely curious as he turns back toward her, face composed.

"Wanda, what's wrong?" he asks. "Is it something I said?"

He feels very far away, even if he's still holding her hand, still trapping her in place. "Did they really print the details of how he died?"

"What?"

"Did the papers print the details of how Captain America died?"

"I'm sorry, Wanda, I don't know where I heard that. Come now, we must go. Our ride to Latveria is leaving very soon . . ."

"No. I'm not going with you until you answer the question, and if you lie, I'll know, sooner or later. You can't cut me off from every newspaper in the world, every telephone line. I'll find out when the Avengers released the details of his death, and I'll know if you lied. So how do you know his throat was slit? How do you know, Pietro?"

"Wanda . . . please, just trust me. None of this is important unless you let it be. We're together, the way we were always supposed to be. You and me. Quicksilver and the Scarlet Witch. We'll be perfect. All you have to do is come with me."

"No," she snaps, and this time when she pulls away her hand slips from his, and she's free to take a step back, out of his reach. He sighs, shoulders slumping, and for a moment he looks truly, monumentally hurt.

"I'm so sorry," he says. "I truly wish it hadn't come to this." He lunges, faster than the eye can follow, and grabs both her hands in his own, pinning them where they are. "You can't hex me if you can't move, sister," he says, and his voice is low and cold—the voice he used when he addressed Peter on the roof.

"If you won't come home, I can't leave you here," he says. "I can't allow you to be an American weapon to be used against your own people. If you won't let me save you, I'll have to destroy you."

His fear makes sudden sense. The affection she's sometimes seen in his eyes, the joy bordering on awe, it's all real. He was sent here to bring her back to Latveria, to his father, because she could be a powerful weapon against Doom's regime if she teamed up with the wrong people—like the Fantastic Four, or the Avengers. How easy it must have been to convince Pietro that it was his idea to go get her. How scared he must have been when she didn't react the "right" way, when he realized he'd have to kill her if she wouldn't come with him.

Wanda struggles to pull her hands free, trying to escape. He holds her fast. Although—with both his hands occupied holding hers, he can't really turn and run away with her. His powers may not precisely follow the rules of physics and anatomy, but momentum says he needs to be able to build up a halfway decent head of steam. Pulling one leg up, she aims a kick at his left knee. He dodges easily.

"Wanda, Wanda, Wanda," he says, slamming her against the glass front of the restaurant. Her head cracks against the glass, hard enough that she feels it in her teeth, and she realizes he's not pulling any punches—he's intending to hit her as hard as he has to in order to knock her down. She stops struggling quite as hard. If she gets a hand free, he'll be able to drag her off immediately, and one or both of them is going to die.

She doesn't want to hurt him. Even after everything he's done, he's her brother, and she doesn't want to hurt him. She wants to see him stand trial for the murder of Captain America, wants to see him pay for what he's done, but she doesn't want to hurt him herself. She kicks again, this time aiming higher, and he blocks her foot with his thigh, smirking.

"Naughty, naughty, little sister," he says, in a snide, oily tone. The affection she'd heard there is gone. He's done pretending at kindness to lure her away; he's showing his true colors now. "Do you hit your American brother like that?"

He slams her into the glass again, and this time it gives way under the impact, sending her toppling into the restaurant in a spray of shards. She bounces to her feet with a speed born of long training. It's not enough: Pietro is faster than any other living thing she's ever seen, and he's already gone. The door is rocking in its frame, either from the impact or because someone has slipped inside too fast for the eye to follow. Her hands crackle red with chaos, and red outlines her pupils, beginning to spread through her irises as she looks frantically around for signs that he's here.

"Wanda?" asks Django, voice shaking.

"Get everyone out of here!" she snaps. "It's not safe!"

He begins to gesture for the staff to come to him, and then his head jerks to the side, accompanied by the distinctive sound of snapping bone. He collapses limply to the floor, revealing Pietro standing behind him, hands still raised.

"Really, Wanda?" he asks. "You thought you could refuse me, and still protect these pathetic little people? Playing at campana while the rest of the world pretends we don't exist, that the Roma all died when they locked us away and said we were monsters? You thought I'd *spare* them?"

Wanda takes a deep breath, staring at him, then at the body of the man who taught her, cared for her, protected her all these years. He's not family the way May and Peter are family, but he's *family* all the same.

Pietro smirks.

Wanda screams.

It's a high, piercing sound, filled with impossible harmonies, echoing off the walls and rattling the glass. It carries chaos in its wake, her magic made sonic and given form. It's not a weapon: It's a beacon, broadcasting her distress to any within range.

⎰⎱

IN HER DISTANT, IMPENETRABLE CHAMBER, HER PLACE OUTSIDE THE BOUNDS OF REALITY as most can understand it, America claps her hands over her ears. The sound goes on, echoing from every inch of the room as a crack appears on the mirror she's been using to watch the Parker siblings navigate their lives. Wanda isn't *here,* but she might as well be: She's screaming like she is, the sound originating from the crystal spires against the walls, breaking supposedly unbreakable mirrors.

America listens, and begins to understand why this iteration of Wanda, nurtured and protected by Doctor Strange, guided to the full scope of what her powers can become, was important enough to flash across her mirror's surface to begin with. This kind of power isn't universal, isn't guaranteed to every Wanda who walks the worlds. This is the kind of power that erases realities if it's not controlled, that breaks the rules of what should be possible. If not for Doctor Strange keeping her from going too far before she fully understood herself, she could have unmade her world long before Pietro came looking for her.

America isn't supposed to intervene in the worlds she watches, is supposed to allow them to unfold according to their own whims and desires, but she has her suspicions about Pietro, the way he vanished at the beginning, only to reappear at the precise moment when he could do the most damage. The scream is fading. She turns to her mirror, attempting to redirect it to Latveria and the king he's mentioned—Doctor von Doom. The glass flickers, first showing the distant outline of a hooded figure, and then showing Doom himself, sitting in his throne with his cheek resting against his hand, bored and regal and menacing all at the same time, a nightmare from someone else's story. The glass flickers again, the hooded figure returning for a heartbeat, like they're standing behind the throne in the scant shadows gathered there, and then the glass goes black.

Someone is concealing Latveria from her. Someone is interfering in a way so profound that it blocks out even a Watcher's eyes, which should be impossible—nothing is supposed to be hidden from her. But Doom is. Somehow, Doom is.

If Doom is being hidden from the Watchers, then someone there has been breaking the rules. Wanda is potentially strong enough to shape realities one day, if she's allowed to grow and develop at her own pace, neither stunted nor forced to channel more power than she's currently able to safely control. Doom adopted Pietro, raised him as his heir, and when the time was right, aimed Pietro at Wanda like a missile.

America is a Watcher. She should be able to see everything this world contains. That she can't is impossible, and yet somehow, Doom is hidden from her eyes. Doom, who wants Wanda. This must be an orchestrated attack, even if she doesn't yet know the exact scope of it. But who? Who could possibly manipulate even a man such as Doom to go to such lengths?

If she's under attack, she's allowed to respond. Every living thing can fight to survive, and Watcher or no, America is still alive.

America takes a deep breath, presses one hand against the cracked mirror, and steps through the glass into the humid air of a New York afternoon. The smells and sounds of the city hit her immediately—frying meat, exhaust, trash gently rotting in piled-up bags along the curb, a sweet dagger of perfume from a passing dog walker. It's all beautiful after the false sterility of her chamber. The smells of roasted peanuts and dog urine are equally wonderful and equally piercing to her under-stimulated nose.

She doesn't have time to enjoy being back in the world, rather than alone and isolated in her chamber. She's here for a reason. Regretfully, America pulls herself away from the sensory explosions happening all around her and turns toward the reason she emerged into this place, on this street corner:

There, in front of her, is a public library. And there, nestled against the library wall and protected by a small overhang, is one of the last public pay phones in New York City. She grabs the receiver, warm and solid in her hand, and even that small sensation, sun-warmed plastic against skin, is nearly overwhelming.

She's a Watcher. She doesn't need a quarter to make a phone call, and she doesn't need to know the number. She just punches keys, and after a few seconds, the phone starts ringing. She holds it to her ear and waits, until with a click, someone on the other end picks up.

"Hello?" says a familiar voice.

"Doctor Stephen Strange," she replies. "This is a concerned friend. Your apprentice has been cornered by her brother at the location where she volunteers her time, and if you don't hurry, a lot of people are going to get hurt. You may never see her again."

"Who is this?" he demands, instantly suspicious.

"A member of the neighborhood watch. You don't have much time."

She hangs up, and she's gone, and it's all up to them now.

It always has been.

CHAPTER TWENTY-TWO

FIND YOUR FAMILY

DOCTOR STRANGE HANGS UP THE PHONE, THEN TURNS TO PETER, frowning. "Do you know where the Black Knight patrols this time of day?" he asks. "Or the Human Torch?"

"I know where to find them both, and Daredevil. Why?"

"Wanda's in trouble. Pietro has her, and if we're to rescue her, we'll need more than just the two of us."

Peter pulls his mask back on with a single sharp gesture, leaping for the window. He shoves it open, and is about to jump out when Doctor Strange lifts a hand.

"We meet at the restaurant," he says.

Peter nods, and he's gone.

WANDA HAS NEVER BEEN THE MOST POPULAR SUPER HERO IN TOWN, even before she was accused of murder. But she's always had allies, people who knew her well enough to know that she's fighting on their side and deserves the benefit of the doubt. Those are the people Spider-Man and Doctor Strange reach out to, gathering them in ones and twos until they feel like they can conduct this battle the way they need to. There's too much risk to Wanda and to civilians: They don't want to be evenly matched. They want to be a devastating force, and to win so quickly and cleanly that there's no chance the battle doesn't go their way.

Doctor Strange and Spider-Man call, and the heroes answer, gathering at a safe distance and awaiting the call to intervene.

The shattered front window of the restaurant does nothing to block the sounds of shouting and breaking from inside, or the occasional bursts of vivid red light. Then the door slams open, and Wanda is propelled through, tumbling down the stairs in a rolling bundle of curls and elbows. She bounces to her feet at the bottom, sweat sticking her hair to her forehead and blood streaking her cheeks, and looks around herself with wide-eyed amazement.

Doctor Strange and the Fantastic Four are closest to where she's landed. Her master offers his hand to steady her, while Johnny Storm bursts into flames and glares at the still swinging restaurant door. Spider-Man is nearby, sticking to the side of a wall, while the Black Knight astride Aragorn waits on the street below him. Kurt is crouching on a nearby streetlight, Meggan hovering nearby. All these people look furious.

Wanda tries to pull away at the sight of the Black Knight. Doctor Strange shakes his head. "He knows you," he says. "He knows you didn't do what you're accused of."

"Pietro did," she says, voice a broken whisper. "He did it so I'd go with him."

Doctor Strange turns his attention back to the rocking door. "Is he still in there?"

"I don't know," she says, miserably. "He could be halfway to Boston by now."

"I don't think he is," says Doctor Strange. "He still doesn't have the prize."

"The prize?"

"You."

As if summoned, Pietro races out of nowhere, slamming into Doctor Strange and knocking him off his feet as he grabs hold of

Wanda. They're in the open now—no walls, and no awkward positioning to keep him from gaining speed.

"I love you," he says. "I would have made you a princess."

Wanda grabs hold of his head as he runs. "You never knew me," she spits, and the ground opens up beneath him, blazing chaos red, as they both fall into her tunnel of memories and broken glass.

(America's window on the scene blurs momentarily, then jumps to another mirror, everything rimed in red as the view shifts into the cascading chaos of Wanda's magic. She watches, still. She is watching until the end.)

Pietro lets go as they fall, unable to maintain his grasp, and slams straight into the first sheet of frozen memory. Wanda has been here before. She evades the panels with easy grace as she falls, maneuvering herself beneath the panel, where she can bolt him as he falls out the bottom. He snarls and grabs for her in the void, and her dodge carries her into the path of another red sheet. She crashes through, Pietro close behind her—

And both of them are standing on snowy ground, dark trees around them, a cube looming before them at the clearing's center. A door is open in the side of the cube, and a snowmobile is parked nearby, footprints in the snow connecting the two points. Pietro recovers first. He grabs for Wanda again, and she blasts him back with a jet of red before she turns and bolts for the cube.

This is her memory. She must have been here before. She just . . . doesn't remember it. It's a paradox, but this is a construct of pure chaos. Paradox thrives here. She runs for the open door, and Pietro tackles her before she can get there, slamming them both to the ground.

"You are—coming—with me!" he says, rapid-fire, and grabs her by the hair. She hits him with another pair of hex bolts, but he shrugs them off, breaking into a run so fast that the world blurs and turns silver-white around the edges, like his speed is its own form of chaos. It's not, she can sense that, but manifesting it inside her magic is giving it some of the same qualities. He runs, and she's dragged with him, and she can't get away.

A sheet of gleaming silver glass forms ahead of them, and he plunges into it, dragging her along with him into a cold palace library, where a little boy with bone-white hair sits by a fireplace, hugging a book to his chest and crying.

He looks young, and fragile, and alone, and Wanda wants to comfort him. It's like, in memory, she can fully recognize him as her brother. A figure in dark armor and a green cape paces back and forth, waving his hands to punctuate his speech.

"—was told only one child might survive, and I *asked* for the useful one," he says. "You were an error, boy. Find the one they lost me, and pay for all you've cost me. Do you understand?"

"Yes, F-Father," whispers Pietro, and Wanda understands but still does not forgive.

Her fist catches the real Pietro, the running Pietro, in the trachea. He drops her, and she tumbles to the snowy ground just in time to see the Parkers emerging from the cube, running at a normal human speed, Richard staggering a little, Mary carrying a baby swaddled tightly in her arms. Wanda bounces to her feet, staring at the impossible ghosts of her parents as they run for the snowmobile and get on, Mary handing the infant to Richard before gunning the engine and roaring away.

Pietro's hand catches Wanda by the hair, pulling hard, and she yelps as she jerks herself away. "Truce!" she yells. "Only here, only for a moment, truce!"

Pietro freezes, looking at her with deep and absolute confusion. "What nonsense are you spouting now?" he asks.

"*That*"—she gestures to the cube—"is where the Parkers found me, and where you lost me. So let's find out what happened. Let's see the truth, Pietro. Was I stolen, or was I saved?"

Pietro hesitates, and that's enough. For what may be the only time in their shared, separated lives, Wanda is faster than he is, because she's already off and running for the cube.

(Whose memory is this? America frowns at the image. Neither of the people it contains can possibly have seen this, but they run through it all the same, children of chaos, caught inside the moment.)

Wanda reaches the cube first, but only because Pietro lets her. They step inside, into the chaos of broken boxes and exploding machinery, and they know two things at once: that they have been here before, and that they are the only living things inside this building. A machine that looks like some sort of complicated incubator stands at the front of the room, and they move toward it, side by side, briefly unified, looking inside.

There are two long troughs, like the channels inside some large and complicated scanner. One contains a tattered baby blanket. The other is empty. Neither holds a child.

"We've been here before," whispers Wanda, and the cube flickers around them, becoming the interior of a wooden wagon, walls lined with shelves, shelves packed with things, all of it shabby but clean in a way Wanda knows from the house where she grew up. There's a cradle there, large enough for two children, and a woman beside it, holding a baby to her breast. She looks up and smiles at Wanda and Pietro, but she can't be smiling at them, can't see them. She's only a memory.

"Ah, love," she says, in a dialect of Romany that Wanda doesn't speak, but knows enough of to recognize a greeting.

A man walks through the twins as if they're not there, and that makes sense, because they aren't. The woman's smile was for him. Wanda knows that. She still feels a pang in her chest at the realization.

He walks to the woman and presses a kiss against her forehead, offering a longer, more complicated greeting. Then he hands her two carved bracelets, each with a large bead at its center. One side of the bead is a wagon wheel. The other is an initial.

W and P.

The woman smiles at him, sliding the P onto the wrist of the baby in her arms. He takes the W and does the same for the unseen infant Wanda.

As he finishes this gesture, there's a terrible crashing sound from outside, and Wanda knows that whoever stole them both from their parents is coming. It's a being she doesn't really understand, meddling with science in a way she can't fathom, that will forever transform the infants who will become Wanda and Pietro. And with that understanding, finally, *finally,* she knows.

She looks to Pietro. This can all be over now, right? The truth is right in front of him. He can stop running toward a fantasy built on lies. But in a face so familiar and so not, Wanda finds no peace, only heartbreak and fear.

"This changes nothing," he says, softly, almost sadly.

"Pietro . . ."

Already the chaos around them is shifting. This moment, this memory, is coming to an end.

And with it, the truce is ended.

"We were both stolen," says Pietro, and grabs her by the throat. "I'm taking you back."

Wanda plants a foot against his stomach and shoves herself backward, falling out of the column of silver, back into the cascade of red, where nothing touches her without her consent. Pietro plummets after her, unable to stay inside the memory without her.

They fall, faster and faster, until they emerge out of the tunnel and onto the ground at Doctor Strange's feet. Pietro tries to rise, but doesn't quite manage it before one of her hex bolts catches him in the side of the head, stunning him. He slumps back to the ground, and doesn't move as Kurt appears next to him, grabbing him by the ankles, and they both vanish in a puff of sulfurous smoke.

Wanda looks around in time to see Spider-Man web Pietro to the wall, sticking him firmly in place. Pietro is beginning to recover from the combined shock of the hex bolt and the fall; he shouts and thrashes against the webbing.

"You'll pay for this!" he shouts. "Both of you! My father has diplomatic immunity—he'll have me out before you know it, and then you'll pay for everything you've done! I know all your secrets, *Wanda.*"

"All your sister's secrets, and you don't know that diplomatic immunity isn't transitive," says Doctor Strange, then shifts to speaking to Wanda. "His father can petition the courts, but I doubt he'll get very far, given that Pietro murdered the very symbol of America. He'll be put into a prison with proper power nullifiers, and remain there for a very long time."

"Django . . ." says Wanda, remembering. Tears rise to her eyes.

Spider-Man appears next to her, leaping from the nearest wall. "I'm sorry," he says. "I'm sorry we weren't faster."

"I'm sorry we couldn't save any of them," says Wanda. She turns to look at Peter. "I'm sorry we couldn't save Pietro. Every time we had the chance, we failed him. I'm so sorry."

Peter doesn't know what to say to that. He just wraps his arms around her, while she does the same for him, and they hold each other while she cries.

Tomorrow is a new day.

They have so many days to come.

ACKNOWLEDGMENTS

—

This book would not have been possible without my fabulous editor, Gabriella Muñoz, and without the wonderful editors I have worked with at Marvel Comics, Devin Lewis and Kathleen Wisneski. I loved these characters on my own. You taught me to understand them on a deeper level, and I am so very grateful.

Thanks also to Joe Field, owner of Flying Colors Comics, who encouraged my love for the Marvel Universe, and to Wing Mui, owner of Outsider Comics, for helping me to keep that love alive. Thanks to my brother, Shawn, who answers any and all questions about obscure Marvel lore, even when asked at three o'clock in the morning. Thanks to my agent, Diana Fox, for understanding why I had to find the time to take this project, and thanks to everyone at Random House Worlds, for making this book possible to begin with.

Finally, thanks to Jay Edidin, who has always been an incredible resource for comics knowledge, and to everyone at Zulu's Board Game Café, for their endless tolerance of my shouty, shouty ways.

And thank you all so much for reading. This wouldn't be possible without you.

AMERICA BRUSHES HER FINGERS AGAINST THE CRACKED MIRROR, SIGHING SATISFACTION
and sorrow in the same breath. No matter what turns her life
takes, at her core, Wanda is always a woman who loves her family, and will do anything to protect them, no matter what it
costs her, or what shape that family takes.

In the image, Wanda embraces Aunt May before she packs
the last of her things, off to her new home in Avengers Manor.
She'll continue her classes both at school and at the Sanctum,
but for right now, she's safest among the rest of her super team,
and still new enough that they like to keep her close. Peter is
there as she leaves the house in Queens for her last time as a
resident, smiling as he waves, and America can almost see the
shadow of Uncle Ben behind them both, approving of this
change. Their lives are moving on.

She's seen enough. It's time for her to move on, too.

As if triggered by the thought, there is a soft ripple in the air,
and she turns to find four of her fellow Watchers arrayed behind her, hands folded in front of them, looking down their
noses at her. She stiffens for a moment, then bows.

"If you'd told me you were coming, I would have baked
cookies," she says.

"You should have seen our approach."

"I was busy."

"You were busy doing things that are forbidden," says one of the Watchers, tone as disapproving as his expression. "You know intervention is not allowed."

"She screamed so hard I heard it here—it cracked the viewing portal! She's terrifyingly powerful, and someone was trying to shield her from me, because they didn't want what they were doing to be witnessed, not even by us. I intervened because failure to do so could have endangered us as well!"

"Intervention is never justified," says another Watcher. "See that it doesn't happen again."

The air ripples, and she's alone. Even for this, she hasn't been punished—unless the isolation is the punishment, which it might well be.

The pieces are too dissimilar. They don't quite fit. Someone pointed the Parkers at the High Evolutionary in time for them to interfere and leave with Wanda. Someone else shielded Doom from America's attention, enough so that she didn't see the threat of Pietro coming. Happy ending or no, it feels like someone's trying to draw her out, like this Wanda's life was a carefully orchestrated plan intended to bring her, America Chavez, into New York. What else would this unseen foe do to bring her to a place where she can be harmed? And how many innocents are they willing to destroy in the process?

She's direly afraid the answer will be infinite.

ABOUT THE AUTHOR

—

SEANAN MCGUIRE lives and works in Washington State, where she shares her somewhat idiosyncratic home with her collection of books, creepy dolls and enormous blue cats. When not writing – which is fairly rare – she enjoys traveling and can regularly be found any place where there are corn-fields, haunted houses or frogs. A Campbell, Hugo, and Nebula award–winning author, McGuire released her first book, *Rosemary and Rue* (the beginning of the October Daye series), in 2009, with more than twenty books across various series following since. She doesn't sleep much.

seananmcguire.com